COLUMBA

"You're not hurt, Colum?" his uncle demanded. "This blood? It is not yours? Thank God! Thank God for all! It is victory, man – a great victory. The unbelievers are vanquished, quite. They flee. All flee. Diarmid amongst the first, I swear! God's cause triumphs."

Colum looked from him to the wounded man at their feet and then at all the bodies lying around, and shook his head, wordless.

But Ernan was not to be deflated. "All is well, I tell you. There was little or no resistance. They knew not what overwhelmed them. Fled without fighting, treading each other down. It has been scarcely a battle, no real fighting. Donald of Ailech has had little to do. Now he pursues Diarmid. But they will not stand, I think, nor rally now. It is victory, Colum – and so greatly thanks to you!"

"Then . . . then Lord forgive me. If even He can! This slaughter . . .!"

PRINCIPAL CHARACTERS

In Order of Appearance

COLUM MAC FELIM O'CONALL: Abbot of Derry and Kells, prince of the Hy-Neill.

DIARMID MAC CERBALL: High King of All Ireland, of the Southern O'Neill.

LUGBE: Student monk, personal attendant to Colum.

PRINCESS EITHNE OF LEINSTER: Mother of Colum.

AINMERE MAC SETNA O'CONALL: King of Donegal, cousin of Colum.

AED MAC ECHOID DRY-FLESH: King of Connaught.

ERNAN, PRINCE OF DONEGAL: Uncle of Colum.

BEC MAC DE: Arch Druid of All Ireland.

ABBOT LAISRAN OF DURROW: Colum's 'soul-friend', known as Molaise.

ABBOT BRENDAN OF BIRR: Notable Celtic Church missionary.

BISHOP FINNIAN OF MOVILLE: Former tutor to Colum.

MACHAR: Monk and ship-master.

BAITHEN MAC BRENAIND: Priest, cousin of Colum.

BISHOP LUGAID OF LISMORE: Usually known as St Moluag.

ANGUS MAC RIAGAN: Lord of Ellary, Knapdale and Crinan.

LADY BRIDGET NIC COLMAN: Mother of above.

CONALL MAC COMGALL: King of Dalriada.

AIDAN MAC GABHRAN: Son of the late King of Dalriada.

EWAN MAC GABHRAN: Brother of above.

DIARMIT: Colum's acolyte.

CATHAL MAC COITIR: Sub-King in Skye.

QUEEN SINECH: Wife of above.

ENDA: Arch Druid of Skye.

ABBOT KENNETH OF ACHABO: Notable Irish missionary.

ABBOT COMGALL OF BANGOR: Notable Irish missionary.

BISHOP CORMAC O'LETHAN: Prince of the royal house of Munster.

RODERICK HEN: King of Strathclyde.

GARTNAIT MAC DOMELCH: King of Fortrenn, of the Southern Albannach.

EMCHAT: Lord of Urquhart.

Nigel Tranter

Britain in 1987
oughton
Headline PLC

1990
1995

identified as the Author of
im in accordance with the
Patents Act 1988.

5 4 3

ary C.I.P.

09-

826 4

in Great Britain by
PLC, Chatham, Kent

Stoughton Ltd
lder Headline PLC
ton Road
NW1 3BH

BROICHAN: The Magus, that is Arch Druid of Alba.

BRUDE MAC MAELCHON: High King of Alba.

PRINCESS NESSA: King Brude's daughter.

FINDCHAN: A priest from Ireland.

BAETAN MAC CAIRELL: King of Ulster.

AED MAC AINMERE: King of Donegal, later High King of Ireland.

DROSTAN: Colum's nephew, later Abbot of Deer.

DONNAN: Irish priest, Abbot of Eigg.

MUNGO: Grandson of King Loth of Lothian. (Also known as Kentigern.) Founder of Glasgow.

BEDE: Mormaor, or sub-king, of Buchan.

MONAN: Missionary priest from Ireland.

ETHERNAN: Missionary priest from Ireland.

PART ONE

1

The tall, yellow-haired man with the vitally grey eyes stared at the younger man, flushed and dishevelled, as he panted out his all but incoherent account. Then the elder held up a quite imperious hand to halt the jerky spate of words.

"You *killed* this man? This player at the hurley? He is dead? At a game!"

"Dead, yes – so they declared. But – I did not mean to kill him. He hit me first. With his stick. A foul blow. Here, at my knee. See – it is swollen. In anger I hit him back. Any man would have done the same, Colum. As he saw my blow coming, he leapt back. Stumbled. All but fell. To save himself, he sank on one knee. My hurley-stick, aimed at his body, struck the side of the neck. Here. He went down like a felled ox. They said that he died at once. Neck broken . . ."

"God have mercy on you both! You, and him. To kill a man at sport!"

"I tell you, it was not intended. I raised my stick in a flash of anger. And this, this happened! Now, now I need sanctuary, Columcille."

The tall man, stroking his shaven chin, said nothing.

"Colum – you *must* give me sanctuary! They will be after me. He was of the Southern O'Neill – the High King's clan. Diarmid hates us of the Northern clan, you know well. He was there, watching, Diarmid the *Ard Righ*. He will have me if he can! I must have the sanctuary of Holy Church. Or I am a dead man this day! I am innocent, but Diarmid mac Cerball will have my life . . ."

"That sanctuary Christ's Church cannot deny you, Curnan. But, dear God – your moment of anger is like to cost us all dear, I fear. You will have to stand trial. And pay the blood-price. But until then you shall have sanctuary here, at Kells . . ."

"Then quickly, Colum! For they will guess that I have come to you. To your monastery here . . ."

13

"You came at once?"

"Yes. I had to. To horse from the playing-field. Riding my hardest. The ten miles from Teltown and the festival." Prince Curnan gestured towards his foam-flecked, quivering horse. "They will be after me . . ."

"So be it. Come with me, to the church . . ."

Colum mac Felim O'Neill, Abbot of Kells and Derry, led the way through the gardens and monastic buildings within the rath or outer ramparts, to the sizeable but simply-designed church. He walked long-strided – but then he always moved thus, vehement and energetic yet without seeming to hurry, a man giving the impression of authority, assurance, decision, even though at times he possessed a deal less than that. The prince hurried to keep up with him. At the church-door, the older man pointed.

"Go – and pray!" he said simply.

The other all but ran into the sacred building.

The abbot strode back, thoughtful indeed – as he had cause to be. He did not require the second-sight, the prevision, with which he was often credited, to foresee dire consequences arising from his kinsman's act. And not only for Curnan. The present High King of All Ireland, Diarmid mac Cerball, would be gravely offended – and he was a violent and difficult man. As chief of the Southern branch of the great clan of O'Neill, he was conditioned to dislike those of the Northern branch, the Hy-Neill, although they were all descendants of the mighty Niall of the Nine Hostages, the most famous warrior-king of Ireland. But particularly he did not love Aed, King of Connaught, Curnan's father. Today's folly would be a stick with which to beat Aed. Moreover, Diarmid had no affection for Colum himself; for, some years before, he had been offered the position of *Ard Righ*, or High King, himself, by the electing sub-kings, but had courteously but firmly refused it, electing the Lord Christ's way, as he said, rather than the monarchial way which was his birthright; and Diarmid had been chosen, as second-best, to sit on the throne at Tara.

Back at the monastery gatehouse, he ordered a student monk to see to Curnan's sweating horse, himself stroking its velvety quivering nostrils – for he had a great fondness for animals and all living things. Then he went outside, to peer down the road to Teltown, from which the trouble could be

14

expected. He was turning over in his mind how best to seek to deal with the High King's men, if they did come chasing after the fugitive, when he bethought himself of prayer. He had told his kinsman to pray – he himself ought to be praying. Colum was a great believer in the power of prayer – although he was all too apt to act first and remember to pray afterwards.

So he went to the elaborately carved Celtic stone cross which stood on a plinth in the centre of the monastic courtyard, and there knelt, monks and students watching from doorways and corners, intrigued no doubt. Not that there was anything unusual about their abbot doing the like at any time of day or night; but a monastic establishment is by its nature a notable place for rumours, tales and gossip, and Prince Curnan's sudden and agitated arrival had not gone unnoticed.

On his knees, Colum sought to marshal his thoughts and petitions in suitable order and humble fashion to put before his Maker. But he had not got far in the process before the drumming of hooves, many hooves, resounded, indeed all but caused the ground to tremble beneath his knees. Hastily apologising to his Creator, he started up, recollected the courtesies sufficiently to add "Thy will be done!" and then turned back towards the gateway.

A large mounted company was thundering up the dusty road, banners flying; and amongst these last, one twice the size of any other. Colum's strong but pleasing features set grimly as he recognised that flag.

The majority of the horsemen reined up as they neared the turf-and-stone ramparts of the rath, but the leaders rode on into the gatehouse entrance. In the forefront, magnificently mounted, was a thick-set, bearded man of about Colum's own age, some forty years, richly clad, with a purple riding-cloak flung back from wide shoulders and a golden circlet around his brows and sandy-grey hair. Those heavy brows were dark-frowning. He pulled up his white, arch-necked stallion savagely, so that it reared, forefeet pawing the air, in front of the dark-cowled, white-robed abbot.

"Is Curnan mac Aed here?" he demanded harshly, without other greeting and remaining in the saddle.

"Welcome to this poor house of God, Highness," the other returned, inclining his head, although not very deeply. "Prince Curnan is here, yes. He is in the church, at prayer. Seeking God's mercy."

"Have him out, then."

Colum raised his own eyebrows in the broad forehead, tonsured, but slightly, in the Celtic Church fashion. "Did I mishear, Highness? Pardon me if I did."

"You heard, Colum mac Felim. Have Curnan out. I want him. He has a debt to pay."

The abbot shook his head. "No, Highness. That is not possible. Curnan is in sanctuary."

"Not *possible*? By the gods – you refuse me? The High King!"

"Until trial and judgement, he is in the care of a higher king than you, Diarmid mac Cerball!"

For moments these two princely descendants of Niall of the Nine Hostages stared each other in the eye. Then the monarch angrily jerked his beast's head aside and spurred on past the other, towards the church. His immediate companions rode after him.

Colum clenched fists and bit his lip – for he also was a hot-tempered man – seeking to control himself. Then he strode in the wake of the horsemen.

It did not take him long to reach the church, but long enough for the mounted men to have got there, dismounted and disappeared inside the building. Not all of them, for the High King still sat on a horse outside. Even as Colum came up, the three of the royal bodyguard emerged, part-dragging, part-carrying the protesting Prince Curnan, to manhandle him right up to the monarch's mount.

Diarmid wasted no words. He jabbed a pointing finger at the prisoner, and then made a plunging gesture with his clenched fist.

Obediently, and grinning, two of his henchmen snatched out dirks from their belts, and without hesitation plunged them deep into their wide-eyed victim, one into his throat, the other between his shoulder-blades.

Prince Curnan mac Aed of Connaught sank to the ground, choking in a flood of blood. His corpse was only twitching as Colum came up.

Horrified, appalled, the abbot stared from the body to his killers and then up at the High King, for the moment speechless.

"He has his deserts!" the monarch said flatly, and pulled his horse around.

16

"Wait, Diarmid mac Cerball!" That was commandingly authoritative enough for even the High King to draw rein – after all, Colum mac Felim was of as royal blood and breeding as was he, and could on occasion show it. "How dare you! How dare you! You . . . savage. You, you have done the unforgivable! Assassin! For this deed, I say, you are accursed . . . !"

"You name this justice? You, the High King. *I* name it murder. And in cold blood."

"What you name it matters nothing to me, Colum mac Felim."

"He slew a man – my own servant, thus *he* is slain. Justice is done."

"You think that? Perhaps that is true. What I may deem it is unimportant. But what Almighty God deems it should concern you. And God is not to be mocked, even by you! For, as well as murder, you have committed the sin of deliberate sacrilege. You have broken God's sanctuary."

"Sanctuary! A device of priests to shelter rogues!"

"Holy Church says otherwise. The Church, in God's name, offers sanctuary to those who seek it, until such time as they may be brought to judgement, men's judgement. You have defiled it, in direst shame."

"Curnan has *had* his judgement. Mine!"

"And now *you* face God's judgement! For the double sin of sacrilege and murder. You are accursed, Diarmid mac Cerball!"

"You curse me? You dare! Me, the *Ard Righ*!"

"God will – that I promise you!"

The monarch hooted a harsh laugh, turning to his watching bodyguard. "You hear this insolent priest? He thinks to curse the High King of all Ireland! In the name of his Christian god. A fool, as well as insolent!"

The others looked away, uncomfortable. Hard, tough men, they were less sure of being impervious to the abbot's curses than was their master; also Colum mac Felim was a prince of the blood even more highly descended than was Diarmid.

The king shrugged, spat at Colum's feet, kicked heels into his beast's flank, and without another word rode off. Glancing at neither the abbot nor the corpse, his people mounted and spurred after him.

Colum stood for a few moments, trembling with emotion. Then he went to kneel beside his fallen kinsman. Clearly Curnan had died almost instantly, one of the expertly wielded daggers having reached the heart. Head bowed and shaking, he stared. Then he rose and stooping, grasped the dead man's shoulders at the armpits, and started to drag the body back into the church. He was a well-made and physically strong man in the prime of life. No doubt some of his monks and lay-brothers watched from windows and corners, but none came to help – for they knew their abbot.

In the church, plain, simple to the point of austerity, Colum dragged the corpse up the single step to before the altar. There, beside it, he sank down on his knees, to pray. At first prayer would not come, only passion, anger, hatred. Fiercely he sought to discipline his all too vehement emotions, thoughts, will, as not infrequently he had to do – but seldom indeed so desperately as now he did. At length he schooled himself to address his Maker in some sort of fashion that he felt might be reasonably acceptable.

Colum prayed for Curnan's soul, for the soul of his victim on the hurley-field, and for his own, that he might learn God's will in this harrowing matter. He even tried to pray for Diarmid mac Cerball also, but failed; but he did ask, beseech forgiveness, if his angry condemnation, his cursing, was wrong. He well recognised that his anger should be against the sin committed rather than the sinner, but found it difficult on this occasion to convince himself.

Eventually he rose and went for his people to attend to the body, prepare it for the burial service and interment. He must send a messenger to King Aed of Connaught, Curnan's father – a message which inevitably would be the beginning of troubles, major and dire troubles, God help them all.

It requires no divine gift of prophecy to visualise some of the troubles which did erupt in Ireland thereafter. The Northern and Southern branches of the great clan of O'Neill, the descendants of the semi-legendary hero, Conn of the Hundred Battles and the later Niall of the Nine Hostages, had long been in a state of mutual antipathy and rivalry, not to say outright hostility. The Northern, or Hy-Neill, to which Colum and the dead Curnan belonged, was the senior and generally more influential, and was more apt to provide the High Kings; but after Colum's refusal of that honour, Diarmid of the Southern branch, a noted warrior, was offered it, and this had given a

18

major lift to his clan – a circumstance for which by no means all the Northern O'Neills had forgiven the abbot. It did not take a great deal to spark off enmity, and this murder of a Connaught prince, in sanctuary or none, was a recipe for conflict.

But as well as this, and totally unexpected by Colum, was a move by Diarmid to strengthen his own hand and at the same time exacerbate the situation by seeking to divide the rival clan. He made a declaration that Colum mac Felim, as well as publicly insulting himself and the office of High King, and harbouring a killer fleeing from justice, had shamefully digressed against his own new Christian faith, in which he arrogantly claimed leadership. The man was a traitor and a danger to both the old faith and the new.

This was a tardy reopening of an old sore, not so very dire and long since healed and forgotten by most converts to Christianity. As a student monk in his twenties, at the monastery of Dromin, Colum had translated, from Latin into the Gaelic, St Martin of Tours' version of the Psalms, and this without the authority of his mentor, tutor and superior, Bishop Finnian. The bishop had been offended, for he had intended to perform this important task himself, copies of the Vulgate Gospels and Psalms being in short supply indeed, and the providing of them, in translation, a distinction much admired. Finnian was scarcely to be blamed, for he himself had earlier brought the Latin copy to Ireland, for safety, from Candida Casa in Strathclyde, when the pagans overwhelmed that mission – and, moreover, it was he who had taught Colum his Latin. So the younger man had been less than tactful, however enthusiastic. But ardent, and seeing the need for the Scriptures as vital for the spread of Christianity, he had refused to halt his work. He had long been forgiven by Finnian. But the bishop had been of the Southern O'Neill, and the old controversy was now remembered and used.

Conditions in Ireland, as in all the northern lands, had changed since Finnian's day. Now, in 561, the Christian faith was endangered, and paganism was reasserting itself almost everywhere. Diarmid was pagan, and the Druid priests were strong and influenced him greatly. He, and they, saw this present trouble as an excellent opportunity to advance their cause by seeking to create division amongst the Christians, by accusing the Abbot of Kells and Derry of schism, heresy and

19

ambition, as well as rebellion against the high kingship. The objective was not only to pit Southern O'Neill against Northern, but Christian against Christian.

At first Colum was scarcely aware of all this; and even when rumours began to reach him at Kells, scarcely believed it, or the scale of it. However, when a friend came secretly to the monastery, from Tara, to warn him that a group under the Arch Druid, including some Christian priests, were planning to come and arrest him, with the High King's agreement, as an offender against both Church and State, to stand trial at Tara before a joint court of the religious and secular authorities, he recognised that it would be wise to be elsewhere meantime. That sort of wisdom did not come naturally to Colum mac Felim, for his was a nature apt to meet challenge head on, too much so, many held; but he realised that he had responsibilities other than personal here, to this monastery and others which he had founded, and which could suffer if he made resistance. Also to the Northern O'Neill clan itself, which might well feel impelled to take to arms to rescue or avenge one of its princes and so precipitate war.

That very night, leaving Kells monastery in the care of its saintly sub-Abbot Liban – whom even the most accusatory would find difficulty in accusing of anything combative – Colum slipped quietly away, on horseback, with only the student-monk and personal attendant Lugbe as companion, both dressed inconspicuously, and headed northwards. Kells was altogether too near to Tara, seat of the High Kings, for comfort in present circumstances, even though that was why he had founded his monastery there.

All night they rode through the sleeping land of Meath, ever northwards, without seeing a soul, although dogs barked at them from sundry villages and farmsteads, seeking to avoid the habitations of men as they did. Lugbe, at only twenty years, had never done anything like this in his life, and was excited and just a little fearful, even his beloved master's presence and spiritual authority not entirely insulating him from dread of the alleged terrors which stalked by night. Colum, to be sure, had travelled thus many a time – not always unpursued, his Christianity being of the sort which had tended to arouse passions of opposition as well as of adherence.

Kells was a long way south of their ultimate destination,

20

Derry in Donegal, over one hundred and fifty miles, where stood the first monastery Colum had founded. He had indeed been instrumental in setting up more than these, for he was a man who did not do things by halves; but Derry and Kells were under his own abbacy, the others not. And one hundred and fifty miles would not be too far to be away from the clutches of the High King and Arch Druid.

In the early hours of the morning they followed the Blackwater River valley out of Meath and into Monaghan, into hilly country now, although the mountains loomed only dimly in the September night. On well into the forenoon they continued, with the young man all but asleep in the saddle, before Colum halted at a lonely hill-farm where they obtained oaten porridge, honey and milk before moving further into the privacy of a birch-wood where they could tether their beasts and sleep unseen. But only for a few hours. If young Lugbe did not already know it, he was learning that life with Colum mac Felim was not apt to be easy, ever.

Across the narrows of Monaghan they took their hilly way, and by now had ceased any looking backwards for fear of pursuit, eventually to ford another Blackwater River, into Tyrone of the lakes and the bogs. They were into Ulster now, Northern O'Neill territory. Colum felt safer here, but only somewhat, for the High King of All Ireland could go where he would, his writ running the length and breadth of the land, in theory, even though one of the Southern O'Neill would be apt to be more cautious in the Northern territory. Colum's concern was not only with his own safety; knowing Diarmid, he recognised that any giving known shelter and comfort to himself, as fugitive, might well suffer for it.

On into another night they rode, the weather kind at least, choosing byways and avoiding towns and villages where possible, even though this involved much fording of difficult streams and bogs. Eventually they had to halt, for their horses' sakes if not their own. But they were now halfway to Derry, and surely they might take it more easily hereafter. That Diarmid and Bec mac De, the Arch Druid, would learn of their flight quickly, Colum was in no doubt; someone would find it worth his while to inform on them without delay. But even so, any pursuit must be far behind, guess as they would that he would almost certainly head for Derry.

It took them three more days, at a more relaxed pace, to

reach that far northern oak-wood on the River Foyle, the gift of Curnan's father, King Aed, where Colum had built his first monastery sixteen years before, as a young enthusiast for the faith, after turning down the high-kingship, impatient to spread the Gospel, almost to force it upon his fellow-clansmen and compatriots. He had learned, in the years that followed, a little of the follies of impatience and the need for forbearance, the acceptance of God's will and timing rather than his own, and so had moderated his pace and all too princely ambitions in the field of religion – even though at times he had wondered whether, after all, he ought to have accepted the high kingship and so been able to *impose* Christianity on druidical, sun-worshipping Ireland. He had learned too, as the years went by, that Derry, in farthest Donegal, was too isolated to make much impact on mid and southern Ireland; and while there were numerous other monasteries and churches scattered over the land, and had been since St Patrick's time a century before, none of these, in his urgent opinion, was in fact making sufficient efforts to stem the rising tide of paganism. So he had founded those other establishments, aided by his princely revenues, in strategic situations, first Durrow, then the one at Kells, near to Tara, the most vitally important; and there, in due course, he had based himself as a missionary soldier of Christ.

They came to Derry on that fifth afternoon, tired but thankful, a lovely place in its woodland setting on an eminence by the riverside, only three miles from the mouth of the Foyle and the great sea-lough. The abbot's unexpected arrival created a great excitement amongst the monks and lay-brethren. Word of Curnan's death, and possible repercussions, had reached even this remote community, but no least notion of personal threat to Abbot Colum. He did not dwell on this, but changed back into his white monastic robe and black abbot's hood, and led thanks for his safe home-coming, for he looked on Derry as his true home still. This small church, his very first building, had been erected largely with his own hands and was the only one in all Ireland facing north-and-south instead of east-and-west. This was on account of a magnificent old oak tree sharing the mound, and which he had refused to have cut down to make room for the church, asserting that it was God's creation as distinct from man's. Now he made the obligatory quick tour of the establishment, commending all and schooling himself to make his sundry criticisms later. Then he set off again, alone, to stride the mile or so along the riverside to another house, not a religious one this time, quite large, indeed more imposing than anything at the monastery where simplicity was the rule. Amidst a flurry of barking dogs and bowing servants, where he was addressed as Prince Colum rather than Abbot, he asked if the Princess Eithne was at home, and was conducted to the orchard, where a number of women were picking apples from the trees for the cider-making. Some of the younger ones were up ladders and one or two even perched on the branches, to reach the topmost fruit; and more than one of these found opportunity to make a great outcry of pretended modesty at a man's appearance, with so much feminine leg on view, Colum waving appreciatively.

One older woman, bidding them to be quiet, came to greet her son, almost as long-strided as was he, with open arms. "Colum, my dear, my dear!" she cried. "Heaven be praised that I see you here! I thank God that you are come. Safe! Safe!" Her strong although melodious voice all but broke – which it seldom did.

They embraced with great warmth, for they were very close, these two. Then Colum held her from him, to eye her fondly, proudly, shaking his head.

"Mother – I swear that you grow but the younger every year! And the more beautiful! How do you do it?" he exclaimed. "Soon your son will look older than you – if he does not already! For my failures and follies but add to my years. Do you have none?"

"Shame on you! Is flattery not a sin? Like hypocrisy? You, a man of God!"

"A man of God seeks – but does not always find!" he amended, in changed, deepened, voice.

"Nor you only, Colum. But at least He has brought you safely here, to me, again. Heard *my* prayers, if not yours. I have been sorely worried for you, these many days. I have seen you in dire need and danger. Evil threatening you. Almost I thought to come to you myself, at Kells. Not that *I* could have achieved anything to your aid . . ."

Still gripping her shoulders, he eyed her. "Mother – you know! Or . . . did some tidings reach you?"

"I knew. I did have word from Aed of Connaught, yes. But

before that, I knew . . ." If Colum sometimes had the second sight, as reputed, it was from his mother that he inherited it, a woman renowned for that strange and not always welcome gift.

The Princess Eithne of Leinster, now in her mid-sixties, was endowed with other qualities in plenty, a woman of beauty, intelligence and strength of character. Hers had been the dominant influence in her son's upbringing, rather than that of his father, for Prince Felim, long dead, had been cast in a gentler mould, studious and retiring – although it was he who had embraced Christianity in his quiet way, leaving it to his wife to imbue their son with the burning zeal which came more naturally to them both.

Curious, he asked her. "What did you know, Mother?"

"Only that you were in danger. That evil men conspired against you. That some whom you would trust would betray you – as Judas betrayed his Lord. That you must flee – or die! So I prayed. And here you are . . ."

He nodded, and as they left the orchard for the house, he told her all that he knew himself, of his friend's warning, of the murder of Curnan, the cursing of Diarmid, the resurrection of that old offence against Bishop Finnian over the Psalms, of the shameful alliance of some Christian priests and abbots with the pagan Druids and Diarmid.

"Diarmid mac Cerball is a barbarian! Quick with his sword but a fool, a witless oaf! Almost as great fools, and much to be blamed, were the kings who elected him High King when you refused, Colum." The Princess Eithne was one of those who believed that her son ought to have accepted the Tara throne; although once he had made his decision she accepted it, supported him loyally and had not kept bringing up the matter. "But Bec mac De, the Arch Druid, is different," she went on. "He is clever, and without scruple. And he can twist Diarmid to his evil will. He hates our Holy Church, and sees you, Colum, as its champion. That he should win over some Christians to his wicked plotting is despicable, utterly shameful." His mother's fine eyes blazed with her indignation and contempt.

"They are, no doubt, some of those hereditary abbots," Colum asserted. "You know their sort. They can be the curse of our Church." The Celtic Church, unlike the Romish, with which it had had no real links since St Patrick's day, did not insist on celibacy in its priesthood; and heredity and clanship being so strong a principle and preoccupation amongst the Irish and the Celtic peoples generally, the notion that an abbot's son could succeed his father had grown up, especially in the south, and there were now even third generation incumbents of monastic seats, some of whose Christian learning and observance was rudimentary to say the least. There were good men amongst them undoubtedly; but Colum, for one, was utterly opposed to the entire concept.

"Those wretches, yes. Their faith can be but skin-deep! So – what do you do now, Colum?"

"I must go see King Aed. Tell him how it was, with Curnan. The least that I can do. Seek to give him such comfort as I may, little as that must be."

"Aed will not accept this murder lightly – nor should he! A proud man, Aed."

"That is what I fear. Yet – the deed is done. Curnan has gone to a better place than Ireland, and nothing will bring him back . . ."

Colum asked after his family, for he had a brother and four sisters, all married and scattered over Ulster and Donegal. He stayed with his mother until late evening, sharing an excellent meal, such as he had not tasted for a long time; for the Princess Eithne lived in some style, with quite a court of women, mainly young – for young at heart herself, she preferred youthful company. Not that she did not enjoy male company also, but on this occasion her son was the only man present, apart from servitors, and he did not fail to derive full relish from the fact. Colum was fond of women, although he had never married, not out of any matter of principle, nor even, at times, lack of desire, but because he recognised all too clearly that the course he had set for himself could scarcely be run in harness with a wife, however patient and understanding. It was a deliberate decision and no easy option, for he was attractive to the other sex, and apt to be left in no doubt of it, and his warm, vehement nature was not slow in responding. So that evening, round the table, and later at the music and song, he played his part in the badinage and playful pleasantry, even mildly flirtatious repartee, giving as good as he got, and had his mother pretending to be censorious, glad to put from his mind, for the moment, the problems and fears besetting him. He had a good tuneful voice and joined in the singing after the meal, even sang them one or two of his own compositions, bardic lays and ballads, both gay and sad, for he had been writing verses and setting them to melodies from boyhood, and still did so, by no means all of them hymnal.

However, when he left that congenial house for the spartan simplicity of his monastery, he did not omit to ask, in no mere formal fashion, God's blessing on it and all therein, nor allowed his benediction to sound in any way incongruous after the jollity, even hilarity, of the evening.

As he walked back through the woodland in the September gloaming, he felt better in his mind and spirits than he had done since Curnan's death. He would spend the next day or two encouraging his people here, and putting to rights certain minor matters he had noted on his brief inspection of his Derry establishment, and then take himself south-westwards for Connaught and King Aed.

2

The journey to the Sligo area of Connaught, where King Aed made his headquarters, turned out to be quite other than Colum had anticipated. As the crow might fly it was some seventy-five or eighty miles from Derry, but as the horseman must ride it meant well over one hundred, to avoid the bogs, loughs and river-crossing which so complicated travel in Ireland, especially in the north-west. He went alone, and being a good horseman reckoned that he could cover the ground in something under three days of steady riding. But it was not to be.

The first day was uneventful, as it was comparatively straightforward, following the River Foyle due southwards the twenty miles to Lifford, where its two major headstreams, the Mourne and the Finn, joined; and another fifteen up the Mourne, in Tyrone now, still southwards, in more hilly country, to a second major confluence where the River Derg came in from the west. This he reached by early evening, without incident or any real delays. But on entering the wide

26

strath where these two rivers joined, he knew an end to his solitary but timely travel. For the long valley was full of armed men, either still on the march or already camped for the night, and all clearly heading westwards, as now was he. The strath was part of the main east-west route from Tyrone, Eastern Ailech, Antrim and Ulidia, the Ulster provinces north of Lough Neagh, all Northern O'Neill territories; and it was all too evident that the Hy-Neill was on the move in a large way. In parties of scores and hundreds the fighting-men were on their way towards the Western Sea.

With a strange mixture of emotion, excitement plus a sinking at the heart, Colum saw and conjectured. He had no illusions that this might be a cause for rejoicing.

A man on horseback, and on a handsome beast at that, and dressed for the road in sober but fine clothing beneath a fur-trimmed deerskin travelling-cloak which could serve, at a pinch, as blanket for sleeping out of a night – his abbatial garb for the present in his saddlebag – he did not fail to attract attention from the marching men. But his air of quiet authority and general appearance, and his riding in the same direction as the troops tramped, ensured that he was not halted or otherwise challenged, although he was the recipient of sundry gestures and not always polite pleasantries from the bored men-at-arms; these he accepted with a smile. When he came up with a larger column, pacing behind an O'Neill banner differenced for O'Conall, he reined in beside its leadership group.

"Friends," he greeted them. "Here is great marching. You are of Donegal with that flag. Where march you, and why? I am Colum mac Felim O'Conall, from Derry." O'Conall was the patronymic of the kings of Donegal branch of O'Neill.

His hearers stared.

"You – you say *you* are Colum mac Felim? The Prince? The Abbot-Prince?" one demanded. "He who, who . . .!"

"I am, yes. I greet you, in God's good name. And would know where you go, and why?"

"But – do you not know? Have you, of all men, not heard? It is war. You must know it. For you it is who is at the heart of it, Prince Colum."

"War, you say! Dear God – *war*! How mean you? What is this? I have heard of no war, sought no warfare. I have been at my monastery of Derry . . ."

The column had halted behind its leaders as they eyed each other and the mounted men, clearly astonished.

"Grianan is none so far from Derry, they say. And you do not know? All Ireland knows, if Derry's monastery does not!" their spokesman said. "The King of Connaught has demanded vengeance for his son's murder – as well he might. And the High King has named you rebel. And all who support you. He has declared war on Connaught and Ailech, and marches westwards. And all Hy-Neill rises to assist King Aed. And *you* know it not!"

Appalled, Colum shook his yellow head. "This is . . . terrible! Scarcely to be believed. War! And in *my* name! Merciful Father – not that! How can this be? In so short a time? I have been gone from Kells for little more than two weeks . . ."

"Much can happen in two weeks, Prince! You have been condemned by some court at Tara, they say – I know not what. But the flaming torch has gone out to all Ireland – if not up to your Derry! The call to arms . . ."

"But – over one man's death!"

"And *your* sin, Prince Colum – if sin it was. Some matter of wrongful writings," another man put in. "I do not understand these things. But those who do are blaming you . . ."

"That old story of Bishop Finnian's Psalms! Twenty years ago, and more. Here is folly, beyond all understanding! I knew that there would be trouble. But not this, never this, outright war. Who first declared it? Aed? Or Diarmid?"

"I know not. Such as we are not consulted! But war it is."

"Our King, Ainmere, is not far ahead, Prince," another said. "With a great company. He will know all, tell you all. He will be camping for the night soon, no doubt . . ."

Nodding, his mind seething, Colum heeled his mount into a canter and rode on.

Passing other parties of men without pause, with the dusk he came presently to the village of Dergbeg, where a broad grassy shelf above the boggy valley-floor provided firm ground. Here the low-browed, turf roofed cot-houses and hovels were all but lost in a tide of men, with cooking fires sending up their blue smoke into the evening air. He could see some horses tethered near one of the larger houses, and for this he made his way through the throng.

Outside the house a group of better-dressed men sat around

a fire of birch–logs, eating and drinking. They eyed him curiously as he came up. Then one, probably the youngest there but wearing the slender gold circlet of kingship around his brows, started to his feet.

"Colum!" he cried. "Colum – by all that is wonderful! Colum mac Felim himself – come to the battle!" Around him the others, hearing that name, rose also.

Dismounting, Colum went to embrace his cousin. Ainmere mac Setna O'Conall was a ruddy, fresh-faced, smiling youngish man. His late father, Setna, although the younger brother of Prince Felim, had been appointed King of Donegal when *their* father, Colum's grandfather, King Fergus had died, because of Felim's gentle and studious character – the Celtic system being elective in the royal families, and the most likely to prove a suitable leader chosen. So Ainmere was now king.

"Come yes, Cousin – but not to battle!" Colum declared. "Not that! But – it is good to see you. Even in these circumstances. This folly."

"What mean you – this folly?"

"War, Ainmere. If it is indeed war, as they tell me. And not but a gesture, a flourish in the face of Diarmid?"

"It is war, to be sure. And not before time. Diarmid, and Bec mac De who leads him by the nose, have been asking for this for long. Now they have it! We will teach them their lesson! Thanks to you, Colum!"

"No – of a mercy! Do not say that. I want no part in war. It is all wrong, I tell you. What happened is no excuse for battle, the death of men . . ."

"Curnan died, did he not? And you cursed Diarmid – and rightly. All honest men hail you for that, Colum. Now that curse will be brought about."

"I said that he was accursed for breaking sanctuary. Murder also – but deliberately to defile God's sanctuary, sacrilege . . .!"

"To be sure. So say we all. So what troubles you?"

"God cannot desire war, the deaths of men, many men, innocent men. Even for the sins of sacrilege and murder."

"Tell that to Diarmid and the Arch Druid! They it is who have declared war, mustered the Southern O'Neill and their friends – of Kildare, Offaly, Leix and the rest. They march. The south against the north. This war has been brewing for long, almost since Diarmid gained Tara. He but required excuse. Now you have given it to him. And he will discover his mistake!"

"Not me. I tell you, I will *not* be blamed for this, for war."

"But you *are* blamed, Colum, whether rightly or wrongly. By our enemies. And not only for the cursing and what Diarmid calls rebellion. But for dividing the Church of God! This convention they held at Teltown, called by Diarmid and the Arch Druid and some of the abbots – a plague on them! They found you guilty of schism and heresy, as well as rebellion. Over some nonsense of the Psalms. Declared that you had stolen Bishop Finnian's property, for your own glory . . ."

"They were not Finnian's property. How can the Word of God be any man's property?"

"Those apostate abbots said that it was. And Diarmid pronounced judgement. 'To every cow its calf' he said. 'So to every book its copy.' Bec mac De's words, no doubt – but Diarmid pronounced them against you. So – they declared war, on you and all who support you. The war they have been wanting for long. And they will regret it!"

The growl of agreement from the listening group was eloquent.

Colum spread his hands helplessly, and held his peace meantime.

He spent the night with the Donegal contingent. They would have had him continue the march with them next day – for astonishing and utterly unsuitable as it seemed to him, they all looked on him as some sort of hero, for having been responsible for the situation. But he preferred to press on faster, for they had to restrain their horses' pace to that of the marching men behind. He wanted to see King Aed of Connaught just as soon as possible.

All day, proceeding up the River Derg, he was passing columns of men, some of whose leaders he knew, from Antrim, Ulidia, Down and elsewhere in the north. He did not allow himself to be delayed more than was inevitable. At midday he circled Lough Derg itself, cradled in hills; and after that it was soon downhill for another ten miles or so to Donegal Bay, with the glittering Western Sea spread before him, a lovely sight which at any other time would have lifted his heart.

There he turned south along the wild and picturesque

shoreline, to reach the Connaught border where the River Erne joined salt water at Ballyshannon. Here there was a great hold-up of marching men at the only available ford and ferry. Not wanting to become involved in more argument and discussion with enthusiastic warriors, he avoided chiefs and leaders and bedded down amongst the ordinary fighting-men, without revealing his identity, sharing their simple fare gratefully. His heart went out to these who, unless he could prevent it, might be called upon to die before long in a cause, mistaken in the first place, and of which they could know little or nothing.

Thereafter he and the marchers left the coast, to cut inland across the fifteen miles of the Dartry peninsula, to the next great inlet of Sligo Bay. Connaught was a large kingdom, one of the largest in Ireland, with many centres of population, wide scattered; but King Aed's favourite seat was in the north-west here, at Drumcleeve, near Sligo; and thither all were making – although having to make it in this round-about fashion on account of the great barrier presented by Lower and Upper Loughs Erne and their related marshlands, which effectively sealed off this Sligo area from the east, for some thirty miles – a defensive feature for which Aed favoured the place. Through the Dartry Mountains, then, the columns wound their way to Drumcleeve.

They found that place an armed camp indeed, men in their thousands congregating around the great hall-house on its mound behind earthen ramparts, which served as the palace. This last was crammed to overflowing with the great ones of Connaught, Ulster, Tyrone and the Hy-Neill. But Colum's arrival and identification gained him prompt entry and lively acclaim, less than appreciated in the circumstances. He was escorted by cheerful chiefs and captains to the great hall, where King Aed sat drinking with his princes and principal supporters.

At the Connaught Sennachie's, or royal herald's, beating of a gong and announcement of the arrival of the Prince-Abbot Colum mac Felim mac Fergus mac Conall mac Niall, a silence descended on the company. Then all who were sitting got to their feet, save only Aed himself – who of course could rise for none, except perhaps the High King, in his own kingdom – but who held out both hands in greeting.

"Welcome, Columcille!" he cried into the sudden quiet.

"A thousand welcomes from all here for Columcille, the Church's Dove Militant!" Columcille, literally Colum of the Church, was a nickname given him as a youth on account of his enthusiasm for the new faith – although few would think so to address him now; and the name Colum meant dove or pigeon in the Gaelic.

Urgent words of denial rose to Colum's lips but he restrained them. This was not the time. He bowed. "I thank you, Highness. And all here. As ever, I come to your house with great esteem. And, I pray, bring God's peace." That was as far as he would let himself go at this present.

"God's peace we can do with! Man's, you will agree, is another matter! Come – sit by me, here."

Aed was a man in late middle years, square of features as of build, thick-set, normally jovial. He was not jovial that day.

Gesturing greetings towards the others, Colum went to sit by the King, the Prince of Tyrone making room for him. Servants were ordered to bring the new arrival food and drink.

"I looked to see you, my friend," Aed said. "Curnan . . . !" He left the rest unsaid.

"Curnan, yes." Colum touched the older man's arm. "What can I say – save that he is gone ahead of you to a fairer land even than Connaught? And will await you there."

"Perhaps. But woe to the man who sent him there, before his time!"

"He, too, will have his reward, one day. Nothing more sure. God is not mocked!"

"Nor am I! As Diarmid mac Cerball will find out, and before long." Aed's fists clenched. "But . . . tell me. Curnan – did he die quickly?"

"At once, yes. Diarmid's ruffians at least knew their trade! Two dirk-thrusts only. One to the heart, the other in the throat. Curnan was gone to his Maker before ever I reached his side – and I was but a few yards off."

"Diarmid, I pray, will take longer to die, I have cursed him – but it may be that *your* curse, Colum, will be the more effective. But I shall do more than curse!"

"I could do no other. He deliberately defiled God's sanctuary. Broke the girth-refuge of the Church. Even an unbeliever knows that to break a girth is forbidden . . ." Colum recounted the sequence of events, from the hurley-field at Teltown, to a grim-faced hearer.

"Aye – that is Diarmid. May he burn in hell! But – before that, Curnan shall be avenged."

"Almighty God will avenge Curnan, in His own good time, Highness."

"Then I shall assist God, my friend!"

Again Colum almost started to urge, plead, against battle as the answer, but he recognised that here, in front of all these drinking, loud-voiced chiefs and warriors, was not the occasion. Instead, he asked for the king's second son, now his heir, his own namesake, although they had appended another letter to his name, Columb mac Aed. He was told that that young man was in fact away leading the scouting-party which was out shadowing the progress of Diarmid's army on its north-westwards march.

It was later, when Aed went out to show himself to the assembled troops, and coming back was ordering singers and storytellers to be fetched to entertain the company, that Colum found opportunity to have a word with him alone.

"Highness," he began, "*must* there be battle? Surely war is not God's way. The shedding of blood, innocent blood. Christ came to speak peace amongst men, not war. Can we not settle our differences, even so grievous, with Diarmid, without bloodshed?"

"Diarmid marches. He is on his way, with a great host. Too late for aught but fighting – even if we so desired."

"But *you* have a great host assembled here, also. And still growing. Let Diarmid know it. Tell him. Send to tell him that you are ready for him. That he will meet more than he bargains for. That he heads for disaster . . ."

"As, I pray your God, he does! He has earned it. Let him pay the price!"

"But . . . it is not only he who will pay, Highness. Scores, hundreds of others will, if it comes to battle. These, your own friends, and mine. And their men. You cannot wish that?"

"Who dies is in God's hands."

"Not so – or not if they die at *men's* bidding. Choosing war when peace could be maintained."

"There can be no peace with Diarmid mac Cerball. I tell you, Colum, he has *declared* war. And on *you*. On all your kindred and all who support you. In truth, it is on all the Hy-Neill, whom he hates. And on me, Aed, of Connaught. He is on his way. And no messenger from me would turn him back, even if I would send one – which I will not! *He* has chosen war. So be it."

"If I went to meet him, myself . . . ?"

"He would slay you out-of-hand! You are already condemned, by this Druids' court. Nothing more sure. Then he would come on, to battle. He is a man of the sword, see you. He will find that I am a swordsman also! But – what ails you, Colum? You yourself are a fighter. In God's cause. Always have been. Why this holding back now? Diarmid is the enemy of your Church. High King he may be – but he has proved himself unworthy. Is it not your *duty* to help destroy him?"

"Not thus. Not by bloodshed and the deaths of men . . ." But Colum recognised that he was not going to persuade his friend. He said no more.

Next day there came a courier from Prince Columb to report that Diarmid's army, reckoned now to be up to ten thousand strong, had passed Enniskillen on the east side of the two Loughs Erne, and so was less than forty miles away.

These tidings much agitated all at Drumcleeve. The size of the enemy force made for serious thinking – for earlier estimates had put it at little more than half that number. So Diarmid had been reinforced, presumably from the southwestern kingdoms, Munster and Clare, of the O'Briens. But grave news as this was, it was the word that he was moving up the *east* side of the long Erne valley which most concerned them all. For the assumption hitherto had been that he would come by the west, the natural route from Tara and Meath in making for the Sligo area. Since the two great loughs, which to all intents formed one thirty-mile barrier, could not be crossed by any army, and the foot of the nearer, lower one came to less than ten miles of Donegal Bay, at Ballyshannon, this must mean that Diarmid intended to attack from the north, the direction least to be expected – the way that Colum himself had come – although it added to the enemy's march considerably. This surprised all.

Aed immediately called a council of war in his hall – and, unsuitable as he himself felt it to be, Colum found himself sitting in at it. Ainmere of Donegal, his cousin, had just arrived, and he sat beside him.

Aed announced the situation tersely, and pointed out that their own strength would barely reach six thousand. More might be on their way to join them, from North Antrim and

East Down, but since Diarmid was advancing on the east side of Erne, any such aid might well be cut off from them by the enemy army – which was probably why Diarmid had chosen to come on that side. And if he was past Enniskillen when Columb sent his rider, he would be considerably nearer by now. So large a force, admittedly, would not move more than some ten miles each day; but even so the enemy would now be only twenty-five or so miles away. So they had but two or three days before battle could be joined. And they could be outnumbered two to one.

There was a period of silence as that sank in. Then half a dozen voices were raised at once. Since two were kings', those of Donegal and Ailech, others restrained themselves; and Donald of Ailech being the older, Ainmere gave place.

"Diarmid chooses the east side of Erne, so must attack from the north," King Donald said, a handsome man in his mid-thirties. "Why? I do not believe that it is only because he might cut off further aid from reaching us here. I say that it is the mountains that he seeks to use against us, the Dartry Mountains, where he can trap us between mountain and sea."

"We need not enter such trap. We can wait for him, here. Leave him in the mountains, while we await our people from the east." Various voices were upraised.

"*We* know our mountains better than will Diarmid, I swear!" Aed said. "Could we not put them to better use than he? If that is his plan."

"It need not be," Ainmere put in. "Coming here, we were greatly held up at the crossing where the River Erne meets the sea. Might not that be Diarmid's plan? To hold the north bank of that river. So that we must cross, to attack him. Giving him great advantage."

"We need not cross. Leave him standing there," somebody pointed out.

"He could do both," Tyrone declared. "Send part of his army over the river and into the Dartry Mountains. Keep the rest lining the north side of Erne, since he has so many. Then, either we split up also, and are the more weakened. Or go into the mountains to deal with those; or else face the river-crossing."

That gave all pause.

"Diarmid is an oaf and a fool in some matters, but he is a cunning fighter," the prince went on. "Else he would never have been appointed High King. There is no such wide river to cross, nor mountains nearby, *south* of here. He has chosen the northern approach I say for good reason. He would divide us in the field, as he has sought to do in clan and Church."

"And if we sit here, at Drumcleeve? Or nearby?" Aed asked him. "Let him come to us, not we to him? Choose our own battle-ground."

"Can we risk that?" Ainmere demanded. "Give him time for more men to arrive, to his support? Suppose that there is another force coming from the south? Not by the Erne valley at all, but up through Mayo or Roscommon. To threaten us from behind. Have you got scouts out on that side?"

Aed shook his head. "Not a party, no. That would be a slow and difficult road to reach Sligo. But . . . my people living there would warn me."

"But not necessarily in time. The ordinary folk of the bogs . . ."

Voices were loud now all around that hall-table, as men argued and theorised. Aed gave them their head, for a little.

Out of it all, the general opinion was that they must wait and see, sending out scouting groups north and south to watch developments; and some into the mountains. Aed accepted that.

Then a new voice spoke up – the Abbot Colum's – and he had a loud and strong voice when he chose so to use it. Almost he was surprised to hear himself speak – although none other there was – for he had had no intention of taking any active part in all this talk of war and battle. But he found that he could not sit there silent when so much was at stake.

"See you," he exclaimed, bringing a fist down on the table – and other voices died away. "Why go north, to meet Diarmid? At the Erne or in the mountains? Let him come south to *you*. South of *here*. This Drumcleeve is no defensive site, no place to stand for a great battle – that is clear. But just south of here – yes! The peninsula of Cooldrevny. *There* you could stand, secure. It is small, but three miles or so long. And narrow, only a bare mile at its neck, the sea all around you, save at that neck. You could not be assailed there, but on that one front. Diarmid would have to attack over that narrow neck of land. And this small stream of Drumcleeve here, entering the bay, does so through bogland, further narrowing that neck. Abandon this house and township, I say, meantime, and occupy the Cooldrevny peninsula – a small price to pay for victory. Go *south*, not north."

All were gazing at him, weighing up his proposition. Aed was frowning, no doubt at the thought of having to abandon his palace and township to the hated enemy.

"We would sit secure there, yes," King Donald of Ailech acceded. "But as good as under siege. Is that what we came here for? We have come to do battle!"

"If you are sorely outnumbered, you may be glad to be only besieged! You could be supplied, on that peninsula, by boat. But here, in the north, amidst your own lands of Connaught, Ailech, Donegal, Tyrone and the rest, you are more likely to have aid coming to you than will be the invaders. Diarmid may well find himself menaced from the rear, at any time. Then you would be in a position to go over to the attack."

There were exclamations for and against this suggestion.

Ainmere of Donegal was in favour. "Here is wise counsel," he declared. "I have more men coming, when they can be mustered from my farther lands. Donald of Ailech also, he tells me. Even your own Connaught, Aed, can raise more men, I swear? A few more days, given us, and we will have as many as Diarmid, if not outnumber him. Even if he does receive aid from the south. I say Colum mac Felim's advice is good. Let it be Cooldrevny."

By the increased murmurs of agreement, it was evident that the majority there accepted that.

King Aed shrugged. "So be it. Although I will grieve to think of Diarmid mac Cerball sitting here in my house. Perhaps destroying it."

"So long as we beat him in the end, we can set your house to rights afterwards," Ainmere said. "And you have other houses aplenty."

"Better to lose a house than many men's lives," Colum said. "You can rebuild a house. But – I do not think that Diarmid will destroy it. He will *dwell* in it, rather, while he ponders how to engage us."

So it was agreed, and the council went on to discuss the movement of men and provisions to Cooldrevny, the collection of boats both for their supply and for the preventing of the enemy using them, and other details.

Colum, while admittedly having involved himself in war plans, had done his best to limit the bloodshed.

A start was made at once, on the task of transferring the thousands of galloglasses the three miles southwards to the low-lying, grassy peninsula which jutted into Sligo Bay. Cattle and sheep were already pasturing there, so meat would be available; but meal and ale and other victual in great quantities would also be necessary, and foraging parties were sent out all around.

Aed and a group of the leaders rode down to inspect the terrain closely, and Colum, feeling in some way responsible, accompanied them.

The peninsula thrust out from the Cooldrevny and Magher-agillerneve area. This, as the name implied, was a low-lying machair, sandy levels and tidal flats, with much marshland; which had the effect of narrowing the neck of the promontory very considerably; indeed to less than half its mile of width for all practical purposes, as a battleground in especial. From there the horn of land projected into the great bay for over two miles, a central modest spine of rock nowhere reaching more than one hundred feet above sea-level, flanked on each side by grassy slopes down to more sandy machairs. The central ridge, if such it could be called, ended in sandhills at the Rosses Point, and at its landward end crouched a few fishermen's hovels at Cregg. There was a small offshore island near the tip of the peninsula.

Viewing all this, the inspecting party had little difficulty in planning their strategy. In effect they had only a bare half-mile of ground to defend, the rest being tidal, undrained marshland. A ditch dug across that half-mile, with the spoil and stones used as a rampart, which they would man, would present a formidable obstacle for any attacker, whatever his numbers; and there was no other access to the promontory, save by boat — which anyway would be quite impracticable for an army of thousands. Diarmid would be held there, all agreed.

So there were three priorities now: to set their men digging that long ditch-and-rampart; collect every boat, curragh and coracle for miles around; and send out urgent couriers to their supporters and hoped-for reinforcements to speed their arrival and threaten Diarmid from the rear. Supplies were also being assembled for what might develop into a siege; fortunately there was plenty of water at Cregg's well and at a small pond halfway along the ridge.

That evening, scouts sent to inform Aed that the enemy had reached Ballyshannon, and finding it undefended had sent across a contingent to hold the south bank.

The next day was busy indeed. Fortunately, although the ditching and digging and piling up of stones for the ramparts was heavy work, they had thousands of men to do it. And all day the boats were being brought in, with peats and wood for cooking fires. The weather, for early October was kind – although this of course would aid the enemy also.

All waited to hear which route Diarmid would choose now. He could advance due southwards from Ballyshannon, leaving the Dartry Mountains on his right, the way that Colum and the others had come; or he could cling to the coast, by Bundoran and Cleevony, round the mountains with their proud peak of Ben Bulban at the westermost tip. In the end, reports came in that he was doing both; no doubt he had his own scouts out, who would inform that no army was seeking to block either route. He would be chary about those hills, however, and hidden forces therein which might assail his flank.

Settled behind their defences at the peninsula neck, the northern host waited, Colum, at least, doing some praying. One or two small contingents of the Hy-Neill reached them, having come up the south side of the Loughs Erne. These included Colum's uncle, Prince Ernan, younger brother of Felim and Setna, with seven-score men.

They heard the enemy, before they saw them, in the constant and eerie ululation of horns, the following forenoon. This was no mere bravado and flourish. The Druids were very strong on horns, from long-horned cattle, using them in their sun-worship and ritual, sacrificial and funerary ceremonies; and the sound of them was calculated to arouse superstitious fears, apprehensions and doubts in an enemy. Christianity was still only a century old in Ireland, much less for most of the present hearers; and the ages-old religion, with all its mysticism and terror, could not be far from the surface in most men's minds. So those horns could have their effect on the rank-and-file of the northern force, if not on the kings and chiefs. Also it meant that the Druids were indeed a prevailing influence in Diarmid's army, something very much to be reckoned with.

Presently the great host began to appear over the Cooldrevny hillocks and grassy ridges, and even the boldest watchers quailed a little at the size and extent of it all, as the seemingly unending ranks and columns and cohorts kept coming into view, under a forest of banners and standards. Soon it was being sworn that there was more than any ten thousand there, that it was as well that they had chosen to sit it out here rather than seek open battle. Even Aed grumbled no more at having left Drumcleeve.

The enemy's scouts must have kept them well informed, for the mighty host came on without pause or hesitation, horns still blowing, right to the Cooldrevny area, and its forefront did not halt until it reached a low ridge facing the neck of the peninsula, less than a quarter-mile from the defensive ditch-and-rampart. There the leadership drew up, and the horsed great ones dismounted. The flags and standards were planted. The two armies faced each other.

Presently a small group came forward from the mass, on foot, all clad in the druidical robes, with four horn-blowers sounding in accompaniment. These advanced to within about one hundred yards of the centre of the defensive line, and the horns falling silent at last, the most handsomely-robed of the walkers raised a hand.

"I am Bec mac De, Arch Druid of this land and nation," he called. "I come in my own name, but also in that of the mighty and exalted Diarmid mac Cerball, High King of All Ireland, here in person. I would speak with Aed, King of this Connaught."

"I am king here – and did not invite you, Bec mac De, nor Diarmid mac Cerball, into my kingdom," Aed shouted back. "Why bring you an armed host into Connaught?"

"Because you rebel against the High King. And because you give shelter and comfort to the man Colum mac Felim, who cursed the High King, and who offends against all religion, the new with the old both."

"The Prince Colum is of my kin. And he offends nothing to honest men. Begone, Bec mac De, with your wailing horn-blowers! And tell Diarmid mac Cerball to leave my territories forthwith."

"You speak loud words, King Aed, which I prophesy you will not be long in regretting! But render up the man Colum, and I shall advise the High King not to assail you with his might."

"I render nothing and no one. Go, fool!"

The Arch Druid turned back, with some dignity, amidst jeers and shouts from some of Aed's supporters, although not all. The horns resumed.

The sun was setting by this time, and Aed ordered wood and peats to be brought, to build fires along the ramparts, and to be kept alight throughout the night to ensure that no assault in darkness could take them by surprise. Soon fires were gleaming from the huge enemy camp also. It was unlikely that Diarmid would seek to attack that night anyway, for his men would need rest after their long marching. However, relays of sentinels were organised, to patrol the perimeter barrier and beyond, before the defenders fed and bedded down. Colum led some hearty psalm-singing around the fires, to help counter all the druidical horn-blowing. He had a great fondness for the Psalms of David – and after all, it was their translation into his own tongue which was being held partly responsible for all this trouble.

Thereafter the night passed relatively undisturbed, save for the calls of the sentinels and the everlasting wailing of the horns, which was kept up throughout and which undoubtedly had its effect on many of the northern galloglasses, other than merely tending to keep them awake; superstition and the fear of magic was by no means dead amongst them.

Sunrise was, of course, the major druidical worship-time, and the southern army made a great show of it, with hailing and chanting and play-acting sacrifices, as well as the unfailing trumpeting. Again Colum responded with psalm-singing, admittedly rather inadequately.

As the light strengthened, however, it became evident that all of the enemy had not spent the night sleeping. For an enormous heap of stones had been collected and piled up there on the ridge facing the ramparts, and was being added to all the time. Since most of the local stone readily available had already been gathered by the defenders and used to strengthen the said ramparts above the ditch, this development indicated an urgent purpose as well as much labour. Presumably hovels and cot-houses had been demolished over quite a wide area to provide all that stone.

Few amongst the defenders failed to recognise the implications. This was a great cairn which was being erected, a burial cairn, to symbolise the defeat and death of the opposition.

It took them until midday to complete that pyramidal cairn, thirty feet high at least. When it was finished, the Druids formed up, to lead a circling procession round and round it, the High King and his lieutenants following on, all chanting, whilst the cow-horns ululated. Those watching and listening, could not distinguish the words spoken but none doubted that they would include the names of those to die, Colum's and Aed's foremost. It was all part of a war of nerves.

Nor was that all that was conjured up. The afternoon was spent by the enemy largely in the creation of another erection, this time mainly in token, and again it was the Druids who were in charge. It consisted of bringing wooden posts and more small stones, to make little heaps, and with these to form a symbolic fence facing the ditch-and-ramparts, for its full half-mile length, although there were gaps between the posts and heaps often as wide as a score of feet. When at length this was finished, the Druid phalanx came forward again, to pace back and forth along its length, weaving snake-like in and out amongst the posts, chanting, and under their strange standards of skulls, human and animal and long-haired scalps, on poles, with sunbursts of polished gold. They kept this up hour after hour, an act of sorcery, the creation of a mystical barrier, well-known to all, across which, in druidical theory, no man might venture without not only dying but incurring everlasting torture, shame and even rejection by his ancestors.

Mummery as it might be named, all this could not fail to worry the defending leadership, Colum not the least. For the cumulative effect on their clansmen and galloglasses was evident. The men-at-arms went about looking apprehensive, not meeting their chiefs' eyes; indeed not all the chiefs looked happy either. The lack of activity on their own part did not help. Colum's psalm-singing was not really an adequate retaliation.

Aed came to Colum in the late afternoon, in some agitation. Could he not think of something to counter all this devilment and sorcery? They required something that men could see. Like those Druids' standards. Was there nothing that he could think of?

"Only Christ's cross. We could, and should use that, carry the cross as a standard."

"That would help, yes. But we need more . . ."

42

"Could we have more than the Lord Christ's crucifix?"

Aed shook his head. "Not for the believers, the faithful. But . . . not all are so strong in faith as you, Colum. These are ordinary fighting men. What will they see? Only two pieces of wood, a cross-bar on a pole! They need something more than that. Or, not *more* but different. Something they can look on with wonder. Something that the Druids have not got. Have you nothing, man?"

"I have only my Psalter. My own copy of David's Psalms. The book I always carry with me."

"A book! Save us – a book! But . . . that might be better than nothing. Few of them will ever have seen a book, writings. How large is it?"

"It is scarcely a book, in truth. Rolled up sheets of parchment. Written on and illuminated with colours. Painting and designs. I have made many such. But this is my own copy. Much worn and tattered, I fear."

"None the worse for that. Could it be hoisted on a pole? For all to see?"

"If so you wish. But crosses would be better."

"Have both. Get it, Colum. We must do something . . ."

So spear-poles were produced, and the sheets of well-thumbed manuscript unrolled and tied to their tops, with cross-bars of wood lashed to others to make crucifixes. Aed commanded their entire host to be drawn up in orderly ranks and contingents, with spaces left between each unit. Then, with Colum, dressed now in his black-and-white abbot's robes, to lead, a cross-bearer and psalter-carrier in front and two more behind, the kings and princes and chiefs following, interspersed with more crosses and parchment-sheets, they commenced a parade through all the ranks, up and down, back and forward, singing the best-known psalm-tunes, Colum's rich and powerful voice resounding – although even he was hoarse before that procession through the thousands was done.

It all took much time, but had its effect undoubtedly, the rough galloglasses eyeing those written and coloured parchments in especial with something like awe, as objects of magic and the supernatural.

Aed and his lieutenants were reasonably satisfied that something of the Druids' display had been countered, even though their wretched horns still sounded. How they kept that up, night and day, was itself a mystery; presumably they had teams of blowers.

Later, round the leaders' camp-fire, as they ate their evening meal, Colum listened to the talk, and impatiently brushed aside congratulations to himself on the successful impact of what was being looked on as demonstration, and what he insisted should have been an act of worship.

"See you," he said, raising his voice challengingly, "has it not come to any of you that all this of the Druids and their demon-craft is not to be feared, but is indeed possibly an excellent augury? Let us thank God for it, I say. For it could well be Heaven's gift to us!"

Men stared at him, in the firelight, incredulous.

"Do you not see? Everything that has been done, thus far, is the Druids' doing. Not Diarmid's. Diarmid is in their hands, clearly. He has made no gestures, or demonstrations of armed force, no warlike challenges. He is leaving all to the Druids, meantime, despite his great numbers. Why? He must have his reasons. I believe that it may be because he has many Christians amongst his army. And cannot be sure of them to fight other Christians with whole heart. Some of his leaders, also, may not be eager for battle against us. The banner of the King of Leinster is there, my own cousin, son of my mother's brother. There are others kin to many of us here. So – Diarmid is cautious, hoping, I think, to avoid pitched battle, if he may. To seek to affright and unman us by his sheer weight of numbers, and all this druidical mummery."

"What then?" Aed demanded. "He must fight, in the end. As must we."

"In the end? I say, sooner, Highness! Here is how I see it. Diarmid, at this present, is holding back from attack, perceiving our position strong, and unsure of some of his support. He and his people are much relying on Bec mac De and his Druids, the spirit of darkness. That is their state of mind. So – let *us*, who have the spirit of light to aid us, take the full advantage."

"What do you mean? How can we? What advantage can we take?" voices asked.

"Attack! Since Diarmid does not!" Colum answered simply He had them silent, now.

"My friends – I believe that God shows us the way. Since this is *His* struggle, as well as ours. If we go down, our

Christian faith goes down in Ireland also. For long, perhaps. So *we* strike."

"How can we strike, man? Attack?" King Donald demanded. "They are double our numbers, on higher ground, with that *airbhe*, that druidical fence between us, which our men will fear to cross and that cairn overlooking all."

On all sides his objections were supported.

"We need not cross that fence. Nor our own ditch. In darkness of night we could divide into two hosts, left and right. Move out quietly round the *ends* of our long defensive line. There is bogland and saltmarsh at both ends, for so we chose it. But, taking our time, and without horses, we can get our people through that marshland. We cannot *hurry* through bog, but we can pick our way, given time. Then, at dawn, we will be on firm ground again, below them yes – but they will not look for us there. Or then. They will be preparing for their sunrise worship of their false gods, unready for battle. Then up with us, and attack, from north and south. We will have them when they least expect it. And, God willing, in God's good cause, we will prevail!" That last came out in quivering intensity and emotion, despite all the man's hatred of war and bloodshed.

The reaction, now, was vehement, vociferous, some loud in acclaim, others in opposition. For minutes on end there was altercation and heated argument.

Then Prince Ernan of Donegal, Colum's uncle, managed to make himself heard. He was the most religiously-inclined of the sons of Fergus, and a sound Christian, only a year or two older than his nephew. "Colum is right. Let us surprise them. The better while they are at their devil-worship. God will be with *us*, not them!"

King Ainmere, his other nephew, felt bound to back them up; and Aed, who was becoming much concerned over maintaining the food supply for their thousands in these conditions, came round to agreement. The thing was accepted.

Thereafter, although some were eager to start the readying of their forces for action right away, it was decided that, even in the darkness, a great stirring of their camp might become evident to the enemy; so they should wait until after midnight, when the other host would have few awake, to make a move. There should still be plenty of time before dawn. But all leaders and captains were summoned and given instructions. They were, above all, to impress on their men the need for silence once the venture commenced.

Only the most carefree slept during those hours of waiting.

At one hour past midnight, with still five hours before the October dawn, they started, in two great columns, King Donald and the Prince of Tyrone leading the north-about one, Aed and Ainmere the south-about, which was likely to be the more difficult, with wider and wetter marshland to cross. Colum went with the latter division.

Both companies retired westwards a little way before turning down from the central ridge, left and right, to the shoreline – this to avoid, if possible, any telltale movement or sound thereof becoming evident to the enemy sentinels. Fortunately, the Druids' horn-blowing, still maintained, would help to cover any unavoidable noise.

Down on the south shore, Colum's party proceeded slowly, heedfully, eastwards now behind local guides who knew every yard of the way, carefully avoiding the village of Cregg, where barking dogs might raise the alarm. The real difficulty began when they reached the actual junction of peninsula and mainland, where were the tidal flats and saltmarsh to cross, fully quarter of a mile of them. They could, of course, have taken the access road from Cooldrevny to Cregg over the higher ground, but this would have brought them dangerously close to the south end of the enemy encampment, and possible discovery. So it was a matter of each man picking his way as best he could, wading, leaping, bog-trotting, plowtering, but trying not to splash unduly. Silence was essential – plus of course safety – and all were told they had ample time. But in the dark it was an awkward, messy and even dangerous business. It was a wet, bedraggled, muddy host, high and low alike, which eventually reassembled on firm ground at the far side, after the slowest quarter-mile march any could recollect.

Even so, they reckoned that they still need not hurry, calculating that they had almost two hours till first light. The plan now was to form three groups, of about eight hundred each, to move forward and uphill from south-west, south and south-east, under Ernan, Aed and Ainmere respectively, Colum going with the centre party. Each group had one of his psalm-sheets, on a pole, as had the north-about host. It all had to be carefully carried out and timed, all three keeping in touch, so that, despite the differing ground conditions and any natural obstacles, all would arrive at their chosen positions approximately at the same time, and silently. They should then be only around three hundred yards from the enemy, and hidden therefrom, it was hoped, by the lie of the land and some scrub woodland of hawthorn and ash – although undoubtedly some of the trees would have been cut down to provide posts for that Druids' fence.

It was at this stage that Colum became aware of a new circumstance – dampness on his face. Too fine for rain – sea-mist. This, he recognised, could be a complication if it persisted. It would make keeping in contact with the other units difficult, at dawn, and hide the enemy's exact movements and positions; but also, to be sure, it could blanket sound and give their own advance cover. He did not know whether to be troubled or the reverse. He chided himself; have faith in God.

From the sandy machair of the shore there was barely two hundred feet of rise to the level of the camp, sand-dunes at first then grassy, gorse-grown slopes, uneven, with occasional outcrops of the underlying rock. Normally cattle would have been grazing or sleeping here, and, bolting possibly before the advancing men, might have given the alarm; but undoubtedly all such had been taken and slaughtered, to feed the enemy. Their progress uphill did arouse some wheepling curlews, as it had done mallard and widgeon down in the marshland, but it was to be hoped that this would not be significantly noticeable to the foe.

Near the summit of that rise, such as it was, a sort of broken escarpment made a brow to the plateau. This, and the scrub woodland, had to serve them as cover. Reaching it, in turn, the three parties settled down to wait.

It made uncomfortable waiting, both physically and mentally. The mist was chill, the grass they crouched on wet; and men were now impatient for action. Indeed some of the leaders proposed that they did not wait. Why not up and assail the sleeping camp right away? Surely that would be surprise enough? Aed was inclined to heed this point of view, but Colum urged otherwise. For one thing, their other north-about force under Donald might not be in position yet; and anyway would be waiting for the agreed start at sunrise when

47

the worship began. But more important, a surprise attack on a sleeping host might well succeed, on a small camp; but not on ten thousand and more. They would reach only the edges of the enemy before all would be roused, giving ample time for the great mass within to rise, arm themselves and resist. Much better to await the worship ceremony, when arms would be apt to be left behind.

So they crouched amongst the branches of felled trees and prickly gorse-bushes, and shivering with the cold and damp, they listened to those horns at their wailing. It seemed a long wait.

Eventually, almost imperceptibly, a vague lightening of the gloom was sensed rather than actually seen, to develop and increase equally slowly. Its effect, however, was not to increase their range of vision so much as to reveal the thickness of the mist. Dark grey at first, this gradually grew whiter, but none the more transparent for that. They could not see a score of yards, much less the enemy positions, or even their flanking friends.

Presently they could hear the great camp above them stirring. The horn-blowing took on a new and different note and volume, and being taken up all over the occupied area, rousing men and calling them to worship. Calls and shouting prevailed.

In agitation, the attackers had to restrain themselves, hearing all and seeing nothing.

When the mist still had not lifted, the noise and stir above lessened somewhat, presumably indicating that Diarmid's cohorts would now be in whatever positions they adopted for greeting the first sign of the rising sun – however much they must take that on trust in this opacity. Colum himself was now perturbed, and suggested to Aed that they might creep forward some way further, since they would not be seen. They might, in the end, just have to attack in this mist – to what effect Heaven alone knew! But none to do so until signalled. The king was only too glad to agree.

One hundred yards further, and then a little more, and it was clear, whatever else was not, that they were now very close to other men. Druidical chanting was going on, with deep chorus responses, rising and falling with the ululating horns, strange-sounding, weird enough to raise hairs at the backs of men's necks. Colum was thankful for the noise at least, for he was all too conscious of their advancing men's mutterings, tripping over fallen branches, rustling leafage, the clink of arms, and the like.

Still there was nothing but white sea-mist to be seen.

"Lord – why, oh why!" Colum whispered. "Why, now, do you hide our enemy, and your own, from us? Oh, God, why do you not clear away this mist, so that we may reap your judgement on the idolators?"

There was no noticeable reply from aloft, and the situation was desperate. Any moment, some member of the two parties might be discovered and the alarm raised. Should they just charge in now, mist or none? There would be complete confusion, their own as much as the enemy's perhaps – and they would be outnumbered two to one.

Then the matter was taken out of their own decision. Noise, different noise, suddenly erupted from the north, distant but vehement, shouting and yells and the clash of steel. Obviously King Donald's force had started the attack, whether out of similar impatience or because they were discovered.

Aed waited no longer. "Forward!" he cried. "Forward!" And the cry was taken up right and left. Colum's more powerful voice was raised also.

"God is with us! In the name of Christ the Lord!" He grabbed one of the psalter-poles from a man at his side and held it high. "Come, and smite! God's Word leads!"

Everywhere men shouted and surged forward, swords and dirks drawn.

What followed was pandemonium, indescribable chaos. All that could be said was that the chaos was worse for the attacked than for the attackers, who at least had purpose, leadership and some faith of a sort – as well as steel at the ready. Into the drawn-up ranks of the enemy, who already were turning in alarm and astonishment to face the north and sounds of conflict, the three southern units flung themselves, smiting at any who loomed up before them. It was a ragged rush, to be sure, uncoordinated inevitably, but even so, surprise was complete. Yells and curses, screams and shrieks, turned the mist-shrouded plateau of Cooldrevny into a white hell.

It was small wonder that panic overtook the lined-up ranks of the sun-worshippers. Unready, they could not see nor know who was assailing them, from where or how many.

Possibly they did not realise that it was in fact their foemen from behind the ditch-and-rampart; it could have been a new host altogether, or two, from north and south. Mainly unarmed and no doubt many sleep-dazed still, men's instinct was to flee from the immediate dire threat – and since they could not flee westwards, into the ditch, they fled eastwards.

Nothing can be more infectious than panic. Here, no one could see what went on elsewhere, no leadership was available, and the attacked were anyway superstitiously concerned in a clash between the gods. A tide of fleeing men crashed into the columns of their fellows, with disastrous results. Little knots of attempted resistance developed here and there, but were quickly overwhelmed. At last the horn-blowing had ceased, superseded by a more horrible din, as men trampled each other down in a flood of terror.

For how long this stampede and slaughter went on there was no knowing – for time, in such circumstances, ceases to have meaning. But presently Colum, at least, came to be aware that the mist was thinning and that the first orange-red rays of the rising sun were penetrating and tinting it with strange, unearthly light. Swiftly, at last, the now coloured mist rolled away.

It revealed a sight of horror, bodies lying all around, still or threshing or twitching, men being beaten down and stabbed, the enemy streaming away eastwards in an unending spate, blood everywhere, even on Colum's abbot's robes, groaning, moaning, screaming, beseeching, mingling with the fiercely triumphant yells of the attackers.

Appalled, Colum halted, still clutching his psalm-standard – and was all but knocked over by the onward rush of their smiting galloglasses – appalled at what he saw and heard, at the agony of men displayed on every hand, at the savagery unleashed – and at his own part therein, the wild exultation which had been his also, and now was suddenly gone. Staring about him as though awakening from some continuing nightmare, he stumbled over a writhing body, to sink down on his knees beside it. Gazing at the staring eyes of the sufferer, he bit his lip and then reached out a hand as in supplication, pleading forgiveness. But he could not long face those tortured, twisted features, and he bowed his head, his own eyes closed.

But he could not pray.

It was thus that Prince Ernan found him presently, and hastened to raise him up.

"You're not hurt, Colum?" his uncle demanded. "This blood? It is not yours? Thank God! Thank God for all! It is victory, man – a great victory. The unbelievers are vanquished, quite. They flee. All flee. Diarmid amongst the first, I swear! God's cause triumphs."

Colum looked from him to the wounded man at their feet and then at all the bodies lying around, and shook his head, wordless.

But Ernan was not to be deflated. "All is well, I tell you. There was little or no resistance. They knew not what overwhelmed them. Fled without fighting, treading each other down. It has been scarcely a battle, no real fighting. Donald of Ailech has had little to do. Now he pursues Diarmid. But they will not stand, I think, nor rally now. It is victory, Colum – and so greatly thanks to you!"

"Then . . . then Lord forgive me! If even He can! This slaughter . . . !"

"Man – what ails you? It is God's victory against the powers of darkness. Christ's Church is saved, in Ireland, this day. You planned it, led all. Your Psalter as standard. Men are calling it the Cathach, the Battle Book! Rejoice, Colum . . ."

No amount of praise could make Colum mac Felim rejoice on that bloody plateau of Cooldrevny, nor thereafter back at Aed's palace of Drumcleeve – which they found little the worse for Diarmid's occupation. As the reports came in, there could be no doubting the scale and completeness of their victory. Diarmid, warrior as he was reputed to be, was leading the flight southwards, and clearly would not halt until he was safely back in his own territories in Meath, his army dispersed and fleeing in all directions. The booty captured was enormous. And the latest count assessed almost three thousand left dead. Their own losses were negligible. Only the one failure was reported – and that was the result of folly. A minor chieftain of Donald's force, one Maiglinde, had ignored instructions and led his group through the Druids' fence and, strangely, met with disaster, dying himself, his people thrown back. As well that this had not become known to the others earlier on, because of the mist, or it might well have had a grievous impact on general morale. Even now, men shook their heads and muttered.

Colum, for his part, finding himself the hero of the hour, withdrew and shut himself up in the little church which he himself had founded there at Drumcleeve years before, and sought to come to terms with his conscience. He was less than successful. Three thousand dead . . .

3

Time heals, it is said – but Colum did not find it to do so, in the weeks that followed. Back at Derry, soul-searchings, fastings and penances gave him no peace of mind. He had long since given up trying to convince himself that what he had done at Cooldrevny was for the best, that it was a service to God's cause, that the pagan faith had been greatly damaged and Holy Church saved and strengthened. Three thousand human souls cried out to him that it was not so, that he who had gone to Connaught seeking to make peace had become responsible for their deaths. He just could not live with himself. He had even sought to allay his nagging self-criticism by compiling a special hymn of praise for the acclaimed victory of God's cause, fine stirring stuff – but whoever else it might convince, it did not convince himself. Small comfort that his mother blamed him nothing; nor did most of his friends and colleagues. But not all. There was an undercurrent of blame. He was aware of folk eying him strangely; even in his own monastery he felt that he was being regarded differently. He found some of the monks and lay-brothers failing to meet his eye. Three thousand souls, his fellow-Irishmen . . .

He was doing little sleeping of a night.

This was all very unlike Colum mac Felim, normally a notably forthright and assured character. Christmastide and its festivities did not help. He almost looked forward to the disciplines and self-punishments of Lent.

Then, one wet and windy February day, a visitor came to Derry, who had the effect of changing Colum's attitude quite remarkably, not in any way purging his conscience but at least

52

causing a reversion to more typical behaviour. This was the Abbot Laisran, a former fellow-student with Bishop Finnian at Clonard, who had helped to found this Derry monastery, and who had been appointed abbot of the second establishment which Colum had founded, at Durrow, in Leinster. But it was not from there that he had come, but from Devenish, on Lough Erne where he had a hermitage on an island. For he had become something of an anchorite, withdrawing more and more to this quiet retreat, for contemplation, prayer and spiritual refreshment, as was the custom of so many of the Celtic clergy. Colum, the man of action, respected such reclusion but could not follow it. Partly because of this, and partly in that he had always esteemed his friend's wisdom and quiet faith, he had come to use Laisran almost as a confessor, at times. All men, he recognised, had need of a confessor on occasion, even though they did not always know it.

Laisran brought no comfort; indeed Colum, in his over-sensitive state, thought that he detected some criticism even in his old friend's greeting and attitude; but he did bring a challenge, which was, in fact, more effective. He came to inform that he, Laisran of Durrow, had been summoned to attend a special synod of the Church in Ireland, to be held at Teltown in six days time, the main objective of which was to pronounce sentence of excommunication on the Abbot of Derry and Kells.

Colum's reaction to this news surprised even his friend in the circumstances, although, despite all the recent heart-searching and self-reproach, it was instinctive. He was suddenly furious, exploding in wrath. Excommunication? Of *him*! Who *dared*? By what right? Hypocrites! A synod of what, of whom? Diarmid's friends and supporters, hereditary abbots so-called, comfortable incumbents of fat manors, who did nothing, nothing of God's work!

Laisran had almost to smile at this abrupt transformation of his colleague. But he also had to point out that there was more to it all than that, not just the enmity of idle men, tribal jealousy and the like. There was real distress and concern amongst many good churchmen. Colum's leading part in the recent battle was deplored, the deaths of so many being laid at his door, the Church's witness for peace and goodwill amongst men put in doubt.

"Do you so judge it?" Colum demanded. "Do you,

Molaise, see me as a man of blood? Preaching war, not love!"
Molaise, short for *mo-Laisran*, my dear Laisran, was his
affectionate nickname for his friend. "God knows me for a
sinner – but not that! I blame myself that I was caught up in the
warfare, yes. I went to Connaught in peace. But Diarmid
invaded, egged on by the Druids. Would you have had me
stand idly by and see Christ's cause go down before the forces
of darkness? Would you?"

"What I think is little to the point, Colum. But others *are*
blaming you. They believe that Holy Church has suffered.
Three thousand dead . . . !"

"Think you I am not tortured by those dead? They rack me!
I never wished any to die. Only that Diarmid's host should not
prevail against the Christians. The slaughter I hated. But – it
was them, or us. Do you not understand? I sought to avoid
battle. By surprise . . ."

"That may be so, Colum. But others do not know it, see it
that way. They see you leading the attack, your famous Psalter
being called the Battle Book! They believe you responsible for
the bloodshed . . ."

"Then they shall learn differently! I myself shall tell them. I
shall attend this so-called Synod. I shall . . ."

"You cannot do that, man! It is impossible. It is to be held at
Teltown. Near to Tara. On Diarmid's own doorstep."

"I shall go, I tell you. They shall not excommunicate *me*!
You are going? I shall go with you. Diarmid will not expect
me to be there. We shall go secretly. I shall not stay long. God
will protect me from Diarmid!"

Wonderingly Laisran eyed his revived friend, who clearly
had found what he needed to lift him out of his so unnatural
dispirited state, a challenge to action. Moping and gloomy
introspection did not come naturally to Colum. He was on the
way to becoming himself again.

They set out next day, on horseback, Laisran borrowing
nondescript garb and packing his abbatical robes in his
saddle-bag. They took no escort, seeking to be as inconspi-
cuous as possible. For the same reason, they followed the
round-about route which Colum had taken, in reverse, those
months ago when he had secretly left Kells, avoiding communities. It would take longer, but they just had time they
reckoned; they must not be early.

So down through Tyrone's uplands, by Monaghan and

Louth, they came to Meath the evening before the Synod, due to start at noon the next day. They put up at a lonely farmstead, about six miles from Teltown.

In the morning, they went together only as far as a wood near the Boyne. There, Colum insisted that Laisran dressed again as an abbot and went on ahead to the assembly, as though he had come direct from Durrow. He, Colum, would make an unheralded appearance soon after the meeting had started. In highly doubtful state his friend departed.

It was strange for Colum to be so near to Kells and not visit his monastery; but that would have been foolish. In that woodland, he had to do some praying. If God did not hear his prayer, then so be it; he would soon know.

Less than an hour after noon he rode up to the fairly small timber church of Teltown, robed now but seeing that his hood part-covered his face. He left his horse amongst many others, with the monkish attendants there, none questioning an abbot latecomer.

Drawing a deep breath, he opened the church-door quietly, and slipped inside, to close it behind him, bowing towards the altar. He threw back his cowl.

The place was packed with bishops, abbots, priors and priests, the senior clergy of all Ireland. One, wearing a bishop's stole, was on his feet, speaking. Colum waited.

It took some time for him to be perceived and recognised, most having their backs turned to him. It was the speaker himself who in the end drew attention to him, as presently his sonorous voice faltered and, falling silent, he gazed. Then his arm rose, to point a quivering finger at the man at the door. He said nothing.

All then turned, to stare, and after a moment or two, hubbub filled the church. Men exclaimed and gestured, few in welcoming or friendly fashion. The name Colum mac Felim was on every lip, mainly in astonishment, hostility, offence.

The newcomer stood there, in appearance at least the calmest man in the building, waiting for the noise to die down, his bearing not defiant but assured, even authoritative. He was, after all, the only prince of the royal house of O'Neill there.

The bishop who had been speaking sat down heavily, and as though recollecting where they were and the requirements of dignity, one by one others who had risen resumed their seats,

55

most now following the lead of the bishop and carefully turning their backs again on the new arrival. Only a single man indeed remained standing. He was dressed as an abbot and was of about Colum's own age, burly of build.

"Columcille, my friend!" this individual exclaimed. "God bless you for coming here this day!" And pushing his way through the seated throng, he came to kiss Colum heartily on both cheeks. It was Brendan, another former student colleague at Clonard, who had later founded the monastery of Birr, in Leinster.

Colum gripped the other's arm, gratefully.

Then slowly, painfully, another rose to his feet, an old man this, white-haired, bent and frail-seeming, wearing a bishop's stole and having to use his episcopal crozier to steady himself.

"Colum, my son," he called, in a quavering voice, "I thank God who has brought you in answer to my prayers."

Colum had to bow his yellow head to hide the tears which sprang to his eyes. For once, he it was who could not find words. For this was their old tutor and mentor, Bishop Finnian of Moville, he of the copied Psalter.

There was much murmuring. But only one other rose in welcome, Laisran.

Somebody raised an accusatory voice. "Abbot Brendan – why do you stand to acknowledge one who has been excommunicated by Holy Church?" It was noticeable that this was not addressed to the old bishop. Colum raised his eyebrows. So he had been excommunicated already; they had been quick about it.

"I will tell you why," Brendan answered. "This Colum mac Felim has done more for Christ's cause than any other in all Ireland. If you could see what our Lord revealed to me, this day, concerning this His chosen one, you would never have excommunicated him. Aye, and I say, God Himself does not excommunicate, in accordance with your unjust decree!"

"How can you say that? What right have you?"

"How does God tell you this?"

"What did you see?"

"What did the Lord reveal to you, Brendan?"

"I saw a bright column, streaming with fire preceding this man of God whom you despise, accompanying him on his journey through the plain. So I dare not slight him. I say that he is preordained by God to live as leader of peoples."

Men exclaimed at that, some impressed – for Brendan's reputation was high – some sceptical, some actually scornful.

"What I tell you is truth."

"He is guilty of the blood of men, many men, thousands," another called. "None can deny that."

"I can!" That was as strong a voice as any there – Colum's own. "You have condemned me, unheard. Is that the justice of Holy Church? Now you shall hear – and judge thereafter. Many died at Cooldrevny, but – but not of my willing. I went to Connaught seeking peace, to prevent war. But King Diarmid and the Arch Druid Bec mac De would have no peace. They came all that way for war, with many times the Hy-Neill numbers. But not only for war. They had come to destroy the Christian faith. Diarmid apostate, the Arch Druid an apostle of the powers of darkness. It was the Druids who led, not Diarmid, at Cooldrevny. They raised all their damnable devilries against us, calling on their heathen gods to destroy us Christians. They blew their horns, summoning evil spirits, night and day. They built a great cairn of the dead for us, and circled it to the sun, cursing us. They erected a druidical fence before us, in challenge. All this, and more, before a single blow had been struck. It was Lucifer against Christ-Jesus! Would any here have yielded to that?"

There was silence in that church.

"We sang hymns and psalms," Colum went on. "We prayed. But the faith of some wavered, in the face of such devils' work. Outnumbered, and many fearful, we could have fallen, when Diarmid's thousands attacked. And Christ's cause in Ireland, *your* cause, would have gone down, nothing more sure. You would not be daring to meet here this day! You, the churchmen, would have fallen also, with the rest, all of you who still proclaimed Christ's name. Many of you would, I say, be dead by this!"

There were protests at that.

Colum's hand stabbed accusingly here and there. "You, hereditary abbots, who are the friends of Bec mac De – *you* would not be dead, no! Not if you had changed into druidical robes, as many would do, as the price of their lives. Deny it!"

The company seethed, but not all in anger.

"*You* attacked. You struck the first blows," someone yelled. "You, Colum mac Felim, led!"

"I struck no single blow. I led, yes. But with the Psalms of David as standard. My own copy." He glanced over at Bishop Finnian. "Those psalms, against the sun-worshippers' skulls and sunbursts! As they greeted the sunrise, with their evil rites. Not to kill but to confound, to disperse, to drive away, in God's great name. As David himself did. And God was with us. They fled in panic and dread, trampling each other down. There was no battle at Cooldrevny. Thousands died, yes, to my sorrow, in the panic and flight. But had there been battle, many, many more would have fallen, Christians as well as devil-worshippers. Can you not see it?"

Laisran raised his voice. "Columcille speaks truth. That surprise at sunrise prevented war, outright war. With near to twenty thousand men fighting, what would have been the toll?"

Argument and discussion took over.

It was the aged and frail Finnian who restored order, by thumping vehemently on the flooring with his crozier. "My friends," he declared, "I say, I urge, I pray, that, having heard the Abbot Colum's words, and knowing his love for Holy Church and all that he has done for her, you now withdraw the sentence of excommunication so hurriedly and inadvisedly passed."

"I so urge, also," Brendan cried.

"And I!" Laisran added.

There was a great shouting, for and against. A count was demanded, for it was apparent that it was going to be a close thing.

They voted, and the count showed twenty-seven in favour, twenty-two against, and a few discreet abstentions.

"It is done!" Brendan the enthusiast exclaimed. "Columcille is restored, God be praised! I told you!"

In the commotion, Colum held up his hand. "My friends," he called. "I thank you. I am a sinner, God knows. But surely I can do more for His cause within His Church than if thrust out? And shall do! But now, I leave you meantime. For there could, I think, be some here at Teltown who will tell Diarmid mac Cerball at Tara that I am come. And he will try to take me, that is certain. And then I would not live another hour! So I go, as I came, secretly. I pray God's blessing on your further deliberations – and ask you all to pray for me." And spreading expressive hands, he turned and left them.

He went for his horse, and without delay rode off again northwards.

Robes hidden again, he made his way back to the same farmery where they had spent the night, there, as arranged, to await Laisran. Although thankful for his deliverance from the terrible sentence of excommunication, and all that that would have entailed, he was uneasy in his mind, the urgent challenge to action over, something of his former self-doubt returning. He had carried the day, thanks to Finnian, Brendan and Laisran. But God? He had prayed, used God's name and cause, and thanked Him. But – how did his Creator and Saviour think of him now? Did *He* blame him for those deaths? That question had to be resolved before he could know any peace of mind.

So he waited. It was dark before his friend put in an appearance.

Presently the two of them were eying each other in the candle-light of the bare shack, before the fire of peats, eating a simple meal.

"It has been a full day," Laisran said. "A notable day for you, Colum – for which I thank God. Are you content?"

"No. Grateful, Molaise. But not content."

"No? You hoped for more? Better than you did achieve? I think that you did sufficiently well, my friend. Better than I feared."

"Yes, yes. It is not that. Not what happened at Teltown. It was good, better than my deserts, no doubt. No, it is in myself that I am not content."

"Are we ever? Should we be?"

"Probably not. But – you and Brendan and old Finnian saved me, this day. But . . . Almighty God? What does He think of Colum mac Felim, I wonder?"

"Who knows that? But He loves you, Colum – that is certain. He loves us all, whatever our failings. And you, to whom He has given great gifts, He must love greatly. I say that it was He who saved you this day, not we three His feeble servants."

"You believe so? That He does not hold me guilty of the bloodshed?"

"Ah, as to that I would not venture to say."

"But you doubt it, Molaise? You doubt it – as do I!"

"I know no more than you do, friend. But this I believe – that out of all this, the bloodshed and today's decision, God will expect great things of you. You have done great works in His cause, yes, already. But perhaps greater than any of these . . ."

"You think so? To purge my sin?"

"I would not put it so. Just say that He has work for Colum mac Felim to do. He has brought you through this fire, for some purpose. A purpose which possibly only *you* can perform. That all those thousands may not have died for nothing."

"So – you do blame me! I felt that you did. Or you would not say it that way."

"I do not *blame* you, Columcille. Who am I to blame? I but recognise the hurt and pain and sorrow of it all. And your own doubts and fears. I do not blame – but others do, still do."

"Aye – that I believe! Was that what was said after I left the Synod? The general feeling? Blame? Even though they had lifted the excommunication?"

"Yes, and no. Blame is scarcely the word. Responsibility, shall we say? Responsibility, not so much for the bloodshed, after your powerful account of what happened at Cooldrevny, but for the possible damage to Holy Church. The linking of battle, war, and Christ's Church. That, and the linking of the Church's cause with that of the Hy-Neill. To be sure it was also recognised that what you did may well have *saved* the Church in Ireland from dire persecution. But a saving by blood and battle could still leave the Prince of Peace's cause open to condemnation. That *Cathach*, that Battle Book, I fear, may have cost Holy Church dear – the Old Testament triumphing over the New! David, not Jesus!"

Colum stared into the glow of the peats. "Jesus drove the traders and money-changers out of the Temple, in His anger."

"But with words, not with swords. He said that he who takes the sword shall perish by the sword."

"So – I am still condemned? Not excommunicated but condemned."

"Not condemned. Say, rather, challenged. You have always been a man for challenges, Colum. Here is one, the greatest. To make good any harm done to Christ's cause."

60

"In what way? What have I to do? What came out of that Synod?"

"It was Bishop Finnian who had the last word. He it was who declared that Brendan's vision, of you with a pillar of fire going before you, on a journey, meant that God had a great work for you to perform. What the work was none there could say. But it would assuredly be revealed, since it was the Divine purpose. All left it at that."

There was a long silence.

"And you, Molaise – what think you this challenge, this task, to be?" Colum asked, at length. "You have advised me well in the past. What now? I need guidance, if ever I did."

"Who am I to say? A weak and sinful man myself, lacking *your* strength and vigour and rank. How dare I say what is in my mind, friend?"

"But something is in your mind? Say it."

"It was the old guide and teacher of us both, Finnian, who led me to it. After the meeting, he said to me that you should consider leaving Ireland for a time, whilst tempers cool and men see it all in a fairer light, with less prejudiced eyes. Make some pilgrimage, he said, some mission in the Church's service . . ."

"Exile! He meant exile?"

"He did not say that, no. A mission, a pilgrimage, he said . . ."

"But that is what he meant. Leave Ireland, my own, my beloved land!"

"For a time, only."

"And you? You say this also? You would have me go? Into banishment!"

"Not that, Colum – never that. Only for a period, whilst this trouble dies down and all is seen more fairly." Laisran paused. "And it comes to me – could this not be what *God* would will? Could such a pilgrimage be indeed the mission, the greater work God has destined for you? Something far beyond what you, or any of us, have attempted up till now. A challenge indeed!"

"What do you mean, man?"

"The tide of paganism is rising again all over Christendom, and not only in Ireland. Elsewhere is worse than here. The Lucifer you named is on the advance! There is work for a man with your abilities and qualities, your powers of leadership,

61

your vigour. Ireland can spare you for a while, after Cool-drevny. Go where you are more needed, Columcille."

"Where?"

"The Church in many lands could do with your aid. Wales, Cornwall, parts of Gaul. But above all, Alba. There are our own folk, in New Dalriada, the Scots as they call themselves. Christians, but under ever increasing threat and pressure, from Brude mac Maelchon, High King of the pagan, sun-worshipping Cruithne, the Picts. If any need help, the Scots do."

"They need swords, I think! Not the Gospel. They need the very aid that is being held against me here! Is that to be my mission? More bloodshed?"

"God forbid! No – but under the Pictish threat, little Dalriada's Christianity is endangered grievously. There has been much inter-marriage with their Pictish neighbours – they are all of our Celtic stock, after all. And there are ten, twenty times as many Picts as these Scots. Their faith is much at risk. The other Brendan, the Navigator, told me of it all. He founded a small monastery on one of their islands, Tiree. Now, an old man, he is back in Ireland, on his island hermitage in Lough Corrib. He is greatly concerned. He says that the Dalriada Scots could lose their kingdom, yes – but worse, they could lose their Christianity. You must know of this, Colum? They are your kin there, the ruling house, are they not?"

"Yes, they are of the Hy-Neill. Lorn and Fergus mac Erc it was, of our own Dalriata in Antrim, went over the sea to Alba near a century ago, and carved out for themselves this little kingdom there. Their father, Erc mac Eochaid, son of the Slave Lord, was brother to Niall Nine-Hostager. So they are kin, yes – their present King Conall a distant cousin. But . . ."

"Then go, and aid your kinsmen. Keep the torch of Christ's cause alight in Dalriada. And more, seek to convert the heathen Picts."

"The Picts? Man – are you crazed? There are thousands of them, hundreds of thousands! As many as in all Ireland. Convert the Picts, you say . . .!"

"Some of them, at the least. Make a start. And if they were Christian also, they would be less likely to attack the Dalriada Scots. See you – seek to bring Christ to at least as many souls as you are being blamed for leading to die! Three thousand!

Bring three thousand to God, Columcille, and thereby aid the Scots also. Here is challenge sufficient for even Colum mac Felim!"

The other stared at him, wordless again.

"Is it too great a project, friend? Even to attempt? If any could do it, I think that you might."

"But . . . a whole nation!"

"Our Lord's apostles went out to convert a whole nation. Ordinary men, not princes! Indeed, to convert the whole world. Think of it."

Colum scarcely slept that night, his mind in turmoil.

The morning saw him heavy-eyed, drawn of feature, no nearer decision, and sour, abrupt, with Laisran, for putting such a further weight, a burden, on his soul. That urge to confession had cost him dear.

Laisran understood, even sympathised – but by no means withdrew his suggestion.

"Go, think about it, Columcille. Alone. You and your Maker. Go to some quiet refuge. I would say come to my island at Devenish, but I go there myself and you should be alone. Alone with God. He will guide you, show you yea or nay. You have gone to the Aran Isles, in the past, for contemplation and spiritual refreshment. Go there, my friend, and discover God's will for you."

Colum bowed his yellow head.

4

Colum strode up and down the shingle beach of Lough Foyle impatiently in the early May sunshine. Typical of the man, now that he had made up his mind to go, and was committed, he was all eagerness to be off, delay anathema. The preparations had taken all too long. But now at last all was ready, their gear was stowed aboard, his party assembled, the tide right, the sun shining, even a suitable westerly wind blowing, God being good to them. But still his mother did not appear. He had tried to say his goodbyes to her at Derry, the previous evening, but nothing would do but that she must come and see them off at the ship. She knew the timing and the tide, but she was late. Women!

A great crowd was there waiting. From all over Donegal the folk had come to see this embarkation, practically everyone from the Derry monastery and others from further afield still, for all recognised that it was a notable occasion. The famous, now notorious, Abbot of Derry and Kells and prince of the Hy-Neill, was leaving Ireland voluntarily, going into exile or banishment, putting all that he was and had laboured for behind him, to go to a heathen land. And taking with him his twelve chosen colleagues, his disciples as they were being called, good men and true, whose loss the Church in Ireland could perhaps ill spare. But that was Colum mac Felim – he never did anything by halves. All watched him at his striding and frowning, none, even those closest to him, daring to join him or speak with him, knowing that they would get their heads snapped off. They had been waiting over half an hour already.

Colum was sorely tempted to delay no longer, to just go aboard and cast off. After all, he had said all that there was to say last night. This coming to wave him away was quite unnecessary. He loved his mother dearly – but there was a time and place for all things, and this was ridiculous. With the weather and the state of the sea so important – for they were going to make one of the most dangerous crossings of those northern seas, where the tides of the great ocean swept down to be funnelled into the narrows between Rathlin Island and the Mull of Kintyre – to hang about here was folly. But he could not do it. Not only because she would be sorely hurt, but he might never see her again in this life; but Laisran would be with her, had stayed behind to escort her, and he had not taken his farewell of the man who had set all this in motion, and come all the way from Devenish to witness their departure.

Machar, the shipmaster, was shouting something from the curragh. They were calling it a curragh, but in fact it was a full-sized long-ship of oak and pine planks, bought from King Donald, with mast and sail and no fewer than sixteen long sweeps or oars. They would require nothing less this day. It even had a name, and quite unsuitable, the *Liath Bhalaidh*, the

Grey Mayor. Machar, one of the youngest of the twelve travellers, was an enthusiast and, having been reared to sea-going, had appointed himself shipmaster. The company of twelve assistants or companions was quite a normal arrangement in the Celtic Church, following the example of Christ's apostles. What Machar was shouting Colum could not tell, with all the chatter going on around, for the vessel was anchored about two hundred yards out, Lough Foyle, with its tidal shallows, allowing it to come no closer without grounding. He turned, and gestured to young Lugbe, the student-monk, who stood nearby, and then jabbed a pointing finger at one of the half-dozen coracles drawn up at the tide's edge, and from it to the ship. With alacrity the youth ran down to the water, pushed out one of the frail little skin-and-frame boats, and went paddling. Lugbe was going with them, not as one of the twelve but as Colum's personal attendant.

This interlude emboldened the priest Dacuilen, who was being left behind in charge of the monastery, to come up with a question about the admission of new students to Derry; for Colum was not resigning his abbacy, not burning all his boats behind him, merely appointing Dacuilen as his Co-Arb. Baithen, his sub-Abbot, had prevailed upon his beloved master to allow him to go to Scotland with him, as one of the twelve.

Colum was reassuring Dacuilen that he had left the fullest written instructions as to the running of the monastery in his absence, when shouting heralded the approach not only of the Princess Eithne and Laisran but of a whole cavalcade of her women and servants, all highly unsuitable, and no doubt the cause of the delay. There was cheering and ribald remarks from the crowd.

Eithne came laden with gifts, choice foods, delicacies, wines, all more than somewhat inappropriate for a penitential pilgrimage. But he could not offend by refusing them; besides, he did not feel particularly penitential this morning.

Restraining himself with difficulty from reproaches, Colum managed to thank her, at the same time exchanging significant glances with Laisran.

"I have remembered something that my father informed me when I was a girl," she told him. "He said that your grandmother, Eirc, daughter of Lorn, King of this Scottish

Dalriada, was meant for another than Murdoch, your grandfather. Lorn had promised her in marriage to Saron, King of the Britons of Strathclyde. But Murdoch, visiting Lorn, and himself grandson of Niall Nine-Hostager, eloped with her back to Ireland – a love match. Eirc bore him four sons, including your father Felim. So King Lorn had only to give his second and less fair daughter, Babona, to Strathclyde's king . . ."

"Mother mine – of a mercy! We are ready to sail, have been waiting for long. No time for tales of family gossip!"

"But this could be important, Colum. It came to me in the night. I had not thought of it for many a year. This Saron of Strathclyde was much displeased. And so was King Lorn. His nephew Conall is now King of Dalriada; and Roderick is King of Strathclyde. They may not love you therefore, grandson of those who caused the trouble."

"That is in God's hands. If He wishes me to do this work, He will not allow such ancient matters to stop me. I cannot be halted now by such . . ."

"I but warn you. You may meet with enmity in both kingdoms . . ."

"Then so be it. I am warned."

"Now – when do you return home? You must have some notion. I asked your Molaise here, but he is equally unhelpful. I must have knowledge of when I am to see my son again! I am an old woman now, and you are the light of my life." That was said in almost an accusatory rather than a sentimental tone of voice.

He shook his head helplessly. "How can I say? I face a great and testing task. It could take years. I have taken a vow . . ."

"*I* have not got years, see you, Colum. And I am not here to say goodbye to you for ever! So – if you do not come home within one year, *I* come to you! Be you sure of that."

"But . . . you cannot do that, Mother. You cannot cross the seas, to Scotland. At your age . . ."

"I can, and shall. Unless you come home. So prepare a place for me where you go. I shall not die here without seeing you again."

"No, no . . ."

"You will not be saying goodbye for ever, Princess," Laisran intervened, with diplomatic intent at least. "You will be rejoining each other, in love, hereafter one day. In a better place than even Derry!"

"No doubt, my friend. But I prefer to see Colum in the flesh, before that! And shall."

Colum, who found partings a trial anyway, sought to bring this one to a close by taking his mother in his arms and giving her a farewell kiss. She clung to him, and he had difficulty in winning free. But even then he was not finished, for three of her young women were waiting close by, and these now came to fling their arms around him and plant their kisses enthusiastically, and not only on his cheeks. And when the others saw this, with much glee they came running to do the same, and the man was all but smothered in femininity, to the vociferous approval of the watching crowd. Normally Colum would not have objected in the least; but he felt the occasion was not propitious, and there would be tales told about this day. Moreover, this farewell procedure proved to be infectious, and promptly all the other travellers were accorded their share also, some admittedly more than others, amidst shouts of laughter, badinage and advice.

Colum shook his head, in an exasperation not devoid of amusement, and saw their solemn departure on the great mission turning into something of a riot of mirth and merriment. He had to regain the initiative. Prince Ernan, his uncle, who was standing by grinning, in the clutch of a notably large lady, was given an urgent signal to help deal with the heap of parting gifts Eithne and her party had brought, lying nearby.

"Come! Come! All aboard!" he shouted, at his loudest. "Enough! We sail. We sail." And himself grabbing up some of the gear, he all but ran down to the water's edge, dodging female arms, to reach one of the coracles.

The move was successful in that while the men were prepared to splash into the shallows, to get the little boats afloat, the women were not; so a separation was effected for some at least – for of course each coracle would hold only three at most, and as well as the chosen twelve there were more than a score of others going, although some were already with Machar, on the long-ship. So the process of disentanglement was distinctly protracted, with the coracles having to be paddled back for second and third loads. Colum himself was sitting in his boat when he realised that he had not taken leave of Laisran. However, his confessor solved the problem by hitching up his abbot's robes and wading out to his friend for a final embrace and blessing.

Thankfully, the exile-in-chief turned his back on all, and paddled his way out to the ship, with his cargo of honey, wine-jars and smoked hams. Ernan was still loading up, with feminine advice.

Colum had visualised sailing off on his mission in dignified fashion, to the singing of a suitable psalm; but somehow this did not seem to be appropriate in the circumstances. When at length the last man was aboard, the coracles were hoisted up. Machar shouted for the anchor to be raised and the oars to be manned, two rowers to each, so thirty-two altogether. There was not much more that Colum could do but wave to the shore, from which cheering arose, loud and long.

As the *Liath Bhalaidh*'s prow swung round to point north-eastwards down-lough, it must have come to many beside Colum mac Felim that this was a strange exodus for a pilgrimage of atonement and danger; but at least it spared them any tearful leave-taking of their beloved homeland.

Machar ordered the great square sail to be hoisted, as the cheering faded behind them.

Three miles down, they passed the notable narrows of Lough Foyle, at Moville, the site of the college where so many of them had learned their priestcraft, and thereafter they were able to dispense with the oars meantime as the westerly breeze reached them ever more fully off the great ocean. The seas increased and by the time that they were right out of the lough-mouth, off Portrush, their craft was pitching and rolling. Out here it seemed a much smaller and frailer entity than it had done in the sheltered anchorage. A few of the travellers became very silent and preoccupied, but most there were used to boating and fairly immune to sea-sickness. Colum sought to cheer the sufferers by pointing out that their voyage would not be a long one. The Scottish coast was, in fact, no more than fourteen miles from Antrim's Fair Head. He did not mention that those miles were apt to be notably unpleasant.

Machar came to ask whether he wished them to sail round Rathlin Island north-about or south-about? The latter was the shorter route, but would lead them into the narrowest constriction of the channel, where tides and currents would run strongest and the waves be steepest. On the other hand, going to the north would leave them exposed to the great ocean rollers for a much longer period, sacrificing shelter from the land-mass of Ireland. Colum advised north-about, for the other would bring them over close to the dreaded Mull of Kintyre. The mighty headland at the southern tip of the sixty-mile-long peninsula where the tides raced notoriously, was a graveyard for shipping; and since they wanted to reach Dalriada, not Strathclyde, they would have to turn due northwards into that tide-race.

They kept a respectful distance out from the Giant's Causeway, and swung away north-east of that strange natural breakwater of basaltic columns thrusting menacingly from the Antrim cliffs into the North Channel, which legend declared had been the commencement of an unfinished bridge of the ancient gods over to Alba. Almost at once they learned what Machar had meant about exposure to the ocean combers; for now, with a south-west wind, they were having to proceed broadside-on to the long seas, and their vessel rolled and wallowed direly, alarmingly, on a scale to make their previous motion a mere jouncing. In any strong wind progress would have been well-nigh impossible, with even today's breeze raising great foaming waves, the white crests of which frequently came splashing inboard. The sail had to be first shortened and then lowered completely and the oars got out again, to keep their bows from swinging round; and Machar called for the crouching passengers to aid the oars-men on the seaward side, in their difficult rowing, others to bail.

Colum was about to move to one of the oars when he thought better of it. If *he* took a hand, all would see it as obligatory to do the same; whereas if he did not, some might refrain from taking part in what was after all manual labour; and he was interested to see how his companions reacted to situations and to each other. Although very carefully chosen by himself from many scores of eager volunteers – and he had been greatly surprised by the numbers who wanted to take part in this strange and hazardous pilgrimage – there were great differences in birth, background and position amongst them. As well as his uncle, there were others of his own kin there, and so of royal blood. Baithen was his first cousin, son of Felim's brother, as was Cobach. Scandlann was a great-grandson of Niall Nine-Hostager. Lugaid, or Moluag, was a well-born bishop; Ciaran, a former fellow-student, a wright's son, was now a prior. The remainder of the twelve were of less exalted position, but all sound in faith, in wits and body, as they would need to be. Colum had his own ideas as to how he would seek to weld them all into a united and effective team, irrespective of blood and status, each respecting the others for their various strengths and qualities. Now, despite sea-sickness, he was glad to see that all without exception responded to Machar's call, at the oars or at bailing – whether out of common danger only remained to be seen. So he himself was able to take a hand likewise, helping Machar on the great steering-oar which served as rudder, and which in these cross-seas demanded strong handling.

They were soon running past the westernmost tip of Rathlin – although running was scarcely an apt description, lurching, dipping, rolling, plunging, rather – a crescent-shaped island some six miles long, cliff-girt, with the seas spouting whitely at their feet, really only an extension of the rock formation which produced the Giant's Causeway. These two towering features they could see, and avoid; but it was what they could not see that was the real danger, the underwater barrier of basalt, stretching far across this arm of the ocean, obstructing the mighty tide-flow of the Atlantic into these narrows and producing the upheaval, turbulence and hazard.

Once past Rathlin, the name itself coming from *rath*, meaning a defensive barrier, conditions became somewhat less trying, as the submarine reef petered out. The seas were still daunting, but longer now and not so apt to fling their crests inboard. Running almost due north, they could see the Scottish coast, the long Kintyre peninsula some fifteen miles away, to the east. Gazing at its blue hills, closer now than their Ireland, some spoke, with just a little dread in their voices, of the heathen and unknown land with its savage inhabitants. Colum corrected them. That was no heathen land. Kintyre was part of Dalriada of the Scots, even though a remote part; and so Christian. Indeed, Brendan of Clonfert, the Navigator, had established a church and cashel there nearly twenty years before, right down at the fearsome Mull – although whether it still survived he did not know. They were not to think that they were bound for a pagan and barbarous land – not in the first instance, at least. The great Alba beyond this Dalriada was pagan, yes, but its Cruithne or Picts, were not savages but of their own Celtic stock, speaking a form of their own Gaelic language, a people of some culture and attainments, well worth bringing to Christ. Let there be no more talk of savages. And this Dalriada was a kingdom of their own folk, where God was worshipped truly.

That stilled the murmurings.

They had not got away from Lough Foyle until about two hours before noon, with all the delay; but even so, by mid-afternoon Machar reckoned that they were almost two-thirds of the way to their destination, with only another thirty or so miles to sail. It kept coming to Colum how short indeed was the actual distance to be covered compared with the momentous nature of their journey, less than one hundred miles from Derry to Dunadd probably, perhaps ten hours sailing, even in these difficult seas. And once they reached the great island of Islay and entered the sheltered waters between it and the mainland, progress would be faster and more comfortable, Machar prophesied. He had never actually been there, of course, but had heard it spoken of by men who had known St Brendan.

And so it proved when, with the May sun westering but still fairly high in the sky, and their sail fully up again, they drew near the green isle of Islay, one of the largest of the Inner Hebrides, over forty times the size of Rathlin. It had been looming ahead of them all along on their northwards passage, but not very prominently for it was fairly low-lying, not mountainous like its neighbours. Indeed as they passed its southern end there were exclamations as to how fair and fertile a place it looked, with rigs of cultivation evident, cattle dotting the low grassy hills and clusters of houses to be seen. All felt better, for it looked very much like Ireland, and the more prosperous parts of Ireland at that.

Once in the sheltered waters of the Sound behind it – these channels between the Hebridean islands were called sounds, Machar told them, the wider seaways, firths, and their loughs, lochs – the vessel's heaving sank to an acceptable level and they made good time. They could have dispensed with the oars, but Colum was concerned to make their landing before actual nightfall if possible – not that in May it would ever be very

71

dark; but approaching strange shores by night was scarcely advisable.

Now, although Islay was not mountainous, all else around and ahead was, with heather and rock hills higher and steeper than any in Ireland, these making the Sound appear narrower than its dozen or so miles. And in front of them, at first appearing as though just the far northern part of Islay but presently becoming apparent as a large and separate entity, was a more dramatic island, with soaring mountains, the two most prominent extraordinarily like a shapely woman's breasts. The company was not so holy as to fail to comment thereon. Machar said that he had heard of the Paps of Jura.

Islay however proved even larger than they had anticipated and passing it took longer, so that Machar had to admit that he had miscalculated and that they were unlikely to be able to reach the Dunadd vicinity, where King Conall had his capital, before nightfall, for he understood that it lay east of the northern end of Jura isle. So Colum decided that they should make a landing as soon as they could find a suitably sheltered spot to pass the night. Better that way, probably, than any unannounced arrival in the half-dark.

So they drew in closer to what they thought was part of the now shadow-slashed mainland shore but which proved to be a narrow islet in the Sound, up the west side of which they sailed until they found a sheltered bay at its north end, where they were able to anchor in shallow water protected by a curving horn of land. There was no habitation of man in sight, but there were cattle grazing, so presumably the island was not unpopulated.

They went ashore in their coracles, Colum falling to his knees on the strand and thanking God for bringing them safely to this his first foreign land. They soon had a fire of driftwood blazing and a meal prepared, more ambitious than the circumstances warranted, thanks to Princess Eithne's provision. Then, most of them, glad to stretch their legs after the cramping hours at sea, made some small exploration of the vicinity – not that they could see much in the half-dark. The island was low-lying and green, proving to be only about one mile wide although perhaps five in length. They had seen no single house on this western coast as they sailed up, but when they climbed the modest central spine of the place, they thought that they could discern the hump-backed outlines of cabins and cot-houses scattered down near the eastern coast. This was no hour, however, for foreign strangers to go rousing island folk who would probably be abed. So the walkers returned to their camp, to bed themselves for the night.

In the morning, after praying, singing a psalm and eating, a few of them climbed back over the little ridge, and confirmed that the island was in fact fairly well-populated on the eastern side, with quite a number of little houses of stone and turf, mainly near the shore, most now having the blue smoke of morning fires rising above them. Not wishing to alarm the islanders by a number of them descending on any one cottage, Colum and his uncle went down to one, while Machar and Baithen called on another, the rest returning to the camp.

Approaching the low-browed hovel, barking dogs greeted them, and their arrival was watched warily by a red-haired man and three young children. The children disappeared into the house as they came up, but the man stood his ground, possibly reassured by their monkish garb. Colum raised a hand to sketch the sign of the cross.

"Greetings, friend, in the name of the Lord Christ," he called. "We are travellers from Ireland, on the way to visit King Conall at Dunadd. This is our first landing in Dalriada. We are men of God." He paused. "Do you understand our speech?"

The man nodded silently.

"Good! What is the name of this island, friend?"

"Gigha," the other said.

"Gigha? And to whom does it belong?"

"Morcant mac Cano." The children were venturing out of the house door again cautiously, a woman peering behind them.

These were strange names, presumably Pictish. The man himself, by his voice and intonation, was probably a Pict. But then, most of the inhabitants of Dalriada would be, the Scots-Irish only a ruling minority.

"How far is it to Dunadd?" Ernan asked.

"I know not, master. What have such as I to do with Dunadd of the King?"

"But it will not be far now, surely?"

"I do not know," the other repeated. "Morcant mac Cano might tell you."

"And where is he?"

The man gestured vaguely southwards, down the island.

Realising that they were unlikely to get anything more out of this individual, they bade him farewell and went to rejoin Baithen and Machar.

These two appeared to have been more successful. Machar declared that they had learned that this island was called Gigha and that it lay about twenty-five miles south of the mouth of Loch Crinan – near the head of which loch rose the Hill of Dunadd, which they would see from afar. They could be at Dunadd by midday.

There being no point in further delay here, they went back to their camp and ordered embarkation. The cuckoos were calling hauntingly as they left Gigha.

They came to realise how long an island was the mountainous Jura, as they sailed past the narrow channel which separated it from Islay, and on mile after mile, up its Sound, in the bright forenoon; and very lovely too, with its coves and sandy bays, its blazing yellow gorse and scattered birch-woods clothing the lower slopes of the high heather hills. But it was to the other side, eastwards, that Machar kept looking, assessing the miles covered and counting the inlets on the mainland Kintyre coast, to decide which was their Loch Crinan. All were in good heart this fine morning, after a night's undisturbed sleep, sailing in sheltered waters, amidst scenes of great beauty, and their first encounter with the Scots folk had proved anything but fearsome.

After a couple of hours pleasant sailing, Machar pointed to a wide loch-mouth half-right ahead about a mile or so, and declared that that would be Loch Crinan. It was opposite a cup-shaped bay on Jura, and well over a mile wide – as he had been directed to look for. Dunadd would be at the head of it.

So they turned in thereat, and, oars out now, pulled up the fairly quickly-narrowing loch, the hillsides coming down close on either side, quite thickly wooded with oak and ash and birch, the cuckoos calling all around, wild duck rising from every creek and lagoon and cranes or herons flapping lazily along the colourful seaweed-hung rocks and skerries of the shore. It all delighted Colum in particular, for he had always had a great love of beauty and of the growing, living things of nature. Birds of course were especially important in Celtic culture and mythology; and the heron was his own symbol, not the dove as his name, if not his nature, might have implied, frequently used by him in illustrations to decorate his writings and gospel translations. The oak-tree also held a notable significance for his family – indeed it was on account of the oak-woods that he had chosen the sites of his monasteries at Derry, Durrow and Kells. So he, at least, began to feel almost at home in this new and fair land, sense of exile fading.

But as they rowed on up the ever-narrowing loch, beautiful as it was, all began to wonder. For the flanking hills were drawing closer and more steep, and there was little or no sign of habitation or cultivation, indeed practically no level land suitable to cultivate, no cattle evident on the hillfoots or clearings in the woodlands. For the capital area of Dalriada this seemed strange. And they had been told to look for the outstanding hill of Dunadd itself. There were hills aplenty, but none more outstanding than the other; in fact, by Irish standards these were mountains rather than hills, thronging mountains.

So doubts grew, even Machar losing confidence. When they were four or five miles up, and at last they saw cattle grazing on the north shore, they decided that if a house showed itself they should land and make enquiries. And fairly soon thereafter, round a slight bend and further narrowing of the loch, two features were revealed – a house set in a pleasant hollow of grassland behind a low jutting headland, not any hovel but a substantial long building of timber; and the fact that, from here, they could see the actual loch-head only a mile or so further, and no community visible.

Beyond the little point, golden with the flags of iris, was a sheltered strand with two boats drawn up. Colum had their own vessel run in close, and lowering two coracles he, with Baithen, Ernan and Machar, paddled ashore.

Their approach had not gone unnoticed, for quite a party were coming down from the house to meet them, led by a young man, little more than a youth, rather evidently carrying a drawn sword, at his back half a dozen men, mainly elderly, with a motley variety of weapons. They managed however to look apprehensive rather than aggressive.

"Friends, friends – we come in peace!" Colum called. "We are men of God, seeking guidance. We wish you only well."

The other party halted, looking distinctly relieved.

"We are from Ireland. Making for King Conall's court. At Dunadd." Colum went on, as they came close. "Is this Loch Crinan?"

"No, no," the youth said. "It is Loch Caolisport. This is Ellary. From Ireland you say, sir? *My* great-grandsire came from Ireland. From Donegal, in Ireland."

"Ha – we know Donegal well. I have kin there. As indeed have Abbot Baithen and Prince Ernan . . ."

"*Prince* Ernan?" That was eager. "A prince? Of Donegal?" Ernan smiled. "There are not a few such, young man!"

"But – my great-grandsire was also a prince of Donegal. He was Angus Mor mac Erc. He came here with his brothers . . ."

"Angus Mor mac Erc!" Colum exclaimed. "Brother to Fergus mac Erc and Lorn mac Erc? You are his great-grandson?"

"Yes. I am also Angus. Angus mac Riagan mac Fergno mac Angus Mor."

"Save us! Then we are kin. God is good! We are all kin. Except Machar, here. I am Colum mac Felim mac Fergus Cendfota, of Donegal. Abbot Baithen and I are cousins, grandsons of the Lady Eirc, who was Lorn's daughter, so niece to Angus Mor. And Ernan is my uncle. Here is a wonder!"

"That we should by mistake sail into the wrong loch, looking for King Conall, and instead find a kinsman, in a strange land!" Baithen said. "Who would have thought it?"

"You are none so mistaken as to King Conall, either," the young man Angus declared. "For he is here, at Loch Caolisport. But two miles off. I saw him yesterday. The royal palace is at Dunadd, yes. But his own house is here, at the head of this loch, at An Tor where he lived, our neighbour, before he succeeded to the throne four years ago. He comes here much. A quiet man, he likes this place."

"So, Machar, you have navigated us well, after all!" Colum said. "At the head of this loch, you say, Angus mac Riagan?"

"The King's house stands within an old Albannach fort, a dun. On top of the hill, An Tor. I will take you to it, if you wish. But, first – come you into *my* house, here – mine, since my father Riagan was slain. In the same battle with the Albannach where died King Gabhran, Conall's brother. So many died there, four years back."

"Alas, yes. We heard much of that. A dire disaster. Your

76

father also? I am sorry. Do the Picts, the Albannach as you call them, still threaten Dalriada? In arms?"

"They do. There are constant raids. No great battles, but small attacks. That is why we greeted you thus!" And he gestured with some embarrassment to his sword, which he held less than handily. "They strike from the sea, as well as by land. We feared that you were Albannach. Brude mac Maelchon, their High King, will drive us out of Dalriada, if he can. He has sworn by the sun to do so."

"Why? You do not threaten him. Your people have lived in fair peace with his for a century now. You have married amongst them. Have been friends."

"To be sure." The young man pointed to the men behind him, watching and listening. "These are all of the Albannach; friends, yes, and Christians. But Brude sees us as enemy – Christians. It is his Druids, they do say, who spur him on. Everywhere the old religions are rising again, so the pagans will drive us out, if they can."

"Aye – so it is the Druids again. As with us, in Ireland. They think that their heathen sun rises again, never to set. But Christ's cause will prevail. It *must*! God is almighty and will not allow it to fail."

The youth Angus inclined his head, but looked unconvinced. "That is our hope. But – come, sirs. My mother awaits us, at the door."

They moved up to the house, solidly-built of oak planks, reed-thatched. It could now be seen that there were a few turf-roofed cabins behind it, with stables and byres. In the doorway stood a woman of early middle age, of striking good looks, still dark of hair as of eye, tall and with a fine figure. As they came up, she put one hand behind her back – but not before Colum perceived that it held an unsheathed dirk.

"The Lady Bridget nic Colman," Angus introduced. "Mother – these are travellers from Ireland. Of the royal house of Donegal. Men of God, they say."

"Then they are welcome to this house," the woman said, deep-voiced. "My own forebears came here from Moville, on Lough Foyle."

That produced exclamations from the visitors, needless to say, and as they were led indoors for refreshment great was the exchange of names and identities and places. Colum's own name was known, as a founder of monasteries, although news of his recent activities, Cooldrevny and what followed, evidently had not reached here yet. The Lady Bridget made her pleasure at their coming apparent, as forthright a character as she was attractive – but she kept her right hand hidden meantime in the folds of her multi-coloured skirt of Pictish tartan; that is, until Colum, moving close, discreetly slipped his own hand down to hers and took the weapon from her gently, to hide within the wide sleeve of his monkish habit.

She turned to look him in the eye. "You are kind, Prince Colum," she murmured. "Kinder than the visitors I feared might have come. Some of us women would prefer clean steel to what our captors would do to us!"

He nodded. "That I understand, lady. And grieve that you had to contemplate it, even for a moment." But he smiled. "And, see you, I do not use the style of prince any more. My friends call me Columcille."

"Then if I may be so privileged, so shall I, Columcille! But – you and your friends are not so saintly that you will not partake of some wine, I hope?"

"Gladly, lady. Did our Lord not turn water into wine? I was sorrowed to hear of your husband's death."

"Yes, he is a sore loss. But . . . Riagan was a fighter and he died fighting."

"You also are something of a fighter, in your own woman's way, I think?"

"Perhaps. And you are a man who understands women, I think!"

"I would hope that I might be given that blessing, in time. Or as nearly as any man may!"

They eyed each other consideringly, and left it at that.

When the Lady Bridget learned that her son was going to conduct the visitors to King Conall's house, she declared that she would go with them also. Since the King's wife had died he was a lonely man. He had young sons, but they were fostered out, as was the tradition in the royal family. Conall had never wanted to be king, but his slain brother's sons were likewise too young to ascend the throne. She liked Conall – who of course was kin to her husband – but, a mild and learned man, he was perhaps not the monarch Dalriada needed, to face the warrior Brude mac Maelchon of the Albannach.

Presently they set out, Colum paddling the woman out to their vessel in his own coracle. She made no over-modest fuss about hiding her white legs beneath her shortish skirt as she stepped into the fragile craft, or thereafter when climbing nimbly up into the long-ship. Those on board were intrigued to be having a female passenger. Young Angus was clearly proud of his mother.

Oars out again, and the visitors gazed onwards to the loch-head to see if they could identify the hill of An Tor, with its royal house. After less than a mile, as they were nearing a little islet, Colum felt his arm touched by the Lady Bridget, who pointed in a different direction, left-handed, towards the shore only a few hundred yards off.

"If you look, up from the little creek there behind the isle, you will see a cave-mouth. You have it? That cave is a strange one. No one will enter it – although I have been in. It was long the retreat of a hermit-Druid, a magician, much dreaded. He dwelt there for years, and although now dead, still haunts it, they say. Dark things were done there. Even my husband would not enter it – and much blamed me for doing so, saying that it would bring us hurt. Do you believe in such things, Columcille?"

"I believe in the powers of evil, yes. But also that the good can overcome them. Satan, the fallen Lucifer, is no myth. But Christ is stronger and will enable believers to overcome the Devil."

"So I told Riagan. But he doubted. As do most, I fear."

"This cave, was it but the Druid's dwelling? Or was it more than that, a temple of heathen rites?"

"Both, I think. There is an altar cut in the rock. And carvings on the walls, strange symbols."

"I must see this place . . ."

Another mile and they were at the head of the loch, where a small river came in over tidal flats. At the mouth of this a number of boats were moored, one a fine long-ship, larger than their own, with a fierce dragon-prow, no doubt King Conall's own. The river emerged from a narrow glen, and to the right of this, amongst the throng of higher but less eye-catching summits, rose a steep, rock-ribbed and wedge-shaped hill, of no great height but sufficiently dramatic-looking, the more so in that it was crowned by buildings rising out of serried ramparts. To see houses skied up there was surprising enough; even more so was the fact that there must be access thereto, although none was evident.

"Your King Conall chooses a strange dwelling-place," Colum commented. "Secure, yes – but lacking all convenience, surely? Once up there, he will be much confined. An eagle's eyrie – but an eagle lacking wings!"

"It well suits Conall," she replied. "He is a studious man, as I told you, and has his writings and parchments and scrolls. You will see, presently, how we reach him."

They moored beside the other boats, and, leaving most of his people there, Colum took only a small group of his closest colleagues, and with Angus and his mother, set off on foot, not for the yawning mouth of the glen, but right-handed, to follow a smaller stream which joined the river just before its confluence with the loch, by a well-trodden path. Bridget nic Colman strode out with the best, clearly used to walking.

Soon they were into a jumble of wooded hummocks and knolls, close country suddenly, and rounding one of these, they found themselves amongst small houses, cabins and barns, with a mill on the stream, a hidden village unsuspected from the loch.

"Achahoish," Angus announced. "This serves King Conall's house of An Tor."

A group of armed men materialised from a barn-like building a little further on but, recognising the Lady Bridget and her son, these caused no trouble. Thereafter they entered a small northwards-probing valley, really only a wedge in the hills, on each side of which, one hundred feet or so up, could be seen man-made ramparts of earth and stone, from which the little pass most clearly could be closed without difficulty, early Pictish fortifications but unmanned now.

A quarter-mile beyond, they discovered the way up to the King's house, at the back and less steep side of the An Tor hill, a zigzag and embanked roadway which climbed in coils and loops and bends, at many of which were more ramparts, behind which defenders could hide and deny access. Whoever built this hold had been an expert in defence.

All were breathing deeply by the time that they reached the summit, the woman by no means the most affected, although her fine bosom did heave in inspiriting fashion. Here they were faced with three tiers of tall, grassgrown earthworks and deep ditches, round which the road had to twist its way, all of which could be manned for effective obstruction, the final tier enclosing the crest of the hill and an area of some acres extent.

This was now filled with later buildings of timber, a fine hall-house of oak, two-storeyed and reed-thatched, surrounded by a huddle of lesser and lower erections, smoke rising from sundry fires. It occurred to Colum that keeping those fires fuelled with peat and logs would demand a deal of labouring up that steep ascent.

Not that this formed any major preoccupation, nor the buildings occupying this extraordinay site, nor even the guards who were now barring their way – for the approach of visitors could nowise go unnoticed on An Tor. It was the view which suddenly opened before them that riveted the attention of that lover of beauty at least. Never had Colum seen anything like what this hilltop revealed, so farflung a panorama of sheer loveliness and colour and contrast, of ocean and islands, sea-lochs and skerries, mountains and headlands, to all infinity, the waters of every shade of blue, but turning to emerald green in the shallows where the white cockleshell sand showed through, the waves creaming, the weed-hung reefs and skerries richly red and olive and yellow, the sun-dappled hillsides slashed with shadow, the cliffs beetling black, the distant mountains dreaming purple, some inland still gleaming with snow. He had heard of the Hebridean seaboard as beautiful, and from the ship had admired it; but never had he conceived of any prospect like this. There could be a thousand islands, great and small, scattered over the azure sea. The West of Ireland has islanded seascapes, yes – but nothing to compare with this. A surge of sheer joy at the sight filled him with emotion and thankfulness to the Maker of it all, his own Maker who had brought him here, by however strange and devious paths, to dwell amongst it all.

"Heaven itself could not be fairer than this!" he exclaimed.

"On a sunny May morning, perhaps," Bridget said, smiling. "But in a winter's storm, or even a grey overcast day, it can be otherwise."

"Nevertheless, this is a foretaste of the hereafter, I say! The Creator of *that* loves beauty with a love beyond all comprehension. Think what that means. God's kingdom will be beautiful beyond all conception. Lovely as well as love-filled. I have never recognised that truth so assuredly before. Praise be for this vision!"

She looked at him strangely – they all did. "I stand reproved," she said, quietly. "I have lived my life here, and

81

had not seen it thus, not recognised the lesson. But then, I think that you are a *man* of vision, Columcille – as well as of other perceptions! But – come, you. These are King Conall's servants, waiting to receive us."

The royal retainers, tough-looking characters, knew the Lady Bridget of Ellary and her son, and made no difficulty about access to the hall-house. One went ahead to inform the king.

After only a little delay they were led from the large hall of the house up a stairway and into a smaller anteroom, where a fire of birch-logs burned on a large central hearth, from which the smoke ascended to a clay-lined hole in the thatched roof, for a chimney. The chamber was full of tables and chests, covered with papers and scrolls, at one of which a man of middle years sat, quill in hand. He was handsome in a grave fashion, spare of build and bent of shoulder, looking older than his years, which would be none so many more than Colum's own. He looked up from his papers and inclined his head towards them, unsmiling but in no hostility.

They all bowed.

"Visitors from Ireland, Highness," Bridget announced. "Come seeking audience. Churchmen, and notable ones."

"They are welcome, then. But what brings notable churchmen from Ireland to this unhappy kingdom?" the monarch asked. He had a strangely light voice, at odds with his appearance.

"We come on something of a pilgrimage, Highness," Colum said. "Sent, we must believe, by God. For His own good purposes. Although ourselves sinners. I am Colum mac Felim mac Fergus. This is my uncle, Prince Ernan. And my cousin, Abbot Baithen mac Brenaind."

Conall put down his pen. "Did I hear aright?" he asked, peering as though short-sighted. "Colum? Ernan? Baithen? These are names I know. As are Felim and Brenaind. Can it be, in truth, that you are Colum the prince and Abbot of Derry? He who refused the High Kingship?"

"The same, Highness. Your kin – distant, but kin."

The King rose and came to them, and on his feet seemed fragile. "Here is a wonder!" he exclaimed. "The kindred of Niall Nine-Hostager – as am I. Come from Ireland. Cousins!"

"Cousins of mine, also." Young Angus pointed out, proudly.

Conall embraced them, clearly much moved. "I do not know what brings you to Dalriada," he said. "But I rejoice to see you. Where did you come from? When did you arrive? What is this you say of pilgrimage?"

"It makes a long story, Cousin, which I will not weary you with now. But we are here on a penance, *my* penance, not these others'. For I am much blamed, in Ireland, for the deaths of many. So I am sent to do Christ's work here. And, if I may, to aid you and your people. We are come to bring the Picts to God.

The other stared, wordless.

Bridget it was who spoke. "I wonder if they know what they propose? A task almost beyond all conception. And yet . . ."

"And yet . . . ?" Colum repeated, almost challenged.

"And yet, if any could do it, I think this man might."

"Not me. Not these, either. But God using us." That was deep-voiced.

Conall shook his greying head. "The Albannach, Picts as you name them, are a mighty nation. In numbers more than all the Irish, I would think. Warriors, fighters, fierce, and wholly given over to idolatry. Pagans of the pagans! Christ-God all but unknown amongst them, devil-worshippers, a fearsome people."

"But God's children, Highness, nevertheless, as are we all. Ireland was pagan none so long ago . . ."

"And could have returned to being pagan had not Colum led at Cooldrevny!" Ernan put in.

"Cooldrevny . . . ?"

"Not all would agree with that! But even these Albannach must be given the chance of salvation. And were they Christian, how much happier, safer, would be *this* kingdom."

"If . . . ! I fear . . ." Conall sighed. "This is a sorry land, doomed, I fear. Perhaps we, the Sons of Erc, should never have left Ireland?"

"Yet this surely is the fairest land on God's good earth!" Colum gestured towards the window, which looked out over all that stupendous panorama. "Here is the very pinnacle of our Creator's handiwork on land and sea. It should be the cradle of His faith in all the north. Pray that we can make it so."

None there had any comment to make to that.

Colum strode over to the window, to gaze out. "See you, Conall mac Comgall – why do you choose to dwell on this hill-top, far from other men? Not for ease nor convenience. It is, I swear, because of *this*!" And he swept his arm towards that prospect. "What you may look on, from here. A sight to gladden the heart and upraise the spirit. *Your* kingdom! Given you by Almighty God. Here you see it. Is it not so?"

"A kingdom is more than land and water, my friend. More than mountains and pasture and islands. It is *men* who make a realm. And men can be less fair than what you see from here! So I dwell, when I can, with the beauty, that I may have the strength to put up with the men!"

"That I can understand, Highness. But the men also are God's handiwork, made in His image, although sadly lapsed. They must be won back to Him, that they may match this beauty."

"And how is that to be done? This Dalriada is Christian in name, yes. But, of a truth, is less than that, to my sorrow. Most of the people here are of the Albannach, still. It could not be otherwise. The old Devil-worship is not banished, only hidden, like deep water below ice. And Brude mac Maelchon and his Druids press us on every hand, and their pagan faith is like to prevail."

"So we come," Colum said simply. "So we are sent."

Conall spread his ink-stained hands, an eloquent gesture, eloquent indeed of lack of conviction – a lack clearly not confined to himself, as the others fell to consider the situation more deeply and what they were seeking to do, what they had had the temerity to think that they could attempt. Faces had fallen during the King's sad recital, expressions become doubtful, if not grim. But not that of Colum mac Felim.

"Twelve men, ordinary men, brought Christ to an unbelieving world," he reminded. "Lit the fire of faith. Can we not at least rekindle the flagging flame, in one land? And tomorrow, have you forgotten, is the Feast of Pentecost. When the Holy Spirit was given to men. For a purpose! Tomorrow we begin, in the name and power of that Spirit."

"How?" Conall asked flatly.

"It came to me as we sailed up your loch, here. When the Lady Bridget told me of the Druid's cave back there, held in dread, a place of ancient evil. Tomorrow we shall celebrate Pentecost and our arrival in this land by banishing that evil and

84

turning the cave into a chapel and sanctuary of the living God. As sign and symbol of what we have been sent to do. So shall we make a start, a small beginning. But pointing the way."

Exclamations arose now, of doubt, wondering and some acclaim, the last most notably from the woman.

"Praise be for a *man* come to this Scotland!" she cried. "Here is a flag, a banner, to follow. What we have needed. Who would have thought that so small a seed as my few words could have borne *this* fruit!"

The King eyed them all, a man out of his depth. "I am put to shame," he said. "I had never thought of the like. It seems that we have need of you here, Colum mac Felim, as Bridget says." He came over to the window. "And after the cave, what? Will you make there your church, your cashel?"

"No, no. That is too small and remote a place. We have not come to hide away in caves! With your royal permission we shall seek a bigger, a better place, where we may establish a great centre, a monastery, an abbey, and work out from there. An island, perhaps, on a waterway for shipping and trade and passage, where many can be reached. Central in this Dalriada, not hidden away. But – that is for the future. Tomorrow we begin!"

"You know *what* you begin? You confront the powers of darkness. And they are strong, strong. *I* know."

"So do I, Conall mac Comgall – so do I!"

5

They stood eyeing the cave-mouth. It did not look in any way menacing or evil, framed by the virginal green of burgeoning birch-leaves and the golden sprays of broom, the gurgle and tinkle of a little waterfall and pool close by, all in the May sunshine. Yet none there was unmoved, unaffected by the aura of the place, the feeling of danger. So strong was the echo of dread and fear within them, from untold generations of superstition, and the worship of cruel and terrible gods and their dark magic, which the new faith of Christianity and love could condemn and triumph over but could not wholly obliterate from the race-memory within them. Even Colum felt it, and crossed himself.

"A prayer!" he announced. "To Him whose day this is. Oh, God the Holy Spirit, Lord of Triune Majesty in Heaven, whose coming to men at Pentecost we celebrate today, come now to this place of ill fame, and by Thy mighty power for good drive forth any evil power which may hide in this dark cavern, that the light of Thy presence may fill it hereafter. For the well-being of man and the glory of God. Amen."

The amens behind were part heartfelt and part unsure.

At his side Bridget took his hand. "Come," she said. "*I* went in, that time, and emerged unharmed!"

Together they moved forward.

The cave was not large, at its entrance about ten feet high and six across, although half of that had been narrowed by walling to form a doorway. Within, the ceiling of rock, slimy and damp, slanted down somewhat, and there appeared to be a lower extension to the place at the far end.

Inside, the dark, wet chill had an almost physical impact, to catch the breath. None spoke. Despite her brave words earlier, Colum felt the woman's hand tighten in his – and in consequence he knew a very masculine excess of strength and confidence. He peered around urgently.

Because of the light being blocked out by his party crowding at the entrance, he could distinguish little or nothing. They should have brought flint, steel, tinder and torch.

"Stand back," he ordered. "Clear the doorway. There is no room for all, here, at one time."

Most there withdrew, with alacrity.

Daylight penetrating again, those remaining could examine the interior. The cave was about twenty-five feet long and half that in width. On one side the sandstone wall had been cut away to form a long broad shelf, a foot above the floor, no doubt the Druid hermit's bed. Across from it another shelf, of similar breadth but much higher, had been built up of stones and topped by flat slabs. Below it, to one side, a distinct basin-shaped hollow was excavated in the rock-floor. Above this second shelf strange diagrams and symbols had been carved in the cave-wall.

"An altar," Colum said. "A heathen altar." He pointed

86

down at the basin. "That, for the sacrificial blood." He leaned forward, to scrutinise those rock-carvings more closely, resting his hand on the cold stone slabbing, and as he did so a lizard darted out of a crevice in the masonry, head high, and scuttled off, down and away, with extraordinary speed.

"Evil!" Baithen exclaimed. "This place is accursed. There has been great wickedness done here. I can feel it. Let us leave, Columcille. It is damned."

"*Was*, not is, cousin," Colum corrected. "We shall change it, not leave it. The evil must be purged out, not left to fester like some rotting wound in this fair land. See you, this was a place of worship, wrong worship but still worship. We must make of it a *true* shrine to the true God and Father of us all. As token of our mission. He has brought us here, of no choosing on our part. We will sanctify this place."

He was still staring at those carvings above the altar. There were three of them. In the centre, upright and skilfully and gracefully executed, was the representation of a strange animal, in rampant stance, with a dog-like head and open jaws, but with a long trunk or pigtail curling backwards, from the top of its head, not its snout. Its legs were only formalised.

"A strange creature," he commented. "What can it represent?"

"I do not know," Bridget said. "But I have seen other carvings of it, on Albannach standing-stones and stone-circles. It must be a sacred beast, of some devising. They much use stones, carved stones, in their worship."

"These on either side are very different, but equally strange." On the right of the animal was a crescent moon, resting on its horns, and superimposed on this, in the form of a V, was what looked like a broken arrow, pointed and feathered; while on the left were twin circles, linked, with superimposed, another arrow, or perhaps a broken spear for it was longer, in the form of a Z. "What can these mean?"

"Who knows? Secret symbols connected with their religion. They are sun-worshippers. Those two circles could represent the sun in two positions, perhaps rising and sinking. Although I have heard it said that they could be women's breasts. For these too are to be seen elsewhere. The quarter-moon could have some meaning connected with the sun. But why the broken weapons, I have no notion."

"Whatever they are, they are sinful, vile!" Baithen declared, a man who was apt to see things in black and white. "They should be destroyed."

"We shall replace them with Christ's cross," Colum said.

They found other carvings around the walling, no more understandable – a variation of the sun theme, with a large circle flanked by two small ones; what looked like stylised flowers in a pot; and two linked designs which seemed to represent a mirror and a comb, Bridget suggesting at least a possible meaning for this last, as representing woman, in women's vanity and concern for their appearance – although what this might have to do with sun-worship or magic spells they could not think.

There appeared to be nothing else of interest in the place, the little extension beyond being featureless, although no doubt useful for storage.

They moved outside, to allow others to inspect.

Colum was eager to hold a service of exorcism and new dedication. He sent young Angus hurrying back to Ellary for candles, steel, flint and tinder. They had brought bread and wine, a chalice and a basin, for the eucharist; and now he used the basin to carry water from the waterfall and used basinful after basinful to wash down the whole cave's interior, paying particular attention to the altar, the oval hollow in the floor, and those carvings. This done, he took a final basinful and, kneeling reverently, blessed it in the name of the Father, the Son and the Holy Spirit and, ringing the bronze saint's-bell which all abbots and bishops carried with them, took the holy water inside to sprinkle on all surfaces, making the sign of the cross, while his company chanted a psalm. This done he set his people to search out hard stones from the shore, harder than the cave's sandstone, and with these to smash and chip and hammer at those strange carvings. Baithen was foremost in this task, though Colum himself knew a certain reluctance to deface notably artistic handiwork, whatever else it was.

When the candles arrived they were ceremonially lit and placed on that altar, with the bread and the wine. Then, all kneeling save Colum and Moluag, as many as could get into the cave but most outside in the sunlight, they sang another psalm whilst the two celebrants moved forward to the altar. Now Moluag was leading, for he was an ordained bishop, with Colum taking the lesser role of acolyte. The Celtic Church differed from the Roman and Orthodox communions in various ways, having developed quite apart for two centuries. It was monastic not diocesan and had no bishoprics as such, its monasteries and abbeys being its centres of authority and its abbots therefore its effective leaders. Yet the office of bishop was acknowledged and revered, each abbey apt to have at least one bishop, sometimes two or three. And although the abbots ruled, those ordained bishop were pre-eminent in the administration of the sacraments, in especial, Holy Communion.

So Bishop Lugaid, or Moluag, a somewhat older man, small but lively, conducted the brief communion service, consecrating the bread and wine on the former heathen altar by the light of the flickering candles, Colum humbly assisting. Then, after kneeling to partake, they rose to administer the sacrament, Moluag the bread and Colum the wine in its chalice, to the others, all receiving.

A final hymn of thanksgiving and Moluag's benediction concluded the service – save for a valedictory gesture of Colum's own, when he stood and went back to the altar and thereon deposited his bronze saint's-bell, handsome with its figure of the crucified Christ and Celtic interlacing decoration, leaving it there to be a token and symbol of the new dispensation. He would make himself another bell.

Laughing now and joyful, all aware of a start made on the great task, and some relief, to be sure, that all had gone well and without any malign interference, they proceeded back to the hall-house of Ellary, where Bridget's women had prepared another sort of Pentecostal feast.

High spirits, high hopes and good will reigned. Tomorrow they would endeavour to carve crosses on that cave's walls, in place of those Pictish pagan symbols; and the next day, as arranged, proceed in company with King Conall, to Dunadd.

The two long ships sailed together down Loch Caolisport and out into the Sound of Jura; Colum, Ernan and Baithen aboard the royal vessel with its dragon-prow and thirty-two oars in two tiers. The Lady Bridget and her son were there also, anxious to help in any way they could. Conall had sent messengers ahead to call a council of his chiefs to meet the missionaries. Opposition was not anticipated but enthusiasm might well be lacking.

They had only some seventeen miles to go up the sparkling waters of the lovely Sound to Loch Crinan, passing the island-separated double mouth of what they were told was Loch Sween, the territory of the descendants of King Lorn. Clearly this Hebridean seaboard was cut into by a bewildering array of sea-lochs, as of islands.

Loch Crinan, when they reached it, was different from the others however. Wider-mouthed and shallower, less of a flooded valley between encroaching mountains, indeed although there were low hills to north and south, at its head, no great distance in, was a wide, level scoop of green plain, the first the travellers had seen in this land, some miles in extent. But even this was not without its prominence nevertheless, for in the midst, perhaps a couple of miles back from the coast, abruptly rose a single conical hill, of no great height but symmetrical and eye-catching. The visitors did not require to be told that this was Dunadd.

They berthed at a fishing-haven, sheltered behind a small island some way north of the loch-head, where horses were available to carry the King's party to his capital. Colum and his immediate associates, along with Bridget and her son, were found mounts also; the others would come along on foot.

The road they followed proved to be an embanked cause-way, man-made, over thoroughly wet marshland, for the green plain they had seen was in fact a widespread bog out of which the hill of Dunadd soared dramatically to beckon them on – a notable defensive feature. The prefix *dun*, signified fort or castle. The strength of its position was further emphasised when presently their road reached a drawbridge over the River Add, which meandered through the marshy plain to form an effective moat. It was explained that Dunadd had been an Albannach stronghold long before the first Scots came from Ireland.

Across the bridge and rounding a shoulder on the north flank of the hill, they found themselves suddenly in the midst of a township of considerable size, hidden from the sea by the bulk of the cone of rock, stone and timber buildings grouped all over the skirts of the hill and some little way up its east-facing flanks. Some of these buildings were large, one evidently the royal palace and another the Moot Hall or meeting-place of the council of chiefs. But there were houses of all sizes, and many cabins and cottages, barns, storehouses and a couple of mills, these served by lades cut in from the river which coiled protectively round township and hill. It was all rather like Tara, back in Ireland, only the rock itself was a deal more impressive. Colum looked for a church or monastery but could not see one.

They rode to the palace where they, and for that matter the King himself, were received with the minimum of ceremony. Colum and his people were allotted quarters in the guest-house nearby, but Bridget and Angus were installed in the palace itself. The newcomers had been a lot better lodged at Ellary; Conall, it seemed, was not a man concerned with creature comforts. Not that the missionaries sought such, but they had been rather spoiled by Bridget.

After a meal, they were conducted up the hill itself, its summit reached, rather like that of An Tor, by a winding embanked roadway up which King Conall rode, although Colum and his companions chose, at Bridget's suggestion, to climb on foot more or less straight up the east side, crossing three times the spirals of the road. Somewhat breathlessly Bridget explained that this important hill-summit was of mixed Scots and Albannach significance. The fort on top, the ramparts of which they could see clearly, was Pictish and notable – as they would see presently – long before the mac Ercs came from Ireland; but Fergus mac Erc had taken it over and made it the centre and inauguration-place of his new kingdom. Probably the Albannach had never really forgiven the Scots for this. So in one way, this Dunadd could be a stone-for-stumbling between the kingdoms.

When they reached the top, within its three concentric rings of ramparts, they found only the one low timber building remaining, where originally there would have been many, this now used as a shelter for illustrious celebrants in inclement weather. Once again Colum was struck by the magnificence of the hill-top vista, a little less dramatic than that of An Tor because of the immediate flats of the surrounding marshland, but in the distant aspect almost finer, for here the lofty Paps of Jura were not central and so allowed the eye to reach further beyond, over Scarba and the Ross of Mull to Coll and Tiree and all the lesser isles. Still breathing deeply from their climb, the visitors were exclaiming over all this when Conall and his mounted party arrived, and the tour of inspection of the knobbly hill-top began.

First of all they were shown the spirited representation of a wild boar carved on an outcropping face of the living rock, fiercely lifelike, hunched with massive shoulder and head lowered, ready to charge. The boar, it was pointed out, was the foremost cult animal of the Albannach and the symbol of their High Kings. Colum forbore to say so, there and then, but it seemed to him the height of provocation for the Irish Scots to have taken over this cherished spot in their mighty host kingdom.

But they quickly passed on to look at other features. They saw nearby a lifelike footprint of a man cut in the level stone surface, very slightly larger than normal. This they were told was the outline of Fergus mac Erc's own foot, implanted here to indicate that he had taken possession of this land. It had been hollowed out deeply, so that it could be used for all the King of Scots' chiefs, leaders and land-holders to come, place soil, from their own territories held of the King, in the imprint and thereafter place their foot therein, so enabling them to take the oath of allegiance standing on their own earth, saving the monarch from having to travel all over his kingdom and islands to receive the homage, an ingenius device. Alongside was a basin, rather like that in the Ellary cave, excavated in the rock for the ceremonial washing of feet before and after. A spring was shown them welling out of the summit stone not far away, which had been essential for the former fort's water-supply. Six kings had held their enthronement ceremonies here – Fergus, Lorn, Domangart, Comgall, Gabhran and now Conall.

Colum asked where the religious coronation service was held? He had perceived no church down there in the township. Looked at a little askance, he was told that this of mounting a throne was not a religious matter, for priests and the like, but for chiefs, warriors, nobles – he, a prince of the Hy-Neill must know that. The said prince had to bite back a strong assertion to the contrary which rose to his lips, contenting himself with saying that God's blessing would be advantageous even to the Kings of Scots! He would return to this, at a more suitable occasion, he told himself.

To cover any slight awkwardness, Conall mentioned that when worship was required it was held in the Moot Hall below. Then he changed the subject, to point out more distant matters of interest, not seawards where the visitors' eyes were apt to turn, but almost due northwards. There, perhaps a couple of miles away, where the ground began to rise out of the plain to the encircling hills, was a populous area, groupings of houses and farmsteads, under a faint film of peat-smoke. There was the main community of this Strathadd, Glassary and Craignish area and province, he pointed out; the capital vicinity being reserved for royal officers, retainers and servants.

It was Bridget, however, who identified for them features not at first evident at that range, tall standing-stones, some isolated and individual but most grouped to form great circles, a dozen and more to each. Tall mounds were also visible, cairns, scattered amongst the circles. Once pointed out, Colum counted at least six of the stone-circles and as many cairns.

"Worship," the woman said. "No lack of worship there! But of the false gods."

"Still worshipped? Even here in Christian Dalriada?"

"To be sure." She glanced quickly over towards Conall.

"So we must start our work nearer home than on the Picts, the Albannach!" Colum said grimly.

"I fear so."

As they moved downhill again, leaving Conall and his mounted party, Colum questioned Bridget about the state of Holy Church here. So far they had seen no clerics, no church buildings however modest, no monastery. The King's remark about worship, when needed, being held in the Moot Hall, did not sound enthusiastic. And paganism still flourished, it seemed. How strong was the Church and Christ's cause in Dalriada?

"Can you not see? It has been sinking, for long. In name we are Christian, but little of true faith remains. Our people have intermarried with the Albannach. *Their* religion is strong, however evil, and threatens terror, cursing and death. So ours has weakened, sadly. King Gabhran was concerned with battle, defending his realm against Brude, not with worship. And Conall is no fighter. Sound enough in his own faith, no doubt, but not the one to take the lead."

"And abbots? Bishops? Who heads the Church here?"

"None that I know of. We hear little of such. Priests are few, and ignorant, I fear. The only bishops that I have heard of, these years, are on a small island off Mull. Iona it is called. I am told that there are two bishops there. But they never leave their island."

Colum halted, to stare at her. They all did. "But – this is beyond all! The sin of it! Christ's cause all but abandoned in this land. Small wonder that the kingdom is in a sorry state. It deserves no better! Two bishops, you say, on some small island? Hermits!"

"There may be others. But we hear nothing of them. You will perceive, Columcille, why I thanked God that a *man* had come to Dalriada!"

Colum looked round at his friends, as they moved on downhill. There was no need for further words.

Words there were, however, in the guest-house that night, as the mission sat up late, discussing, declaiming, arguing. They had come to convert Alba, but it seemed that the Albannach would have to wait.

The chiefs and princes of Dalriada were arriving all morning, or such of them as lived within a day's journey or sail of Dunadd – for many in the outlying territories and farther islands could not be summoned in time. Observing them as they came in, with their armed bands, the visitors were not impressed. They looked a fairly rough and uninspiring lot – but perhaps the onlookers were prejudiced, after what they had heard.

At noon King Conall convened his council in the Moot Hall, and quite soon thereafter sent for Colum and his twelve to appear before them. There were about two dozen present, and the newcomers were struck by the disparity in ages, from old men to beardless youths, with very few men in their prime – no doubt as the result of dire casualties amongst the Scots leadership in the recent warfare with Brude of Alba. Some indeed were mere boys. Angus mac Riagan was there, but not his mother, women not being admitted to councils however high-born.

Conall had presumably already given the company some account of the visitors and their purpose, for his introduction now was brief. "Prince Colum mac Felim of Donegal, Abbot of Derry, his uncle Prince Ernan, Abbot Baithen of Durrow, Bishop Lugaid and these others, have come to this land on a mission of sorts. Men of religion, they believe that there is a task for them here. Their principal concern, I understand, is to bring Christianity to the Albannach. I think perhaps that they do not fully grasp the size, indeed I would say the impossibility, of such a task. But if they can do anything to lessen the savagery of our enemies and attackers we shall be grateful, and wish them well. Prince Colum?"

Almost starting by declaring that he was here as abbot not prince, Colum thought better of it. Their cause required the co-operation of these men and youths, or at least non-hostility, and they were more likely to be impressed by his royal blood, at this stage, than by any clerical status. So he began by saying to them that he brought greetings from their friends and kin in Ireland, informing that their difficulties and problems here were known, and declaring that his mission was to try to bring them aid both in matters of religion and in their defence against the heathen Albannach, the latter not by warfare and battle but by seeking to bring Christ to these Picts and thereby replace hatred by love and the brotherhood of man.

That produced only undisguised scepticism and no signs of gratitude.

He went on to assert that their purpose was neither empty posturing nor impractical day-dreaming. After all, these Albannach were a Celtic people of the same racial background as themselves, with similar traditions and customs to their own in Ireland a century before. If the Irish could be Christianised so could the Picts. The true faith had been brought to numberless nations, by God's good grace, many of these much more barbarous than Alba, which had a name for culture and the arts of painting, carving, poetry and the like. Was it not so?

That produced no sort of reaction from the company.

Had they not a *duty* to bring Christ's message of hope to their heathen neighbours, he went on? That was at the very heart of the Gospels. And did they not agree that the Albannach, Christianised, would become friends rather than enemies, and so end their attacks on Dalriada?

He got reaction now, but only smiles and snorts of disbelief, which would have been jeers had it not been a prince of the Hy-Neill speaking.

Noting it, Colum's temper, never of the most patient, surged to the princely rather than the abbatial. "You, you men of Dalriada – have *you* sought to advance God's cause here? Have you carried the message of salvation to these Picts? You have married their women but have you considered their souls? Have you even considered that as Christians they would make better neighbours, you in Christian Dalriada?"

Complete silence greeted that.

Colum leaned forward, almost threateningly. "Have you even sustained the faith here, your own selves? How does Holy Church in Dalriada? Since landing, we have not seen a priest, a monastery, a church! Is that why the Albannach remain ignorant of Christ? Because the Scots themselves are forgetting Him?"

There were frowns, murmurings and shufflings of feet.

He changed his tone again. "Friends, do you not see it? If you neglect God's cause, can you expect Him to prosper yours? You have suffered greatly of late, in war and raiding. Might it not be a judgement on you? Your fathers carved this small kingdom out of the side of Alba, yet managed to live in peace with the Picts. They brought with them from Ireland the faith taught by St Patrick. That faith, if it scarcely flourishes today – could that not have much to do with your troubles?"

"We need swords and spears today, not just faith! Soldiers, not words and prayers!" That was the first interjection produced, from a very young man, of hot eyes and strong features. And it raised a growl of agreement.

"The Prince Aidan mac Gabhran," Conall mentioned, from his throne-like chair.

"Soldiers, you say? You will never beat King Brude with swords, my friend. For he can field a score of his soldiers for every one of yours. It is the sword of the spirit you must use – something he has not got! *We* are soldiers, yes – but soldiers of Christ! Or try to be."

"How do you think to go about this, this spiritual warfare, Prince Colum?" an old man asked. "It is easy to speak great swelling words, I think. But less easy to turn a mighty devil-worshipping nation to a new and gentle faith. How do you think to start?"

"Gair mac Fergna mac Angus Mor, Lord of Islay," Conall identified. "Uncle to Angus mac Riagan."

"Easy it will not be, no," Colum agreed. "But with God's help we shall do it, Lord of Islay. Time, it will take, to be sure. First we will establish a monastery, an abbey here, in some convenient place. As witness to the renewal of Christ's cause in Dalriada. There train ourselves and others for the task ahead. Seek to set up other centres and churches. *Then* move out into Alba . . ."

"That will take long years," the young Prince Aidan interrupted. "By then Brude mac Maelchon could well have driven us into the sea!"

"Time, yes. But meantime, I will have gone to see the High King Brude."

That left all speechless, even Colum's own people looking somewhat alarmed.

He did not elaborate. "So we require a place to plant our monastery."

"Where do you look to do that, Prince Colum?" someone asked.

"We are in your hands, in this. The land is yours. We do not know it. Somewhere from whence we can reach all parts, with least difficulty. And since we have learned travel here is most conveniently done by water, it would probably be best on an island – of which you have so many. Moreover, we have a tradition of worship on islands, as you will know. But . . ." he paused. "It would be best, I think, if from such island we could not see Ireland."

That produced some surprised glances, but no suggestions.

"I am told that you have a thousand islands in the Hebrides," he challenged them. "Do not say that there is not one, however small, which you would not offer in God's service?"

"You are welcome to come to Islay," the lord of that isle said. "But I fear that on any clear day the Irish coast is visible. Why do you not wish to see it?"

Colum hesitated. "Say that it were better not. Ireland is our beloved home. To see it, daily, beckoning, could perhaps weaken our resolution."

Curiously, that admission of weakness from so authoritative and challenging a man, had the effect of lessening the somewhat hostile atmosphere. There were smiles again, but betraying something like sympathy not scorn.

"I have the islands of Colonsay and Oronsay," a youth said, almost diffidently. "You are welcome, sir, to build on one of them."

"*I* have seen Ireland from Colonsay," the Prince Aidan

exclaimed. "But then, I have better eyes than you! And I would not wish to see monks on Colonsay!"

"Ewan mac Gabhran, Aidan's brother," the King said. "The elder."

This older youth scowled but said no more.

"I thank you, Prince Ewan," Colum said, looking thoughtfully from one to the other of the late King's sons.

"I own Tiree, most fertile of all the Hebrides," a man of late middle years said. "St Brendan the Navigator set up a monastery there many years ago, but it has failed. You could have it, Prince Colum. But I fear that Ireland is visible from Tiree on many days. I am Ferchar mac Tulchan."

"You are kind, all kind," Colum acknowledged. "Brendan of Clonfert I know and have heard of his foundation on Tiree. I sorrow that it has failed. Is there none out of sight of Ireland?"

Various voices spoke, naming islands to the north – Kerrera, Lismore, Muck, Eigg, Rhum, Coll and others; Colum uncertain whether they were offering him sites on these or merely asserting that they were out of sight of Ireland.

King Conall intervened. "Mull is my own – the largest of all our isles. It could be that I could find you a place on Mull. And there is Iona, off Mull. But there are already monks on Iona."

"Ah, yes, Highness. We were told of that. Indeed, the only monastery we have heard of. Two bishops there? This interests us. Who are they? Who consecrated them? Brendan was not a bishop and therefore could not have ordained bishops."

"No. These succeeded to their positions. Hereditary bishops."

"Hereditary bishops! But . . . that is impossible! We suffer from hereditary abbots in Ireland, yes – but not bishops, never bishops. Bishops must be especially ordained and consecrated, by other consecrated bishops. As Bishop Lugaid here." He turned. "Moluag – have you ever heard of a hereditary bishop?"

That little man shook his dark head. "Never! It is against all reason! Now we know why Holy Church in this land is in such poor state."

"Did not St Patrick found a church of seven bishops?" someone demanded. "These will be of that foundation."

"St Patrick was a bishop himself, and so could do so. But they were not hereditary. None could do that."

Most there made it evident that they were not interested in ecclesiastical niceties, and began talking amongst themselves. Conall probably felt the same, for he sought to bring the meeting to a close.

"It is enough," he declared. "Prince Colum and his friends have our good wishes. They have been offered sites for their monastery on various islands, from Islay northwards, including two where there are, or were, already monasteries or monkish settlements – Tiree and Iona. They must now go and see for themselves, and choose. We will hope that they may achieve some success in their self-sought tasks." That did not sound optimistic. "If there is no other matter to discuss, I shall declare this council over."

"I thank Your Highness, and all here," Colum said. "I hope and believe that this day will prove to be a memorable one for us all." He raised his hand. "I pray for God's blessing on you all."

A feast was to follow, but Colum, concerned for his people left back at their ship, and anxious that his company should not become divided into privileged and under-privileged, sought that his party should be excused. The Lady Bridget was not invited to the all-male junketing, and Angus wanted to remain with the missionaries. So they took their leave of King Conall meantime, promising to inform him as to their progress thereafter, and set off westwards along the causeway across An Moine Mhór, or the Great Moss, as the flooded plain was called.

Colum gave some account of the council proceedings to an interested Bridget, as they rode. She declared that she could have foretold most of what had transpired. She had not heard about the desire not to be able to see Ireland, and recognised that this would complicate their search. She suggested that Colonsay or Oronsay, twin islands in the main seaway, might suit their purposes.

Colum explained that this had been offered by Prince Ewan but vetoed by his brother Aidan. He was interested in these two, sons of the late King Gabhran, who did not seem to love each other.

She agreed that this was so. They were very different characters; Aidan, the younger one by two years, forceful, hot-tempered, resentful of his quieter and less vehement brother's seniority. When their father had been slain three years before, Aidan, although only fourteen, had claimed that one of them should succeed to the throne, preferably himself as the most able, but Ewan had said no and voted for their kinsman Conall. So there was bad blood between them. Aidan hated Conall and had proclaimed that, when he was older, he would replace him on the throne. A less gentle monarch than Conall would have had Aidan disposed of ere this, she thought.

"And does Conall have no son to succeed him?"

"He has no fewer than seven sons!" she told him. "All under twelve years, however. When his wife died, he had them all put out to fosterage. He is no more a proud father than he is a warrior-king."

Colum shook his head. "I fear for this realm."

When they were about halfway back to the coast, where there was a fork in the causeway, the woman reined in her horse and pointed left-handed, due southwards.

"You were interested, Columcille, in the footprint and boar carved on the rock up on Dunadd's hilltop, and in the Albannach worship and stone-circles we saw from there. Perhaps there is something which might further interest you, yonder. It is little known, but intrigues me. Would you care to see it? I was reared in these parts, at Cairnbaan, where this road leads. And discovered this, as a girl. It will not take long."

"If *you* find it of interest, then I think that I shall. Lead on, Lady."

They took the left fork and rode a mile southwards, until the ground began to rise to low wooded knowes. Here the causeway ended in an ordinary roadway, which wound off through the hillocks. But Bridget turned her beast's head off to the right, on no defined track but clearly knowing where she was going amongst the hawthorn and birch knolls.

Having to twist and turn and climb, she led the little company part-way up one of the hillocks, little different from the others, but rioting in golden broom, with much outcropping rock. All around them the cuckoos were calling hauntingly. Presently, amidst the outcrops, she halted and was about to dismount when she perceived that Colum made haste to do so first and came to aid her down. She waited.

"You are courteous, Columcille," she murmured. "It is long since any man, save a servant, has so served me!"

"Then they have been the losers!" he said, as he lowered her in his arms to the ground.

"And this place will now remain even more memorable to me," she told him.

"It is a good place, yes, and fair," he acknowledged quietly. "And the cuckoos love it, I hear. I trust the birds. They know much that is hidden to men."

"You say so? I had not thought of that. But shall remember it now." She moved a few yards only, and then pointed. "Can your birds tell you what that means?"

She was indicating just one amongst many outcropping stones, by no means the largest thereabouts. But on this one, plain to be seen now, were the imprints of two left hands, man-size, cut skilfully in the living rock, as deep and effective as had been the footprint up on Dunadd.

They all looked at those strange symbols in silence, wondering. Then Colum went forward, and, stopping to make the sign of the cross over them, placed his left hand in one of them. It fitted him perfectly.

"Is that wise to do, Columcille?" Prince Ernan asked. "These could be evil, devil's work."

"We are not here to dread the old religion and devilries but to change them, Uncle. But – what can it mean?"

"They are both left hands," Bridget pointed out. "Not a pair. There must be some significance in that".

"The right hand is usually taken to betoken honesty, friendship. So the left could be the opposite. But why two? And why engraved in stone? Deeply. Was soil to be put in these, also. As in the footprint? I cannot think why?"

"The stone is stained in the print. Reddish, whereas the rock itself is grey. Could soil have done that, red soil from elsewhere? Or . . . blood!"

Men eyed each other at the mention of that word, the age-old fear of human sacrifice, terror and death none so deeply buried in them.

"It could be that," Colum acceded. "The left hand of blood. The blood of the victim. Or the threat of blood. Or for swearing a blood-feud. But why two?"

"Evil, whatever," Ernan insisted. "I say that this place is accursed, however fair."

"Then we must lift the curse. Why else did we leave Ireland?"

"Whatever it signified, it is ancient," the woman said. "Albannach. Which makes me to wonder, Columcille. So near to the Dunadd footprint. So similar in the fashioning. Could it be that the footprint also is ancient? Not Fergus mac Erc's at all but there long before the Scots came from Ireland? Albannach. Only *adopted* by Fergus and his successors, for their own purposes?"

"That could be, yes. I have never heard of that in Ireland, putting earth in a footprint." Colum looked around him. "This is a place of beauty and flowers and trees and birds. *They* worship God in their own way. It should be a place of true worship for men also, not an ancient evil. One day I shall come back here and build a shrine, a little church. As we did at the cave on Loch Caolisport."

"That would be good," Bridget said, although the others looked doubtful.

They returned whence they had come, to the causeway, and on to the shore of Loch Crinan and their vessel.

They were back at Ellary well before nightfall, to hospitality which more than made up for the feasting missed at Dunadd.

But Colum mac Felim had not come to Dalriada for comfort and good cheer, however attractive its dispenser; and although he was not by nature an ascetic he was eager to be about their business, the Lord's business. He declared that they must sail on the morrow.

So next morning it was leave-taking, sorry as they all were to depart from Ellary and its excellent mistress. But their link therewith was far from severed, for young Angus mac Riagan came to Colum and asked, pleaded, to be allowed to accompany them, to become one of his band, at least meantime. He believed that God intended this, had brought them to Ellary for a purpose. His mother did not stand in his way in this, although she did not hide the fact that she would greatly miss him. Indeed, she asserted that she could wish to go with them herself, but realised that this was impossible; but one day, perhaps, there might be a place for a woman in their mission?

Kissing her, Colum said that he would not forget that suggestion.

Down at the shore, seeing them off, in her good wishes, Bridget had a final warning for them. On the way out from the Sound of Jura into the main Sea of the Hebrides, making for Colonsay and Oronsay and Tiree, just past the northern tip of Jura they would see a fair channel between that great island and the next one, Scarba, leading to the open ocean. Not to take it, for although it looked fair and innocent, it was not. It was in fact highly dangerous, even evil, much feared. It was called the Gulf of Corryvreckan, the Cauldron of the Evil One. Unseen until a vessel was within the drag of its circles, was a great whirlpool of the tides, which had sucked down many ships to their doom. It was said to be a servant of the Storm God, one of the most powerful of the heathen pantheon. And most cunning and deceitful, for although it could howl and roar its threat, of a wild night, so that it could be heard even at Dunadd ten miles away, of a calm summer's day it gave no sign nor sound until it was too late for shipmen to avoid its terrible clutches. They must avoid that channel, go on up the Sound beyond Scarba and Lunga another five miles, although this looked a less good seaway, amidst a great clutter of islets. But it was safe enough. Angus would guide them.

Colum thanked her, but said that Christ's soldiers did not need to fear the storm god any more than the other false deities. But they would be careful, he promised.

So they left good Ellary and Loch Caolisport, to face the challenge of the future.

6

"This beauty of land and water, these fair colours of the sea, the sun and clouds and islands – I have never seen the like, Angus," Colum declared. "Days of sunshine. The weather – are we especially blessed with the weather? Ireland is a country of much rain."

in late spring and early summer it is often like this, with much sun and little rain, this May month in especial. Later it is less kind, at times. You come at the best time."

"God is good to bring us here so that we quickly come to take this land to our hearts. For His purpose, I believe."

They were well up the Sound of Jura, past the mouth of Loch Crinan, opposite a still more lovely sea-loch, which Angus named Craignish, dotted with islets, as was the sound ahead of them in bewildering array, all dominated on their left by the northern headlands of long Jura, with its crags, heather hills and skirting woodlands; and beyond that was the soaring mass of a different kind of island, really only a great mountain-top thrusting up from the sea-bed, in mighty cliffs and steeps and rocky screes, with no low ground evident at all at this side. This was Scarba, the cormorants' isle; and to be sure it looked uninhabitable by other than birds. Although he told them that it belonged to himself, Angus made no suggestion that the missionaries should establish their monastery *there*.

Most of the party, less interested in natural beauty perhaps than was their leader, were gazing half-left ahead, in especial Machar their shipmaster. For there was the channel between Jura and this Scarba which the Lady Bridget had told them harboured the dread Corryvreckan whirlpool of the Storm God, and all were agog to see it – but from a distance, only from a distance. No roarings or boomings came to them, this fine morning, only the slap-slap of the waves against their hull, the creak of the oars and the mewing of their escorting seagulls.

When, presently, they passed the last foreland of Jura and could look directly into the half-mile-wide passage between it and the frowning cliffs of Scarba, all were part disappointed, part relieved, to perceive nothing to indicate menace, turbulence or even larger waves and broken water in its two-mile length, only the warm sunlight on the sparkling surface. Angus assured them that at most times and tides there was little to be seen, but the menace was always there. The roarings in a winter gale could give due warning; but the danger was the more dire on a calm day when all seemed inoffensive.

"Perhaps we shall see something when we draw near," Colum said.

After a moment, when what he had said sank in, all turned their gazing from the channel to himself. None spoke.

"What causes such a whirlpool?" he asked Angus interestedly. "Do you know? There is said to be one near Rathlin Island, called after a son of Niall Nine-Hostager who was drowned there. We did not see it as we came."

"I do not know," the youth said. "Devilish powers beyond our ken . . ."

"But why just here? Between *these* two isles, when there are a thousand islands? One place, only. Your mother said, did she not, that it was on the north side of the channel?"

"Yes, the Scarba side. Towards the far end. I have looked down on it from a Scarba hillside."

"And saw what?"

"A darkened circle of water, that is all. Darker towards the rim, the outside, paling towards the centre. But . . ."

"We shall see. Machar – steer in."

A number of voices were raised now, none more urgently than their skipper's own.

"Columcille – no! Not in there! That would be folly. The lady said to pass it by, to go on up this Sound of Jura . . ."

"Lady Bridget meant us well. But I say differently, my friends. We are here to challenge evil and the powers of darkness, not to acknowledge and flee them. If this whirlpool is indeed evil, we shall show that God's power is a deal more potent. If it is but some strange trick of nature and the tides, as I suspect, then Christ will still not let it injure His cause."

"Columcille – be not foolish!" Ernan exclaimed. "Deliberately to endanger all, to provoke the dark powers, to tempt God . . . !"

"Not to tempt but to trust, man! Do you not see, all of you? Here is our first real test. Since those of the cave and the hands were small, of little danger. This of Corryvreckan is otherwise, dreaded by all this people. Are we to flee it? Acknowledge the powers of superstition, the pagan spells? This Storm God – did we come all this way to let him rule this lovely land? If he exists. I say outface him now, and men shall hear of it and learn and take heart. Steer in, Machar."

Muttering, that man swung the great steering-oar over, but kept on swinging it, so that their craft came round and in very close indeed to the Jura shore.

105

Colum smiled. "We are more like, I think, to wreck ourselves on these Jura rocks than to be sucked into this whirlpool," he commented.

Heading due westwards now, the breeze was against them and the sail had to be lowered. The oarsmen, however, made very sure that they remained close inshore. The remainder of the company were notably silent.

It was a strange experience to approach that danger area so aware of the menace yet unable to gain the least impression of conditions in any way out of the ordinary. All around, on land and water, was only beauty and harmony of nature this sunny forenoon.

Half-way along that channel and still with nothing to be seen nor sensed, Colum turned to Angus. "Where?" he demanded.

"A little further. Not far, Prince. See you yonder inlet on Scarba. With the dark mouths of caves. It was from above there, on the hill-face, that my father showed me the whirlpool. Out from there."

"How near that shore?"

"Not far. The outer edge of it quite near. But it is large, the circle of it. So that the other edge is in mid-channel."

"Then, over here, we are not near it? We are a quarter-mile from mid-channel."

"Ye-c-es . . ."

"Machar – steer over some way. Here we will see and hear nothing."

The helmsman opened mouth to protest but recognising that anything such would be pointless, shrugged, and did as he was told. The oarsmen, however, visibly slackened their pulling.

There was still nothing of significance to be perceived.

"Soon, now," Angus declared, in some agitation.

"I see nothing. Hear nothing. Feel nothing."

"No. But . . ."

"*I* feel it!" Machar exclaimed.

"What, man?"

"A pull. A drag on this steering-oar. To that side."

"You are sure? I think that you imagine it."

"No. It is true. A strong drag. Come, feel it yourself . . ."

"Yes, yes. I can feel it," one of the rowers asserted, and others began to shout in agreement.

"Then wait you. Stop rowing," Colum commanded. "Oars up, for a little."

There were objections, but the long sweeps were all raised.

It took no time. In only seconds their bows swung round to the right, to point towards mid-channel.

"You see!" Machar cried. "We are being drawn in. Row again, all of you! Quickly. Pull her back round, shorewards."

"Wait!" Colum barked the order. "Not yet. We cannot be sure that we are being drawn in." He stooped and picked up a small piece of woven cloth, which one of the rowers had been using as a sweat-rag, and threw this overboard to the right side.

Immediately it went dancing and swirling away from them at speed out towards mid-channel.

"We are drifting, Columcille!" Machar shouted. "Our boat. Look! I can see it, if you cannot. Fast."

"I see it, yes. So it is true. Oars, then – but only to back-water. How far, Angus, to the centre of it?"

"I do not know. It could be a quarter-mile across. But – turn back quickly, of a mercy! Before it is too late."

"Hold us steady," Colum called to the oarsmen. These had the bows of their craft pointing to the near shore now. He moved to the stern, beside Machar, and climbed on to the bench there. Facing the whirlpool area, he raised his right hand.

"In the name of God the Father, God the Son and God the Holy Spirit," he called, his powerful voice at its strongest, "You great and troubled waters, I charge you be still! Cease from your turmoil and ferment. Cease, I say! From strife and welter and malice! There is only one God, the God of love and order, of beauty and truth, the God of all power in heaven and on earth, who made you, the waters and the lands. No other power may prevail against that of the Creator of all things, no spirit of evil or spleen or strife. So quiet you, unquiet waters, I say, in the name of the Lord God! Peace!" And he made the sign of the cross, west, north and east.

None spoke in the boat as it rocked there on the tide.

Colum turned and stepped down. He bent to pick up another scrap of oarsmen's cloth, and making something of a gesture of it, dropped it over the side. The rag floated and bobbed on the surface, but remained by the boat's side, not drawn away towards the north.

A great sigh went up from the watching men.

"Praise be to God!" Colum said. And in a different tone, "Row on, my friends."

A gabble of exclamation and comment broke out as the oarsmen bent to their task. Not a few rather strange glances were turned on their leader, as the long-ship surged on westwards for the open sea. None now complained of drag or hindrance.

Out on the wide waters beyond the channel they swung a few degrees north of west, for Colonsay and Oronsay. Angus pointed out the islands, about a dozen miles away. From this angle there appeared to be only the one, but they were told that Oronsay was only a half-tide isle, close to the other and perhaps one-fifth of the size. It was said to be a holy place; indeed it was named after St Oran, it was said.

"St Oran? I have not heard of him. Has any here?"

None had, and Angus could give them no more information. Perhaps he had been one of Brendan the Navigator's people, left behind on Tiree?

All were in cheerful and indeed elevated mood now, as they pulled their way over the azure and emerald sea, doubts and criticism of their leader gone, hopes for the future soaring. They sang as they rowed, a rhythmic chant in time with the strokes of the oars. The breeze, which they had assumed to be due west, now proved to be south-west, the bulk of long Jura the cause of the previous deflection, so that now, heading west-by-north, they were able to hoist sail and tack their way, which was a help.

They reached Colonsay by midday, to find it a fair island of about seven miles in length and averaging two in breadth, with some modest grassy hills but quite a lot of low ground for pasture and even tilth, and a serrated coastline of little bays, some sandy, islets and weed-hung skerries. Only when they were close-in could they see that Oronsay, at the south end, was a separate entity, T-shaped and disjoined by only a narrow, shallow channel.

Angus directed them to pull in at a major indentation of the eastern coast of the main island, at Scalasaig as he called it, where there was a boat-strand, with craft beached, and behind it a community of cottages and shacks clustering round a fair-sized hallhouse, Prince Ewan mac Gabhran's home according to their guide. All agreed that it looked a fair and attractive isle.

No islanders came to greet them as they landed, but Angus declared that they would not be going unwatched, the folk no doubt always fearing Albannach raiders – as he himself had done a few days before. To allay any such fears, Colum, with only a few of his people, moved from the vessel up to the hall-house, clearly unarmed. A stone-circle was to be seen nearby to the south.

Angus went ahead, and being known here, was able to reassure the occupants. Prince Ewan, it transpired, had not yet returned from Dunadd. But no objection was made to the visitors surveying the island, when they said that they had the prince's offer of a site.

All were glad to stretch their legs after the cramping limitations of shipboard, and in almost holiday mood groups were formed for exploration. But Colum himself asked to be directed to the place's highest hill, first of all; and since that proved to be not far off, a mere half-mile to the north, and named Ben nan Gudairean, it seemed, he left the others to wander at will while he set off, long-strided, with Angus, Ernan and Baithen.

It was no great climb, for the hill's summit was only a few hundred feet above sea-level; cattle and sheep indeed grazing right to the top. And there, looking round, Colum shook his head, and pointed.

There, far to the south-west but clear in the midday sunlight, was a darker line than any sea horizon with, just discernible, a slightly more evident hump in the centre.

"Malin Head, I think," he said. "Sixty miles and more away – but still visible!"

"You are set on this of not being able to see the Irish coast, Columcille?" Baithen asked. "Is it so important? This is a goodly isle. And it seems that there has been Christianity here before us, this Oran . . . ?"

"Cousin – today we feel filled with God's strength, His purpose with us in this lovely land. All around us is beauty – aye, and challenge too. But days will come when our spirits are less high, when they flag and sink, when we see around us not sun and loveliness and colour but only grey skies, pain and weariness, men's hardness of heart and our own sorry weakness. *Then* the sight of our beloved homeland across these waters, none so far off, could sap our remaining strength, tempt us to doubt and yield and go back. The good Laisran especially warned me. of this. He said not to believe that any of us are spared the assaults of the Tempter. Even Christ Himself had to fight them off, in His wilderness. Laisran said to go and keep going until we could no longer see Ireland. I think that he was wise."

In chastened mood they descended that hill.

But that did not prevent them from making some survey of the islands, noting that, scattered amongst their attractions and assets of good grazing, fertile corners and shelter, were a large number of stone-circles, burial-cairns and standing-stones, proof that here men had been long settled. On Oronsay, to which they sailed presently, they found more relics of past settlement, including the ruins of some beehive-shaped huts within an earthen rampart, and in the centre one more standing-stone, but this enhanced with the rough carving of a cross. Much moved by this, many argued that here was the place to set up their monastery, on ground already sanctified, and so reverse its sad abandonment. But Colum shook his head. They would go on searching, he said. Who knew what further opportunities they might uncover? And they could and would come back here later and revive this forsaken shrine. In token of which he knelt and led an impromptu service of rededication, before heading back for their long-ship.

There followed some debate as to whether they should now make straight northwards for Mull and Iona, or head further westwards for Tiree, considerably further away. Colum decided that since it was now afternoon, they should visit Iona first. It would take them fully three hours, probably, to reach Tiree; moreover, that island, which they could just identify as a long and level outline some thirty miles distant, was clearly sited some way off the main traffic route for travellers; also, placed where it was, Ireland might well still be visible.

So they headed north-by-west over that isle-dotted sea, Colum at least still under the spell of its beauty, with the mainland mountains and sea-lochs to their right and the long promontory of what Angus said was the Ross of Mull some fifteen miles ahead, scattered skerries and islets intervening. Machar, as navigator, was less appreciative of the scenery, eying all the reefs and atolls, colourful as they were with multi-hued seaweeds and alive with birds, warily indeed, especially watching out for what Angus described as another death-trap ahead called the Torran Rocks, a great cluster of reefs, some just submerged at high water, round which the tides swirled and eddied, where many a vessel had struck and foundered. The Sea of the Hebrides might be of surpassing loveliness but it could be something of a mariner's nightmare, he asserted, with the hazards of whirlpools, cross-currents, tide-races, reefs and islets and the down-draughts of winds from the encircling hills.

Ten miles on from Colonsay they gave the Torran Rocks a wide berth to the east. And now what most of them had assumed to be part of the mainland half-ahead proved to be the great Isle of Mull, the second-largest of all the Inner Hebrides, with as high mountains as any in sight, and separated from the mainland by only a mile-wide sound or firth, which Angus said was one of the principal waterways of all that seaboard, sheltered passages for fifty miles and more, but with strong tide-races. The long and lower peninsula of it, directly ahead, twenty miles long, was known as the Ross of Mull, and at its very tip was the small island of Iona, not to be seen from here because of the cliffs and hills of the Ross.

Presently they were skirting those jagged cliffs and islets, where the seas broke in white foam, and all remarking on the grandeur but savagery of that coastline, with its yawning caves, thrusting rock-stacks, and spectacular waterfalls like white horse-tails dropping hundreds of feet. Then they rounded the ultimate headland of the Ross, at Erraid – and abruptly all fell silent, gazing, everything changed before them.

Ahead, only half a mile away, an island basked in the afternoon sun. Fair beyond the dreams of any of them, not large but green, and fertile, it rose to small shapely hills, indented with little bays of gleaming white cockle-shell sand, these backed by sandy machairs and dunes, with the white shining through the green grasses and likewise through the sea's shallows, to produce colours of every shade of green and blue and purple distinguishable to the eye of man. No single dwelling could they perceive from here, only a sublime atmosphere of peace and tranquillity and sheer comeliness, such as even the least imaginative amongst the voyagers could not fail to recognise.

"Glory to God!" Colum got out. "Here, here is a glimpse of Paradise! A foretaste of Heaven itself! Is this it? Iona?"

"Iona, yes," Angus said. "That is our name for it. The Albannach call it merely I. Their word for Island."

"You mean, just I? *The* island. Amongst a thousand islands?"

"Yes. Strange, is it not? One island . . ."

"I do not think it strange, no. They see it so. This is the isle of isles!"

"Yet it is but small. Not important. With few people. But three miles long. I have never been on it."

"A jewel can be small but can be priceless."

Avoiding a scatter of skerries, Machar was for sailing right round the island to find the best haven or boat-strand, but Colum was all eagerness to land at once. And when, as they approached the first of those lovely bays, at the southern tip, and were scanning its translucent purple-and-green pale waters to see if they were deep enough to take their long-ship, a heron arose before them from the tide's edge and flapped away lazily round the shoreline, Colum cried out.

"A crane! A crane! See – my bird! A sign, it is. Here we land. On this Iona. In, Machar – in here."

"It shallows quickly, Columcille. Look – it will not give us depth."

"It matters not. We will land from the coracles. Go in, as far as you can, man. I must land where my crane awaited me!"

"We call these birds herons, here, not cranes," Angus amended.

Actually they got further into that bay than Machar had anticipated. The water was so clear and the sand below so pure white that it seemed shallower than it was, with every pebble and tendril of weed and wrinkle showing as through a window. They got to within seventy yards of the beach before Machar had to anchor; and by then Colum already had one of their coracles ready to put overboard. He was going to be the first to set foot on this Iona.

The long-ship was barely halted before he was over the side and paddling, shouting for joy like any boy. Not even waiting for the coracle to ground, he kilted up the skirts of his abbot's robe and jumped into the lapping wavelets, to splash ashore. The noise he was making was complemented by the plopping into the water of seals from nearby rocks.

On the dry sand he fell to his knees and kissed the ground, gasping praise and thanks. Still kneeling there he picked up handfuls of the glittering white sand and let it dribble between his fingers, beaming, laughing towards those in the boat and in the other coracles which were now following his lead. None had ever seen Colum mac Felim so happy.

Moluag was first ashore after him, then Ernan and Baithen's brother Cobach, an active character; and without waiting for others, Colum led these three up the beach, through the flanking dunes and into the grassy machair levels beyond, almost at a run. Presently, panting, he halted, to point, wordless. There, ahead of them, set like a sapphire in silver and emerald, was a small loch, dotted with birds, wild duck and eiders, oyster-catchers and other waders around the edges and another heron, or perhaps the same one, pacing the shallows on its long, stick-like legs. Sand-martins and swallows were darting above, larks singing their praise and from near and far the cuckoos were calling, calling. For any who loved nature and beauty, words were not only unnecessary but inadequate.

Beyond the little loch the land began to rise in true grassland, with scattered hawthorns and yellow gorse-bushes, lifting to a modest ridge seen to be crowned by the monoliths of a stone-circle, and further, to a succession of slightly higher hills, the loftiest perhaps a couple of miles away towards the north end of the island, with low ground on either side to the coasts, about a mile apart, with some open woodland. Colum gestured towards that stone-circle, and set off again round the loch. Strung out behind were half their ship's company.

Breathless with all this compulsive haste, the four in the lead climbed to that first ridge, although it was scarcely a climb, no more than two hundred and fifty feet, to reach the ring of tall standing-stones, thirteen of them, spaced each some five feet from the others, and with a flat table-like stone in the centre. They all made a hasty sign of the cross over this ancient monument to sun-worship, with its sacrificial altar in the middle.

"This we . . . must cast down . . . if here we bide," Ernan panted. "An idolatrous blemish . . . on a goodly place."

"Perhaps," Colum said. "Or perhaps not. It was a place of worship once, however much in error, see you. Worshipping the Unknown God through the moon and stars and imagined

113

demons. Better to *use* it. Convert it to worship of the true God. A shrine here . . ."

But his words died away as his eyes took in the scene which had now opened before them. For from this ridge they could see most of the east side of the island and its features. And there was much to see, to take in. Clearly this eastern half, sheltered from the prevailing westerly winds, was where men had planted their habitations. There appeared to be no actual township but a number of houses, sheds, barns and the like were scattered behind a central bay where a jetty projected and a few boats and curraghs were drawn up. Further north some way were two larger buildings, seemingly of stone, and a few hutments, with a farmery beyond which was as far as they could distinguish details. Nearer at hand they could see what appeared to be a mill, where the stream from the loch reached the eastern shore. Dotted here and there amongst all this were more stone-circles and standing-stones and the heaps of cairns. And behind all rose the quite prominent and attractive peak of what was obviously the island's highest hill.

Three youngsters, Angus, Lugbe the student-monk and Diarmit, Colum's acolyte, the most nimble of the company, caught up with them.

"These stones," Diarmit said. "They should not be here. And see, there are more yonder. These spoil all."

"Not so," Colum told him. "They represent man recognising that there are powers infinitely greater than his own. Mistaken, but worship nevertheless. We can build on such, use these, and so meet the pagans part way, to lead them to Christ's truth."

That assertion aroused no marked enthusiasm in his hearers. Angus pointed out that his father had told him that the Druids had thought highly of this island and had had a college here. That highest hill, which they called Dun I, held some importance to them.

"Then we shall *keep* it important. A sign that Christ has taken over Iona."

"Then – you intend to bide here, Columcille?" Ernan said. "We search no further?"

"To be sure. Can you think of anywhere better? This beauty. Fertile land. The birds – my heron! We have been *brought* here. And it is placed rightly for our travels."

"What of these so-called bishops?" Bishop Moluag asked.

114

"They will not stop us, never fear! Let us go seek them out."

They turned back for their ship. When they had all got back aboard, the anchor was raised and they sailed round the southern tip of Iona, threading the seal-dotted skerries, to follow the eastern shore up to the central bay that they had noted. Nothing was going to stop them now.

They were able to berth their long-ship at the stone jetty, where a barge was already tied up, with a few curraghs and coracles beached on the nearby boat-strand. Disembarking, they eyed the scene. They had observed people about the houses and cultivation-strips as they sailed up, but now all such had disappeared, no doubt to watch the visitors suspiciously from cover.

Colum led his twelve up to the first of the houses of timber and turf, the croziers of the bishop and two abbots carried now, the rest of the company following on some way behind. No one emerged to greet them, although sundry dogs barked and even a pet lamb came running and bleating. When they knocked on the first door, a youngish man did appear, notably cautious, opening the door only partially. Colum addressed him in reassuring tones, declaring that they were God's servants from Ireland, come in peace and friendship, and asking where they might find whoever was in authority on this island.

The man blinked and shook his head, apparently at a loss.

Angus spoke, in a slightly different tongue. The Albannach language was similar to but not identical with the Gaelic spoken by the Irish and the Dalriadic Scots. This produced some comprehension, especially when he gave his own name and style, and the man pointed northwards. Bishops Artan and Bran, he said, were the ones they would be looking for, up at the temple and college. He would take them there, if they wished it.

Availing themselves of this offer, they were conducted by their guide, and now followed by an increasing little crowd of interested islanders and children, from other houses, on a track through cultivation patches, pastures where tethered milk-cows grazed and sheep wandered at will. Poultry-sheds and barns were in evidence, ducks and geese dozed in the sunlight

115

amidst rows of beehives. Iona appeared to be an island of plenty.

After about half a mile they came to the two larger buildings they had seen from the ridge above the loch. These were stone-built and thatched with good reed-straw, not turf like the others, and from one the smoke of a fire arose. The other gave no impression of habitation.

A man and a woman, both of middle years, were watching their approach from the house doorway, and as they came up, these were joined by a second and older man. When nearer still, the first man disappeared inside and then came back with two bishops' croziers, one of which he handed to his companion. It was obvious that they had noted the newcomers' pastoral crooks.

"Who are you who come bearing those staffs?" this man called.

"We are the Bishop Moluag of Lismore, the Abbots of Durrow and Derry, the Prince Ernan of Donegal and others of God's servants from Ireland," Colum answered strongly. "We come, on King Conall's invitation, to this his island."

That gave the questioner pause. He turned to consult his older colleague.

That man raised a somewhat quavering voice. "Bishops, abbots, princes, you say, sir? From Ireland? Why, why do you come to Iona?"

"To further God's work, friend. You will be glad, surely? I see that you bear croziers. So you must be God's good servants also. Abbots, perhaps . . . ?"

"Bishops, sir – bishops. I am Bishop Artan. This is Bishop Bran."

"Bishops? This is . . . interesting. Then, we greet you both, in Christ's name. And the lady."

"What do you think to do here?" That was carefully said. "This visit?"

"Why, we come to set up a monastery. For the futherance of the Gospel message, my friends."

"A monastery? You would . . . remain here, then?" the younger man, Bran asked. "We need no monastery on Iona. This is but a small island. Why come here?"

"Because we have been led here. And King Conall offered it, amongst others. Our monastery and mission will not only

116

be for Iona's needs, but for the blessing of many. Do not say that you will not welcome that, friends?"

"You would be better elsewhere, I think, Irishmen. On a larger island. Or the mainland."

"We two are quite sufficient for the needs of this island," the older man added. "We wish you well – but Iona does not require Irish priests."

"You do not want us here, then?" Ernan challenged. "You are turning us away? Is this *your* island, or King Conall's?"

"The temple here is ours. By inheritance. The King has never disputed our place here."

"You inherited it from whom?"

"From our fathers. The bishops before us."

"But you yourselves were never consecrated bishops?" Moluag charged.

"We *inherited* our bishoprics. As did our fathers."

"That is impossible. The office of bishop may be bestowed only through consecration and the laying on of hands by an already consecrated bishop. All of Holy Church so orders it. There can be no bishops by inheritance."

"So you are imposters!" Ernan said.

"Scarcely that," Colum intervened. "Mistaken, but honestly so, no doubt. As were their fathers. My friends, we cannot accept you as bishops. But your tenure of this island? King Conall said that it was his, as is Mull over there. You say that it is yours?"

The pair eyed each other. "The land of it may be the King's," Bran said. "But the charge is ours."

"Charge . . . ?"

"It has always been a holy isle. From long ages. The Druids esteemed it so. They had their college here." Bran pointed to the other building. "In due time the Church took it over, our forebears. There were seven bishops on Iona, once. We remain. It is the Church's island, in our charge."

"Then it is suitable that *we* should come to it, since we are accredited ministers of Christ's Church, ordained and consecrated. King Conall offered it, and we shall stay to build our monastery here. You can aid us, if you will. Not as bishops but as our helpers, companions in Christ."

"And if we say no?"

"Then you will leave." That was simply said, but with all the authority of a prince of the Hy-Neill.

For moments there was silence, the older man, Artan, wringing his hands, the younger scowling. Then Colum resumed.

"Come – we need not quarrel. There is room on Iona, I think, for us all. And enough of God's work waiting to be done. Where, my friends, is your church?"

Artan pointed to that second building.

"But – did you not say that was the Druids' college?"

"It was. Until the Church took it over."

"Ah, you used their place of worship? Or your fathers did. That could have been wise. May we see it?"

The older man shrugged but began to move in that direction. The younger, Bran, turned abruptly and re-entered the house. The woman followed him.

The visitors looked at each other, and followed Artan.

The air of neglect about the building they approached was entirely evident. Stones had fallen from the walling and the reed thatch was in need of repair. The door stood open, but by the dead leaves and straws lying in the entrance, it looked as though it had not been closed for long.

Inside it was dark, bare, chill. And there was little to see. There was a flat altar-stone, but it was placed centrally, not at the eastern end as was customary. Also there was a scooped-out basin in the stone-flagged floor nearby, which could have been a font – but which equally could have been for sacrificial blood, as at the Ellary cave. Again, as at Ellary, there were strange Pictish carvings on the walls. Admittedly, at the far end, a cross had been hewn out somewhat crudely. That was all.

The newcomers gazed around. "This – this is your church?" Colum demanded, to the exclamations of his party. "Is this . . . all?"

Artan nodded. "The Reilig Oran, the Temple of the Blessed Oran."

"But you use some other? For your services?"

"There is no other, no. There are but the two of us now . . ."

"But, man – this is beyond all! You call yourselves bishops and this sorry place, this barrack of the Druids, is your church? And but little used, it seems."

"We can worship in God's open air, sir."

"True. And rightly. But this, this speaks more of the Druids than of Christ!"

118

"It is a notable place, of much sanctity," the other asserted, with a touch of spirit. "It is the *Reilig Oran*. Where the Blessed Oran worked his miracle."

"Oran? Miracle? He came here also? We have just sailed from his isle of Oronsay."

"He died here. Some score of years ago. And lies buried there." Artan pointed to the far end, beneath the rough cross, where the stone-flagging stopped and there was only earth. "There the miracle took place."

"What miracle was this?"

"You have not heard of it? Of Oran's return? I would have thought that all knew of it, even in Ireland." There was reproach there. "It was a great wonder. Oran was sick and like to die. This Druids' college was then to be turned into a church for this island. And it was good that one should die for the blessing of a place of worship." Artan's quavering voice took on some strength of fervour. "So Oran offered himself. To die, and be buried here. That this place might be the more holy. So we dug a grave there, and laid him in. He lay, eyes closed. Then raised his two hands, one on either side of his head, to bless all. Then he stopped breathing. We filled in the earth over him, praising God."

They all stared at the old man.

"You buried him? Alive!" Colum cried.

"He had offered himself. For the good of this place, and all."

"But this is folly! Sin! That is an ancient pagan rite. Devil-worship. Well known to all. A living sacrifice. To be buried alive under an altar or a building. The Druids always have done it, for their heathen temples. And *you*, you who name yourselves bishops, did this!"

"It was for good. The good of many. And good, great good, came of it. And quickly. For but three days later, when a service was being held here, the earth of this grave was seen to move and part, and Oran sat up. He still had both hands raised in blessing. And he spoke. He said that death and the grave were none so ill. That there were no deities and devils, no fires of hell, but only joy and light hereafter. Then he blessed all, lay back, closed his eyes again, and stopped breathing once more."

"You saw this, man? You yourself saw and heard it?"

"No-o-o. I was not there, sir. But others were, who told me."

119

"I do not believe it. Nor *accept* it! That it truly happened so. Or, if it did, it was the Devil's work, I say."

All around him Colum's people were eying each other and that patch of bare earth, some in fear, some in alarm, some in doubt, some crossing themselves.

"We left the grave open for some time, in case Oran should come back," Artan went on. "But he did not, and presently we filled it in again. But we have never put the stone slabs over it. In case . . ."

Colum frowned, looking at his friends. That they were impressed was evident — and to be deplored. Here was superstition that could much damage their work and mission, he recognised, an echo of pagan belief and practice. Let this take root in their minds, and it could gravely weaken their resolve; for they were going to be much exposed to heathen influences of this sort.

"This Oran," he said strongly. "If there is any truth in this, his mind must have been troubled, an unquiet spirit. You knew him, before? Did he live on Iona? We heard that Oronsay, the isle called after him, was his dwelling place."

"He came here from his other island, yes, left his monastery a year or two before his death. Lived in a cave beyond Dun I, a life of great privations and rigours, fasting and beating himself. Even cutting himself with knives, they said . . ."

"Ah! One of those! So that is it. He left his monastery on Oronsay for that? A man possessed of a tortured mind, surely. Disturbed, unquiet, a prey for Satan. A good man lost, for a while. So we have this manifestation, of wrong. Here is a lesson for us all." He raised his hand to make the sign of the cross over that grave. "Now rest in peace, Brother Oran," he intoned. "Be no more troubled. In the name of the Father, the Son and the Holy Spirit. Amen." And wheeling about, he led the way out of that place.

Outside, in the afternoon sunlight, warm and benign after the atmosphere of the *Reilig Oran*, he looked about him, back whence they had come and northwards towards the high hill.

"We go on, I think some distance from . . . this!" He turned to Artan. "I thank you, friend, for showing us your, your temple. Perhaps some good may come of it."

They left the old man there, to move further on up the island, on the levelish ground a little way inland from the indented shoreline.

In less than half a mile they came to a fair place where a small stream came down off the high ground through something of a meadow, with a scatter of trees, hawthorn and alder and one larger, an oak. As they considered this, another heron could be seen to be stalking down by the burnside. Wordlessly Colum pointed to it and to the tree, and then glanced back over his shoulder. An intervening knoll hid the *Reilig Oran*.

"Here," he said. "This is our destined place. Is it not a place of promise? See – my crane and my oak! Here our journeyings end and our labours begin, my friends."

Eying it all, none there questioned his choice. There was running water, level ground, pasture, shelter provided by the high ground to west and north, and the beach no more than two hundred yards away to the east. There was a little rocky knoll to their left nearby, and up this Colum climbed, to use its eminence as a viewpoint.

"See," he told them, all eagerness. "There, from the oak-tree to the stream and to those gorse-bushes towards the shore, we shall raise our rath, our cashel, dig our ditches and raise our ramparts. There is ample space. On yonder knowe we shall build our church. The hospitium near it, and the refectory where is that flat outcropping rock. We could build it round that, indeed, as our God-provided table. The kitchen by the waterside and the sleeping-huts around those hawthorns. So, in this place of flowers and birds and beauty we shall make our home. And from it go out joyfully to bring Christ to all this land. And we shall not pine for our Ireland! Come, you . . ."

7

Colum straightened up, a hand to his aching back. Admittedly he was not used to this labour of digging and dragging and building. But it was important that all his company, of whatever rank or status, should participate equally in their great task, whether they were princes or the humblest monks and students. And sore as his back was, he gazed around him with gladness in his grey eyes. For everything was progressing, taking shape, his vision developing. The ditch-and-rampart for their rath or boundary, where he was digging now, was not far from finished, enclosing fully three acres in its square. The refectory was half-built only and the foundations of the hospitium levelled and dug, the hutments going up. Local folk, islanders willing to help and being duly rewarded, were bringing reeds for thatch, straw, poles and saplings for wattling and turf for infilling. Best of all, the church, his own especial care, was well advanced — for he wanted it to be finished first. For one week's work it was satisfactory.

Stooping again, he picked up the two corners of the old blanket he was using to drag the soil he dug from the ditch, and turning, pulled his load away backwards, along and through a gap in the rampart and then over the levelled ground to the church, panting. There Ernan, Moluag and Baithen were working — or at least the last two were, for the prince was sitting on a heap of poles, mopping his brow.

"Come, Uncle," Colum rallied him, in gasps. "Do not say . . . that you are . . . wearied of good works! You were sitting . . . at my last load."

"All right for you, Nephew — a mere forty-two years! I am forty-five — which makes all the difference! This Iona earth is devilishly heavy."

"He finds bedding in the poles equally unsuitable!" Baithen declared, smiling. "And that pleating of sapling-boughs injures his princely fingers!"

Moluag chuckled. "Ernan sees his proper role as giving good advice, bless him! One of the latecomers to the Lord's vineyard!"

It was considered right that these four seniors of the company should build the church. It was to be a wattle and daub structure, since their stone-masonry was elementary indeed and would nowise rise to anything larger than the beehive huts. The method was, once the site was levelled, to drive in upright poles, of birch, these being straightest, about two feet apart, with a second line of them a foot within, to form the outline of the walling. Then pliable sapling boughs were woven into hurdles, and these attached to the outer and inner pole-walls, tied in place. Then earth and turf were poured into the gap between, to make a solid infilling. Finally, when the wallhead was reached, with the sapling hurdles left out where the windows were to be, the outer and inner surfaces would be smeared with clay-mud, or daub, and whitewashed, before the roof thatching was added. This was the traditional Celtic building style, of proven efficacy, sufficiently long-lasting and a deal easier and less costly than quarrying and cutting stone for masonry. This weaving of sapling boughs, which showed through the clay-daubing, was the origin of the interlacing pattern which so typically made the background for most Celtic carving and illustration.

Baithen left his pole-hammering and came to aid Colum hoist up bucketfuls of the earth from his blanket, to pour into the walling cavities.

"They are having difficulties at the refectory, Columcille," he reported. "Because of the outcropping rock, there. They cannot hammer the poles in sufficiently deeply, with stone so near the surface. Some are saying that a new site ought to be chosen."

"I will go speak with them."

Glad enough to have a brief break from digging, Colum went over to where the monastery's second-largest building was to be, the eating-house. Here some ten of his people were labouring, and some cursing. The old man Artan was sitting watching them and shaking his grey head. He was taking quite an interest in this entire project, but his colleague Bran was keeping his distance.

There was an immediate volley of complaint about this site. The north side of the building had not been so bad, and was nearly completed to the wallhead. But the south and west sides were giving them no depth of soil to dig in the upright posts, because of the underlying stone. The general opinion was that they should either find a new site altogether or change the position here somewhat, and use the completed north wall as the south, and erect the refectory on the other side of it.

"But that would mean leaving this great rock-table outside," Colum objected. "It is just made for us all to sit around, to eat at. You must see that. A God-made table for our company. Whenever I saw it I recognised it. A symbol of endurance, not to be moved. And our mission with it. We should use what is provided."

"But if we cannot raise the posts . . . ?" somebody asked.

"Then we must use the wits which God also gave us! Build up this south side of stone, so far. High enough to make a firm setting for the poles, bedded in. Then the wattles above. All daubed over. That should serve."

They were doubtful but none was so bold, or unwise, as to argue.

Artan spoke up. "The Druids had a village for their college, down at the beach there, Port an Drubhaid. Many little houses, part stone, part turf, now ruined. You would find much usable stone there, easily to hand, to save you the toil of quarrying."

"Thank you, my friend. That is kindly thought on. We shall use that."

"Stone is heavy to handle, Prince Colum. Hard on men's backs, to carry. I have an old horse, which could draw a sled. We use it for the kelp, the seaweed, for treating the earth for the oats. And for harvesting. You could use that. Bishop Bran has one also."

"Excellent! You are good. And . . . my friends call me Columcille, not Prince, Artan." He turned to Angus mac Riagan, who was working there. "Go with our good Artan, Angus, and fetch the horse and sled . . ."

Colum went back to his digging, well pleased.

The day following was Sunday, a day of rest – from building work, at any rate. But there was other work that Colum was intent upon. In the morning, after prayers, he sent his people around Iona to invite the islanders to attend a service of praise, thanksgiving and worship, at midday. How many would come he had no idea. Artan said that as many as one hundred folk lived there. Not all would respond; but Colum guessed that many who might have no great interest in worship might come along just to see the newcomers and what they were doing. No doubt the island would be agog with tales.

There was some discussion as to where the meeting should be held, with the church unfinished and too small anyway. *Reilig Oran* was felt to be unsuitable, although Colum himself was for using existing places of worship, even heathen ones, such as stone-circles, as being part-way towards a recognition of God as the Supreme Being. But this was an allegedly Christian isle, not pagan, however inadequate and mistaken its devotional disciplines hitherto. The weather remaining

124

excellent – they had had only one wet day since landing – it was decided just to conduct the service in the open air within their rath or cloister, where there was ample room.

In the event, quite a large crowd turned up, fully sixty, men, women and children too. Some of the men were those who had been helping with the building work and fetching materials. Colum and his lieutenants made a point of greeting all warmly, and announcing that after the service there would be food and drink, however simple, for all. Artan was there, minus his pastoral-staff, but it was noticeable that the man Bran was not, although his wife was spotted in the background.

When all was ready, Colum led his missionary company from their improvised kitchen-area in procession, to the refectory-site, all singing a psalm, with Lugbe and Diarmit clashing the two pairs of cymbals they had brought from Ireland, in a stirring beat of time. At the flat outcropping rock which was to be the monastery's common table, he mounted it, as did Bishop Moluag and Abbot Baithen, while the others grouped themselves around. As the singing and clanging went on, Cobach came up with the basket of oaten bread and flagon of wine for the communion; and as a considered gesture, Colum invited Artan to join them up on the table, although Moluag had been doubtful as to the wisdom of this.

When the psalm-singing ended, Colum began by announcing that they were met together to praise God, thank Him for the giving of His Son Jesus Christ to be the saviour of men, all men, to ask His blessing on this fair island and on their work here, and hereafter to prosper their labours in seeking to bring Christ to the whole of the nations of Dalriada and Alba. After a short service of praise and prayer there would be an administration of the holy sacrament of Christ's Body and Blood, in which all were invited to partake, men, women and children too. Thereafter, in friendship and fellowship, they would eat and drink more earthly but belly-filling fare – this last added with a smile. Colum was a great believer in the need for joy in worship, holding that solemnity could be overdone, and often was, and that their Creator was bound, like man made in his image, to have a sense of humour.

That he believed in brevity also, especially for the present company, was proved by the prayers which followed, simple and to the point; and his enthusiasm infectious as his hearty singing of the psalms which punctuated the prayers demonstrated. He made no reference to the previous dispensation of the so-called bishops. Then, before any could grow restive, even the children, he pronounced a comprehensive benediction, and called on Bishop Moluag to consecrate the bread and wine for the Eucharist.

It had been agreed beforehand that this too should be reduced to its essentials, although in all reverence, and Moluag was similarly brief. Then Colum, who acted as acolyte, announced that they brought here, to all, the Body and Blood of Christ their Saviour, to be received in faith into eternal life; and after partaking themselves, he led the little group of the stone-table down, with the bread in its basket and beakers to be filled with wine from the flagon, to distribute to the assembled company, most kneeling but not all. Some of the children did giggle – and were awarded a pat on the head and a conspiratorial grin by Colum.

The service over, all in no more than thirty minutes or so, the missionaries went singing back to the kitchen-area, followed by the crowd, good cheer the order of the day. The victuals provided thereafter were not and could not be ambitious in the circumstances, but they were adequate, cold meat from beasts the visitors had purchased from the islanders, more oaten bread and cakes, honey, ale and milk. Machar, who had now exchanged his role as skipper for chief cook, beamed on all and pressed second helpings on the hungry. The Iona folk were clearly much in favour of it all, and in no hurry to depart for their homes.

Satisfied that they had made a good and wise start, Colum, in late afternoon, decided to make a tour of the island, something he had not had time to do hitherto. With Ernan, Baithen, Cobach and Moluag, and Angus mac Riagan as interpreter and guide, he set off north-about in the golden sunshine.

Their chosen monastic site was slightly more than halfway up the eastern coast, so there was a full mile still to go to the northernmost tip. This stretch of fairly level ground between Dun I and the Sound of Iona proved to be the most populous part of the island, with another mill, many farmeries and crofts and scattered cot-houses, cultivation-strips, cattle and sheep much in evidence on a sheltered and fertile tract with some trees. The shoreline was quiet but pleasant, the views east and north to Mull and the mainland mountains highly scenic. The headland itself was low, with a shallow *caol* separating it from a group of islets.

Once round the corner, however, all was changed, for the western, ocean-facing coast was very different, with the hillsides coming down close to the fretted seaboard of small cliffs, stacks, reefs and skerries interspersed with many little bays of the pure white cockle-shell sand, picked out with crimson and olive seaweeds. No single house was to be seen, although cattle grazed on the hawthorn-dotted slopes, and sheep amongst the grassy crevices of the cliffs. Westwards the isle-strewn sea was a complementary breathtaking vista. Look south by west as they would, they could see no sight of Ireland.

Gazing, Colum gave renewed thanks for the beauty of it all.

Walking along the cliff-tops, the air was perfumed with the scents of bog-myrtle, broom and sea-pinks and loud with the calling of the cuckoos which they sent off in looping flight from hawthorns and scrub-oak, whilst the eiders below crooned their accompaniment to the sigh of the waves. Colum was like any schoolboy released, exclaiming, pointing, gesticulating, to the amusement of his friends. Was there anything on earth as fair as this Iona, he demanded? None had the heart to suggest otherwise.

Two miles down this west coast, the land sinking now to the sandy machairs, dunes and pastures of the southern end of the island, they came to a great bay, almost a mile across, a lovely place of painted shallows, paddling ducks, flitting waders and seal-dotted rocks. Ernan said that this so attractive place, with no single house in sight, might have been an even better site for their monastery; but Colum made the point that, a delight as it was, facing west and open on every hand, in less kind weather than this it would be very exposed to the prevailing winds, which was no doubt why there were no houses here. But it was a place to come to and enjoy, to be sure.

Rounding this, they came to the southernmost tip of all, and the smaller bay where they had first landed, all agreeing that it was almost as beautiful. Here, Colum said, they would bring the coracle in which he had landed, and bury it in the sand, symbol and sign that here they had come to their appointed destination, here come to stay.

So they returned up the south-east shore, which looked across to the Ross of Mull, well pleased. They would climb Dun I one day soon, and erect a cairn thereon, in thanksgiving.

It was ten days later, June now, with the church and refectory completed externally at least, the hospitium going up, the kitchens recognisable as such and most of the sleeping huts erected, that they had a visitor – the Lady Bridget. She arrived unannounced in a sea-going curragh, crewed by fishermen, ostensibly to see how her son was faring, but not seeking to hide that her interest went considerably beyond that. Angus was not the only one happy to see her.

It happened that Colum was working apart from the others when she appeared, up on the summit of a little rocky mound to the west of the rath, where he was building a round beehive-shaped hut detached from the rest, for his own use. This he was doing, not in any prideful attitude but because he perceived that there could be drawbacks as well as advantages in his policy of always working closely with the others, as just one of the company. He would continue to do so, but there were occasions when he needed to be alone, to wrestle with his own personal problems and worship; also to counteract in some measure the familiarity in which all now held him. He was their leader, and leadership implied a certain distancing now and then, he recognised. And there undoubtedly would be times when he would have to exert his authority in no uncertain terms, to make unpopular decisions – and a certain withdrawing of himself would help. So, kneeling on the round wallhead, to lay thatch on the roof, he raised his head to a hail from below. It was accepted that nobody mounted what was already being called Tor Abb, the mound of the abbot, without being invited to do so.

Angus stood down there, with his mother.

Surprised, Colum straightened up, waved, smiled and beckoned. The woman climbed the slope alone.

"Here is a joy!" the man exclaimed. "How good that you should come. Welcome! Welcome to our new abode on this fair isle. A humble abode, but making progress. I think of you often, and wish you well."

"I, also. You are kind. You do not mind, that I come? Uninvited." She came up, to kiss him frankly.

He held her to him for a moment, and then, well realising that many eyes would be on them, stepped back a little but still held his hands on her shoulders.

"Mind? I am glad, Bridget, very glad. I did not know that you would wish to make the journey, or . . ." He shrugged. "I should have sent to ask you to come. I think no other in this land is greatly concerned for us and what we do!" He grinned, then. "Not yet. But they will be!"

"That I can believe, Columcille! I had come to see how you fared. Angus sent me word where you had settled and of what was being done. Some of it. Your labours. And that of Corryvreckan . . ."

"Aye. Your Angus is doing well. He works as hard as any."

"As you do, I see!"

"It is necessary. I must lead, in more than word and command. This hut that I build up here – this too is necessary, I think. Not to separate me from others, but to let me be myself at times, not always playing the leader, the abbot. You understand? You do not think it unsuitable?"

"Far from that. It is right. But . . . this lowly hut? For you who could have been High King of all Ireland."

"It will serve me very well. I chose a different course. And if it is poorly made, that will be my own fault!"

"I shall help you. I can thatch . . ."

"No, no. That *would* be unsuitable."

"Because you think that I am handless? Or because I *am* a woman? A woman must not interfere in men's work. Or even God's work!"

"Not so. Never that. But you are here on a visit. Our guest. We do not set our guests to work!"

"Nevertheless, I would wish to aid you, Columcille. On *this* little hut, which is to be your own. Some small labour of mine, in it. That I can think on . . . hereafter."

"You are kind. Very well. But, later, Bridget." He smiled, chuckled indeed, and turned her round to head her down that slope again. "First, something other. Something we must do, I must do." He laughed. "And some will grudge me it, I think! Oh, yes, they will. But there are benefits in being leader, as well as responsibilities."

"What do you mean?" she asked, as they went down together.

"We have made a number of rules, for our monastery, see

129

you – good and necessary rules. Agreed on at a conference of all. And one is that we welcome visitors in God's good name. Treat them worthily. And wash their feet – as Christ Jesus washed His disciples' feet. *I* am going to wash yours."

She paused, to eye him. "But . . ."

"No buts, Lady Bridget nic Colman. You are our first real visitor. Therefore your feet must be washed. And I claim that privilege!"

It was her turn to laugh. "Then so you shall, Colum mac Felim."

They crossed the rath diagonally towards the kitchen area, which had been erected where a small burn came down off the higher ground, for water supply. As they went they gathered a little crowd leaving tasks to greet the guest.

At the burnside, just above the kitchen, two little dams had been constructed, to form pools, the upper one for the monastery's drinking-water. Colum led Bridget to the lower pool and sat her down on a flat stone there.

There were exclamations all around. Undoubtedly when the foot-washing rule had been established, it had occurred to few that women would be included in the custom. Louder exclamations still greeted Colum's call to Machar for towelling, and his kneeling down at the pool-side, clearly himself to do the washing.

Waiting for the towel, he assisted Bridget in removing the fine deer-skin boots she was wearing. She kilted her multi-hued Albannach skirts up, already shorter than apt to be worn in Ireland.

"I admire," he said gallantly. "Feet are not always of such delight!" Not that he confined his gaze entirely to her feet.

She laughed. But some there looked disapproving, and Angus somewhat embarrassed.

Colum did not make merely a gesture of the washing and drying process, but did the task thoroughly, Ernan taking the opportunity to declare that such assiduity might be taken to imply that the lady's feet were in sore need of washing. Her tinkle of laughter robbed the occasion of any flavour of unfitness.

That over, a group of them took the visitor on a tour of inspection, in which she expressed herself as much impressed by all she saw. A modest feast in honour of guests was another of the monastic rules, and Machar, whenever he heard of the

130

lady's arrival, had set about preparing the best that was to be had. Normally their fare was plain to the point of basic needs, sufficient but little more, oat-bread, fish, cheese, honey and milk; but today, with the hospitality provided for them at Ellary to be acknowledged, a soup was added, with smoked mutton and curds-and-cream, Bridget's fishermen-crew were summoned to take part, the refectory crowded. Whilst they ate at the flat table-stone, various members of the company entertained by singing songs and reciting tales of old Ireland, Colum included. Lugbe and Diarmit produced their cymbals and gave a spirited rendering of St Patrick's Challenge.

The hospitium or guest-house being far from completed, and there being no question of Bridget being able to return to Loch Caolisport that night, accommodation had to be found for her. She declared that she would be perfectly happy in one of the beehive-huts, but all agreed that to be unthinkable. Artan stepped in and declared that, since his wife had died, there was a spare room in the large house he shared with Bran and his Eilidh, and he would be honoured if the Lady of Ellary would occupy it, with the other woman to ensure her comfort. So that was arranged.

In glorious Hebridean sunset of scarlet and gold and palest green, against which the scattered islands stood out in purple silhouette, Colum and Angus escorted their visitor to Artan's house. But at the door there, Bridget, kissing her son goodnight, dismissed him in kindly but no uncertain fashion, back to the monastery. When he had gone, she turned to Colum.

"Let us walk a little further, Columcille," she suggested. "The night is so very pleasing. I . . . I have a word I would wish to say to you."

"Gladly," he agreed.

"I had to speak with you, alone," she said, after a moment or two. "It has been much in my thoughts, since you left Ellary. And the more so since I have seen what you are doing here, heard what you attempt. I greatly admire." She paused in their walking and laid a hand on his arm. "Columcille – have you no place for a woman in your great work? No task for such as myself to do?"

He eyed her urgent upturned face in the sunset's glow, which amplified its strong features in light and shadow. He did not speak.

"Surely there must be something? A small part to play, humble enough but of use, for a woman to offer? It is a great and noble work that you have begun. I would wish that I might assist, in however small a way. With my husband dead and my son joined your company, I am left alone at Ellary. I am not old, yet. And fit for something, some useful duty. No?"

For once Colum was at a loss. "I do not know," he said. "It is good, kind, that you should think of it. But . . ." He wagged his head.

"God's work is not only for men, is it? He made women also, did He not? For more than just child-bearing, I think!"

"Surely. I know it. But – what do you think to do? What work do you have in mind, Bridget?"

"Whatever requires to be done, that a woman can do. You know what is required here, not me. And you understand women, Columcille, that is clear. Better than most men, I think."

"I greatly appreciate womankind, yes. Enjoy what women have to offer, their many qualities and, and delights. What they have that men lack. But in this of our mission . . ."

"You are not against women in the Church's work? As many men are, I believe."

"No-o-o . . ."

"May we not have our own contributions to make? Our Lord did not reject women and their contributions. What of my namesake, St Bridget? She was sufficiently active in God's service!"

"Yes. Oh, yes – women have added much to Christ's cause. It is but that I do not see, at this moment, any fit place for you, or any other woman, in our undertaking. I had not thought of it, I confess. Later, who knows? One woman, in a company of many men, would scarcely be . . . acceptable."

"Other women than myself might join you."

"Perhaps. But – doing what?"

"Not merely cooking and feeding you! Acting the house-keepers. There must be more worthy tasks than that? I can work with my hands. I am no frail weakling. But I can also use my wits and voice in worship. As well as my son Angus, I say! You wish to convert many to Christianity. Of that many, half will be women, will they not? Could such as I not serve in this?"

132

"I will have to think on it."

"Do that, if you will. The Church has its nuns and nunneries, has it not? Not that I would wish to be shut up in any nunnery! That would not be my choice. I wish to *aid* you, in your mission, Columcille. Perhaps God has some task even for Bridget of Ellary?"

He nodded, slowly. "I shall consider this, never fear."

Again she touched his arm. "You do not think it amiss for me to put this to you, Columcille? You will not hold it against me? Find offence in it? I do not wish to be a nuisance to you. You welcomed my son to your good company. If you could find some place for his mother . . ."

They walked on in silence for a little, to a slight ridge from which they could look out over the great west bay and watch the day sinking into the colour-stained Hebridean Sea, before turning back to walk, unhurriedly through the gloaming, speaking little now but without any tension between them, accepting each other.

At Artan's door Colum would have been disappointed had he not been accorded a goodnight kiss, as had Angus.

They did not see each other alone again, although Bridget did put in a half-hour's thatching on the hut on Tor Abb, as she had asked to do. Then, in mid-afternoon, the entire company escorted her down to the jetty for her embarkation, to wave her off. She assured them all that she would be back.

Colum went to his labours, thoughtful.

8

As that summer progressed, Colum – and not only Colum – grew increasingly impatient to be about their primary task. This was not building work, setting up the monastery and making arrangements for its upkeep and supply; it was the bringing of the Gospel to the peoples of this lovely but benighted land. They must be about God's business. But where to start?

133

Undoubtedly the key to any major success must be Brude mac Maelchon, the warrior High King of Alba, for if he actively opposed them, it would be very hard to make any headway amongst his people; also, he represented menace to Dalriada, and the smaller nation, preoccupied with attack and invasion, was not in the best state for religious regeneration. But Brude's capital was far away, at Inverness on the other side of Drumalban, a lengthy and dangerous journey by land, through fierce mountain-passes and hostile peoples. For this they were by no means ready yet. Some of the island clans probably would be better tackled first, much more easily reached, by boat, and not likely to be in any close touch with Brude. Mull and Iona were almost the last of the Dalriadic-possessed isles; all north of these were Albannach and still pagan.

However, a gesture towards Dunadd first of all might be wise and seemly; and anyway, Colum wanted to see King Conall, to obtain from him permission to expand their activities on Iona. They desired to be self-sufficient, to grow their own crops, pasture their own beasts, grind their own corn and cut their own wood. So, first a visit to the Dunadd area, and then a sally into the northern isles.

On a showery day of mid-August, then, the weather less kind than in late spring and early summer, Colum and a small group of his colleagues left Baithen in charge at the monastery and set out in the long-ship south-eastwards for the Sound of Jura. This time they were not going to challenge the Gulf of Corryvreckan, but take the shortest and accepted course for Loch Caolisport, making for Ellary in the first instance, where they knew that they would be welcome. It would represent a sail of some fifty miles.

Between the heavy rain-squalls the scene was still beautiful, the colours changed somewhat, the cloud-shadows darker, the sea responding, the yellows of the gorse and broom on the islands replaced by the purple of bell-heather and the young green of the bracken deepened. The seas tended to be steeper, snarling around the dangerous Torran Rocks; and when they had passed the attractive little chain of islets which Angus called the Garvellachs, and skirted the east side of upthrusting Scarba, they crossed the mouth of the channel between it and Jura, the muted but menacing roar of the whirlpool was very evident. When Colum made a rude gesture towards it, all laughed.

134

In the sheltered waters behind the length of Jura they made better time, for the prevailing south-west winds had not been helping them greatly and it was continued oar-work. At Loch Crinan they could see the cone of Dunadd rising out of its plain; and a couple of hours later, with the sun already sinking behind the Paps of Jura, they turned into Loch Coalisport.

Bridget was delighted to see them, and set about providing a welcome-feast to outmatch the one to which she had been treated on Iona. She laughingly offered to wash any feet in need of ablution, but please, not the entire ship's company. Colum rejoined that it must be all or none, to deal with that sally.

Before retiring for the night, she asked him whether he had thought more on her plea for some part for her to play in his mission. He told her that he had indeed discussed the matter with his senior colleagues, and they had agreed with him that some female participation might be right and advantageous, in time; but just what, was unclear. There was a fairly strong feeling that any nunnery or the like on Iona itself, such a small island, would be apt to be a distraction and source of problems, men being men and women, women; and for a woman, or women, to come to be part of the monastic group itself was hardly to be considered. But it might be that a nunnery or woman's establishment could be set up, at some future date, either over on Mull or on a nearby island, to assist in the mission. With this scarcely enthusiastic reaction Bridget had to be content – although Colum's rather apologetic, indeed almost affectionate manner of conveying it, helped her to accept it equably.

Next day they sailed up-loch, to call at Achahoish and An Tor, and found King Conall just as they had done on the previous occasion; indeed this visit might have been merely an extension of the other. Conall had clearly no real interest in what they were doing. However, nor was he hostile, but was more concerned with the princely status of his callers than their mission. He agreed that they should have all they desired on his island of Iona, so long as they did not infringe on the rights of his other tenants. As to their holding some sort of religious exercise at Dunadd itself, he had no objection, provided that his own attendance was not expected, for he had a sufficiency of matters to occupy him here and demanding of his time.

135

With this Colum had to be satisfied. However unsuitable a monarch Conall mac Comgall made for them or Dalriada itself, at least he put no real obstacle in their way. They took their leave and returned to Ellary.

There they made plans for what they might attempt at Dunadd. The main problem was how to obtain any worthwhile attendance of the people. It was apparent, from the first council meeting, that few if any of the lordly ones were sufficiently interested to put in an appearance. Their appeal, therefore, in the first instance, must be to the common folk. How to reach them?

Bridget, sitting in on the discussion, volunteered that here at least was something that she could do. She could send messengers to summon the folk to a meeting or service. Colum said that since they could expect few chiefs and leaders, they should hold the meeting not at Dunadd itself but at that area to the north, which she had pointed out from the hilltop as the place of population with the stone-circles and cairns.

So, two days later, they all sailed up to Loch Crinan, to its northern head, at the boat haven of Port an Deora, where there was quite a sizeable fishing-community, with only a couple of miles to walk to the township of Ballymeanach. As they went, they collected quite a crowd of fisherfolk, which was a hopeful sign.

There was no church nor Christian shrine at Ballymeanach, and although Moluag recommended using a fairly central knoll for their service, Colum had no hesitation in selecting the largest of all the stone-circles. This would serve very well, he asserted, a worshipping-place, now to be purged, redeemed from error, and used. In the centre of this he took up his stance, backed by his colleagues and Bridget. The local people gathered round to gaze and chatter; but none ventured within the mystic circle.

There was the usual flat altar-stone in the middle, and when presently Colum climbed to stand on this, there was a distinct stir and murmur amongst the onlookers. Clearly this was something that was not done, an offence presumably to the old gods. He told Diarmit, who always had the duty of carrying it for him, to hand up his special preaching-cross, and this he now held up high, with both hands. It was not the usual representation of the crucifix, but a triple cross, the two arms and head each crossed themselves by another bar of wood to form the Jerusalem Cross, representing the Holy Trinity. Being almost man-height, it was quite heavy, as Diarmit had reason to know, and took some strength to hold high for any time. Normally its pointed base was planted in the ground, but this could not be done on that altar-stone.

Colum raised his powerful voice, as well as the cross. "Oh, ye people of Ballymeanach and Dalriada," he cried. "We come to you, in love and peace, and in the name of God the Father, God the Son, Jesus Christ and God the Holy Spirit, the one, true and only God, who loves you all, sinners and just alike. *We* are sinners also, but joyful sinners, for we know that Christ Jesus has bought us with His shed blood, saved us, and you, from evil, sin and death. So – you are God's saved children, all of you. We call on you, with us, to praise His holy name."

Lowering that cross, for even his strong arms were beginning to tremble with holding high its weight, he started to sing the psalm:

O come let us sing unto the Lord,
Let us heartily rejoice in the strength of our salvation;
Let us come before His presence with thanksgiving,
And show ourselves glad in Him with psalms.

His little company joined in heartily, though it is to be feared that none of their audience did; but at least the cheerful, tuneful noise brought others hurrying to join the crowd around the circle.

When the psalm was finished, Colum raised his voice again. "I am the Abbot of Derry and Kells, in Ireland. Here with me is the Bishop Moluag, the Prince Ernan, Prior Ciaran and others. We have come from Ireland to your Isle of Iona, to preach the Gospel of Christ here, and to bring light and salvation to the Albannach. With us we have the Lady Bridget of Ellary and her son Angus mac Riagan, whom you know. Now, I charge you, join me in prayer to the Almighty."

"Wait you!" a voice called. "By what right do you strangers come here to trouble us? To thrust your Christian god upon us! We have our own gods, more ancient and powerful, by far. And how dare you to set your feet on the sacred altar of the sun? Leave us, Irelanders! Go! We do not want you here."

"Want, friend? Perhaps you do not want us. But you *need* us! That you make most clear. And we have come to stay." Colum spoke almost mildly. "As for the sun, it is God's servant, as are we all. It is not to be worshipped any more than you are, friend. Or myself. Look, how it shines kindly on me as I stand here on this stone. If our sun is indeed a god and resents my feet on its altar, then let it strike me now! In the name of your sun's Creator, I challenge it!"

There were long seconds of silence as people waited, staring, many undoubtedly in real fear and dread; indeed some of the missionaries crossed themselves – for it had not been so long since their fathers were sun-worshippers. Colum turned to look skywards, smiled, but still waited wordless.

Then the sunshine suddenly faded. A great sigh went up from the crowd.

Colum's laughter was joyful, as he raised his cross high again. "See," he cried, "the sun hides its face before the Cross of Christ! Bowing before its God and ours. But – now see it smiles on us again, in love." And he gestured as the small cloud he had noted passed on.

Everywhere men and women relaxed, exclaimed, smiled, many turning to look in the direction of the objector.

"So, friend," Colum went on, "so much for the old gods, the imaginings of ignorant men. It is the Son of Righteousness that we worship, with healing in His wings, as the prophet said. Come you and join us here, if you will?"

But an elderly man was seen to have turned his back on them and was walking away, watched by all.

"Now, we pray and praise!" Colum called, lowering his cross. "On your knees, friends . . ."

There were no further interruptions in a lively succession of prayers, hymns, psalms and recitations of Scripture, lasting for perhaps half an hour with, in time, some of the crowd joining tentatively in the singing. At the end, Colum announced that they intended to set up a church here at Ballymeanach, with his colleague Ciaran in charge, the first to be established outside Iona; and they would value all the help in the building work and support thereafter. Meantime, Bishop Moluag would hold a service of baptism down at the nearby burnside. Some of them were probably already baptised into Christ's Church; but for those who were not, or were unsure as to whether they were or not, here was

138

invitation, indeed urging. A second baptism would be of no harm.

So, singing again, he led the way to the stream which flowed into the River Add, followed by practically the entire company. There Moluag, with Lugbe acting acolyte, found a fair-sized pool and waded straight in, handing his crozier to the younger man and taking in exchange a beaker which he filled with water, blessed, and held up invitingly to the crowd.

At first there were no volunteers, all hanging back. Colum cheerfully sought to encourage, pointing out that they were all sinners, as he was himself, and even Bishop Moluag indeed, and so all needed baptism. At that a middle-aged woman came forward, hesitantly, and Colum smiling and taking her by the arm, led her into the water, to present her to Moluag. Then another and younger woman stepped out, and seeing that her predecessor had got her skirts wet, hitched her own up high – to the vocal satisfaction of some of the men there, at whom she made a face. Grinning, Colum gestured for others, challenging the men not to be so backward.

After that there was some movement, a steady trickle rather than a flood, with most there still only watching. In all about a score received baptism, Moluag liberally pouring water over their heads and getting very wet himself in the process, but all in the best of spirits.

When the supply of candidates dried up, Colum pronounced a comprehensive blessing, thanked all for attendance and announced that Ciaran would build his new church actually within the stone-circle where they had held the service, as sign that Christ's rule of love had taken over. Then, forming up his little team, singing again, they set off back towards Port an Deora.

When presently the singing died away, Bridget came to walk beside Colum. "That was well done," she said. "A notable start. That of the old man who objected – how well you served him! To bring the sun to your aid was well thought on. And to use that little cloud. Many there, I could see, were much moved in spirit."

"God provides the way," he told her simply. "I am but his inadequate mouthpiece. Was that man a Druid, think you?"

"I do not know. But you, you are quicker than others I think, to hear the divine prompting!" She smiled. "And, that other prompting, to come forward for baptism – you would note that it was the women, not the men, who heard it first, and responded!"

He laughed. "I noted! You make your point, Bridget. I will not forget."

Presently they were sailing back to Ellary.

The next two days were busy with planning the new church at Ballymeanach, its staffing and arrangements. Ciaran, a quiet man but determined, was eager for the task and proud to be the first chosen for a semi-independent charge. He would have two of the company back at Iona to assist him. Colum paid another visit to King Conall, to ensure that there was no royal objection to their siting the church in the stone-circle – and found no difficulty there.

Thereafter, leaving Ciaran with Bridget, who assured that she would do all that she could to assist him, the others set sail again for Iona.

Colum was anxious to get his first mission to the Albannach going before the winter storms limited their travelling. So it was not long before he set out again in the long-ship, for the north this time, and with a larger company. They had decided that the large island of Skye should be their main objective, some sixty miles away; but first they would have a look at Tiree, which everyone told them was supremely fertile, indeed known as the Granary of the Hebrides. Colum was concerned about continuing supplies for feeding their base at Iona, which he intended to grow into a major establishment, an abbey indeed. That island was too small to provide a sufficiency of grain. Also, by becoming established on Tiree they could use corn to exchange with the Mull and mainland folk for other things they needed and could not themselves produce, and to pay for timber, wattle-saplings, skins and hides and the like. They envisaged a thriving trade in grain up and down that seaboard, to finance their activities.

So it was north-west that they sailed on the second day of September, leaving Echoid, one of his original twelve, this time in charge of the monastery. It was some score of miles to Tiree, the most westerly of the Inner Hebrides and notable as the flattest.

Because Tiree was so flat it was not prominent on the horizon like the other islands, and even half-way there it showed as little more than a dark line ahead. Yet it was quite large, some ten miles long, hammer-shaped and varying from six to one mile in width. The reason for its renowned fertility was two-fold; one, its overall levelness, which meant that most of the area was tillable, and that allied to the prevalent sandy soil meant that there was not a great deal of bog and peat, although there were a number of small lochs; and secondly, that its lack of hills, save for a few modest heights at the south-west end, allowed the rain-laden Atlantic clouds to pass over unpunctured, to drench the mountainous mainland seaboard further east. To some extent this applied to little Iona also, but much less so.

They landed at a wide sandy bay, well towards the east end of the island, backed by a large scatter of houses, evidence of a considerable population. There was a jetty here to which they could moor the long-ship. As elsewhere, their arrival was greeted warily, the danger from Albannach raiders and pirates never far from the islanders' minds. But their monastic habits, and Diarmit carrying the large cross on disembarking, quickly reassured, and people emerged from cot-houses and cow-sheds. These Tiree folk were somewhat more concerned with Christianity than were most, for it was only some thirty years before that Brendan the Navigator had established his monastery here, although it was now apparently abandoned.

The visitors' first concern, naturally, was to examine this site. The people of Scarinish, as they found this community was named, not only directed them but not a few came along with them in friendly fashion. Baithen, who had always said that they ought to have used Tiree as their base, muttered further to that effect now.

They were led off along the wide white-sand bay on the right, eastwards, admiring all, but noting that there seemed to be no trees on this island. Remarking on this to one of their guides, Colum was informed that it was too windy in winter and early spring for trees to grow, the man laughing, and bending forward walked thus for a few paces, before explaining that all over the Hebrides a Tiree man could always be identified by his forward-bent gait, from battling against the winds. Colum observed that it did not appear to prevent grain crops from growing, and his informant agreed, adding that to some extent the wind actually helped in this, for it blew the powdery cockle-shell sand all over the island in winter, from the west-coast beaches, thus conveniently liming the ground and improving fertility.

They had not gone far when Moluag drew attention to a strange sight. Although they were still on the edge of the eastern beach, they could actually see the great Atlantic rollers breaking on the skerries of the western shore, two miles away, so level was the intervening ground. Their local guide said that this was why one of the names given to Tiree was *Rioghachd bar fo thuin*, the kingdom whose summits are lower than the waves. At particularly high tide storms, it had been known for the said seas to pour right across the island, at this waist.

Turning inland, after a mile or so they reached a circular lochan of no great size, which Angus was interested to hear was named Loch Riaghan, his father's name, and wondered whether there could be any connection. However, his speculations were cut short by their arrival, rounding the loch, at Brendan's former monastery – although the local people called it St Comgall's, Comgall having apparently been the prior left in charge of it by Brendan. It had been a typical Celtic monastic establishment, similar to what they were erecting on Iona, although smaller, all within an earthen rampart or rath; but now it was being used as a farm, with what was no doubt the refectory converted into a farmhouse and other wattle and daub buildings used as barns and cowsheds. The little stone church, however, still stood intact, with its burial-ground nearby.

They found the installed farmer to be a youngish giant of a man, a cheerful soul with a buxom wife and a clutch of noisy children. He did not seem in the least to resent the newcomers, and informed that he was a son of the owner of the whole island, Ferchar mac Tulchan, and had been farming here for some years. He said that the monastery had been abandoned after a particularly grievous Albannach raid about a dozen years before he came, when some of the monks had been slain, others carried off and much of the property damaged. Not only the monastery, to be sure. Colum told him that his father, Ferchar, had indeed offered them a base on Tiree, at the Dunadd council-meeting, and they had come to inspect. From what they had seen of the island it seemed an admirable place as a grain-growing supply for Iona. He added, that, of course, they would not think of seeking to repossess this site, or to disturb the farmer, but would seek a location elsewhere. The young man, Cathair mac Ferchar, declared that he would be glad to help them in any way he could.

The rest of that day they spent exploring Tiree, finding many indications of ancient occupation, the remains of fortified strengths, brochs and duns, the stone walling of one of the former no less than twelve feet in thickness and honeycombed with mural passages; also cairns, stone-circles and standing-stones. They found the west coast much more rugged and cut into than the east, with innumerable offshore skerries and islets. But what interested them most was the ground itself, and how suitable it was for crop-raising, level in the main, dry, grass-grown, with little or nothing of the heather, bog-myrtle, marsh-iris and other growth so normal on the islands, so colourful yet indicating waterlogged land. There was comparatively little outcropping rock either, save along the western shores, where stone was to be had for quarrying. They noted that no very large proportion of the available ground was in fact under cultivation at present, so that there was scope for much more. Cattle roamed everywhere but there seemed to be few sheep.

Colum was of course looking for a suitable site for another monastery. If it was not to be close to Brendan's, then it seemed wise to place it somewhere reasonably sheltered from those threatening winds – so on the east side. Also, if there was much blown sand to be contended with, plus the possibility of tidal flooding, the lowest parts of the island were not advisable. Therefore the south-west corner, the claw of the hammerhead as it were, seemed to be the area to be considered. They could not at present examine it all closely, but a prospect from one of the little hills might help. It was important, too, that there should be a landing-place for vessels nearby. So they turned back across the central waist of Tiree, which for some odd reason the locals called the Reef, although it was the lowest and flattest part of all, to Scarinish, where they had left the long-ship. Cathair mac Ferchar came with them, glad to help.

They sailed on down the coast in a south-westerly direction, to round a headland and skirt the shores of a very large bay called Hynish. Ahead they could see the place's highest eminence, Beinn Hynish – although that seemed an over-ambitious style for so modest a summit – at the southernmost tip of the island. After a mile or two of skerries and rocks they

143

found two distinct sub-bays of white sand within the main Hynish Bay, the second, Soroba, having what looked like an ideal boat-strand and a protective horn at the south end. Cathair said that a little further on, at Hynish itself, just below the hill, there was a jetty, part natural rock. This Soroba, then, seemed a good site for them, with a stretch of level land behind it, before higher ground sheltered it from the westerly winds. Colum picked out a standing-stone on a small mound a mile inland which attracted him in his preference for using existing worshipping-places. But they would go on and climb the hill, for a wider prospect, before deciding.

So, about six miles south-west of Scarinish they put in at the jetty at Hynish fishing community, and landing, set off up the hill, no very taxing climb, led by Cathair. From the top they did get a splendid prospect of this end of the island, and liked well what they saw. There was quite a large loch immediately to the north, half a mile perhaps in diameter, and a lot of level land around it which looked promising as arable and as yet seemingly untilled. The coastline around this southern tip of Tiree was in the main rocky in a modest way, with many little inlets and islets, which should be good for lobster-fishing; but further round, to the west, was considerable sand-dune country. They could see, from here, far beyond to the north, but could identify no place which looked more hopeful than Soroba Bay and its strand and standing-stone. So back to the boat and round to Soroba again, where they found a suitable shallow anchorage, sheltered by the horn of rock, and went ashore once more. All accepted that this would make an excellent location for their second monastery, Baithen being particularly enthusiastic – and he was normally an enthusiast. Colum told him that, if he so wished, he could be its prior and take on responsibility for its establishment.

So they marked out a suitable site, where there was fresh water, half-way between the shore and the standing-stone and about a mile from the large loch. Then Colum pronounced a comprehensive blessing over the chosen ground, paying particular attention to the standing-stone. Then, with the sinking sun, they returned to their vessel and sailed back to Scarinish.

There was no problem about accommodation for the night, with the friendly islanders glad to give the visitors hospitality in their homes, Colum himself in Cathair's farmhouse, the former refectory.

In the morning quite a crowd came down to the jetty to see them off.

It was said to be some fifty miles from Tiree to Skye, with many other islands to pass on the way – all no doubt worthy of their attention; but Skye was the largest of all, larger even than Mull, and for their purposes the most important. If they could make an impression on the Albannach there, the effect would be felt throughout the Hebrides.

Only a couple of miles north of Tiree was the sizeable Isle of Coll, some ten miles long, but narrow, and this would repay attention in due course. Thereafter was quite a lengthy stretch of open sea, a dozen miles, to the next, Muick, the Isle of Pigs. They were heading north by east now, and with the south-westerly breeze behind them, made good time without the oars. So all were able to take in fully the prospect before them – and it was sufficiently eye-catching and dramatic. For now, far ahead, the entire seaway appeared to be blocked by great and jagged mountains, peak upon peak seeming to rise out of the sea in saw-toothed ranks, beautiful but somehow menacing, and different, in a sort of frozen violence, from anything they had seen hitherto. Those were the Cuillins of Skye, Angus explained, named after the legendary hero Chulainn mac Sualtain, of the Knights of the Royal Branch of Conchobar, fearsome mountains of which the Skye folk lived in dread, for they were known to be the haunt of demons and evil spirits.

That made Colum sit up on his stern bench, kindling a light in his eye.

Angus pointed ahead again, but further to the left, west-wards, to what seemed to be a part of Skye nearer than the rest, and with high but less rugged mountains. That was the Isle of Rhum, he said, separate, indeed some miles from the nearest part of Skye, smaller but less ill-famed. Nearer, half-right, was Eigg, smaller still but with more cultivable land, it was said. Eigg was shaped like a long-ship, with its great thrusting prow facing them, the Sguir or Buck-Tooth of Eigg.

It was a heartening and indeed exciting experience for them to be sailing through this kingdom of islands, all so varied in size and outline and character, yet so consistently beautiful.

They had their islands off the west coast of Ireland, especially Donegal and Connaught, but nothing like this wideflung galaxy. Colum felt almost guilty that his notable exile and penance should have fallen in such fair surroundings.

But such euphoria tended to be counteracted, as they progressed, by Angus's apprehensions as to their Skye mission, for, he declared, and not for the first time, that the Skyemen were notorious for their harshness, cruelty and savagery. It was from Skye that most of the pirates and sea-robbers came, and all the Hebridean seaboard went in fear of them. Cathair mac Ferchar had indicated much the same. Colum had to silence these forebodings lest general morale be affected.

So they sailed on past modest Muck and the mighty soaring tooth of green Eigg and the magnificent shadow-slashed Rhum, and ever those fierce Cuillin mountains of Skye grew closer and the more threatening, seeming to bar all ahead. Something of a silence fell upon the crew of the long-ship, as the sun began to sink and the shadows lengthened.

In the early evening they came to what looked like the end of their seaway, with only upheaved land before them. None, including Angus, had been here before, their course now unknown. Those serried, jagged peaks stretched far ahead westwards whilst to their east front, although high, the mountains seemed less fearsome. Directly in front, what looked like the headland of a peninsula loomed, with a narrow channel opening to the east, which might be a sea-loch; the opening to the west was wider, but seemed to make straight for those Cuillin mountains. Almost without debate they chose the narrower eastern waterway.

Very quickly it became necessary to get the oars out, for now they had to counter a strong current, and the encroaching hillsides cut off that helpful south-west wind. Machar became somewhat alarmed, but Colum pointed out that this current at least proved that they were in no dead-end sea-loch but in a tidal channel which must communicate with the open sea beyond.

Spirits were not raised by the increasing gloom, for although it was a fine evening, the further they rowed up this sound the higher soared the flanking mountains, even on the east side now, and the more shadowy grew their course. Skye was assuming an ever more unwelcoming character.

146

Colum began seeking a landing-place to pass the night, for in this half-darkness the racing current in a narrowing channel could be dangerous – as Machar did not fail to emphasise. But to find anywhere suitable, indeed possible, was another matter, peer as they would. The sides of this long channel were consistently inhospitable. They passed the dark mouth of what was probably a sea-loch on their right, which looked particularly uninviting, but the hills ahead on that side did look lower. So they rowed on.

The sound quite suddenly narrowed further, to not much more than a mile across, with the current inevitably the stronger. Machar was for turning back for that sea-loch but Colum pointed out a bay on their right-front, with lower ground about it, although cradled by the hills. In there.

Having to work hard at the oars to make headway once they turned all but broadside on, they made for that bay. As they entered it they saw that there were three or four houses there. Thankful for that, and with the current slackening off here, they pulled in to land.

Aware that their arrival might be arousing fears, Colum took only Ernan and Moluag, with Angus to interpret if necessary, and walked up from the shore to the nearest of the cot-houses, where a group of men had gathered to watch their coming, staves and axes in hand. But, on calling his usual reassuring words, they were allowed to approach.

These were the first Albannach that the missionaries had spoken to outside Dalriada. But when Angus spoke to them, they responded in a tongue so similar to the visitors' own, although the accent and intonation was different, that only the odd word required interpretation. That was a major relief.

Colum took over, therefore, and explained briefly who they were and what was their purpose, touching only lightly on the Christianity issue, since almost certainly these would be pagans. The reaction was a certain obvious bewilderment but no real hostility. They said that the travellers could spend the night, if so they wished, in a hay-barn nearby. And, yes, they could provide oat-bread, dried fish, honey and milk, but in no great quantities.

Whilst Ernan and Moluag went back to their vessel to supervise disembarkation, Colum and Angus remained to talk with the men, now joined by others, with women and children and the usual barking dogs. They learned that this place was called Glenelg, and was not on Skye at all but on the mainland, in the territory of Knoydart and Morar. The waterway they had come up was called the Sound of Sleat, and that was Sleat, a horn of Skye, across the water.

Later, after they had eaten in their barn, Colum and one or two others went back to the houses, to try to gain information about how and where they should proceed thereafter on Skye. They were respectfully accepted as some sort of Druids, their hosts having heard vaguely of Christianity but knowing nothing of it, yet quite prepared to listen. Glad to do a little missionarising here, Colum was nevertheless more anxious for the needed guidance, at this stage, and with Angus's help questioned them closely.

It transpired that these Glenelg folk were by no means fond of the Skyemen, indeed lived in some dread of them and of Skye itself, which evidently to them was a place of evil spirits as well as of dangerous men. The great island was ruled by a sub-king, under the High King of Alba, named Cathal mac Coitir, whose main seat was at Portree, on this east side of the island – as its name declared, the haven of the king. He was a dangerous and hard man, and his people took after him. But then, to live on Skye, they would have to be, for it was an ill place, in the thrall of demons, and always had been. They themselves had to pay tribute to King Cathal, in cattle and corn, for their safety's sake, although they were not his people; but their own chief, Gartnait of Knoydart, was far away on Loch Nevis-side and could not protect them.

Colum said that they would go to see King Cathal. But what was this about demons and evil spirits? Was it some druidical talk, or threat?

No, no, he was told. The Druids were themselves afraid of the Fell Hound, the chief of the demons. All recognised its power, went in awe of it, and made sacrifices to it and its lesser devils. They themselves had had children stolen to be sacrificed to the monster.

"The Fell Hound?" Colum asked. "What is this nonsense?"

"No nonsense, Master, as we know all too well," their principal informant, an elderly man named Leot, assured, looking scared at the very suggestion. He pointed westwards. "Beyond those first mountains there is a mighty and dread range, the Cuillins of Skye. There is where the Fell Hound dwells with its horde of supporting devils, and from there lords it over all the island, and far beyond. When we hear it baying of a night, all men hide themselves, even the king. It brews great storms amongst those high tops, makes thunders and lightnings and sends down floods on those who do not appease it. Its packs of lesser hounds take men's cattle and sheep, horses and even children . . ."

"These sound like wolves, to me. We have them in Ireland also."

"No, they are hounds, devil-hounds. That is why those mountains are so named, from *cu*, the dog, Cu-Chulinn . . ."

"My friend – you have it all wrong! I know the story of Cuchulinn. I should, for it happened in our own Ireland, not in this Skye. Before Ireland was brought to Christ, there was a King Conchobar, very powerful, who set up a renowned group of warriors known as the Knights of the Royal Branch. One of these was the king's own nephew, Setanta. Arriving late at a great feast given to the king and his court by one Culand, a noted smith and worker in metals, Setanta found the door shut and the hall-house guarded by a fierce house dog, let loose to keep out intruders. It would have kept out Setanta also, but bare-handed he grasped the huge beast, wrestled with it and eventually slew it by main strength. But its owner, Culand, was angry and demanded *eric*, or recompense. Unable to pay, Setanta agreed himself to act the watch-dog for Culand's house each night until a pup of the hound grew large enough to take over. So he was nicknamed Cu-Chulaind, or Culand's Dog, and became a famous hero under the name of Cuchulinn. Somehow this tale has been brought across the sea to Skye. Perhaps Cuchulinn may have come here himself, at some time? If we could, so could he. And had these mountains named after him. And all the stories of his devil-hound grow from that."

His hearers were scarcely prepared to accept that, however respectfully they listened. So Colum went on to tell them something about the true God Almighty and His son Jesus Christ, who made children's bogles of all such supposed demons and fears. He did not go into it all at any length, this hardly the time and place. They heard him out politely enough, but that was all. Reverting to matters they knew about, they said that if the visitors were for sailing north to Portree and King Cathal in the morning – which clearly they did not advise – then they should wait until mid-forenoon when the tide would start ebbing and the current running through the narrows ahead, called Caol Rhea apparently, would be much reduced.

The travellers spent a reasonably comfortable night in the hay-barn. They heard no ghostly baying.

In the morning, eating their breakfast of oat-porridge, milk and bread, and waited on by the Glenelg herd-dogs, one particular animal gave Colum an idea, as he patted it. When they went to say farewell to the cottagers, he asked if he might purchase this somewhat ugly but affectionate creature; and this was agreed to readily enough, for apparently there were over-many dogs about the place. So in mid-morning they set off again, with an extra passenger, which Colum immediately christened Gaul after a particularly plain-faced and awkward monk at Derry of whom they were all fond. They were seen off by a barking chorus of Gaul's fellows.

If the current in the sound was slackened by the change of the tide, it must have been fierce indeed before in that ever-narrowing channel which became the Caol Rhea. It was all hands to the oars, as many as three men to each. With the mountain-sides soaring to left and right all but straight from the water's edge, almost seeming to lean over them, it was a fearsome place to be the gateway to Skye. Yet the Glenelg folk had told them that cattle from Skye were frequently swum across here, for droving to mainland pastures. Apparently the beasts were driven into the water, on the Skye side, through a little pass which could be seen, fully half a mile above where they were intended to land on the mainland side, so strong was the current bearing them down; there they were collected and rounded up, to be taken onward by the Glenelg men, hence their numbers of cattle-dogs.

The abyss-like strait fortunately extended for only about two miles and then began to open out to a wide loch ahead, entirely landlocked it seemed at first, which they had been told was Loch Alsh. From this they got a different view of all the enclosing mountains. In the forenoon light both clarity and colours were enhanced and there was much of beauty as well as strange menace in that widened prospect. To the west, the nearest range of major mountains were seen to have a distinctly red tinge to them, no doubt from underlying red granite. But beyond them the main Cuillin massif rose blackly towering, seemingly in a vast horseshoe of pointed fang-like peaks, where mists hung, bare of vegetation apparently and more threatening than ever.

They had been told that there was another strait to get through to win out of this Loch Alsh into the main Inner Sound of the Hebridean Sea, this called Caol Akin, and guarded by a fort on either side, between which a massive iron chain was stretched at surface level, so that no craft could pass without paying toll to King Cathal. When they reached these narrows, Colum ordered Machar to pull in on the Skye side, in response to shouts and threatening gestures from guards there. Outshouting the Skyemen, his powerful voice at its strongest and most penetrating, he declared that he was a prince of Ireland, come to visit Cathal mac Coitir, and demanding that this ridiculous chain be lowered at once to give him passage. On being told that toll was required, he replied in seeming outrage that Irish princes of the blood-royal did not pay toll or tribute to any man, especially when they were on their way to greet an Albannach kinglet. After a little pause, a loud clanking sound indicated that some iron rollers were being turned, to slacken the great chain. As it dropped deep below the surface, the long-ship was rowed over without hindrance and without further acknowledgement of the forts, into the open waters of the Inner Sound. Its crew chuckled and eyed their leader the more admiringly.

The great waterway proved to be as much as a dozen miles wide, separating Skye from the mainland, although there appeared to be a long and narrow island in the midst, which the Glenelg folk had called Raasay; but that was fully another dozen miles north-west. They were to head for its southern tip and then swing in between this and a lesser isle, and they would be in the channel which led to Portree.

It took them well into the afternoon to get that far, passing many fishing-boats on the way but no challenges. They duly found one more *caol* between Raasay's foot and its satellite isle, Scalpay, and turned therein. Now they had only some six miles to sail up this narrow arm of the sound to the deep bay at the head of which lay the so well-guarded Portree, their destination.

As they reached that bay, which was backed by a green valley but otherwise surrounded by hills and cliffs, two long-ships larger than their own came out therefrom, oars sending up a mist of spray, to head for them. As they drew near they could be seen to be bristling with armed warriors. Colum ordered his people to strike up with a psalm, cymbals beating the time and the oarsmen pantingly contributing and pulling in unison. Thus, in such differing fashion, the two parties approached each other.

Colum, as ever, took the initiative, shouting cheerful greetings above the singing and asking if they were on the right course for King Cathal of Skye whom they had voyaged far to meet?

A voice from the nearest vessel answered. "*I* am Cathal mac Coitir. Who are you who dares to come into my waters uninvited?"

"Ha – greeting, friend. I am Colum mac Felim, Prince of Donegal. And my uncle here Prince Ernan. And others of note in Ireland. You will have heard of us." That was statement rather than question.

"I do not know you. I have heard of Donegal, across the seas. And heard no good of it! Why do you come here?" The voice, even shouted, had a pleasant lilting intonation at variance with the unfriendliness of the words, and came from a heavily-built youngish man who stood high in the prow of his vessel beside its fierce figurehead, bare-headed but dressed like all the others in a long leather jerkin above a multi-coloured kilt which left knees bare, his person hung about with barbaric jewellery and a great chain of hammered silver.

"We come only for your good, that I promise you. You may not know us – but all know of King Cathal of Skye!" And might God forgive him that lie.

The two local ships manoeuvred to place themselves one on either side of the newcomer, near enough almost for oar-blades to be touching. There would be perhaps fifty men on each vessel, armed with axes, throwing-spears and swords. None looked friendly. King Cathal pointed ahead, wordlessly authoritative.

Colum was more vocal but equally authoritative. "Lead on," he directed. "It was kindly thought on to come and escort us in, Skyeman."

Cathal hooted a laugh but did not otherwise answer.

So the three craft were rowed side-by-side up the deep bay of Portree, to quite a sizeable township at its head, in the mouth of the glen, quite the largest community they had seen since coming to Alba, considerably greater than Dunadd,

152

Ballymeanach, or Scarinish on Tiree. But what held the travellers' attention was not so much the township as the establishment which crowned a soaring steep bluff high above on the right, a fortress of ramparts and ditches, stone walls and building surrounding a tall, circular broch, frowning over all. Obviously it was the King's house.

There were three long jetties projecting into the bay below the township, as well as an extensive boat-strand where many fishing-craft were drawn up. Two of the jetties were occupied by no fewer than eight long-ships tied up there. The third was vacant except for a smaller and highly decorated craft moored there, its upreared prow carved in the representation of a wolf's or perhaps hound's head, jaws wide, and a doll-like human figure, realistically red-painted with bloody wounds, held in white teeth, no doubt this some sort of royal barge. Colum eyed the unpleasant figurehead thoughtfully.

Their escorts pulled in at what was clearly the king's jetty, and the newcomers were curtly gestured to moor beside the smaller craft. Colum was first ashore – or almost, for he held the dog Gaul on a length of rope, and it managed to precede him. Immediately, he and his followers were closely hemmed in by armed men from the long-ships.

King Cathal came up. "Come!" he jerked briefly, and strode off along the jetty.

Colum deliberately held back until all his people were off their boat, but found himself jostled by members of the royal bodyguard in no gentle fashion. He was about to rebuke them suitably when he was amused to find the dog doing it for him, growling and snarling, so quickly had it adopted its new master.

It was, in fact, the dog which caused the next incident. Beside the first houses, the King pointed up towards his hilltop fortress. "Come!" he said again. Apparently he was a man of few words. "Not all."

Colum nodded and turned to sign for all but his closest associates to wait where they were meantime. Then he moved on.

Cathal, looking back, barked, "Not that dog."

"Of your indulgence, King, yes. Where I go, this dog goes. It is . . . an especial animal".

The other turned to eye him levelly, and he had a hot eye. Then he shrugged and strode on.

So the little group of six and the dog, flanked on either side by the armed retainers, were marched off northwards, very like prisoners, behind the monarch.

Quickly, rounding the bay-head, they began to climb, and quite steeply. There was the expected winding and zigzag road up, but Cathal scorned this and led the way up a route, part track, part stone steps, which mounted directly towards the summit of the castle-hill. Ernan, the eldest there, was soon panting, and the others not far from it. They were all fit men, but they had been cooped up in the boat all day and the day previously, and this abrupt climbing was taxing. Undoubtedly Cathal knew it but did not slacken his pace; and Colum was not the man to avoid a challenge. Actually the dog Gaul was quite a help to him, pulling eagerly on its rope.

When, breathless, they reached the hilltop fort and palace, the newcomers were surprised to find that the guards here were all women, dressed exactly as were the male warriors in short kilt and long leather jerkin but with their breasts both protected and emphasised by a kind of harness of bronze cups and straps. They had heard rumours that the Albannach sometimes used women to fight side-by-side with men, but had scarcely believed it. These young females looked much more than merely decorative.

Up here, with the township dwarfed far below, the prospect was magnificent, the views in all directions farflung and tremendous – save due southwards where, only a few miles away, the mighty black Cuillins reared their savage barrier, more dominating here than ever. It was obvious from this viewpoint that the approach of their long-ship would have been seen for a long distance, giving ample time for their reception. The large banner flying over the fort was now seen to bear as emblem the same bloody-jawed hound's or wolf's head and victim.

Passing between the ranks of women-warriors, the visitors were led through the outer ramparts and between an avenue of poles, on one side bearing foot-high phalluses with blood-painted tips, on the other actual human skulls, scores of them. Some of the missionaries crossed themselves at the sight.

Cathal made straight for the hall-house, which stood beside the great central broch which soared like an enormous stone beehive fifty feet or so in height, with round its summit-walk more female guards pacing. In the hall-house doorway two persons stood awaiting their arrival, an elderly man in rich druidical robes and a handsome, raven-haired woman as richly clad and bejewelled.

Cathal himself marched past both, and inside, without pause or making any introduction; so Colum halted and raised a hand.

"I pray God's mercy on all here," he intoned. "I am Colum mac Felim, a prince of Donegal. This is Prince Ernan of Leinster. And the Bishop Moluag of Lismore, son to the Lord of Derry, my cousin Cobach, and Ternan mac Fircetea, also a prince. We greet you in friendship."

The Druid and woman eyed each other doubtfully. It was the former who spoke. "This is the Queen Sinech," he said. "I am Enda, Arch Druid of Skye. We have heard of Donegal, in Ireland. Also Leinster. Why come you to Skye, Irishmen?" As a welcome that lacked warmth.

"We bring you good news, friend. And our greetings and admiration for you, Highness." And Colum bowed to the lady.

She inclined her dark head, unspeaking and turned to lead the way inside.

But when Colum moved to follow, the Arch Druid pointed at Gaul. "That animal . . . !" he exclaimed, shaking his grey head.

"Friend, I told King Cathal that where I go this dog goes with me. You here, on Skye, are much concerned with hounds, I understand? I would have thought that you would have welcomed such."

The other looked shocked. "Do not speak of this, this cur, in the house of the Hound Lord!" he rebuked, and he glanced with a curious mixture of pride and dread southwards to those ever-menacing mountains.

"This is an especial animal, Druid," Colum said sternly. "You will treat it with all respect." He hoped that the creature, all untrained for houses, royal or otherwise, would not let him down too sorely.

The queen turned to look him up and down in frankest appraisal, and with a half-smile moved on into the house.

In the large hall there was no sign of Cathal. A great table had food and drink spread on it. The woman gestured towards it.

"Refresh yourselves," she invited.

"I thank you, Lady Sinech." Colum moved to the table, selected an oat-cake, and deliberately making something of a flourish of it, fed it to the dog, which wolfed it down in one gulp. Then he took one for himself, and gestured towards his companions.

The woman tinkled a laugh, but the Arch Druid frowned darkly. Colum noticed that the man was turning a sort of ball in one hand, black, round and round.

"You feed the dog first!" he charged. "Why? Is it your house-god, that, that animal?"

"Not so. There is only the one God, the Father of our Lord Jesus Christ – and of us all, you, Druid, and you, Lady. The dog is but a creature of that God Almighty – a chosen one."

"This dog looks to me like any common herd-dog," the man Enda said. He had now transferred the ball to his other hand. "How then does your god choose it?"

"*I* chose it, Druid. To do God's work."

"You chose . . . ? Then you are a Druid?"

"No Druid, but a priest of the Most High. As are these my friends. All humble servants of Christ God."

"I have heard of Christians," the Queen Sinech said. "But never seen one. What brings you here, Prince-Priest?"

"We come to bring you the good tidings of great joy our Lord brought *us*. Believing that you need them. From what we have heard of Skye." Colum paused. "And to rid you of your incubus and werewolf, which holds you in thrall. The Fell Hound!" That was said with emphasis and quiet assurance.

She stared at him, wordless, as he heard the gasps from his own friends.

The Arch Druid raised a hand to point at him. Then putting down his black ball on the table, clasped both hands above his head in a strange gesture, part-plea, part-imprecation. "You . . . you fool!" he got out. "Insolent fool! You shall pay for those ill words, I promise you! The Hound will have you, have you all. Cathal, the Hound Lord, will ensure that. You will suffer."

"I think not, friend. The days of fear of your Hound are over. That is why we are come. To bring you to Christ and His Father, in Heaven above. Higher than any Cuchulinn mountains!" Colum moved over to pick up that curious ball from the table, to examine it. He had never seen the like. Still warm from the other's hands, it was of some very smooth stone but with its surface not smooth but carved all around. Looking at it, he saw that it was in fact engraved with likenesses of a wolf's or dog's face, jaws wide. Smiling pityingly, Colum tossed the thing up into the air, caught it, and then with a shrug, stooped and gave it to the dog Gaul, who took it and wagged its tail.

With a sort of strangled yelp, Enda darted forward to retrieve his ball. But the dog, growling deeply, warned him off.

"So much for your Fell Hound!" Colum observed, smiling.

"You are a bold man, I think!" the woman said.

"Too bold for his own good!" That voice turned their heads. King Cathal stood in an inner doorway. Presumably he had been watching and listening.

"*My* good is not of importance, Highness," Colum said. "It is your good that we are concerned with. And the boldness is not in ourselves but in the power of Almighty God."

"You will need all that power, Irishman, to save you!"

"From what, Cathal mac Coitir?"

"From the power of the Hound of Skye."

"Since it is that so–called power that we are come to end, we are not afraid."

"And when do you seek to show your god's power?"

"So soon as may be. Tomorrow, perhaps? If your Fell Hound will present itself!"

"Watch your words, loud mouth! Lest you do not live to see tomorrow!" The king had come near, his fists clenched in anger. And in one of them was another of those black balls.

"My life depends not on myself or my words. Nor on you, King Cathal. Nor on your Hound. But on Christ, the Son of God. *He* decides what shall be. And I am content with His will."

"Tomorrow your Christian god will face the test! How do you think to show its power?"

"That, Highness, you will discover in due course. Wait, you!"

They eyed each other for long moments. Then Colum inclined his head. "Have we your royal permission to retire, King?" he asked. "We shall meet again in the morning."

The other nodded curtly.

Colum bowed to the queen and was turning away when he recollected. Stooping to the dog, he patted it and reached to take the black ball from its mouth. All slobbers as it was, he handed it back to Enda.

"You are going to need this, tomorrow, to give you courage, I think, Druid!" he said mildly, and moved to the door.

Sinech came to see them out. On the doorstep she spoke quietly to Colum. "I would watch your backs this night, Prince-Priest!" she murmured.

"I had thought of that, Lady," he told her. "But – I thank you."

Past the lines of female guards, who eyed them with interest, and walking down the steep track to the township, Colum had to bear with considerable expressions of doubts and fears from his companions, even some implied reproach for the dangerous predicament they now found themselves in. Was this head-on challenge necessary? They were now obviously in dire danger. Ought they not just to sail away, during the night, while still they might?

He asked them what they had come to Skye to do? Was it not to bring Christ's saving grace to these benighted pagans? Would that be served by fleeing now? Shameful defeat for Christ's cause?

Ernan asked how did he propose to prove Christ's power? Did he have any notion? Or would he just await the moment?

Colum pointed away southwards to those black Cuillins, their jagged tops now mist-shrouded with approaching night, and looking none the less grim for that.

"Those mountains," he said. "There is the seat of all this evil. There we shall outface it, with God's help."

Down at the jetties, they found the rest of their party relieved to see them back, but themselves having encountered no problems. Indeed they had managed to obtain some bread and fish from the Portree folk.

As a safety precaution Colum had their long-ship moved out from the jetty a little way into the bay, where they anchored. There they left the long oars out, on either side, lashing them firmly in position with ropes, so that no other vessel could come alongside without due warning. The light was failing now, but they could see armed men pacing the jetty and shore, watching them.

158

After eating their frugal repast, they sang a psalm or two, the chanting echoing out over the still waters, with Colum's resonant tenor strong. Then committing themselves to God's good keeping and setting guards to keep watch, they bedded themselves down as best they might in the cramped and uncomfortable cradle of their vessel, but with the tide to rock them to sleep.

There were no man-made alarms during the night; but more than once men wakened to hear a strange, faint wailing sound, uncanny, rising and falling, seeming to come from the south. When Ernan roused his nephew, who was sleeping soundly, to listen to this, while some of his companions were crossing themselves, Colum told him to go back to sleep. It was only the Fell Hound bewailing its coming end tomorrow.

9

In the morning light they pulled in again to the jetty, where they found the royal long-ships fully-manned, waiting. Presumably they had been so all night, to prevent any attempted flight by the visitors. Landing, some of them went to bargain with the locals for more bread, smoked fish and milk, the warriors eying their every move.

Breakfasted, they were holding a little service of praise and prayer on the pier-head, watched with interest by quite a proportion of the Portree population, when they perceived a large company coming down the hill from the fortress – which they had learned was called Dun Torvaig. This proved to consist of King Cathal himself and his queen, with Enda and a group of other Druids, escorted by a double guard of men and women warriors. Finishing their hymn, Colum went to meet them, Gaul alongside.

"Ho, Irishman – you sing! You will not sing again, I think!"

"We sing to God's praise, Highness. And shall here and hereafter, in joy. We would wish you, and your lady, and all here, a similar joy, in Christ Jesus."

"*Your* joy is like to be short-lived! This day will be your last."

"No day is any man's last, Cathal mac Coitir. For we go on to the next life. We all do. For better or for worse."

"Then be you prepared to go on this day!" That was grimly said.

"Only if it is God's good will. Which I doubt. It is your false gods which will pass away today."

"We shall see. Show us your Christian god's power."

"We shall. But not here."

"Where, then?"

Colum turned and pointed southwards. "Yonder. In those mountains."

They all stared, with varying expressions, of astonishment, disbelief, dread.

"No!" That was the Arch-Druid. "Those mountains are the Hound's territory. Sacred heights. No man goes there."

"*We* do," Colum said simply.

"It is forbidden," Cathal said.

"Only by your own fears. We have none such. They are only rocks, see you – hills of black stone. So we climb them, conquer them. And your false hound god with them."

"You would not dare!"

"We would and will. And you and yours come with us, to see it done."

"We do not. We do not set foot on the Cuillins. It is forbidden, I tell you."

"Then come as near as you dare. And watch us ascend. You will be in no danger, I promise you. And if your Fell Hound exists, and is more powerful than our Christ God, then you will see us destroyed. When we give your Cuillins to this dog Gaul!"

That brought forth much exclamation and anger amongst the royal party, with the Druids voluble, some apparently in favour of going, others against. Cathal himself, it transpired, accepted the proposal.

"We shall come and see your destruction, Irishman," he announced.

"It would be quicker and wiser to see to it here and now," Enda advised.

"He fears that his false powers over you will end this day,

King Cathal. With that of his Hound's. It is all fear. We offer you love instead, God's love. And freedom from fear."

"Love . . . !" That was a snort. "We will come see the end of you, fool! And you will know fear before you die."

"We shall see. Now – to go there? It will be quicker by water, I think? But you will know best."

"We sail, yes. To Loch Sligachan. Ten miles. Then walk. To the foot of Sgurr nan Gillean. Not far."

"Good. Lead the way, King Cathal."

They all moved down to the jetties, however reluctantly some of the company. Cathal and his wife, with Enda and some close attendants, boarded the smaller royal barge moored beside the missionaries' craft, the rest embarking on various long-ships. It took some time before all was ready to cast off. Oars out and sails hoisted, five craft moved down the bay.

Turning southwards at the mouth, it became all oar-work, with such breeze as there was now against them. Gazing ahead, Colum pondered. Those Cuillins were still mist-covered – which did not suit his requirements. He murmured a prayer for help in this, as in all. Because the tops were not to be seen, the mountain-range seemed even higher than ever, presenting what looked like a dark and quite insurmountable barrier cutting off all ahead. All in their boat who were not actually rowing, and therefore with their backs to the view, eyed it askance, with probably only a little less dread than did the occupants of the other craft.

Presently, passing the *caol* between Raasay and Scalpay, by which they had entered this sound, the flotilla almost immediately turned into the entrance to a narrow sea-loch, only a quarter-mile in width, a gloomy place with those mountains overhanging closely. On the left was the red range, rearing hugely, even these looking fierce enough this dull morning, and so near. But directly ahead all was black and menacing as the jaws of hell itself, for no sun could shine in here because of the mist canopy above the narrow funnel of Sligachan.

This loch was about three miles long, its head proving to be at the mouth of a chasm-like valley probing due southwards and dividing the red from the black Cuillins, Glen Sligachan. There was no jetty here and disembarkation had to be by coracle. Whilst this was proceeding, suddenly the strange, ululating wailing sound came down to them out of the mountains, so much louder and more unpleasant than back at Portree. Its effect on the hearers was dramatic. None was left unmoved, some raising hands above heads, some actually falling prostrate on the ground, some kneeling. Even the missionaries looked thoroughly unhappy. All except Colum that is, who, about to step down into a coracle, with the dog, managed to produce a loud laugh.

"Heed the poor dying Fell Hound!" he exclaimed. "It's reign is over, and it knows it." Lower-voiced he said to Ernan, "It is only some trick of the wind amongst those peaks and corries, I think. And I thank God for it – since it means that the wind is rising. And wind will blow away this mist."

Ashore, he made for Cathal. "Where now, King?" he asked.

The other pointed up the funnel of the south-probing glen. "There," he said. He gestured, but frankly winced as the howling sound came again. "Glen Sligachan. If still you dare!"

"Lead on, Highness."

They made a large party as they moved off, keeping to the east side of a swift-flowing river, on the red mountains' side, not the black. There was little talk amongst either section of the company, under that oppressive, savage rampart. Colum kept glancing up, if few others did. The wailing sound was intermittent and obviously came from high on their right, hidden in the mist. It seemed to be happening more frequently – which, if it was caused by wind up there, as suspected, was all to the good.

They walked for something over two miles up that dark valley, with no complaint thereat from Colum; the longer the better, not because he sought to put off the test but to give the wind time. He could not be certain, but he had an idea that the mist up there was thinning.

At length, on a grassy shelf of the valley-floor opposite where a sizeable burn, almost a waterfall, came down on the other side, Cathal halted. He pointed across, and up – but did not *look* up, none of the Skyemen did; that appeared to be either forbidden or at least inadvisable.

"There," he said. "That is Sgurr nan Cu-Chulinn, the Tooth of Culand's Hound."

There was, of course, nothing to be seen, only the swirling grey mist and the black rock. But actually it was not at the

162

hidden mountain that Colum was looking but higher and south-westwards. Timing now could be all-important.

"If it is your Hound's seat and dwelling-place, then we will climb it, conquer it," he declared. "Prove to you that our Christ is lord of us all, that no hurt can come to those who believe in Him, whether from hounds or demons or the fears of men. You will see it."

"See!" That was Enda, the Arch Druid. "I would wish to see your end, yes, Irishman. But once you are gone into that mist, we shall never see you, any of you, again. Other fools and doubters have gone and never come back. But our eyes shall not see it."

"That would be a pity, Druid. For to see can be to believe! We must endeavour to let you see your deliverance from fear." He glanced up again. Nearly, but not yet. "We shall sing a Christian psalm to God Almighty before we start." Colum turned to his far from confident-looking group. "Unto the hills!" he cried. "I will lift mine eyes unto the hills, from whence cometh my help. Sing!"

Loudly then he led them in the psalm, so well-known to them all – but he kept his eyes raised heavenwards and southwards.

After a somewhat hesitant start, they took it up vehemently, so that the narrow walls of that valley re-echoed with the singing. They got as far as 'the sun shall not smite thee by day, nor the moon by night . . .' when suddenly Colum raised a hand and shouted. "Enough! God hears!" And with a further wave of that hand gestured upwards and westwards now.

As all eyes were raised, the mist rolled away, as though a curtain had been drawn back, and a pale sun shone through, irradiating high above them the jagged black shoulders and thrusting peaks of the mountain and its neighbours, daunting and malevolent but clear.

"So you shall see, Druid – you shall see!" he declared, but his words were lost in the wondering exclamations and clamour of the company.

"King Cathal," he went on, whilst the impression was still having its effect, "we now climb your Hound's mountain, to banish any power it may have over you. It will take us some time to reach yonder summit. We will carry up some wood from those trees," and he pointed to small scrub oak alder and birch growing above the opposite riverside. "When we reach the top, you may not see us, from here. So we will light a fire of it, and you will see the flame and smoke and know that we have triumphed."

Cathal said nothing.

"This dog, my Gaul, will go with us. And will swallow up your Fell Hound. It will have no more dominance over you." He turned to his own people. "It will be a steep and hard climb," he warned. "Not all need come. Only those who have good lungs, strong muscles and a head for heights. You, Ernan, will remain here with King Cathal and his lady. Tell them about our Lord Jesus."

"I could do it, Columcille," his uncle protested. "I am none so aged and decrepit!"

"Some must stay. You amongst them. The fewer we are, the swifter."

Ernan was still objecting when Colum felt pressure at his side, almost nudging, and looked to find Queen Sinech there.

"I said that you were a bold man, Prince-Priest," she murmured. "I hope that you are a wise one!" As she spoke, he felt her hand slip into his, at his side, as she pressed something therein. He did not need to look down to see what it was; obviously it was a slender dirk or dagger. Her voice dropped momentarily to a whisper. "Take this. It might aid you."

Almost he rejected it. But on second thoughts did not, but hid the knife in the folds of his robe. It was kindly meant. Why offend by refusal? Especially as any handing it back would make evident to others, and to her husband, what she had done. He inclined his head.

"Thank you, lady," he said quietly.

Some debate was going on amongst his party, and out of it only about a dozen of the total decided to tackle the daunting climb, although others said that they would at least come part way. The dog Gaul at least was eager to start.

Any sort of over-emphasised leave-taking might have implied a fear of not returning, so Colum merely gripped his uncle's shoulder, waved to the others who were staying behind, bowed to Cathal and his wife, and strode off without further ado, hitching up his robe and being almost dragged onward by the dog.

They had first to get over the river, a wet start to the climb. No doubt in rainy weather it would be all but impassable, but this day they were able to pick a way across, zigzagging, with

164

the notably cold water never higher than mid-thigh, the dog paddling. There was some stumbling on the rounded stones of the bed.

At the far side, waiting for the others, Colum eyed the challenging prospect ahead in more detail. Sgurr nan Cu-Chulinn, now wholly clear of cloud and mist, was seen to consist of no fewer than five soaring pinnacles, the highest the second from the south end. No direct assault on any of these was possible, he decided there and then, owing to the fierce steepness of their east faces, sheer, naked rock cliffs. But between the southernmost pinnacle and that highest peak was a col or saddle; and by slanting over to their left they ought to be able to reach there without too much difficulty, although the final lift would be taxing. By making a half-circle approach leftwards, they would make the ascent more gradual. He reckoned it about one mile, an upheaved and awkward mile, to the col. Loosing Gaul, for he was going to need both hands hereafter, he started off through the oak and birch scrub, for the first hazard, to get across that plunging burn, a foaming cascade indeed; and found it more difficult to negotiate than the wider river below, this because it had cut for itself a deep gully in the underlying rock, with wet beetling sides. In the end it was Gaul who showed them the best way over.

Colum was a man of much physical as well as mental energy and he actully enjoyed this striding out, and in some measure the challenge ahead. Glancing back, he counted eleven followers.

Climbing now, but at an angle, they were into dwarf woodland, quite extensive but ragged and with the trees twisted and contorted and never much more than man height, witness to the harsh growing conditions and shallowness of the soil. He noted however that there were deer-paths in and through it, so life did exist here. The said paths were a help to the climbers.

Panting somewhat, for Colum was setting a fair pace, they came out on to a minor ridge, and found a loch in the corrie ahead. Looking back, they could see the large company at the riverside, dwarfed now and settling down to wait.

"What are they expecting to see?" he asked of Moluag, who was keeping up well, being small but wiry. "They dare not look on their precious Hound's territory. So how think they to witness our destruction?"

Breath precious, the little bishop spread one eloquent hand. He had not, like Colum, left his crozier behind and was finding it a useful support on rough ground.

Rounding the loch on the west and upper side, they gathered bundles of dead wood, for their fire, from the last of the stunted trees, and faced the first real climbing, on scree and fallen rock, difficult going, this the ascent to the col between the southmost summit and the main peak. It steepened all the time, and unused to serious climbing, they all found it heavy going indeed. That they were not really clad for this sort of exercise was quickly evident; and the wood was a nuisance to carry. It was here that harsh reality began to separate the physically tough from those less so. With the utterly daunting and all but sheer rock pinnacles towering ahead, the latter came to a recognition that most would never get higher than the col, and that they were holding the others back even now.

The col reached at length, even trembling weariness was momentarily forgotten in the face of the utterly stupendous and breath-taking vista which suddenly opened before them. From this lofty viewpoint almost the entire Cuillin range was visible, seeming almost to burst upon them in overpowering grandeur, scores of fierce peaks jostling each other in savage rivalry. It could be seen now that the formation was like a vast horseshoe of naked black stone, opening to the south-east and cradling deep in its dark cold heart a stark and lonely loch, far below, long and narrow. But not only this; almost as overwhelming was the prospect to south and west, seawards, the limitless ocean and Sea of the Hebrides, alleged to contain a thousand islands, all, it seemed, to be seen from here. Spellbound, they stared.

Colum, probably the most appreciative of them all of scene and beauty, did the least staring. His present concern was with what lay close at hand, the up-thrusting bare cone of Sgurr nan Cu-Chulinn itself. From here it could be seen that the east and west faces of it were utterly unscalable, all but perpendicular, soaring up a thousand feet higher. But between these was a narrow climbing ridge, steep yes, broken and fissured. If there was any way up it was by that ridge.

When he barked a word or two and pointed to it, all fell silent. It was the moment of truth. Only four others who had got this far could in fact face that ridge. Moluag, Cobach and the youngsters Diarmit and Lugbe. The others bowed to reality.

The five now discarded their robes and jerkins, to wear only their shirts, already sweat-soaked. Moluag even laid aside his pastoral staff. There was the problem of the firewood and the dead bracken they had brought to make smoke. Some of it they left here and tied up the remainder into tight bundles, with girdles, belts and even Gaul's leash, to strap to their backs. Then, without delay, they faced the ascent. They were going to need hands and knees almost equally with feet.

The farewells of their friends were heartfelt.

They had not climbed far when up to them came the singing of those left behind, psalms to help them on their way.

They needed all the help available. Once they were on that knife-edge ridge every foot presented new problems, dangers, difficulties – and always the dizzy drop on either side grew the more of a preoccupation. One careless move, one miscalculation, one slip or mistaken hand-hold, and they would be entering the next life. Those bundles on their backs were a handicap. Even Gaul went warily indeed, often whimpering.

They had to pause and rest often, but never for more than a couple of minutes at a time lest muscles and determination both relaxed. It occurred to Colum that coming back down was going to be almost worse. The faint singing continued to come after them.

How long it took them to reach the base of the final pinnacle they had little idea. They had been so concerned with every rock and step and grip of their way that they had had no eyes for the ultimate challenge. But at length it towered before them, at first sight utterly inaccessible, perpendicular naked rock, perhaps one hundred and fifty feet of it.

Moluag panted. "Will this here not serve, Columcille? Enough? A fire and smoke here and it would be seen as near enough to the top, from down there. That is . . . impossible!"

Colum was not listening. He was scanning that cliff-face foot by foot, noting crevices, cracks, ledges, and faults in the black stone. There had been no least crumbling of the rock all the way up; it was hard unyielding stuff that would not give or break away under their grasp as some rock might. He had never seen rock like this, not granite nor felspar nor sandstone, but something unknown – and at least reliable.

He pointed. "I think, if we moved round half-left. Then

right again. You see that little ledge? Edge along that. Then up slantwise. To that crack, like a chimney. Then left once more. We could do it."

He got no response. They could not hear any singing now.

"*I* am going to try it," he went on. "God has brought us this far. He will let us finish the task. Wait here if you will. I could make a little fire up there. And the larger one here."

He went on.

It was crawling now, like a fly on a wall, every inch to be considered, almost as much sideways as upwards, sometimes even having to descend a little way again, finger-tips work, toes also, eyes busy, every sense at stretch. And at the back of his mind, all the time – coming down, coming down . . . ! Ropes – they should have had ropes. He looked down only once, and that was at the sad wailing and yelping of Gaul. The dog could by no means get up here, and was in a sorry state of abandonment, alone at the base of the pinnacle. For that glance downward showed the four others all crawling up after him.

At one point, clinging on desperately, Colum stopped to pray. There was an overhang directly above him and he could see no way of getting past it and no way over it. Forehead against the black stone, he knew doubt, fear, even terror, something hitherto almost unknown to that man. Was this the end, then? Failure? Did God not hear him. Was He deserting them . . . ?

He heard heavy breathing half-right below. He opened his eyes to look down. Moluag was about a dozen feet lower and edging along to the right, inch by inch.

"Is there a way? There?" he gasped. "I . . . I am held. Here. A way?"

"I think so," came up to him. "The foot of that crack. Your chimney. Only a score of feet. A ledge, small but . . ." Moluag left the rest unsaid.

"Thank the Lord! Then . . . I come down . . ."

"Have a care, man – have a care coming back . . ."

That was scarcely necessary counsel. Prospecting every cautious move with fingers and the toes of his leather brogans, Colum crept back whence he had come, telling himself that it would be like this coming back down hereafter, and wondering. Perhaps that wondering helped him, for a word almost at his ear startled him. It was Cobach, and he had descended practically on top of him. So he was clear of that false approach and overhang, God be praised.

Moluag was already some way along and up, on the right, Cobach moving slowly after him, Diarmit and Lugbe not far below. In the middle now, pride in abeyance, Colum followed on.

They found that chimney actually less difficult to ascend than the rock-faces, by putting their backs against one side and pressing against the other with feet and knees, so hoisting themselves up. And when they reached the top of it, there was only a score or so of feet more, of less steep climbing, before they found themselves at the summit of all.

Their sudden arrival at the topmost pinnacle, nearer to the heavens than any of them had ever been – and Colum third up, not first – affected them all with an elation that verged on exultation, almost light-headedness, so that they could only gasp laughing incoherences, stare about them in wonder and shake their heads. It was as though they had risen out of this world, translated abruptly from grievous trial, danger and effort to ecstasy, limitless and free. Somehow, from up here, the Cuillins did not seem of menace any more. Whether this was the highest of them all they did not know; but in conquering this one they felt that they had conquered all.

Colum brought them back to reality, with the fire to be laid and lit. At least there was no problem as to where to put it, for the peak had only a tiny summit platform. They built the sticks and twigs up in a pyramid over the dead bracken fronds, as tinder, and struck sparks from the flint and steel carried in the little leather pouch round Diarmit's neck. The dry material caught quickly and the bracken at least sent up a satisfactory plume of smoke. There was quite a steady wind up here, and the smoke blew off north-eastwards; but surely there would be enough of it to be evident from down in Glen Sligachan. Looking down, they themselves could not see into the valley-floor, the rock-formation intervening; but they thought the smoke would be visible.

Concern about getting down from this dizzy height was now preoccupying Colum's mind. He ordered the five cords, belts and leash, which had been round the wood-bundles, to be tied securely together. This produced an odd-looking but serviceable rope of over twenty feet, which he hoped would be

169

of help, providing some support both actual and moral. Then they moved, almost reluctantly, back to their chimney.

Descending it, by the same method they had climbed it, was not difficult – although now they were looking downwards, and the frightening drop was unnerving indeed. Colum advised that they keep their eyes firmly on the rock beside them. At its foot they decided to use the rope. Moluag, who seemed to have the greatest aptitude for this spider-work, would go first, the rope tied round his middle, Colum attached to the other end and using any rock projection to strengthen its hold. Moluag would go only a few feet, then pause, and the others would follow, holding on to the rope as they descended, Colum bringing up the rear – all of course going down backwards and facing the cliff.

Slowly, much more so than ascending, they crept down, feeling the way with toes and hands, each aiding the others in a heart-stopping progress, Colum ever counselling no hurry, no hurry. There were many pauses, whilst breaths and nerves were recovered.

It was at one of these pauses that they heard Gaul's howls, mixed with offended yelps. And it was only then that Colum, for one, recollected the Fell Hound. He had totally overlooked the alleged haunting of this mountain by the phantom in all the excitement of the ascent and achievement. He laughed aloud at the thought – to the others' alarm.

Gaul's delight at seeing them again was touching. Colum feared that in the creature's joy it might get into trouble going down the long ridge. He spoke sternly to it, to doubtful effect.

In fact, the men were probably in more danger than the dog in that descent, for after what they had experienced on the pinnacle they tended to look on this part as easy and took more chances than when coming up. But when Cobach slipped and only saved himself from a dire drop by grabbing a knob of rock and being assisted up again, they all took more care.

Down at the col they found their colleagues lying in the sun around the embers of another fire – so there had been two smokes for the Skyemen to see. There was much acclaim, question and answer; but since those others had not experienced the full rigours of the ascent, they could not altogether appreciate the feat to the full.

Without delay, after donning their robes again, they all set off downhill, well content.

They were more than halfway down when that self-satisfaction was rudely shattered. They had passed the loch and were in the scrub-woodland, Colum leading, when in a birch-clad hollow a roaring grunting sound assailed them. Peering around, with unbidden thoughts of hounds and demons, they were frozen in their tracks by the sudden appearance of a great wild-boar coming charging out of the brushwood, head down, tusks gleaming. Gaul, ranging in front, had presumably aroused it, in its lair. The dog, at sight and sound, turned and bolted back to Colum, to hide behind him. The boar charged on.

Colum had only the briefest moments for reaction. The brute was coming straight for him. On that narrow deer-track he would inevitably take the full force of the attack. There was little room, with the scrub around, for any avoiding action. What could he do? Those tusks . . . !

It was instinct which took charge rather than conscious decision – for he had never been in such a situation, nor considered it. As, head down, the animal rushed at him, he side-stepped, as far as he could. But the boar was more native to this scrub-woodland than was Colum, and swung round in turn. Jumping back and aside further, the man recognised that this dodging would not save him, especially when he stumbled, all but fell, over Gaul hiding behind him. Squealing with fury, the boar reared up to the attack, those up-thrusting tusks deadly.

Colum managed to twist away from that lunge, but only just. Something to counter those tusks. If he had had his staff . . .

He had only his own arms. Something made him thrust his left forearm out, waving it round to twist the wide sleeve of his robe more thickly about it. Only just in time, as the creature leapt at him again, jaws open, tusks curving up. Into those jaws he plunged his arm, all that he could do.

He reeled back under the impact, for that boar was a heavy brute. It was Moluag, at his back, who saved him from falling. But the boar was now clamped on to his arm, snarling. Its weight would pull him down. He knew no pain in his arm.

Help came, in some degree, on two sides, Moluag's pastoral staff belabouring and Gaul, recovering courage, launching itself at the boar's hind legs, biting. But the great pig was not to be distracted. Chewing on Colum's arm, its tusks thrusting up to his chest, his neck, his face, the stink of it strong, the man was held upright only by the pressure of friends behind him. This could not go on.

Then he remembered. The dirk the woman had given him. He was not totally unarmed, after all. Thrusting his free right hand into the pocket of his robe, his fingers closed over its slender steel. So slight a thing to pit against this huge, snarling brute. A woman's knife. But sharp, sharp.

Raising the weapon, he plunged it down in behind the boar's heavy front-quarters, drew it out and plunged again. The heart should be somewhere there. The creature squealed in a mixture of pain and rage. Held up from behind, Gaul biting and Moluag smiting and poking, Colum thrust and thrust again with all his remaining strength, to the throat now.

Suddenly his arm and robe were soaked in a flood of blood, not his own. The knife must have severed the brute's windpipe and jugular. With a bubbling, choking roar, the grip on his forearm slackened and the animal slumped forward on to the man, inert now although jerking. The sheer weight of it bore Colum down, support at the back notwithstanding. Man and animal collapsed to the ground together, the knife still lodged in the boar's throat.

Shaken, bruised, trembling, Colum was aided to his feet, amidst a clamour of concern, praise, thanksgiving. Blood-spattered, unsteady, he unwound his torn sleeve. Beneath, his arm was mauled but not apparently seriously damaged, thanks to the tough woven homespun of his abbot's robe. He looked down at the boar, dead obviously but still twitching. Stooping, he drew out the slender knife from its throat.

"Their Hound . . . was but . . . a pig . . . after all!" he got out, with a shaky attempt at a laugh.

"God be praised!" Moluag said, for them all. Then he pointed. "That dagger? How . . . ? Where . . . ? I have never seen it."

"The woman, Cathal's queen. Gave me it. Secretly. God must have moved her to it."

After a little pause to let Colum recover his breath and strength, they were for moving on when a thought occurred to him.

"Let us take this animal with us," he said. "Who knows, it might serve a turn. Something to bring back. Proof of conquering . . ."

172

"It will be heavy to carry, Columcille . . ."

"Drag it. Use our ropes again. There are a dozen of us . . ."

So, taking it in turn, four at a time, they proceeded on their way, downhill, the carcase delaying them considerably. They all but abandoned it more than once. But Colum insisted, and took his turn at the dragging.

Getting it across that torrent of a burn at the foot was beyond them however. At Cobach's suggestion, in the end, they merely pushed it over the edge of the sheer drop, into the burn itself, and a few of them then got down into the rushing water themselves, to pull it down the steeply-falling bed, the strong flow of what was almost a cataract actually aiding them. Right to the river they got it, this way.

Their arrival there, needless to say, created a great to-do on the other side, with much shouting and exclamation, Ernan and his companions coming running down to the waterside in enormous relief and thankfulness – though when they saw the blood on Colum's white robe there were cries of alarm. The sight of the climbers' party manhandling a large tusked carcase across the river, half-submerged and dragged by ropes, left all speechless.

It was the dead boar, undoubtedly, which brought Cathal and his company down to the waterside, to stare if scarcely to greet them, the Druids looking notably unhappy. Safely across, Colum raised his hand. "Hail, Cathal mac Coitir!" he cried. "You are saved, all of you. Free men and women now, no longer in thrall to your Hound. Christ God reigns supreme in Skye, *you* his representative! All is well."

The king said nothing. He was gazing at the boar, as were they all.

"We climbed to the top of your Hound's Tooth. You would see our smoke? Vanquished all your demons. This dog Gaul is now kindly keeper of the Cuillins! It seems that your Hound was, in fact, no more than a poor pig!"

Cathal, clearly bemused, pointed at the carcase. "That . . . !" he got out, "You slew that!"

"Why, yes. The blood is the boar's not mine. We brought it down for you, and your lady. As token. A gift." And he glanced at Sinech, standing beside her husband. "A little knife did that!"

The woman's eyes widened.

"So now, king, you can forget your Fell Hound. Aye, and

these Druids' power over you! For their gods are false, their incantations of no value, their maledictions void." Colum waved a dismissive hand towards the scowling Enda and his little group.

But Cathal had moved still further forward, to peer down at the boar. "You slew this with a knife? This great beast, lord of the forests?"

Colum drew out the slender dagger from his pocket and held it up, the blood on it now dried brown. "With this, and God's help."

The king, shaking his head almost in disbelief, looked over to Enda and then to his wife. "You see what this can mean? A sign!"

Sinech nodded. "I see well," she said.

Colum was surprised. Cathal seemed much more interested and impressed by the killing of this boar than by the matter of the Fell Hound, the prime victory of the day.

"You give this to me, Prince?" That was the first time Cathal had accorded him his title.

"Yes. If you want it."

The king stooped to stroke, almost to fondle, those tusks. Then he waved forward some of his guard to take over and carry the carcase.

A move was made down the glen, the Druids drawn apart now. Colum's arm was beginning to ache. Walking with Ernan, he mentioned his surprise at Cathal's seeming greater interest in the boar than in the disposing of the Fell Hound myth. His uncle admitted perplexity also, but suggested that the king might have had time to get over his first shock on the matter of the Hound, in some measure. He had been much concerned when they saw the smokes up on the mountain, sufficiently awed then. He and the Druids had argued for long over that. Enda had wanted to leave, to go back to their ships, but Cathal had forbidden it. Clearly he was impressed by the Christians' power. He had spoken of the matter of the mist-banishing too; he seemed to believe that to have been achieved by the psalm-singing. It had all been very interesting, highly encouraging for their cause. Now Ernan wanted to hear the details of the climbing adventure he had missed.

Down at the sea-loch the new state of affairs was emphasised by Cathal's insistence that Prince Colum should travel back with him to Portree in the royal barge, whilst Enda was dismissed to one of the long-ships. The dead boar was placed in the prow of the barge, as though to challenge the hound-figurehead there. Launched out, with Cathal all but gloating over the ugly, shaggy corpse, Colum spoke low-voiced to Sinech, in the stern.

"I am grateful for your kind thought, lady, over the knife. I carry no such thing. Without it, all might have been . . . otherwise!"

"That is good," she said. "But I had not thought of the boar."

"No? Are there many on Skye?"

"Some, yes. They are a danger. Many have died because of them."

"Yet it was this phantom Hound which all seemed to dread. None spoke of boars. And now, your husband is much concerned with the creature. Why?"

"For good reason, Prince-Priest. The boar, you see, is the emblem of the *Ard Righ*, the High King of All Alba. So none seeks to slay them. But Cathal would wish to be High King after Brude mac Maelchon. He is not content to be King of Skye. Long he has had this ambition. Now, you present him with this slain boar. And you are a powerful worker of wonders. He sees it as a sign. Something Enda could not give him."

"Ha! Now I see it. I sought only to free him, and you all, from the power of the Hound, and to bring you to Christ-God instead. Now – this! God has His own methods, it seems!"

Back at Portree, the missionaries' treatment was markedly changed. Nothing was too good for them. All were to come up to Dun Torvaig, where they would occupy quarters in the guards' barracks. Food and wine would be theirs in plenty. Women would be available. Prince Colum should have his own room in the hall-house.

Their mission seemed more likely to prosper, now, in Skye.

Later, after what amounted almost to feasting for these normally abstemious monastics, Colum sought his couch in the luxury of a room to himself. He was tired, after the day's exertions and excitements, but sleep eluded him, his bruised arm aching and throbbing. That was not the only impediment to slumber he had to contend with, however. Presently the door of his chamber opened quietly and then closed again. He had company.

Sitting up, in the half-light he saw that it was a woman, Queen Sinech, one more surprise for this eventful day.

"You are not asleep, Prince-Priest?" she asked softly. "That is good. I have come for my dirk."

"Ha! I had thought to keep it, lady. In remembrance of a woman's thought and care," he said. "It was a timely gift. Most kind. And my name is Colum."

"I can be kinder than that, Colum!" she declared, and came to sit on the edge of his bed. He saw that she was wearing a loose bed-robe of fur; and more than that, as she leaned a little towards him and the robe fell open, that she wore nothing beneath it.

"You are . . . generous," he conceded carefully. "The knife is still in the pocket of my habit, there." He pointed to his pile of clothing across the chamber.

"Since you thought to keep it, in memory of me, do so, Colum. Take it. And, see you, why not take me, also?" And she shrugged off that bed-robe from her shoulders. Slipped to her waist, it left her upper half bare, gleaming palely, lovely.

The man drew a deep breath. "Lady Sinech, you are beautiful as you are kind," he got out. "But . . . you have a husband. And I am in his house."

"Cathal will not miss me. Nor care," she assured easily. "He is even now sleeping with one of the many women of his guard – with two, probably. He does so, most nights. Fear not Cathal, my friend." She came closer.

He cleared his throat. "I esteem you, lady. But . . . I think, not tonight, if you will bear with me."

"No? You are not a man-lover, Colum, I judge! Or I would not be here. Some are that way – but not *you*, by your every look!"

"No, not that. But tonight I am tired, weary." The excuse came to him. "And in some pain, Sinech. This arm . . ."

"Ah, yes – your poor arm. Let me see it." She rose, to stoop over, closer still, and her bed-robe fell to the floor leaving her entirely naked. "Hold out your arm, Colum."

As the queen had shrewdly guessed, or perceived, that man was far from impervious to the charms of women, nor lacking in full appreciation of the other sex. And this woman was very handsome, and her body, so near to his own, almost irresistible – and he was himself naked in bed. How to restrain his sudden urgent desire? And at the same time avoid offending? A voice in his head said that this woman could greatly assist his mission here in Skye. And celibacy was not a rule of the Celtic Church. Was that Satan's voice?

She was peering at his outstretched arm, and one of her full and shapely breasts was brushing against his shoulder. "I see no break in the skin," she announced. "Only bruising. Tooth-marks, or tusk-marks. A lotion will help. A lotion of puff-ball powder and the juice of blaeberries, with honey. I will have some made tomorrow."

"I thank you." Pain would not be an excuse which would serve indefinitely. "Sinech, I must tell you. In the matter of man and woman, I am wed to Christ's Church. You may find it difficult to understand. But I am vowed to keep myself apart from women. Until I have accomplished my task. It is a great task and demanding of all that a man has and is. This of bringing Christ to those who know Him not. All else must be sacrificed, meantime. Only so may I do what I am set to do. Can you understand?"

She was silent for a little. "So you are little better than one of those who have no use for women? I would not have believed it!"

"No, not so. I find women desirable. *You* I find desirable. Could it be otherwise, with you here, and, and offering yourself? But . . . I am committed. Vowed. I am sorry."

Sinech stood for a moment or two looking down at him. Then she sat on the bed again, beside him. "So great a waste!" she said. "But you can hold me, at the least. A woman has her feelings and desires also! I shall not trouble you for long."

"It is scarcely trouble," he told her. "If matters were otherwise, it would be . . . pleasure." He moved a little aside, to give her room, but did not draw aside the bedclothes.

She disposed herself against him, and he carefully put that aching arm around her warm and so yielding person. So they sat silent, save for heightened breathing on both their parts.

Presently she gave an uncertain little laugh. "I have never done such as this before, Prince Colum. It is . . . trying!" And she turned to kiss him.

"I know it, woman."

She slid a hand down the hairs of his chest, and then lower. "Ah, I see that you are indeed all man, even though you say otherwise!" she commented.

He gently but firmly raised that hand again. "Would it not

177

be kinder, Sinech, to us both, if you were to leave me?" he asked, but not sourly. "Why trouble each other so? There is scarcely profit in this."

"You are a hard man. Aye, in more than the one way!" She took his hand now and raised it to her breasts.

"Not hard. Only set on a great purpose." Finding his fingers automatically curving round and cupping her breast, he stilled them with an effort. "Can you not understand? I am held to it." Unbidden, before his mind's-eye, he saw the features and form of Bridget of Ellary. Almost roughly he drew his hand away. "My arm pains me. Too much for this," he lied.

Sighing, she kissed him again and rose, picking up her robe. "I go, then, since you send me. This Christ-God of yours is a stern master, I think."

"Not stern, no. Loving, Sinech – loving. But – there is more than the one kind of love. Tomorrow, I will tell you of Him and His love. Now, I must needs sleep."

"Sleep well then, Colum. I think that I shall not!" And slipping on her robe about her, she moved to the door.

Despite the queen's injunction, and his own need, the man did not sleep well that night. Over and over in his mind he turned the events of the day and this evening, and for all the vital importance of the former it was the latter which preoccupied him most. How was he to be judged on his behaviour? He had resisted temptation, after a fashion. Had he hurt the woman by it? And she, as queen, could aid or injure their mission. He had resisted adultery – but he had most certainly *wanted* her body. And he had used Bridget's person and image to aid him reject Sinech. Was that in itself sin? And Bridget . . . ?

It was not of hounds nor boars nor demons that he dreamed when at length he slept, but of women.

In the morning, Colum besought Cathal to allow him to tell him and his people about Jesus Christ, the Son of the Most High God, and His sacrifice for men and desire to reign in their hearts. The king, who clearly was not of a religious turn of mind, one way or another, was not enthusiastic but made no real objections, even when Colum urged that his instructing should be done not up here in Dun Torvaig but down at the

Portree township, where all the folk could hear him. Sinech, who revealed no signs of the previous evening's events, to his relief, supported him, and a move was duly made downhill. Many of the palace-guards and servants came too. Gaul, who had passed the night in Lugbe's care, was a happy dog to be reunited with its master. It could scarcely realise its strangely enhanced status in the eyes of these islanders, who were now apt to view it with some awe, warily.

The king's command assembled a great gathering on the beach beside the jetties, from which, after a session of psalm-singing, Colum addressed them. It was not the occasion for any deep, theological exposition, and he kept to the simple Gospel story, only prefacing his talk – for it was that rather than any preaching – with a brief reference to the day before's happenings in the Cuillins, and Skye's new-found freedom from the fear of the Hound and related demons, assuming that it all would already have been the talk of the township. He had an attentive audience, although possibly disappointed in seeing no more wonders. Cathal looked somewhat bored. There was no sign of Enda, although some of the other Druids could be seen at the back of the crowd.

When it was over and most of the crowd dispersed, Colum held a council in their long-ship. They had made a start, he declared, but Skye was a big island and their mission was to it all, not just to the king's Portree. He proposed that he and perhaps two-thirds of their company should go off on a tour of the island, spreading the good news, whilst Moluag and most of the other seniors should remain here to teach the Portree folk a fuller knowledge of the faith. Then, when he came back, in a few days, they could make an end, or a beginning, baptise the new believers, and set up the nucleus of a church and small monastery.

None could better these suggestions; but Moluag asked about King Cathal. He did not seem very interested, yet so much could depend on his attitude. Colum said that they must work on Cathal, however unpromising a convert. Ambition was his weakness, it seemed. He wanted to be High King of Alba. If they could instil in him the notion that embracing Christianity would help in that cause, then he might well be persuaded. Moluag's reaction was that this was scarcely a worthy line to take; Colum countered by declaring that they had to use the tools which came to hand. Besides, it could be true. They would go, hereafter, to seek to convert Brude mac Maelchon; and another Albannach king, as Christian, would be in a strong position in the hierarchy. And they must use Queen Sinech's influence. She had more wits than her husband, and could be very useful. Already she was sympathetic – Colum did not say how much so.

That night he asked Ernan, who had been bedding down with Moluag and Cobach, to share his room with him. They were not disturbed.

So next day the travellers set out in their long-ship again. They had gained from Cathal and Sinech information as to the main centres of population elsewhere in this island kingdom, and the king – or more truly his wife – had allocated to them a couple of warriors of the guard, who would accompany and guide them and ensure their safety – also, no doubt keep an eye on their actitivies to report back. They left Moluag in charge at Portree.

They sailed off, on Sinech's advice, north-about, up the Sound of Raasay, to make their first call at the inlet of Loch Arnish on Raasay island itself, where they found Cathal's younger brother as chief. They did not spend long with him and his people, for he seemed unresponsive to what they told him; but they left Scandlann there, with one of the student monks, to see what he could do, and if unsuccessful, to return to Portree. Then they sailed on for their next stop, Staffin, on the northern, Trotternish, peninsula of Skye.

Staffin itself was not impressive, a mere huddle of hovels around a small fort of stone and earthen ramparts; but the adjacent scenery was spectacular indeed. Never had the visitors seen anything quite like it, a fantastic regiment of rock towers soaring up hundreds of feet, not mountains these but isolated fangs, steeples, bastions, called the Quiraing, they were informed. Small wonder that Skye had such a reputation on all this seaboard for wild strangeness and savagery. All the way up the sound from Portree they had been sailing past a huge, spinal escarpment and range of rock crags, a score of miles of it, with but few landing places or levels for settlement. Staffin Bay, with its fluted cliffs, appeared to be the only one capable of supporting a population.

Once they had turned the head of the peninsula however, to proceed down the western shore, the scene changed, with a picturesque coastline of sandy bays, offshore islets, green machairs and considerable lower ground, more typical of the rest of the Hebrides, and here there were people. They spent their first night at a fair-sized township called Uig, on its own large bay. Their two warrior-guides ensured for them a reasonable reception from the chief. So next day they did not do any sailing but spent it visiting the scattered communities in the Uig area, seeking to spread their message of faith and hope. They could scarcely make any major impression at this stage, of course, but they could give an indication of their mission, seek to make friends, lay the foundation for future developments, and as it were, spy out the land. All this took time, to be sure, but it was what they had come to Alba to do.

As they proceeded on down that coast, this matter of time passing began to concern Colum. He just had not realised that there was so much of Skye, the overall task so great, so many communities large and small. They landed at Snizort at the head of its long sea-loch, Vaternish, Dunvegan, Pooltiel, Durinish and Idrigal of the table-top hills, and their royal-guard guides – who were becoming their friends – told them that they were not yet half-way round this great island, with the most populous areas of all, the Strath district and the southern Sleat peninsula, still before them. Colum realised that he would have to cut their circuit short, or at least make fewer landings, since there was no way of actually shortening the journey. Moluag and his helpers might be becoming seriously worried as to their safety.

It was two whole weeks in fact, and the October days beginning to shorten noticeably, before they won back to Portree, having to traverse the narrows of the Sound of Sleat and Caol Rhea once again in the process. They found that Moluag had met with considerable success in his efforts, and had already baptised some thirty new Christians. But he had been anxious about his friends. Sinech had been one of the first to accept baptism and had encouraged others, although her husband still held back. There were many more almost ready to take vows, despite the Druids, who were engaged in what amounted to a campaign against it. Fortunately King Cathal, whilst not committing himself to Christianity, appeared to have lost all faith in the Druids and was not obstructing the missionaries. Moluag, with Sinech's help, had even chosen a site for their first church and cashel, on the north side of the hill of Dun Torvaig, a mile north-east of the township.

Scandlann had returned from Raasay, afraid that there was little progress to be made there meantime. So Colum sent him off, with two assistants, to Snizort, where the ship-party had found their most hopeful reception, to set up a mission there. Snizort, although at the head of the west-coast sea-loch of that name, was in fact less than ten miles from Portree, and to be reached, on foot, by a central valley. So the two first foundations on Skye could keep in close touch and give each other mutual support. Moluag was so involved with his little flock already that Colum suggested that he should remain at Portree, at least until the spring, so as to ensure that all was firmly established, and to try to work on Çathal. It would leave Iona without a bishop meantime, but they would be only two days' sail apart, after all. Moluag, a natural leader himself in a quiet way, and who sometimes found Colum's type of forceful leadership somewhat trying, was nothing loth.

Colum, beginning now to become concerned about conditions on Iona, after their long absence, delayed no longer. He had a final interview with Cathal, seeking to impress on him the temporal as well as the spiritual benefits of an adherence to Christianity, asserting that with God's help he would turn all Alba to Christ, and that those of the ri or lesser kings already converted would be in an advantageous position. Not all Colum's colleagues approved of this worldly-wise approach, but he insisted that kings were in a special category and required special treatment, for they could either greatly assist or greatly hinder missionaries.

Sinech joined the throng of his own people and local converts to accompany the Iona group down to their ship. Walking side-by-side, there was a strange bond between them, yet also a shadow. Few words were exchanged on the way down.

"You will be back?" she put to him, when nearing the jetty.

"To be sure. I shall come to Skye as frequently as I may. Having set amove something here, I shall not desert it."

"You perhaps set amove more than you know, friend!" she said.

He glanced at her sidelong. "I am in God's hands, in that, as in all."

"God's hands are loving hands, you teach?"

"Always that," he agreed.

"So – He will not deny *you* all love, Colum?"

"No-o-o. Far from it. But . . ."

"But not the love of women?"

He did not answer; he could not.

"You will think of me, on your Iona?"

"Oh, yes – that I can promise you, lady."

"With that I must be content, then. Over the distance."

"Iona is not so far away, Sinech."

They had come to the long-ship's gangplank, the others thronging close around. He turned to her, and she came into his arms. He kissed her cheek and brow.

"God keep you!" he said deeply.

"For whom?" she demanded, almost roughly. As abruptly, she thrust him away from her, swung about and strode off.

Sadly, he shook his head after her.

The parting with Moluag, Scandlann and the others was less dramatic.

The wind was rising all the way down the Sound of Sleat, but the hills of that long peninsula sheltered them. However, once level with its southern headland, they ran into the beginnings of their first real Hebridean gale, and were forced to put into the mouth of Loch Nevis, in Knoydart, for shelter. That night and all the next day they were storm-bound in the bay of Inverie, with nothing to do, not even any population to seek to convert. Even the second morning, although the wind had dropped considerably, the seas were still high; but Colum, impatient for activity as always, insisted that they should set out again.

They thereafter made a rough, uncomfortable, even alarming southwards journey, in steep and sometimes enormous seas, ever on the lookout for reefs and skerries. To some extent, presently, the islands of Rhum, Eigg and Muick provided breakwater, but once past these, and with the mighty thrusting headland of Ardnamurchan to get round, they felt the full unhindered fury of the Atlantic waves, against which the long-ship seemed puny indeed and man of no account. But Colum assured them all that God had not brought them this far to abandon them now, His purposes in Alba just begun; and thus heartened they went on their way singing somewhat breathless hymns and psalms. Anyway, they could not do other, for the Ardnamurchan peninsula was the last place to look for shelter, as savage a coastline as they had seen, the most westerly point in all mainland Alba, this day part-hidden in a mist of spray from the breaking seas.

Once round it, however, with Mull ahead, they chose, for relief, to go east-about round that great island, down the sheltered Sound of Mull, rather than face more of the raging ocean's battering. They had heard about this lengthy water-way, twenty miles of it.

It was by no means calm, even in the Sound of Mull. They sailed its length, interestedly examining both sides of the two-mile wide channel. Each looked attractive, that of Mull itself, on the south side, clearly the more populous, Morvern, actually a remote part of the mainland, less so but dramatically the more scenic. Anxious to get back to Iona, there was no time to explore. They would come back one day.

The sound ended in a great hub of land-enclosed waters, highly picturesque, with the major Loch Linnhe coming in from the north, Lochs Etive and Creran opening to the east, and the wide Firth of Lorn reaching southwards, all mountain-girt and isle-dotted. One large and comparatively low-lying and fertile-seeming island, lying in the mouth of Loch Linnhe, particularly attracted; but again there was no time to land. They pressed on down the southern firth.

The now early dusk found them where the Firth of Lorn opened to the wider sea, with the islands of Scarba and long Jura ahead and the south coast of Mull bearing away to the west. It was apparent that by no means could they hope to reach Iona that night, against a still stiff westerly breeze and seas. Young Angus pointed out that once in the sheltered waters of the Sound of Jura, they would not be so very far distant from Ellary, and Colum was tempted; but he decided that this was not the occasion. Yet they would have to land somewhere, to spend the night. Directly ahead only a couple of miles was an isolated group of rocky islets. They were appropriately called the Garbh Eileach, Angus told them, or Garvellachs, the Rough Isles, not the most welcoming of names. However, for one night, one of them surely would serve.

Closer inspection revealed that four were large enough to be called islands, two about a mile long, amongst a scatter of rocks and skerries, all crags and cliffs of grey slaty stone, with no trees or bushes but, surprisingly, patches of very green grass. They made for the east-facing side of the largest, sheltered from winds and seas, and found there a little bay, with two houses behind it and a few cattle and sheep evident. So they might get food here.

Aware now of the alarm of a long-ship's unheralded arrival was apt to produce amongst little island communities, Colum, Ernan and Angus alone, with the dog Gaul, landed and made for the cot-houses, in the evening half-light. Four men awaited them, armed with the usual staves and axes. But these were quickly reassured by the visitors' looks and greetings, and agreed that they could pass the night in their hay-barn, and to sell them milk, cheese and honey, although not in any large quantities. They said that, yes, this island was called Garbh Eileach; but the other three larger ones had their own names, A'Chuli, Eilean Dubh Mor and Hinba, that furthest south. None of these was inhabited however.

The travellers spent a comfortable night amongst the hay.

Colum rose early, as so often he did, in order to have a little time to himself before the others awoke. Fond as he was of his colleagues and fellow-men, he liked to get away from them all at times, to be alone. And he felt the need of exercise, with so much of boat travel. It was just dawn, and he set off, with Gaul, to climb to the top of the highest point of this island, quite a craggy hill not unlike the Sguir of Eigg in miniature, rising to fully three hundred feet he assessed. As he climbed, the half-dark gave way to the smoky red-gold of sunrise, casting purple shadows westwards from every rock and hummock. The wind had dropped to a mere zephyr and the seas were moderating noticeably. They would have no difficulty in getting back to Iona that afternoon.

At the summit of the hill, panting, he stood and watched the sun in splendour lift from behind the eastern mainland mountains, and thanked his Maker for the sight and beauty of the scene, for bringing them safely to this place, for the fair success of their mission so far and for much else of blessing. And doing so, his eyes were drawn to a strange sight. A level beam of the new-risen sun had found a gap through the distant mountains, to penetrate almost horizontally to the very topmost tip of the most southerly of these little isles, Hinba they had named it he recollected, there to strike on some glassy rock, quartz perhaps, or even the marble which was to be found on Iona, and to blaze on this with a dazzling unearthly brilliance. He stared, although the brightness actually hurt the eyes. Was it some sign? It was extraordinary, and only he was there to see it. Could it mean something especial, something personal to himself?

He waited there and gradually the dazzle faded, but was replaced by a rose-red glow which seemed to bathe all Hinba in warm effulgence, lovely, peaceful yet somehow sternly so, for it was as craggy and rock-bound a place as its neighbours. Could it be . . . ? Was this to be his own place? His *diseart*? An uninhabited isle, only a half-day's sail from Iona. He could come in a coracle. Be alone there. All the Celtic saints had their retreats, their *disearts*, usually on remote islands, where they could withdraw for prayer, contemplation, renewal of spirit, quiet. Could Hinba be *his*, shown to be his by the Son of Righteousness?

Thoughtful indeed, he descended to his friends.

When presently they left Garbh Eileach, Colum had Machar steer their craft south-about round that Hinba – and approved exultantly of all he saw there. The island was about a mile long but only a quarter of that in width, crags and cliffs and the hill to the south and west but with some level ground, with grass, broom, gorse and wild-thyme to north and east. So cattle could graze there, or at least a cow or two. Bees could make their honey. The eider-ducks in a little sheltered bay were there for company. He said nothing of it at all to his companions.

They were back at Iona by midday, only a score of miles. All proved to be well there, with no major problems, although Echoid, left in charge there, had begun to be anxious. It was good to be back. But now horizons had widened.

10

Although winter, with its short days and frequent storms, restricted them in travel and mission-work and outdoor activities, there was no lack of indoor work for Colum's people to tackle. There was the interior of their buildings to finish off, whitewash and decorate; new barns, store-houses, byres and the like to make; wood-carving for church furniture; leather-work and tooling for shoes and jerkins and girdles, but also for outer bindings of books; and more important, the transcribing on to paper of the Gospels and Psalms, many copies being required for the churches they were going to found, these illustrated where the scribes were competent to do so, both in picture and with coloured Celtic traditional interlacing designs, things of beauty as well as instruments of faith and love. Colum in particular spent much time at this work; after all, he had been doing it all his life, not only on the celebrated occasion of St Finnian's Psalter.

They found the Hebridean winter less trying than they had anticipated. It was very windy admittedly, but there was less of rain than in Ireland, and little or nothing of snow and ice. Some days indeed were so calm and quiet that only the shortness of daylight hours reminded them that it *was* winter. On one of these days Colum actually risked a solo visit in a coracle to Hinba, skirting the Mull coastline heedfully and ready to paddle for cover in his light little craft if the seas became rough. Baithen disapproved – but then Cousin Baithen was Baithen. Colum in fact encountered no difficulties, and spent a cold night wrapped in blankets in a sort of cave on the little isle, falling quite in love with it all and plotting just where he would build his cell and shrine.

Yuletide was joyfully passed, in praise and thanksgiving and modest feasting; Bridget of Ellary arriving on a brief visit, to the pleasure of not only her son. She still asked whether there was no place for her here; and regretfully Colum could think of none which would be suitable.

On a calm day in early February, Baithen went to Tiree, with two helpers, to begin to set up the nucleus of their monastery there, and to prepare the ground for the spring ploughing – for this island was going to be their main supplier of grain, for their own consumption and for selling to others. All their missions, in the end, must be mutually supporting.

On Iona itself they started feeding the land with kelp, manure and cockle-shell sand which was almost pure lime, preparatory to ploughing. The local folk said that it should not be ploughed until April; but Colum held that a month earlier should be possible and ought to make for earlier and better harvests. It was laborious, back-breaking work for those not used to it, especially wielding the *cas-chrom* or hand-plough, although on sandy ground this was easier than on heavy soil and clay. They would never grow as much, or as good crops, on Iona as on Tiree, however, for of course the native islanders had already taken the best plots. Colum took his share in this toil. Also he bought himself another animal friend, a shaggy, white garron, or short-legged tough work-horse, useful for this ploughing, for bearing loads and for carrying the portable altar-cum-font on missions. They trained this amiably docile creature to travel in the long-ship, standing patiently in the stern, where they contrived a special kind of stall. It would, however be very much a fair-weather voyager.

In March they had a visit from Moluag, who came for further helpers. His efforts on Skye were proving very successful and he wanted to open new missions. Queen Sinech was being helpful, and sent her salutations to Colum. Colum gave him Fechno and Grillan, to assist him.

His band of seniors was now much reduced on Iona, with Baithen needing help on Tiree. Somehow they must attract recruits, and not just students and lay-brothers or local converts. Colum decided to send Echoid, with Machar, back to Ireland to ask Laisran his soul-friend to find him some volunteers. It was almost a year since they had come to Dalriada.

They scoured Mull for cattle to purchase, especially milk-cows. Colum wanted Iona to become the centre for cheese-making, as a source of income. He would like to put a couple of cows on Hinba; but that would mean someone permanently there to tend and milk them. He compromised meantime by leaving a pair with the crofters on Garbh Eileach, who would look after them for the extra milk.

Hinba occupied his mind considerably. Short-handed as he was, he was unable to go there as often as he would have liked. He had had no opportunity to do more than mark out the sites for what he wanted to build, in stone necessarily. He could hardly leave Iona, especially at spring ploughing-time, to spend days on what was really a selfish project, the providing of a little sanctuary for himself. So he was consoled with the thought that if God approved of him having a *diseart*, He would show the way, after that flash of sunrise light.

And He did, in totally unexpected fashion. One year and two weeks after their arrival on Iona, Echoid and Machar returned from Ireland in the long-ship, and far from alone. Laisran had done them proud. He had prevailed on three quite prominent and vigorous clerics to turn missionary, at least meantime, two of them indeed abbots, Kenneth of Achabo and Comgall of Bangor; also Bishop Cormac O'Lethan. These had brought with them about a dozen monks and students as assistants. The seniors could not remain there permanently, of course, since they had responsibilities back in Ireland, but they would stay for some time. Colum was overjoyed. He knew them all, indeed Cormac was a personal friend. They would be of enormous help. But if their arrival was a surprise, much more so was that of a fellow-passenger – the Princess Eithne.

Colum had rather forgotten his mother's assertion that if he did not come home to her in one year she would come to him on her own. And here she was – and she declared that she had come to stay. She had brought a middle-aged maid with her.

To say that Colum was nonplussed would be an understatement. He was fond of his mother and admired her; but what to do with her? An elderly woman on Iona, in very much a man's establishment, no sort of nun but a royal princess who acted like one. He welcomed her, of course; but her regal announcement that she would not return to Ireland until he did, left him in a quandary. A visit, yes – but . . . ?

Then he thought of Hinba. She could go there. Build her a house on Hinba. She could keep his *diseart* for him. Only a few hours' sail away. An excuse for him to visit the island frequently. But . . . was it practical? To maroon a woman of her age, used to courts and high company, on an uninhabited island. Even with neighbours only a mile or so away. Her maid would scarcely be sufficient company.

Bridget! Was Bridget the answer? Would she come to Hinba? Not just to keep his mother company – he could scarcely ask that. But to set up some small women's chapel, cloister, nunnery? A little convent there. Something of the sort would complement their main work suitably. At the other end of the isle, of course, from where he planned his own cell. It would hardly do to have the women close-by – however pleasant on occasion. But they could have their house at the northern end, almost half a mile from where he had his own cell.

189

Colum was sufficiently honest with himself to recognise that there could be wishful thinking in all this, and even possibly some putting of temptation in his own way. That must be withstood. But the idea could help to solve two problems.

He put it to Eithne. She was not enthusiastic, seeing no good reason why she should not remain on Iona itself, only doubtfully accepting that to have a women's establishment attached to the monastery would have a distracting effect on the men. And she was nowise prepared to play the abbess in a nunnery here. Her son reassured her. That would be for another.

With the arrival of Bishop Cormac and the Abbots Kenneth and Comgall, all men of experience and authority, Colum felt more free from daily duties and services on Iona. The spring sowing could go ahead without him. He decided to pay a visit to Ellary, and to take his mother with him. It was important that, if the Hinba idea was to come to anything, she and Bridget would have to get to know each other and, it was to be hoped, get on together.

Taking Angus with them, they sailed in the long-ship, and went by Hinba, Colum taking the opportunity to show his mother the isle, its amenities and attractions – and its drawbacks – where he proposed her house should be sited and where he planned his *diseart* cell and shrine. It was a breezy day of sun, great towering white clouds and sparkling seas, the Hebridean scene very lovely, and Eithne found it all very much to her taste, to her son's relief. The smallness of the island did not seem to worry her, nor its unhabited state; what did was the apparent lack of fuel for heating and cooking. Colum promised ample supplies of peat and firewood.

The sail down the Sound of Jura to Loch Caolisport and Ellary took them the rest of the day, so that it was late evening before they presented themselves at Bridget's hall-house. Her pleasure at their unexpected visit was undisguised and her hospitality open-handed as ever.

The two women got on well from the first, and after much genealogical probing decided that they were probably cousins eight times removed. Colum was almost hesitant to interrupt this, tentatively to put the Hinba proposition to their hostess. To his surprise she accepted it almost without discussion, as though it was an obvious development, with Colum seeing the light at last. Bridget knew Hinba, although she had never landed on it. As to details, her main enquiry was when did they start?

After Eithne retired to bed that night, Bridget and Colum sat up late discussing it all; he found himself wishing that young Angus would go seek his couch also instead of sitting there listening interestedly – before reproving himself for the thought. He would have to watch this particular concern with and fondness for this woman, or at least a desire to be alone with her. It could become a danger to his work and his example to others. The Church by no means forbade love of women; but it could be a notable distraction. It had long used women and their persons deliberately to test the strength of men's wills and their command of their basic passions. And there was the yearning amongst all Christians for some feminine side of the Deity, more than just the notion of Mother Church. Where was the line to be drawn? When did the love of women, for women, change from being normal, natural, even a virtue and joy, to a sin? If ever. The danger, surely, was in the risks of distraction. And *he* must not allow himself to be distracted on the misson God had given him.

When Bridget showed him to his chamber, and he kissed her goodnight, holding her for a moment, he said, "You are going to have to help me, at times, woman. In more than turning souls to Christ! I am learning my weaknesses. Do you understand?"

"I think that I do. But . . . I am none so strong, either. And do we know for sure what is right and what is wrong in this matter, Columcille? As on many others."

"Aye, who knows indeed? But that we will be shown, I think, I believe."

They left it at that.

When, two days later, they sailed back to Iona. Bridget said that she would follow in a few more days, after she had had time to settle her affairs at Ellary, and had left all in good hands. One day, Angus would have to come back, to take over the chiefly duties of their house – but not yet.

It was May, and the sand-martins were back, the broom and gorse in blazing gold and the cuckoos calling from isle to isle. The long-ship, laden now with gear, implements, building material and food, as well as the men and the three women, came to Hinba. Thus they arrived, some of them to stay; a significant occasion.

On landing, Bishop Cormac blessed the island – although, to be sure, Colum had done so himself more than once, in less formal style – and a psalm was sung before all went about their various tasks and the unloading of the ship, which was to go and fetch the two cows from Garbh Eileach.

Colum's first concern was to escort Bridget, Cormac, Kenneth and Comgall round the isle. He showed it off with a sort of boyish pride, its every feature now dear to him, telling them of the sunrise beam which had so impressed him – actually, walking, or rather clambering round, they saw much quartzite rock outcropping, which accounted for the dazzlement.

Their tour demanded the expenditure of much energy, for the isle was a rough and rocky place, almost sheer on the west side, cliffs and crags rising to a central spine with many little summits, the highest to the south which the sun had picked out that first morning. They went south-about so that he could show them the exact hilltop spot where the beam had struck; and by the time that they reached there, the three visitors from Ireland, unused to climbing, were panting heavily, Bridget seeming in better shape – although it was her shape indeed which revealed her exertions, her fine bosom heaving.

They found various east-facing outcrops of glassy rock which could have reflected the sun. But the newcomers were more interested in the magnificent prospect from these rocky heights, which although only about two hundred and fifty feet, gave a much loftier impression. The Sea of the Hebrides, seen from here, was beyond all description.

Colum took them along the serrated ridge, for they could by no means follow the precipitous shoreline on the west side. As it was considerable scrambling was involved, and Colum was proud of Bridget, who made a better job of it than did the three others, creating no fuss about the hitching up of her skirts.

About halfway along, he halted where they could view the island in its entirety. Looking down on the much less steep east side, he pointed out the area near where they had landed. It was there that he proposed to build his cell and shrine, near the southern end. Then two-thirds of a mile to the north, indeed near the northernmost point, where there was a wide grassy shelf protected from the westerly winds by a shoulder of hill, that was where he suggested the women's house should be. There were springs at both localities – indeed water was no problem on Hinba.

They continued on their lofty traverse, with the other isles of the group now tending to attract their attention with their striking outlines, shadow-filled hollows and crevices and sea-torn bases. With the wheeling gulls around them, the guillemots and puffins nesting on the cliffs and the cuckoo's calling drifting up to them from the lower ground, it made a memorable walk, all agreeing that a more attractive *diseart* would have been hard to find. And when they slanted down, at the northern extremity, to the shelf area Colum had spoken of, which was almost a little plateau of grass and broom and sea-pinks, facing across a scatter of skerries to the next isle, A'Chuli, Bridget expressed herself as well-pleased with it as the site of the new home she was to share with the Princess Eithne. It was sheltered yet with fine prospects, easily accessible from the shore and even had a tiny beach from which they could bathe. Colum pointed out the spring of delicious cold water, at which they drank to refresh themselves, whereafter Bishop Cormac blessed it suitably. Then they returned along the east shore to their landing-place, passing the two cows being driven up to their pastures on the plateau.

Thereafter, it was all hands to work. They had brought ready-made hurdles or wattle-frames of interlaced saplings, from Iona, and these were carried along and up to the plateau and there erected in the chosen position to form the walls of what they were already calling the *Tigh Chailleacha* or nunnery – although Eithne had her reservations about such a name. Filling in the spaces between the hurdles with small stones and earth was no problem; but Hinba seemed to be devoid of clay, so they would have to delay the plastering, outer and inner, until later. Meanwhile they made five apartments, a small bedchamber for each woman, a wash-room and a large living-room, with a double stone fireplace which would serve for both. A byre for the cows, a barn for hay and storage and a henhouse were also erected out of the pre-fabricated hurdles, doors and window-frames, and a garden plot was marked out. Beehives and their occupants would be brought later, also poultry. Almost before the turfs were in place on the plank-roof, the women were inside arranging the simple furnishings, bedding, skin rugs for the floor, and the like. The wall-hangings would have to await the plastering.

When the long-ship sailed back to Iona in the early evening, it left five new residents for Hinba, well pleased with progress achieved. Angus mac Riagan was going to stay on the isle for a day or two to help the women settle in, dig their garden ground and make himself useful. He and Colum would pass the night in the new barn, and tomorrow make a start on the *diseart* cells.

Weary but happy they watched the sun set over the isle-dotted sea. Colum knew a great satisfaction and sense of well-being – and had to remind himself that that was not really the object of a *diseart*, which was rather the seeking of solitude, spiritual revival. But perhaps his Creator, the God of love, would understand.

In the morning, having made the women's breakfast for them, he and Angus repaired to the other location, to start a different kind of work. The *diseart* was to be built in the traditional style of unmortared stone beehive-shaped cells, with arched vaulted roofs and no windows, in imitation of Christ's sepulchre, stark, comfortless but enduring. Colum had helped to build more than one of these in Ireland and knew the craft of it. This one was to be all his own work. Angus's help was to be restricted to the back-breaking task of collecting the stones. At least there was material in plenty.

In selecting his site Colum had chosen a spot midway between his spring and a great square outcrop of quartz, flat-topped, which would serve to remind him of the hilltop vision. He decided that his cell should be a double one, linked, one for living-quarters, one for devotions. He had intended to erect a shrine nearby for outdoor worship, a simple cross beside the well of blessed water; but on second thoughts decided that a little church would be more suitable. The women would require a chapel of some sort, especially if their establishment grew somewhat; and it would be pointless to have two such places on so small an island. But that could wait, meantime.

Building in stone was an infinitely more laborious and time-consuming process than in wattle and daub, especially of these beehive-shaped cells, since the entire construction

194

depended on vaulting and the keystone principle. So the selection of the right stones to use took longer than the actual laying, especially of the upper half. The circular walling had to be very thick at the lower half, then tapering off as it began to curve over for the roof. No mortar was used, and all was held together by the weight of mutual support, and above by the wedge-shaped stones which, fitting into each other and by their own weight, shape and downward pressure, made a solid roof. There would be a low doorway and no windows. This building, so basic and severe, would last for ever; whereas the hurdle-filling-and-clay structures had only a limited life.

So Angus went stone-gathering, on the beach and below the cliffs. The difficulty was in transporting it all to the site. This the youth overcame by dragging all on an old ox-hide brought for carpeting. Colum meanwhile sorted out the stones into piles, depending on shape and size, large for foundations, flat ones, square-sided for outer walling, small, rounded and odd-shaped for infilling, and of course the precious wedges for the final vaulting. This all took a deal longer than might have been anticipated, for a great quantity and weight of stones was necessary, many tons. The walling was to be almost three feet thick at the base, although thinning as it rose; so that to gain an internal floor space of say eight feet diameter, the main cell had to be some fourteen feet across. The secondary cell, opening off by a little vaulted passage, could be slightly smaller.

By midday, when Bridget came to summon them for a meal, the builders were sore of back, indeed Colum hardly able to straighten up. On feminine advice, almost orders, after a bathe in the sea, fishing from a coracle was prescribed for the afternoon. Moderation, even in *diseart*-creation, not one of Colum's more obvious attributes, was called for.

When, two days later, the long-ship arrived again with more materials, some poultry and three hives buzzing with imprisoned bees, the main cell walling had risen as far as the springing of the vault for the roof. Some inexperienced commentators remarked that progress was slow – and earned an appropriate rejoinder from their aching-backed leader, and were bidden to go collect more stones.

Angus returned to Iona with the ship that late afternoon. Colum would follow in two more days.

In the evening, Bridget suggested a walk and climb, to

watch the sunset from the summit ridge, and tactfully invited Eithne to accompany them – who as tactfully declined on grounds of age and infirmity, not obvious to the uninitiated.

They set off uphill, unhurriedly. The climbing inhibited conversation but called for frequent male hand-offering for female assistance. At the rocky ridge the silence tended to persist – as did the intermittent hand-holding, for it still made uneven going. At length they sat down, their backs to a quartzite rock, to face westwards over all the spread of the red-gold Hebridean nightfall. Presently Colum broke the quiet, and waved his free hand.

"Beauty!" he said. "There, whether men see it or no. If all were to die this night, tomorrow the beauty would still be there, in sunset and scene, in flower and scent and animal and movement . . . if not any more in woman!"

She was slow to reply. "What *is* beauty?" she asked. "Some see beauty in this, some in that. Some, I fear, in nothing."

"God pity them, then."

"Yes. But if none sees it, is the beauty still there?"

"To be sure. *God* sees it. He makes the beauty, therefore He must love it. Indeed it is one of the four attributes of the Creator – love, order, beauty, truth."

"Love. Order. Beauty. Truth," she repeated. "I had not thought of that, Columcille. Love, yes. Truth, yes. But beauty and order . . . ?"

"Was not order the first of all? Out of chaos and darkness God created order, light, beauty, before truth or even love was necessary, since there was only Himself and eternity. Order is of the essence; without it there can be only confusion, storm, disaster. Without order those pale stars we see appearing would collide in their courses. This earth would smash into the sun. The seasons would not follow each other, nor night follow day. Seedtime and harvest would fail. The grain of oat would not grow into an oat-stalk and head but into a thistle, the oak-tree bear no acorns and so perish. Have you ever thought of muscles, Bridget, the ordering of muscles, our own and others? Think of the muscles of a great stag which can race over the mountains like a drifting cloud. Or those of a galloping horse bearing a man. Or of a wild-boar charging. Then think of the muscles of a flea, which you can barely see, yet can make it jump hundreds of times its height. Think if *you* could do that, with your muscles! Or a spider spinning its web and climbing it, swinging on it, strength all but invisible. There is order for you. In everything created."

"I see it now."

"Order and beauty, I say, are closely allied. Although it might not appear so at first thought. Without order there would be little of beauty. Both are of God and make delight." Colum sounded all but carried away – but not quite. "You are a beautiful woman!" he declared deep-voiced.

She did not answer.

Carefully now he went on. "Your beauty is a delight to me, Bridget. I think that you know it."

"I am glad," she murmured.

"A delight. An inspiration – I have composed poems about it, and you. But also . . . a temptation!"

"So-o-o! Need it be so?"

"This I ask myself, of many a night. And I fear that the answer must be yes. In many ways I am a weak man."

"You are the man God made you, Columcille."

"Perhaps. But we are to overcome our weaknesses. And must pray for strength to do it."

"But also – forgive me if I am wrong – for wits to know what is weakness and what is not. What is sin and temptation and wrong, and what is not. Is that not so?"

It was his turn not to answer.

"Truth. Another of your four attributes of God. To discern truth. Each man and woman must surely decide what is true for them, God's truth. And all men and women are different, born different, made different by life. So what is true for one may not be true for another. Is *that* not true?"

"What are you seeking to say, Bridget?" he demanded, a little thickly.

"Only that perhaps you should not flog yourself, with this of temptation and sin. Not in . . . this matter. You are a whole man, made very much so by God. Does He wish you to behave as though you were not? Might not that even be to criticise your Maker? You know better than He?"

"God forbid!" he exclaimed. "But, see you, I have taken on a mission. A great and demanding mission. To help absolve me from something of what I did, which resulted in the death of many men. This task, to bring the Albannach to Christ, will take my all. So I may not, cannot, must not risk distraction. And, and . . ." He left the rest unsaid.

She sighed. "In your great task, there are times when you will need refreshment, rest, comfort, encouragement, to continue. Why else this *diseart*? The comfort and help, yes help, that a woman can give a man, is something not to be despised."

"Despised, never! But . . . how far may it go, woman? That is the question. The kernel of it. How far?" That was almost harshly said.

"That, Columcille, is not for me to tell you. We will . . . know, I think. Love, order, beauty, truth. We have spoken of beauty and order and truth. What of love?"

That silenced him. For long, holding each other's hands, they stared into the glory of the sunset, unspeaking.

"Love," he said, at length. "That word covers so much."

"As it must. Since it is the very essence of God, is it not? So you preach. Love in *all* its aspects we must seek and cherish, must we not? Can we choose, select, one kind of love, and discard another?"

"I do not know, I do not know!" Abruptly he rose to his feet. "You confound me – you, a woman, confound me! Am I sounder on order and beauty than on love and truth, lass? Come – it grows chill. You must not get cold!"

"I do not feel cold at this minute, Columcille . . . !"

He raised her up and put his arms around her. "Bear with me, Bridget – and pray for me. That I may come to know what is truth. And God's will with me."

"I do. And shall, always. As you for me – for I also am weak. And a weak woman is weakness itself!"

They turned and kissed, as the last smoky refulgence of the dying day silhouetted Ben More of Mull and its satellite mountains; and then picked their careful way back through the gloaming to *Tigh Chailleacha*.

Two days later, with the main cell roofed in, Colum returned to Iona.

11

Colum found himself with little opportunity for profound cogitation on matters of truth and love in the weeks that followed. For the day after his return to Iona, they had a visitor, and no ordinary visitor on no ordinary visit. Three long-ships arrived, one of them containing none other than King Conall.

He came with a purpose, not out of any real interest in the missionaries or their progress. He came with a request. Would the Prince Colum mac Felim go on a mission for *him*? Not a religious one, or only incidentally so. To the kingdom of Strathclyde. An important mission, on which much might depend. Would he be Dalriada's envoy to King Roderick of Strathclyde?

This surprising request found Colum doubtful, however intrigued. He had planned to make his major attempt on the Albannach realm this summer, a journey up through main-land Alba to the High King Brude's capital at Inverness – for which the Skye venture had been but a testing of the water. Here, to go to Strathclyde instead, would be a distraction indeed.

Conall explained. Roderick of Strathclyde was a Christian, converted by the famous St Mungo many years ago. But he was no friend of Dalriada. The two kingdoms had been hostile ever since the unfortunate matter of Lorn's daughter Eirc, Colum's grandmother, all those years ago – Colum recol-lected his mother's warnings about this. But now it was important that there should be co-operation, important for both kingdoms. And Colum mac Felim, an Irish prince and notable Christian, as well as grandson of the runaway Eirc, was the ideal ambassador. Roderick would listen to him, where he might not to a Dalriada envoy.

Colum wondered and waited.

It was the Angle, Athelfrith, who was the trouble. Nephew of the aged King Adda of Northumbria, and grandson of the mighty Ida who had invaded Britain and carved out for himself the dual kingdoms of Northumbria and Bernicia. This Athelfrith was a warrior-prince, intent on conquest. His Anglian armies had overrun parts of Deira to the south, and Lothian and parts of Albannach Fife to the north. He had boasted that when he was King of Northumbria he would rule from Deira to the northern ocean, to Orkney and Zetland, an empire. In Fife already, he would have to be stopped. If he won the Southern Pictish kingdom, of which Fife was part, based on Abernethy on the Tay, then all Alba might fall – and Dalriada with it, for they could never hold out alone. These Angles were vicious, terrible fighters. Heathen, of course. Worse than the Saxons of the south.

Colum had heard much of the Angles, Germanic tribes of great ferocity, who had conquered so much of south Britain, which they were now calling Angle-land or England. But what had this to do with a mission to Strathclyde?

Roderick of Strathclyde held the key, Conall went on. Although his capital was at Dunbarton on the Clyde estuary, his kingdom extended right down to Lancaster and the great river Ribble, marching with the Welsh border, thus including all Cumbria. So he flanked Northumbria on the west, and could menace the Anglian homeland if so he wished. Meantime he had a treaty of peace with King Adda. If Roderick could be persuaded to annul that treaty, even if he did no more, it would offer a powerful threat to this invading Athelfrith. He would have to pull back, watch his rear. Roderick himself was no warrior, but he had many men. He could field many thousands if he wished. So he could hold the key to the situation. And Colum, a fellow-Christian and notable persuader, might persuade him.

That man asked for a little time to consider; but Conall pointed out the urgency of it all, for they had received information that Athelfrith was even now back in Fife across Forth, the lower half of the Southern Pictish kingdom, slaying and ravaging. If Colum could persuade Roderick, then perhaps he could also return by Abernethy and inform Gartnait who ruled that kingdom. He would be grateful, and might well listen to the message of Christianity. It might help with Brude, the High King, also, for he was known to be anxious about Athelfrith's ambitions; and was meantime one reason why he had been making no further attacks on

Dalriada. Conall, when he wished, knew how to make an appeal. He ended by declaring that if Prince Colum would do this, he would make over to him the whole island of Iona, in gift.

Whilst the king was being given refreshment in the refectory, Colum came to a decision. It did not demand a great deal of deciding. His task was to convert the Albannach. It did not greatly matter, after all, if he made the attempt on the southern kingdom first. Indeed it might well help to have done so, if successful, when he approached King Brude mac Maelchon at Inverness. And if he could also act the peacemaker in the process, and gain the regard of this Roderick of Strathclyde, so much the better. Presumably he was a far-out kinsman of the man, a grandson of *his* grandmother's sister. Moreover, it would be interesting to learn about the celebrated St Mungo, who had converted Roderick. Was he still alive? And, to be sure, the outright gift of Iona was much to be desired.

So within the hour he told Conall that he would attempt it.

The king sailed away with a promise that a start would be made within the week. It greatly eased Colum's mind that he would be able confidently to leave Iona in the care of Kenneth of Achabo and Comgall of Bangor. He would take his friend Bishop Cormac with him.

Three days later he set out in the long-ship with Machar and only a small party, for the south.

On their way he called in at Hinba, not only to take his leave but also to confer with his mother on the details of his grandmother's elopement and its consequences.

If Bridget was unhappy about Colum's departure for what would obviously be quite a lengthy absence, she managed to hide it, and indeed found words of encouragement; but also made urgings to take care. Eithne told him all she could recollect on the Eirc-Murdoch-Saron affair, and the Strathclyde reactions which had mounted to all but war; but she added that she had heard no ill of the offended Saron's grandson, Roderick.

So, after only an hour or so on Hinba, they proceeded onward for the Sound of Jura.

Their voyage, in part, was just a reversal of their original journey from Ireland, passing Gigha on the east and then Islay on the west, and on down the so lengthy peninsula of Kintyre to the Mull thereof, some fifty miles. They put in at Gigha for the night, at the same lonely inlet they had used on their way north. Next morning the weather was poor for late May, with drizzling rain and a fitful wind. But the seas were not high and Machar did not object to the rain, in the circumstances, so long as it kept the waves down and did not end by blowing a gale; for rounding the dreaded Mull of Kintyre was allegedly one of the major navigational hazards of all this seaboard, what with cross-tides, under-tows and currents, where the Atlantic Ocean, the Sea of the Hebrides, the Irish Sea and the Firth of Clyde met.

So around midday they approached the tip of the longest peninsula of the Isles of Britain, warily, with the rain dying away and the breeze freshening. But, to the surprise of all, under the mighty frowning headland, from which they kept their distance, they encountered nothing worse than a great slow swell; which, making their craft rise and fall in long, rolling, twisting motions, caused some of the party, including Bishop Cormac, to feel distinctly sick. At the very point of the Mull was the low, offshore island of Sanda, with its attendant reefs and skerries, scene of shipwrecks innumerable, no place to near in bad weather or darkness; but in today's conditions Machar decided that they could risk the inshore passage, for the sound was almost two miles wide and visibility was good.

In the event, with the wind favourably west behind them, they were able to speed through the channel and beyond in fine style, the seven miles, oars shipped, until they passed the last cliffs at the south end of Kintyre and were into the more sheltered waters of the Firth of Clyde. Vastly relieved, the sufferers forgot their sickness.

Now they were only halfway to their destination, for this firth was long, intricate and isle-dotted. The greatest island of all, Arran of the mountains, lay some fifteen miles to the north-east, and for this they headed, much impressed with the towering majesty of its shapely peaks, so very much kinder-seeming than those of Skye. They were interested to see that there was quite a lot of shipping using the firth, something they had not come across before.

It took them until early evening to reach Arran, where they put in at an east-facing bay all but hidden behind a dramatic island, shaped like a detached mountain soaring to over one thousand feet they assessed. On the inner shore of this they landed, to spend the night, their first in Strathclyde. They made something of a ceremony of it, of praise and thanks, and prayer for the success of their mission.

They found fishermen on this island, whose language, although differing somewhat from their own and from the Albannach's was also a Celtic tongue and not difficult to understand. These told them that Dunbarton, their king's capital, was still some forty miles away, past the islands of Bute and the Cumbraes, where the firth narrowed and thereafter turned round to the east. They would see a great fort-crowned rock where King Roderick's palace was.

In comparatively sheltered and enclosed waters, and sailing north-east with the wind directly behind them, they made excellent time, and were at the narrows between Bute and the two Cumbrae islands before midday. Again they were struck by the amount of traffic in the firth, craft of all types and sizes but few that looked like war vessels. Presumably, therefore, this Strathclyde was a great merchanting nation, something new to the visitors.

Past the islands, with the firth now narrowed to a mere three miles, a number of sea-lochs opened on the west, while the firth itself made a great bend eastwards. And there, ahead of them, unmistakable, a huge pointed rock rose right out of the water, dominating all, its steep sides ringed by tiers of walling, its summit crowned with building, clearly Dunbarton, the Fort of the Britons. They eyed it with more than mere interest, for as well as their destination, and a famed place in its own right, this was the birthplace of St Patrick who had brought Christianity to Ireland; also the scene of St Mungo's successful conversions.

As they neared the rock, they saw that all around its base, on the sheltered sides, were quays and jetties and docks, filled with shipping, and backed by warehouses and stores, with a large town stretching away to the north, larger than anything they had seen, even in Ireland. Colum's task suddenly seemed to grow the more onerous as he gazed. This was a greater nation than he had realised, its king evidently rich and powerful. What had he, Colum mac Felim, to offer Roderick?

Landing at one of the quays, they met with no difficulties as to their reception here; indeed they had no reception at all, it apparently being no concern of anyone as to who they were or what their business. Clearly the inhabitants of Dunbarton were entirely used to the presence of strangers amongst them. There may have been some glances at their unusual monastic garb, but that was all.

There was no need to ask the way to the palace – it was fairly obvious on its rock-top. Leaving their crew and oarsmen at the long-ship, Colum led his little party in that direction.

The lofty rock of Alclyde, which appeared to be conical from some directions, in fact had twin summits, with quite a dip between, both crowned by stone building. But since these were only accessible by stairways cut in the rock, they would make less than convenient accommodation, however secure. So there were other and more commodious buildings lower, which could be reached by a steep roadway. The rock itself was guarded by tiers of fortified walling wherever it was insufficiently sheer to be unscalable, with gateways in these for the road, each with its guardhouse. However, none of the guards so much as asked the newcomers their business, much less held them up. The impression gained was of an unusually open if not friendly establishment. Colum was pleased to see a little church, stone cross at the door, on a sort of ledge some way below the main hall-house.

On an apron of grass before the hall-house door a group of young men and women were playing some romping game which involved much laughter, squealing and a deal of hugging and clutching. This the visitors watched with some surprise, their arrival scarcely noticed, or at least ignored. When this appeared to be going on indefinitely, Colum moved forward to tap one of the men on the shoulder, to seek directions, interrupting something of a wrestling match with a flush-faced, wild-haired and clothing-disarranged young female.

"King Roderick?" he asked. "Where do I find the king, friend?"

The other half-turned. "I know not," he gasped. "He is not here." He laughed, to the woman.

"Not here? This is his house, is it not?"

"What do you want with Roderick, priest?" the woman said, panting. "He is from home."

"We are come to visit him, lady. On an embassage, of a sort. From Dalriada."

"Dalriada!" Her rather fine eyes widened. "We do not often have to do with Dalriada. What is your mission, priest?"

"A matter of some importance, lady. But . . . that is for King Roderick. Where shall we find him? Is he gone far?"

She shrugged, further disarranging her bodice, which was gaping open anyway. She pushed the young man a little way from her. "He will be back tomorrow, it is said. I am Langueth."

"Tomorrow? Then we must wait."

"You must." She laughed, not to Colum but to her partner in their game. "As must all."

Colum looked towards the hall-house door. "I shall inform someone as to our arrival. And come back tomorrow."

"No need. I told you, I am Langueth."

"Perhaps, lady, I should see some other? The King's chamberlain, or such?"

The remainder of the players had now gathered round. One of the other men spoke. "You address Queen Langueth, sir," he said.

Astonished, Colum managed to sketch a bow. "I had no notion, Highness. Forgive me. I am Colum mac Felim, Abbot of Derry and now of Iona. Of the house of Donegal."

"Donegal? And Felim?" she repeated. "These names sound familiar . . ."

"No doubt," he said, almost grimly. "But that is an old story. We shall come back tomorrow, Highness. And hope to see King Roderick."

"Yes. Where will you go meantime, Abbot?"

"We shall find lodgings in the town, no doubt."

"If you are of the royal house of Donegal, I think perhaps that my husband would have you better housed than that." That was not exactly cordial but somewhat more gracious. "There is a guest-house here. Down beside the church. Go there."

"I thank you, Highness. I regret having disturbed your . . . play!"

She laughed. They all did. "I will send servants," she said dismissively.

They bowed, and turned back downhill.

"A strange queen for the King of Strathclyde," Cormac observed. "How old a man is he?"

"I know not. But not young. For St Mungo converted him years ago. In Wales I understand. After the saint left this Dunbarton. So – a young wife . . . !"

They found the guest-house commodious and comfortable, on another rock-shelf opposite the church; and soon servitors appeared to cater for their needs. They saw no more of Queen Langueth, but had no complaints as to their treatment.

They presently held a little service in the church, their singing bringing a few of the castle staff to watch and take some part, older folk these.

They ate well and passed a good night. It all seemed entirely casual, informal to a degree.

In the morning, they went down to the town and were much impressed by its size, busyness and evident wealth. While they were there they saw four large long-ships put in to the quays, their square sails painted with the Green Dragon device, almost certainly the royal emblem of Strathclyde. That could be Roderick returned.

Indeed, back at the fort, they were not long in the guest-house before the King himself arrived on their doorstep, unannounced. He was a man of middle years, heavily-built, a little corpulent and florid in feature but with a pleasant open face, a genial expression and no regal formality.

"Which is the Prince Colum mac Felim – the Abbot?" he demanded. "My wife tells me that he has come. Here is a surprise indeed."

"I am he, Highness. I greet you, in Christ."

"So! We are kin, are we not? Far removed."

"I understand that our grandmothers were sisters, yes. And their husbands scarcely loved each other!"

"I have heard that, friend. Heard also of *you*. Of a great battle in Ireland. And that you had come to Alba, doing great works in Skye."

"You are well informed, Highness."

"Traders are great bearers of news, Prince Colum. And we do much trade here."

"So we perceived. We greatly admire. Now – here is Bishop Cormac O'Lethan, of the royal house of Munster . . ."

Colum presented his people. Then explained that they had come on a mission from King Conall of Dalriada.

"I have heard less good of Conall than of yourself, friend!" Roderick observed. "But we will talk of that later. You will dine with me in my hall. And lodge in my house, you and the Bishop . . ."

In the evening, with the rest of the party brought up from

the long-ship, they were escorted up to the hall-house, where a feast was prepared for them in the great hall. Roderick set Colum at his right hand at the high table, and Cormac on his left. Queen Langueth sat on Colum's right, looking very different from before, splendidly dressed and bejewelled and managing to seem almost demure. At the long table which reached down the hall, where the others sat, were to be seen sundry of the lady's former playmates.

Roderick made an excellent and attentive host, providing a banquet such as Colum had not enjoyed for years, with great variety of fish and fowl and meats, with sweets and wines. Clearly he himself appreciated his food, partaking hugely and pressing more on his guests. Langueth however, only toyed with hers. There were entertainers, to sing and dance and tell stories. Colum perceived that this was no occasion to talk of his mission.

He did ask about St Mungo, however, and found the king very ready to inform. The famous missionary, born in Fife, was still in Wales where, with another convert, Asaph, of the royal house of Gwynedd, he had founded a great monastery and seminary at Llanelwy. The Welsh had given him a new name, which he appeared to be using, Kentigern, which in that tongue meant Lord of the Hounds – Roderick was unsure of the reason behind that, although it might mean leader of the hounds of God. Himself, he had more than once urged the saint to come back to Strathclyde, where he had set up his first church, as a young man, before being driven out by the pagan King Morcant; and perhaps he would one day. But meantime he was helping to unite the Welsh Christian kingdoms to withstand the tide of the invading heathen Angles and Saxons.

This would have provided a good opportunity to introduce the subject he had come to discuss, but Colum forbore, with further entertainment proceeding. He endeavoured to engage in some conversation with Queen Langueth but gained little encouragement.

Presently he noted that Roderick had fallen asleep at the table. Langueth perceived it also, and presently rose and took her leave, without comment. Colum and Cormac exchanged glances. It was hardly suitable for guests to wake up a king in his own hall. After a little longer, with their host still sleeping and snoring gently, they rose and bowing to the monarch's back, moved quietly away, to return to the guest-house, their party following their lead. Roderick had said that the two leaders were to have quarters in the hall-house; but that could wait. The evening's entertainment seemed to be becoming distinctly rowdy as they left the building.

They held a brief service in the church before retiring for the night.

In the morning, not too early, Colum presented himself at the hall-house again and found Roderick at the table, almost as though he had never left it, eating a hearty breakfast. Nothing would do but that Colum must join him, although that man had already eaten hours ago.

Eating only sparingly, he broached the reason for his visit. "You said last night, Highness, that your friend St Mungo was helping to unite the Welsh kingdoms against the onslaught of the heathen incomers, the Angles and Saxons. As, to be sure, is his Christian duty. But the Angles menace more than Wales, do they not? They have overrun Lothian and now attack Fife, in Southern Alba. We hear that Prince Athelfrith is ravaging and slaying there at this present."

"So I am told," Roderick admitted, mouth full. "Heathen slaying heathen."

"It could be Strathclyde's turn next, could it not? These Angles are determined, ravening. Athelfrith, they say, is insatiable."

"I have a treaty with his uncle, King Adda."

"Adda is an old man. As is his brother and heir, Athelric. Athelfrith could be King of Northumbria at any time. And boasts that he will rule an empire, from North Wales and the Trent to the Isles of Zetland. Will he deny himself Strathclyde, treaty or none?"

The other eyed him thoughtfully. "He would find Strathclyde less easy to take than Lothian. Or Fife. Or even Deira."

"No doubt. But he could try. And begin by invading your Cumbria. You must have considered all this, Highness?"

"Is this what Conall of Dalriada sent you to speak of, Prince Colum?"

"Yes. He is concerned that Dalriada, like Strathclyde, could be endangered by these Angles. And I am concerned that these Christian lands, Dalriada, Strathclyde, Cumbria, and Wales, could fall to the heathen, the pagans triumph again."

"So . . . ?"

"A Christian alliance, Highness. Gwynedd, Strathclyde,

Dalriada. Cardigan and Gwent also perhaps, since all Wales is now Christian."

"Would that halt Athelfrith in Fife and Alba?"

"It would give him pause, warning."

"I have no desire, friend, to become involved in war. I am a man of peace."

"And well so. It is to *prevent* war that we suggest this. See you – if you were to annul your treaty with Northumbria meantime, you might need to do no more. It would be a warning to Athelfrith that his flank was endangered. A mere letter to King Adda. And another to King Maelchon of Gwynedd offering a treaty with *him*. When Athelfrith heard of these, he would have to reconsider, I say."

"Maelchon is dead. He has died of the plague. Cadwaladr now reigns in Gwynedd."

"Maelchon dead? I did not know it. God rest his soul. St Mungo converted him, after your royal self, did he not? This Cad . . . I did not hear his name aright?"

"Cadwaladr."

"Is he Christian?"

"To be sure."

"Then send to him, Highness. A treaty. Instead of with Northumbria." Colum paused. "This could reach further than Wales. Brude, High King of All Alba, was son to Maelchon, was he not?"

"Yes. The Cruithne, or Albannach high kingship descends through the female, a strange custom. Brude's mother, daughter of the previous High King, Drust, married Maelchon of Gwynedd."

"Then an alliance with Gwynedd could aid King Brude also. For he is said to be concerned over Athelfrith's invasions. His southern sub-kingdom of Fortrenn, containing Fife, is already assailed. It could be himself next. You, Highness, therefore hold the key to Athelfrith's containment, do you not?"

Roderick scratched his chin. "I would require to consider this. Consult with my advisers."

"I shall await your decision, Highness. And pray that it may be favourable. For Christ's cause, as well as the safety of all these nations. We must stem the heathen tide."

"Was that what you were doing in Ireland? At your last battle?"

"I believed so. I still believe it. The bloodshed I grieve for. But the forces of darkness had to be halted. There, as here."

"Very well, my friend. I shall consider well . . ."

Colum and his people spent two days with the local Bishop Eogan visiting churches and monasteries around Dunbarton, up the Vale of Leven into the Levenachs, reaching the great mountain-girt loch of Lomond with its many islands. When they returned, it was to be told by King Roderick that he was prepared to do as suggested, to annul the treaty with Northumbria meantime and to propose a defensive alliance with Gwynedd and, by implication, with Dalriada also. Over another feast, he declared that he was agreeing to do this largely for St Mungo's sake and the debt he owed to that good servant of Christ. He, Roderick, was a man of peace still, however, and would be loth indeed to have to take up arms in this matter.

Colum, somewhat chagrined to find himself looked upon as something of a man of war, was nevertheless much gratified over the decision, and assured his host that he believed that these moves would be sufficient to halt Athelfrith, without recourse to actual warfare, at least so long as his father, Athelric, still reigned.

Then Colum broached the subject of Gartnait of Fortrenn, King of the Southern Albannach. Suffering as he was from Athelfrith's invasions, he would surely be greatly heartened to hear of this alliance against Northumbria. He was Roderick's nearest neighbouring monarch. How did he esteem him?

Gartnait mac Domelch was a young man, he was told, a pagan but not aggressively so, and well enough disposed towards Strathclyde. He was no warrior-prince, being, it was said, more interested in the chase, women as well as deer, wolves and boar, than in religion. But undoubtedly the Northumbrian raids on Fife, one of his most fertile provinces, must greatly concern him.

Then a visit to Gartnait might be useful, profitable, Colum said. In the cause of Christianity. This Christian alliance of Strathclyde, Cumbria, Gwynedd and Dalriada could be a strong influence to make him listen to the Gospel message. If Gartnait could be converted, and allow missions to be sent amongst his people, then this could greatly help in the mighty task of bringing all Alba to Christ. He was senior of the seven *ri* or lesser kings, under the High King, was he not?

Roderick conceded, and said that Gartnait was kin to Brude himself. A visit to Abernethy on the Tay might serve the Christian cause, yes.

Colum in his accustomed urgent fashion, was for going right away. How far away was Abernethy? Could they travel any of the way by boat?

The king laughed. No, there was no going by water – save by sailing right round Alba to the Tay estuary, a thousand miles! They must go north by east, through the hills of Kilpatrick and Campsie to the headwaters of the Forth. Then, keeping north of the Great Moss of Monteith, make for the Allan Water. Following this up would bring them to the hills of Ochil, pierced by the Glen of Farg, which would lead them to Abernethy, seventy or eighty miles. He would provide them with a guide and horses. But it would be difficult going, much of the way, through mountains and much bogland, with many river-crossings. Three days it would take, he reckoned, perhaps four.

Colum assured that they were used to boggy country and river-fording in Ireland. They would start in the morning.

So next day, leaving most of his party with Machar and the long-ship's crew, with only Bishop Cormac, Echoid, Diarmit and Lugbe, they set out, with a guide and a small mounted escort provided by Roderick, on the first real mainland journey they had attempted. It made a strange sensation, for ever since leaving Ireland they had been essentially ship-travellers, moving around the Hebrides and the western seaboard, with overland travel for only short distances. Now, leaving their ship, and even the coracles, behind, they would be out of sight of salt-water for days, probing through wild and mountainous country into a heathen land. It demanded something of resolution – but that was a quality of which Colum mac Felim was seldom short.

At least there were no mountains to contend with at first, for instead of proceeding up the Vale of Leven to Loch Lomond, as they had done before, they rode due eastwards along the north shore of the Clyde, now quickly narrowing from firth to mere river. There were lowish wooded hills to the north which, the visitors were interested to hear, were now called after St Patrick – who of course came from hereabouts – but there was ample low ground flanking the river, with a quite large population. Across on the other side, too, less hilly, was settled land with much farming evident. After some five miles they left the Clyde, where it began to bend southwards, in the vicinity of a place called Bolline, and here their guide, a cheerful young man named Ferchar, a nephew of Roderick's, pointed away south-eastwards up-river. Another eight miles, he said, was the place of Cathures, on the Molendinar Burn, where the blessed St Mungo had established his first church and monastery when as a young man he came west from Culross in Fife, the start of his missionary activities. A community had grown up at Cathures thereafter, now being called Glascu, or Glasgow, the dear place, as Mungo named his Molendinar site. From there the saint had sought to convert Strathclyde, and been sufficiently successful as to be driven out by the pagan King Morcant. He had gone to Wales, where he had converted Roderick, who had come north to succeed Morcant when that evil monarch had died, his foot withering after he had kicked Mungo with it. The visitors were much interested.

A few miles on, east of Bolline, they were halted by armed men at a fort named Duntocher, demanding toll for the local chief; but these were quickly put in their place by King Roderick's escort. Thereafter they unfurled a flag bearing the Green Dragon of Strathclyde to travel under, to save further such interference.

Now they rode into more hilly country, but still by fair tracks and with no difficulty, cattle country, with great herds in evidence and much tilled ground to feed them. There were mills too, on the many streams which flowed down from these East Levenach or Lennox hills, to grind the corn of what was clearly a prosperous countryside. Roderick ruled over a very worthy kingdom. At one of these, the Mill of Gavie, they turned due northwards into quite a major pass between the Kilpatrick and the Campsie Hills.

Progress slowed, with innumerable streams and rivers to ford and flooded valleys to negotiate. But still the lower slopes were cultivated after a fashion, in strips and terraces, and the hillsides above dotted with sheep now rather than cattle. They halted for the night at a milling township on the Endrick River called Balfron, their guide well satisfied with their first day's progress of nearly thirty miles. They would do less well hereafter.

Next morning they were commencing their slow climb out

of the great vale or strath of Clyde to reach that of Forth, one west going the other east. The River Forth was the border, the dividing line between Strathclyde and Alba.

At the ultimate low ridge between, they reined up to stare at the prospect opening before them, sufficiently dramatic. Immediately ahead, below them, was a vast waterlogged plain, many miles wide and stretching eastwards out of sight. Beyond, to north and west, rose great purple mountains, no mere hills these but soaring majestic peaks, tier upon tier, a mighty barrier.

"Alba!" their guide said simply, and left it at that.

Although they were still to proceed north-eastwards for many miles, at this stage they had actually to swing westwards. This was to work round the head of the so extensive flood-plain of the infant Forth, this known as the Great Moss, for there was no crossing it apparently. From a distance it looked as though there was as much land as water in its farflung levels; they were assured that this was an illusion and that the entire extent, some eight miles wide by twenty-five long, was permanently flooded, impassable and the haunt of the wildest of wild beasts. This was the barrier, as much as the mountains, a mighty moat which sealed off Alba and all the north from Strathclyde and Lothian and Bernicia. This was why Athelfrith the Angle attacked the Albannachs by sea, from the Fife coast away to the east. No armies could cross west of the Snowdoun of Stirling, where the River Forth became an estuary or firth.

Much impressed, the travellers proceeded round the western edge of this watery sump, slowly now, for even here the ground was wet, with streams innumerable draining in. Amidst it all they had to ford the River Forth itself, here only some nine miles, as the crow flies, from its source on the side of the mighty Ben Lomond, and surprisingly modest-seeming to be the cause of all the subsequent flood-plain. The skirts of the mountains were very close, and Colum and his colleagues eyed them warily. They were now in Alba.

However, before they reached the foothill slopes, they swung off due eastwards, along the north side of the Moss, to avoid a township named Aberfoyle. Strathclyde was not at war with Fortrenn, but there was little coming and going between the two, and these border Albannach communities might be touchy.

They got as far as a large loch, really only a more honestly open part of the Moss, by evening. It was called the Loch of Monteith. The hills above were less than mountains here, as they progressed eastwards, and were known as Monteith, the Mounth of the River Teith, another major stream to the north which they would have to cross the next day. Apart from the odd cot-house and small farmery, they saw no villages or even hamlets; clearly this outlying part of Fortrenn was much less populous and prosperous than was Strathclyde.

They camped at the lochside, where Colum and his friends went swimming, to wash away the horseback smells and stiffness – to the wonder of their escort Ferchar, who expressed no desire to join them. They were making good time, and Ferchar reckoned that they should reach Abernethy in two more days.

Their third day's journey proved to be the beginning of something of an eye-opener for Colum. He had tended to think of the Albannach, or the Picts, as a somewhat backward and even barbarous folk, warlike but uncultured. Now he learned differently. As they moved on up the Carse of Forth and over into the valley of the Teith, through more populous country now, it was to see much that was unexpected and significant. Stone was the dominant theme – stone buildings and houses, stone monuments and carvings, and of course the stone-circles and standing-stones to be seen everywhere. To visitors, coming from lands where construction was almost wholly of timber or wattle and daub, plus turf, this masonry, dry or mortared, for even cottages, byres and sheep-pens, was surprising. Something of the sort they had seen in Skye, but not with such prevalence. The massive round towers, which Ferchar called brochs, particularly interested them, used apparently not so much as residences but as places of refuge for the local population in case of attack. They explored one of these, for in times of peace they stood empty, and found it a major construction, barrel-shaped and rising as high as forty feet to a parapet and wall-walk, with an overall diameter of as much as one hundred feet, enclosing a circular cobbled courtyard of half those dimensions. The enclosing walling, although sufficiently massive, was not all that in width, but was a double circle of wall, pierced by windows on the inner side and containing many chambers at differing levels, stairways and even fireplaces. Many people could dwell in these strongholds for limited periods, and their beasts could be penned in the open courtyards.

But it was the carvings and monuments which most intrigued, not only on these brochs but met with frequently, at typical ramparted forts, at roadsides, fords and burial-cairns, as well as on the monoliths and stone-circles. Clearly the Albannach were most notable carvers and designers, as well as stone-masons. The designs, both incised and in relief, were frequently most elaborate and decorative, as well as mysterious, of men and animals, fish and snakes, abstract forms and figurations, with recurring strange symbols. The human figures were variously dressed, some in long belted robes, Druids presumably, some in smocks and breeches, some in quilted or leathern armour with shields and spears, some on horseback as warriors or huntsmen chasing deer or wolves, all entirely lifelike. The accuracy of the clothing depicted was fascinating, even buttons and brooches and arm-rings being shown. The people who made all this were no barbarians, Colum recognised, and adjusted his ideas accordingly.

The symbols mystified, and their escort could not help to explain them, strange designs, some geometrical, of circles linked or superimposed on what seemed to be broken arrows or spears in the shape of Zs or Vs; some rectangular with indentations, some like flowers in a pot, some seemingly decorated horseshoes. The mirror-and-comb and curious trunked creature designs they had seen on Skye were common, indeed most of the figures were to be found repeated on stones innumerable, so were of evident if unknown significance. Of the animals, the bulls and boars were of particular vehemence, the eagles likewise, and the geese looking warily over their shoulders amusing.

Examining all these delayed the travellers considerably. They had no trouble however with the inhabitants. At forts and stone hall-houses they were sometimes halted by armed men; but the Green Dragon ensign of Strathclyde and the declaration that they were come from King Roderick to visit King Gartnait always gained them passage. There seemed to be, in fact, comparatively few youngish men to be seen, working on the cultivation-strips or herding beasts; Ferchar was of the opinion that many must be mobilised to go and withstand Athelfrith's invasion of Fife.

When they crossed from Teith to Strathallan, where the Romans had built a marching-camp at Alauna, Ferchar declared that he knew a better way to reach Abernethy-on-Tay than by threading the Ochil Hills by Glenfarg, as Roderick had suggested. They would keep on up Strathallan and round the western perimeter of the said hill range, through more settled country, now that they saw they were not being denied passage, thus avoiding many of the hazards of the inevitable bogs and fordings of the valleys and glens. Also, there was a royal palace at Forteviot, on this line, notable for its hunting, and it was possible that King Gartnait might be there rather than at Abernethy.

They camped the third night at a hillfoot community called Dunning, overlooking Strathearn now, where, as the sun set, the local Druid was conducting a service of worship of a sort at a large stone-circle. The visitors went to watch, and Colum restrained himself from attempting any pronouncements as to error, recognising that until they had seen Gartnait this would be unsuitable. Indeed he was interested to watch the ceremony, and even pointed out to Cormac that it had its good points, the worshipping of the Unknown God, in the shape of the sun, the reverence to a supernatural power and the confession of human inadequacies. The sacrifice, on this occasion, was only a sheep; if it had been a human-being Colum could not have stood by inactive. The visitors had a word with the Druid afterwards, and found him interested, if rather scornful, in their Christianity, of which he had some mistaken ideas, but not really hostile.

The large River Earn ran into the Tay near Abernethy, and three miles north-east of Dunning they came to Forteviot on its south bank. There was a major township here, around a fort and palace, with not very high hills coming down close on the east, wooded foothill country ideal for hunting. However, Gartnait was not present, being presumably at his capital awaiting news from his army in Fife, and seeking to mobilise additional levies from his chiefs.

They pressed on.

They came in sight of the great Tay, already beginning to widen from river to firth, silver set in green, from the shoulder of Balmanno Hill; and there, to the east some four miles away, on a similar shoulder of hill, rose the Southern Albannach capital, terraces and ramparts and towers of grey stone, with

216

the smokes of fires innumerable drifting towards them on the east wind off the firth and the Norse Sea. Below the town, for it was clearly that, and cut through the level carseland, was a long inlet from the Tay, straight and at least partly artificial, leading to a harbour, with shipping, nothing like Dunbarton with its great docks area and warehouses, but still a useful haven.

Unlike Dunbarton, too, the visitors' approach did not go unnoticed. A mounted company came out to meet them half a mile from Abernethy, under the Black Boar on silver ensign of Alba. A handsomely-clad warrior in leather-plated armour studded with silver and stones, wearing a jutting pointed beard, hailed them civilly enough, to ask what brought men of Strathclyde to Fortrenn in these evil days.

When Ferchar announced a mission from King Roderick to King Gartnait, and Colum added envoys from King Conall of Dalriada, the other raised his eyebrows. He informed that Gartnait mac Domelch was at present gone to Dunnechtan across Tay, but was expected to return at any time. He added that he was Talorc, Chamberlain to the king.

It had not occurred to Colum that Albannach kings would have chamberlains. He gained other unexpected impressions as they were conducted to the town – for it was certainly that rather than any mere community or castleton. It held no aspect of a fortress or citadel however, without enclosing walls, its many houses arranged in terraces climbing a modest slope above the plain of Tay, but not mounting up to any ramparted fort on a soaring rock, as at Dunbarton, Dunadd or Duntorvaig. The name itself was, to be sure, significant – *aber* meaning at the confluence or mouth of a stream, *nethy*, flowing into the greater river; not the dun of a fortified place. This seemed to imply a capital not preoccupied with defence and war. But what interested and surprised Colum most of all, as they rode up through the terraces, amongst all the other stone buildings, was the sight of what most surely must be a church, not large, but with a fine stone carved cross at its door. This Christian symbol, so completely unlooked for, much intrigued the visitors.

At the head of the slope they were brought to an open space, quite wide and surrounded on three sides by two-storeyed buildings with arched roofs of stone vaulting. Three high flagpoles here flew boar banners, so this was obviously the royal palace. In the centre of the open space was a large stone-circle of thirteen monoliths.

The travellers were installed in a guest-house to the rear of the palace. As on the previous evening at Dunning, an assembly of folk gathered presently for the sundown service around the circle, with blowing of horns and parading of skulls and fertility symbols on poles. This time it was a calf which was slain for sacrifice.

Afterwards Colum, Cormac and Echoid approached the Chief Druid, a venerable white-bearded figure, who did not eye them with any hostility. He said that he had met other Christians, indeed that there had been a number here including his own uncle, but all were now dead.

This led Colum to question the old man as to the obviously Christian church building they had seen on the way up. They were told an interesting story. It seemed that Gartnait's mother, Domelch, was the daughter of a previous king here called Nechtan Morbet. At some stage in his reign he had been ousted by a usurper and had fled to Ireland. There he had fallen ill and had been nursed and restored to health by the famous St Bridget, Abbess of Kildare. Later, when he had returned to Alba, Bridget herself felt called upon to make a missionary pilgrimage in heathen lands – the visitors knew of this – and not unnaturally had included Abernethy in her visiting, where she was well received. The Druid did not think that Nechtan Morbet himself ever actually embraced Christianity, but he had let the abbess seek to convert others, and in gratitude for her kindness to himself, built this church for her. It had not been used for years, of course; but Nechtan had been a good king and the place was allowed to remain in his memory. St Bridget had died in 521, the year of Colum's birth.

Much moved by this account, the missionaries retired for the night. Could all this be a good omen? These Fortrenn Albannachs seemed a reasonably friendly people and perhaps ripe for conversion.

In the morning, they visited St Bridget's Chapel. It was, of course, neglected internally, with pigeons having taken up their abode therein – these Colum declared to be the Holy Spirit's representatives. But they had made a considerable mess, needless to say, and nothing would do but that the visitors must get water and brushes and set about cleaning the place up. They were much impressed by the two splendid stone crosses inside, which, not having been exposed to the elements like the one outside, still retained much of their colourful and attractive paintwork. Needless to say, the Strathclyde escort did not find itself called upon to take part in this cleansing process.

It was whilst so engaged that King Gartnait arrived and was, not unnaturally, astonished to find high-born envoys from the kings of Strathclyde and Dalriada so employed. He proved to be a slender and good-looking young man of evident character but somewhat diffident manner, but as evidently much worried. Whilst welcoming the visitors kindly enough, his attitude clearly was that he had more on his mind than entertaining unexpected guests.

Colum, recognising the situation, quickly came to the point and as quickly had Gartnait's attention – the point, of course, a defensive alliance against the aggressive Anglo-Saxons. He could, indeed, hardly have had a more attentive listener, or a more enthusiastic supporter of the idea. Although Gartnait was somewhat doubtful as to the practicalities of the proposal, and how it would help him in his present problems of repulsing the invading Athelfrith in Fife. But when Colum told of the breaking off of the treaty between Strathclyde and Northumbria and the reaction that significant move was bound to have on Athelfrith, Gartnait saw the point immediately and was visibly heartened. When he was assured that King Roderick would have already sent messengers to inform Athelfrith's father at Bamborough, his relief and gratification were apparent. After all, Athelfrith's invading force was little more than twenty miles away at the moment, and although probably not intending to venture far inland from their shipping in the Forth estuary, might well be planning their next venture into the Firth of Tay here. He, Gartnait, had his chiefs and lords assembling men, but they were not a warlike folk and were little match for the ferocious Angles.

The emissaries were well entertained that night in the palace. Colum decided to avoid broaching the subject of Christianity until the morrow. This time they did not attend the evening sun-worship ceremony.

In the morning, by asking Gartnait if they might hold a service of praise to God and His Son Jesus Christ in the little church, the wider approach was made comparatively simple and unforced, especially when the young monarch requested to be allowed to come and watch the proceedings. Indeed, so many of his people, especially young women, with which the palace seemed to be particularly well provided, came to see what went on also, that most could not get inside and had to peer and listen from the open door. Even the old Chief Druid was there. The Iona group was very small, which meant that the psalms and hymn-singing and responses were less rousing than they would have wished – although Colum's powerful voice filled the church resoundingly – and they lacked the cymbals which always appealed to the uncommitted spectators. But Colum seized on the opportunity to preach vehemently on the theme of Christian love as distinct from hatred, peace instead of war, and mutual respect instead of aggression, as well as a kinder and more joyful life hereafter, sentiments which went down well with the present company. There were no interruptions or walkings-out; and in fact some actual enjoyment seemed to be generated. At the final hymn, one of his own composing, Colum urged all to join in with the refrain, to hum the cheerful tune at least, and not a few did, admittedly with a certain amount of giggling and laughter. Laughter was in short supply at Abernethy at this period, and so was welcome.

Afterwards, at a repast, Gartnait was full of questions about the Christian message and practices, particularly how it affected rulers like Roderick, Conall and the Welsh kings, as well as the Irish, so that Colum did not really have to make excuses for expounding the Gospel teachings, and Christ's promises for the here and the hereafter. For his part, he learned more about Nechtan Morbet and Bridget the abbess – with whom, he gathered, Nechtan had actually been in love. He had never apparently become a baptised Christian himself, however sympathetic, but had given leave to the lady to make any converts that she could. Some hundreds had in fact been turned to the new faith, but as time wore on, with St Bridget departed, there were few new adherents and gradually the old ones died off. There were now, so far as Gartnait knew, no Christians in Fortrenn. But they kept St Bridget's Chapel as a memorial to a notable and spirited woman; and the idea of Christianity held a sort of romantic tradition in consequence.

From there, of course, it was easy and natural for Colum to ask if he too might be permitted to seek converts in Fortrenn, and, grateful for the good news the visitors had brought,

Gartnait agreed. He pointed out that there might well be some opposition from the Druids, but said that he would give orders that the missionaries and any converts were not to be harassed.

So far, so very good.

For four days thereafter, then, Colum and his little party moved about the south and north shores of Tay, preaching and spreading the word to those who would listen, meeting with no real opposition and with varying acceptance. The general preoccupation with invasion and war told both for and against their efforts, but on the whole probably apprehension as to the future helped their message.

Well satisfied with progress, Colum felt that it was time that he was on his way back on the long road to Iona. Moreover, he did not like to leave Machar and the long-ship's crew for too long idle at Dunbarton. So, returning to Abernethy, he asked Gartnait if he might let Echoid and Lugbe remain there meantime, to continue the good work and seek to spread the Gospel in Fortrenn, whilst he and Cormac went back to Roderick and informed him of the Southern Albannach agreement to the defensive alliance. The latter met very much with the young king's approval and he agreed to the former quite readily.

So partings were the order of the day, next morning, and amidst mutual good wishes, farewells were said and blessings exchanged, and the long journey homewards – for Iona was now feeling very much home to Colum at least – commenced.

He was very much aware as to how scattered now his various colleagues and helpers were becoming – but that, after all, was an essential part of their mission. But it did mean that he would either have to recruit more qualified missionaries in Dalriada and Alba, or else get others to come from Ireland to help. Success, even qualified success, brought its own demands.

12

Happy as Colum was to get back to Iona, and to find all well there under Ernan, Kenneth and Comgall, although scarcely admitting it to himself, he found himself almost more looking forward to visiting Hinba and recounting progress – and by no means only to his mother. All on Iona were very busy, with field work in progress, new building, small-scale missions out to parts of Mull, and the islands of Colonsay and Coll; and even the preparing of a sort of harbour at the north end of the island, not for boats but for seals; for at Skye they had learned that it was possible to breed seals as it were in captivity, and these would provide a welcome source of food and more important, lamp oil. Colum, lover of animals, was at first somewhat doubtful about the ethics of this; but food after all was vital, and on an island could be difficult in the long winter months, and oil was as necessary; also the skins were most useful for a variety of purposes.

While he had been away, Moluag had arrived back from Skye, having set up a number of mission-posts there, with the help of Queen Sinech – they could hardly be called churches yet – leaving Scandlann, Fechno and Grillan in charge. But as the Iona community's only bishop, Moluag felt that his place was here – he had not known of the temporary presence of Bishop Cormac. The trio on Skye needed more helpers, he declared. Altogether, the manpower situation was becoming critical. Colum at least persuaded Cormac, Kenneth and Comgall not to return to Ireland yet awhile.

Feeling slightly guilty about it, despite all this, within only a few days of his return, Colum set off alone, save for the dog Gaul, in his own curragh, for the little island-group of the Garvellachs and his *diseart*, shamelessly using filial duty as an excuse.

He could not complain about the warmth of his welcome on Hinba. Eithne and Bridget were getting on very well together, but were delighted to have company, more especially

Colum's. They were turning their little establishment into a very pleasant home, admittedly with little of the nunnery or sanctuary about it; but then, neither of them was really nunnishly inclined. They seemed to be on excellent relations with their neighbours on the larger Garbh Eileach.

Over a repast, making much more imaginative use of the available basic foods than was apt to be the case on Iona, they listened to Colum's account of his travels and doings in Strathclyde and Fortrenn, being particularly interested in the St Bridget connection, not unnaturally. Eithne knew more about the renowned abbess than did Colum, for she had been a young woman when Bridget was at the height of her fame. In fact mother and son got involved in some slight argument over the lady, when Eithne referred to her as *Bishop* Bridget, Colum immediately protesting about the title, pointing out that there was no such thing as a female bishop. But the princess insisted. In this case, there was. So far as Eithne knew, Bridget had been the only woman-bishop in Christendom. What had happened was this When she decided to set up her first monastery and nunnery at Kildare – and be it noted that it was to be monastery as well as nunnery, men as well as women, frowned upon by certain stupid folk – she had gone to old Bishop Mel to be ordained abbess. But, growing forgetful with age, he had in error read out the wrong service and ordained her bishop instead. It was considered impossible to undo this, once done; and because Bridget was so beloved, and famed for her good works, bishop she remained although she but seldom exercised the episcopal function.

Colum continued to express doubts; but his mother pointed out that there were various paintings and carvings of the saint, in Ireland, showing her bearing a bishop's crozier and not an abbot's pastoral staff.

Their own Bridget asked how her namesake had managed to make the name acceptable to Christians, since she had always understood that the original Bridget or Bride – after whom she herself was called – was a semi-legendary Celtic pagan heroine, half-goddess, wed to a sea-god, renowned in myth and story.

Eithne explained. The child was of the humblest origin, daughter of a Christian slave, Brocessa, belonging to a well-known bard and storyteller called Dubtach. The bard had named the girl Bridget after the heroine of one of his favourite stories. She was married off young, to a Druid, but she grew up strong in the faith of her mother, who had been converted by St Patrick; and in time, by her goodness and grace and beauty, so captivated her husband that he too turned Christian and freed her mother from slavery. After his death, her rise as a missionary had been extraordinary, God most evidently with her.

Their Bridget was more interested in the account of a monastery and nunnery combined, and wanted to hear about this, with a glance at Colum.

Eithne could not tell them much more on that theme, save that the abbess believed that since God had made men and women to be together, live together and work together, He could not have intended that His Church should separate them as though they somehow were at enmity. So Bridget trained her young monks and nuns – if nuns they could be called – to learn together, and understand each others' different problems, difficulties and yes, temptations, as well as all that they had in common; so that they could be better ministers of God's word to men and women alike. Indeed she held that if the young people learned, through constant association, how to use and yet control their bodies and urges, they would be a great deal less likely to give way to sudden temptations thereafter. Also she held that there was much less likelihood of carnal affections arising between men in her monasteries than in others. She showed the way, herself, by having as her coadjutor-bishop, St Conladh, yet without scandal.

To all of which Colum listened and pondered. He had heard some of it all before, of course, but not in detail. He was especially interested when his mother pointed out that he should be a follower of Bridget's teachings since she, like himself, had been a lover of oak-trees, which was why she had chosen Kildare as the site of her first monastery, meaning the Church of the Darrach or Oak-Trees, just as he had at Derry, which meant the same thing.

Later, Colum and Bridget, with the dog, went together for an evening walk round the isle, visiting first his *diseart*, to offer up a brief prayer of thankfulness. The twin cells and the shrine, he noted, were kept clean and tidy, with even some fresh-picked flowers in a bowl in the living-hut. He had no doubt as to who kept them there, and was touched.

Moving on, and he pondering the sequence of events which

had brought them there together, pointing up to where he had seen that flash of light that sunrise morning, the sign which had brought him to Hinba, the woman spoke up.

"Columcille – this of St Bridget, so unexpected a find and surprise at Abernethy. Could this not also be a sign? Something of a message for you? And for me, perhaps, with the same name."

"A sign of what?" That was just a little wary.

"A sign that women have their due place in God's work. A more active place than you and your friends have been prepared to allow? Not just shut up in nunneries, or even on an isle like this! But working. And working with men. Why not? Bridget of the oaks showed the way, did she not? And she got to Abernethy before you!"

He shook his head. "I do not say that she was wrong. But I think that she may have made too light of the problems. And the problems are there, Bridget – as *I* know all too well! Men and women! Celibacy in itself I do not advocate. For most men, even priests. But missionaries – missionaries cannot truly marry. They cannot be true husbands, I think. A wife means a home. And children. The missionary must marry the Church."

"I was not talking of marriage. But working together. As missionaries."

He sighed. "Think you that I would not like that? That it would not much please me. And others likewise. But . . . *there* is the danger. Distraction. The attractions between men and women are strong, as we do know. Journeying, encamping, working together closely – think you that the men would not become distracted from their missionary zeal? Have their minds on other matters too much. Possibly even make enemies of each other in rivalry for women's affections. I have thought much on this, Bridget, and know my own mind sufficiently well to perceive the dangers."

"I think that you make too much of them."

"Perhaps." He touched her arm. "It may be that I am myself more apt to be affected than are some others! I know my weaknesses, you see!"

"I would not call it weakness, Columcille."

They walked on in silence for a while.

Presently, at the extreme southern tip of the island, he did not exactly change the subject but gave it a new direction, to emphasise the need for dedication of the men to their great task and the ever-growing shortage of manpower as the missions expanded. Echoid and Machar had brought back his three senior colleagues from Ireland, and some others, yes, but far more than these were needed. He was even considering whether he ought himself to go back to Ireland, on a recruiting visit – although he would greatly grudge the time that would take up, when he was eager to press on with the major project of converting Alba. Somehow they must get more men.

"Or women . . . ?" she asked, smiling.

"It is really priests that we need, ordained men, who may be left on their own to establish missions and churches, to baptise and convert and convey the sacraments. Not just enthusiastic helpers. In time, to be sure, these must come from the Albannach converts themselves – but that is not yet. We cannot turn converts into priests before they are ready."

"Your mother and I have spoken of this problem," Bridget told him. "Indeed it has been obvious from the first. It was bound to happen, if you were successful at all. We feel that perhaps you have not always made the best use of what you have, Columcille. Apart, indeed, from the women!"

"In what way?"

"Forgive me if I seem to criticise. My admiration for you and your labours is beyond all my poor words. But, because you are a born leader, your nature is always to lead, to act, to *do* it yourself. I think that perhaps you plan ahead insufficiently, do not sit and think out the future. Here, on Hinba, we have much time for thinking! Perhaps you should use your *diseart* more! You will not change your nature. But you might plan to better effect."

"As how, Bridget?"

"This of manpower, in especial. How many of your men, brought from Ireland, are at this present labouring on Iona? Ploughing, sowing, reaping, tending cattle, building, carving, writing the scriptures, leather-working, even breeding seals! Many, I think. Could not most of them be better employed, turned into priests, to go forth from Iona?"

"Iona is the base we must have. The monastery and its activities are essential to our mission. It is the centre round which all turns."

"To be sure. But all that labouring work, however good for the soul, could be done by others, new converts, hired workers, Albannach, leaving your own people, or many of them, free to be the missionaries you need."

"M'mmm . . ."

"Then there is the island itself, Iona. It is a fair place and you have made it flower and sing. But, it is small and not very fertile. That is why King Conall allowed you to have it. I know that you grow more grain on Tiree, but that is a wind-swept place in the wide ocean, and good only for that. There are other places, where your labours would be rewarded better, fourfold. I do not mean for the monastery to leave Iona, but for you to use others for the growing of crops and fruits and the herbs you require, the pasturing of flocks, fuel for the smoking of fish and meat. And much else. Sheltered, kindly places, if not on the principal routes for ships. Is it not so?"

He stroked his chin. "You have some such in mind?"

"Yes. A number I can think of. But one, in especial. Which you would not require to bargain for with some chief. Lismore."

"Lismore? What do you mean? Lismore is in Ireland. Moluag's own monastery, which he founded."

"Is there a Lismore in Ireland also? I did not know. But, after all, it but means the Great Garden. *My* Lismore is an island, very fair, sheltered in the Firth of Lorn, where the Sound of Mull joins it, no great distance from Iona. And five times Iona's size, ten miles long. Fertile indeed."

"Such a place must belong to others."

"That is the point. It belonged to my husband, Riagan. But it was snatched from us by Brude mac Maelchon in the Albannach invasion, when Riagan was killed, when they overran so much of Dalriada. But that tide has ebbed meantime, with this threat of the Angles. I have sent men to Lismore and they tell me that there is no Albannach occupation there now. So it belongs, in fact, to my son Angus. There are a few folk living there but not a great many for so fertile an island, ten miles long by almost two across."

"All that? But – wait you. When we were sailing back from Skye we went down the Sound of Mull and into your Firth of Lorn. I remember Angus pointing out an island, as fair and fertile."

"That would be Lismore. You could have it, Columcille. Angus would give it to you."

"And need *more* men to manage it!"

227

"Not necessarily. You could use our own people, the islanders. And get others. And a small mission there could be of great help in converting the nearby Albannach territories of Appin and Morvern."

"Ye-e-es." Colum paused. "This much interests me, Bridget, I admit. In what you say. But in another matter also. Moluag. Perhaps I should be not be telling you this – but I trust you beyond all. It could be . . . of matter. The fault is in myself, no doubt. But . . . Moluag and I do not always see alike. We differ at times. See you – he is a fine man, a good priest and bishop. Yet we can clash. So it would be best, I think, if we were not always together. Yet I need a bishop nearby. Cormac will not always be here. So – this Lismore!"

"You mean that Bishop Moluag should go there?"

"Yes. He founded the monastery of Lismore in Ireland. Let him found another here. A small one. Near enough to Iona for coming and going. But not having to share a small isle with me!"

She laughed. "Dear Columcille – you are the cunning one!"

"But – no harm in it? Only good. He would be happier. Could do good work from there. And manage that island, if it is fertile as you say, for the benefit of all. If he will go."

"You think that he might not be agreeable?"

"Perhaps not. He might see it as a sort of banishment. Cause offence. I cannot *command* him to go, a bishop. But the name, Lismore, should affect him, challenge him. It will have to be done with care . . ."

"Another matter needing your care, my friend – Angus. I have been thinking of speaking to you on this for some time. Angus is greatly admiring of you and what you are doing. He would, I know, devote his life to you and your mission. But . . . is it indeed for him? Is being a priest what is best? He is, you see, Angus mac Riagan, Lord of Ellary, Knapdale and Crinan. Lismore also. His father's only son. As such he has responsibilities, duties to his people. He is almost a man now. I have looked to matters for him, as best I might, since his father died. But I am not doing so here on Hinba. I think that it is almost time for him to become what he was born to be. *He* may not think so, but . . ."

"I see it – yes I see it. I have thought on this, myself. He is a fine lad and has been of the greatest help to me. He would make an excellent priest. But . . . as you say, he has other responsibilities. Which, I suppose, only he can carry out? There is no other kinsman . . . ?"

"None close. Two cousins were also slain by the Albannach. It was a costly invasion indeed, for Dalriada. We lost most of our best and strongest, as well as our King Gabhran. Angus will be needed."

"I shall greatly miss him."

"And he you. And your Iona. But – he may be able to do much for the Church still. As one of the leaders of our kingdom. More, perhaps, than as a simple priest."

Colum smiled grimly. "I myself had that question to answer, that decision to make, once! To be High King of Ireland and *order* my people to be Christian. Or to be a simple priest and seek to *persuade* them! Did I choose wrongly?"

"I think not. But *you* are Colum mac Felim, an especial man. The man God required for His task. Much as I love my son, I do not see Angus in that light."

"Who knows? But, yes – I will recommend that Angus returns to Ellary and his duties there. With regret . . ."

By now they were high on the west-facing ridge of the island, and as before, they settled to watch the sun at its sinking into the isle-strewn ocean – of which, surely, no sight on earth could be more beautiful and inspiring. Hand in hand they sat to eye it all, silent now, thinking their own thoughts but occasionally turning to consider each other. When, at length, they rose, it was to kiss, but controlledly, too controlledly, before moving northwards, the dog Gaul at least carefree.

After conducting Bridget to her door and saying goodnight to his mother and her maid, Colum returned to his own little cell at the *diseart* for the night, wondering, wondering.

He left Gaul with the women when he went back to Iona in the morning.

In the event, he had no difficulty in persuading Moluag that his Dalriadan Lismore was awaiting him, indeed asking for his presence. Probably that man was as well pleased as was Colum to be going to have a separate establishment not too far away, for of course he had been used to running a large monastery in Ireland, and always playing second fiddle here in Dalriada would undoubtedly gall at times.

Young Angus was happy that they should have Lismore, but sad that he was to be sent back to Ellary, pleading to be allowed to stay with the missionaries. But Colum, while understanding and sympathising, was kindly firm, in deference to Bridget's wishes and advising. They would still see much of each other; and Angus might well be of more value to their cause acting the chief than the student-monk.

Never one for delay once a course was decided on, Colum set out, with Moluag, within the week, in the long-ship. Angus went with them and would stay with Moluag on Lismore for a short period to assist in the settling-in process and ensuring that the islanders were helpful. Two other students were also included as aides; and Colum decided to call in at Hinba, in the passing, to ask Bridget whether she would care to accompany them on this venture – for he had rather gathered that she was finding her present life just a little constricting. Besides, Lismore was her idea, and as the late lord's wife there she could probably play a useful part, a woman's part. The seed that she had sown had not fallen on wholly stony ground.

She was delighted with the suggestion, and was ready to depart within the hour. But it took longer than that, for nothing would do but that the Princess Eithne came too; and since they could scarcely leave her maid Ertha alone on Hinba, she and the dog had to embark also, amidst much fuss. So they made a larger and mixed company as the long-ship pulled out from the Garvellachs and headed north-eastwards up the Firth of Lorn.

They had only some seventeen miles to go, past the inshore islands of Luing and Seil and Kerrera, and with the prevailing south-westerly wind behind them, made good time. They were steering clear of an isolated rock where the Sound of Mull forked off on their left and the great extension of the firth, called Loch Linnhe on the right, when Angus pointed ahead to a jutting narrow headland.

"Lismore," he said.

His hearers looked, and then at each other – for this was nothing like the picture they had conjured up in their minds of a green and pleasant garden-like isle. It glowered grey rock, rising to quite a steep and bare hill, higher than Iona's little peak, nothing but naked stone in sight. Moluag turned an accusing frown on Colum.

Behind them, Bridget spoke quietly. "Wait you," she

advised. "This southern end is different. Something of a fist of defiance shaken at Mull and the mainland, to protect its garden! The rest is otherwise."

Moluag said nothing.

As they drew nearer they could see that behind the hill a long narrow peninsula was stretching; but it too was bare and inhospitable, rising to a central ridge, with little of grass showing, and no trees, the shore rocky. Even Colum eyed it doubtfully.

"You will see," Bridget said.

"I had not thought to come to such as this," Moluag declared shortly.

The headland and its northwards extension was like a grey wall dividing the firth in two, and Bridget explained that the sound on the east side was known as the Lynn of Lorn whilst that wider to the west was the Lynn of Morvern, hence the name Loch Linnhe, the loch of the lynns or channels.

For fully a couple of miles up the east side of the island there was little alteration in the scenery of ridge and naked limestone rock. Then, after passing a quite major hill where the island began to widen out, and negotiating a cluster of offshore islets, all quite suddenly changed. The ground-level sank, although it seemed to be furrowed still by low escarpments of projecting limestone, grass grew richly and there were trees everywhere, not dense forest but scattered and in clumps.

Colum peered, pointing. "Those are oaks, I swear! This should by *my* island, I think, not yours, Moluag!"

"Perhaps you should indeed settle here, and I go back to Iona," the other commented.

Bridget, glancing from one to the other, nodded. "Yes, why not, Columcille? Here is the larger, richer island. And nearer to the Albannach lands. You could have a greater monastery on Lismore."

He looked at her, and she raised one eyebrow significantly. Clearly she was seeking to spur on Moluag. "Perhaps," he nodded.

Moluag frowned.

The further they went northwards the more attractive Lismore looked. It had not the sheer loveliness and brilliant colours of Iona, which were largely caused by the pure white cockle-shell sands and their translucent effect on the water and the multi-hued seaweeds. Here the shores were rocky and pebbly. But there was infinitely more grass and meadow, cultivable ground, woodland and verdure generally.

Colum summed it up. "Iona is a sparkling jewel, but this is a silver chalice!"

"Where do we land?" Moluag demanded.

"Not far now," Angus said. "There is an old broch at Tirefour. You will see it on a mound. It stands above a pebbly strand at a shallow bay. In the old days the broch was to protect the landing-place. There is a more sheltered haven round at the north-western corner, a fine natural harbour, called Port Ramsa, but it is too far off, some miles from the township and the best parts of the island."

Soon they saw the tall, barrel-shaped outline of the broch towering above the shore, part broken down but still impressive. There was a scattering of offshore reefs and skerries to be avoided.

Machar had the sail lowered and the oarsmen pulled the ship as far into the shallows as he thought safe.

"Who is going to be first ashore, and have Lismore?" Bridget asked, looking at Colum.

"Ah! My coracle!" that man exclaimed.

Moluag slapped hand on wood. "Mine!" he cried.

The two light craft were hastily put over the side and both men clambered in – although Colum seemed to be less agile at it than usual. So the bishop had his paddle out and had his boat moving first. There was laughter and cheering from the long-ship.

Colum made a great splashing, but the other's paddling was more effective and he surged ahead. So far so good. They were about thirty yards apart.

Then Colum, preparing to admit defeat, perceived something which Moluag would not, being that much further to the south. The pebble-and-rock point for which the bishop was heading with all speed, was not in fact part of the main strand but a detached skerry of a sort, quite close to the land. There was water all round it, so that it was not truly part of the island. Whereas Colum, by making a small circling movement, could have a straight run in.

This could ruin all, he recognised. Hurriedly he calculated. Then shouted aloud. "This is only a skerry! A skerry, man. Not the island. *My* flesh and blood will be first on Lismore!"

Moluag called back something incoherent, and swung his

coracle round to the left. But he had further to go to get round that skerry than had Colum at his end.

The latter was in a quandary. He could, of course, delay deliberately; but Moluag was a proud man and would perceive and resent anything such, in a challenge such as this. There would be only a moment or two when they would be out of sight of each other at opposite ends of the skerry. He could only make the most of that.

In the event the two coracles emerged almost at the same moment, now some sixty yards apart, Moluag paddling furiously. To urge him on, Colum shouted, "Flesh and blood! Flesh and blood! The first ashore!" He was handling his paddle less than dexterously still, but there was a little jut of pebbly beach thrusting out nearer to him than to Moluag.

With only yards to go, the latter saw it.

Giving a last mighty heave to his paddle, Moluag tossed it aside. He whipped out from a pocket the eating-knife they all were apt to carry on journeys. Almost in the same movement he slashed this down on the very tip of his little finger and, spurting blood, hurled knife and small piece of himself ashore. The two coracles thereafter grounded almost simultaneously.

"Flesh and blood! Mine!" the bishop cried exultantly. "Lismore is mine!" He leapt out, waving his bleeding hand.

Colum stared, astonished, and more slowly clambered over and ashore.

Moluag was all but dancing on the pebbles in holy glee, ignoring the bright red flood. "You did not think of *that*!" he exclaimed.

"I did not," the other agreed. "Nor need you have done, my friend. That was . . . overmuch!"

"Not to win this island for God."

"Perhaps not. Although *I* had some such intention also! But – it is yours, Moluag – all yours. With its people, its oaks and meadows, its pastures and tilth, its fruits and favours – but also its demands and difficulties." He pointed. "See – there are alders as well as oaks, less kindly trees. And these jagged limestone ridges look sharp and are edged upwards. These will not always offer you so smooth a pathway."

"Do I look for a smooth path? The Lord will smooth them for me! And make the alders kind as oaks. He has brought me to this second Lismore for *His* good purpose."

Colum nodded. "So be it. I wish you well. May you, and Lismore,. prosper."

Others were coming ashore now, and coracles being in short supply, Colum paddled his back to bring Bridget.

"Did you see what he did?" he demanded, as he helped her over the side. "Chopped the top off his finger, to throw ashore! Can you believe it? His flesh and blood, first. Took a knife to his finger."

"He did that? Of a mercy – I did not think to bring him to such a strait! I but sought to rouse him, to urge him on. He seemed doubtful. He is not sorely hurt?"

"No, I think not. Only bleeding like any pig! You can bind up his finger, Bridget – and feel no guilt! But – you once accused *me* of being the cunning one!"

"You did not require much guidance from me, here . . . !"

On the beach, she was tactful enough to congratulate Moluag on his victory and not to fuss or chide over his odd behaviour. But his little finger was still pulsing out blood, and she hastened to tend it as best she could, tying a leather thong from his pleated girdle tightly below, to stem the flow, and binding it up with a strip of woven stuff from his shirt. Clearly the bishop himself was in too elevated a state to care, at this stage. His one concern appeared to be that no one had thought to bring his crozier ashore from the ship.

They started off inland, Moluag rejecting any suggestions that he should sit awhile, past the ruined broch and up over the succession of little limestone ribs which formed terraces of rich deep grass on the gentle slopes. It was the lime which made this land so fertile, in the same way, although on a much greater scale. as did the cockle-shell sand for Iona. Wildflowers bloomed everywhere, not just the usual sea-pinks, wild thyme, crowsfoot-trefoil, clovers, buttercups and viper's bugloss, but speedwell, blue periwinkle and tormentil and harebell, a. favourite of Colum's, all fluttering with butterflies. It was obvious why the place was called the Great Garden.

The terraces rose to a low rounded spine about half a mile inland. From here they could see far and wide. There was a central plain running the length of the island, lower than this ridge and the similar one on the west side, but nowise to be called a valley. They noted two quite long lochs in this, and were told that there was a third, well to the south. One, which

Angus called Balgowan, the loch of the buttercups, almost a mile long, was close at hand and allegedly full of trout – to Moluag's delight, for he was a keen angler. Down at its reedy edge, where an excited Gaul put up mallard and squattering coots and other wildfowl, and dignified heron stalked the shallows amongst the golden marsh-marigolds, they were again expressing delight when Bridget pointed half-right to a scatter of houses, the main township or clachan of the island. But Moluag's glance went past these to something actually closer, a single tall standing-stone on a slight elevation near the north end of the loch.

"There!" he declared. "That stone, the pagan stone. That will be my challenge, my whip and goad, to remind me always of my task. Lest the peace and beauty and kindness of it all – aye, and the trouts – lure me from my duty. Between that stone and this loch I will build my monastery, and from here spread the Word."

"There are other good places, Bishop," Bridget said. "With more shelter of trees, better land. Perhaps you should see more." And Angus pointed out that there was a particularly fine well halfway down the west side of the loch, apt for holy water and baptism, always important for monastic establishments. But Moluag was determined, obstinate. That standing-stone was going to act as his constant reminder. It represented the sun-worship and human sacrifice which was the curse of the Albannach, and that was what he had come here to fight. The stone would be his taskmaster.

So they all trooped over to the monolith, where the bishop, seeming none the worse for his damaged finger which must have been throbbing fiercely, after pointing out suitable plots for his church and other buildings, performed a brief, preliminary service of dedication, leading all round the perimeter singing a psalm and sprinkling water from the loch, duly blessed, right and left. Thereafter he went over and splashed more water on the standing-stone, intoning it washed from its stain of blood and sin and now to be a monument to the true faith. In all this, Colum kept, as it were, in the background, this to be very much Moluag's day.

Presently Bridget and Angus led them down to the clachan, from which already people were watching them warily, to present the missionaries to the local inhabitants and tell them that fullest co-operation was looked for. Lismore, like the rest of Dalriada was of course nominally already Christian; but with no church nor priest on the island, it was in fact barely so. But there was no hostility, and with their young lord and his mother making their wishes felt so clearly, co-operation seemed assured.

These owners did not themselves have any actual house here, but their headman, one Erip, lived at Port Ramsa, two miles to the north, in a dwelling large enough to put up the principal visitors for the night. Eithne made no fuss about the walk there, although her maid grumbled. The long-ship's crew for their part, tucked themselves away into the many entire and reasonably clean mural chambers on the abandoned broch at Tirefour.

Moluag went to bed a happier man than he had been for long, and Colum and Bridget took their usual evening stroll together before turning in, this time accompanied by Angus, well satisfied with their day.

In the morning, the energetic ones commenced a tour of the island, or much of it, missing out the extreme rocky southern end. Unlike the true Hebridean isles, Lismore did not face the wide ocean on its west side, but the mountains of Morvern, highly scenic in a different way. As a consequence, that shore was no more exposed than that on the east. Nevertheless, it was little populated, and with much fertile land unused, was ripe for Moluag's eventual development. There was a good natural harbour and inlet about halfway down, An Sailean, so that boats could be used to transport farm produce and the like instead of having to carry it overland.

They found quite a large offshore islet down towards the southern end of the west coast, called, it seemed, Bernera – as were other Hebridean islands – this one a mile long and rising to fully one hundred feet, tree-clad and attractive. Only a mere eighty yards of water separated its nearest point from the main island. They saw no fewer than eight herons parading its shore – to Colum's satisfaction, these long-legged birds being his favourites. Moluag said graciously that, with Bridget's permission, he would grant this little Bernera to Colum, in compensation for having lost the race for Lismore. Perhaps he could turn it into another *diseart*, of which he might well be in need? On this genial note, weary but well pleased, they returned to Port Ramsa.

Next day, leaving Moluag, Angus and the student-monks to commence their labours, with much well-wishing and mutual blessing, Colum embarked on the long-ship with the women, to journey back to Hinba and Iona, another blow struck, they hoped, in Christ's name.

PART TWO

13

The great day dawned at last, the start of the prime and major effort of the entire mission and venture, after so much of preparation and planning and prayer. Colum had said his goodbyes to his mother and Bridget the day before, after a two day solitary vigil at his *diseart* on Hinba. Now they were off to assail the Albannach citadel at faraway Inverness.

They had taken all the advice they could get as to their journey, routes, problems and dangers. No one on Iona or nearby had ever actually been to Inverness, at the other side of Alba, but one or two had been part way. It seemed that there was a mighty valley running slantwise north-eastwards from the head of Loch Linnhe, extending for almost seventy miles, known simply as Glen More, the Great Glen. It spawned many lochs and rivers on its way, and at its northern end produced the largest of them all, Loch Ness. Out of this loch flowed the River Ness, eight miles to the northern sea; and where the river reached salt-water was Inverness, Brude mac Maelchon's capital.

Put that way, it had sounded a fairly simple journey, just pressing on and on along the miles. But there were a sufficiency of difficulties apparently – apart from the probable hostility of the people they would meet on the way, wild animals and other hazards of travel through fierce mountainous country. Unfortunately the aforesaid chain of lochs stretching up Glen More were not all linked up by rivers; so the long-ship could take them only to the head of Loch Linnhe, whereafter they would have to go on afoot. Nevertheless most of the going would have to be by water, for there were few known tracks; so coracles would be needed. But these must be of sufficiently light construction to be carried on men's backs. They had therefore spent considerable time and ingenuity in designing and constructing canoe-like craft of waterproof sealskin stretched over slender but tough frames of oak saplings, a very fleet of these, for each man would require one. This inevitably must limit the size of the party.

There was much competition to be part of this great venture, despite its obvious dangers; but in the end Colum took only the three visitors from Ireland, Bishop Cormac and the Abbots Kenneth and Comgall, Lugbe and Diarmit and two student-monks. Machar and his crew would turn back at the head of Loch Linnhe.

So amidst the farewells of practically everybody on Iona, they cast off, the long-ship so laden with coracles as to look almost twice its size, and headed south-about round Mull and up into the Firth of Lorn. They would call in at Lismore in the by-going.

They found Moluag already quite well advanced with the construction of his monastery beside Loch Balgowan and the standing-stone, nothing completed but all beginning to look like a unified establishment, the church itself the furthest ahead, all wattle and daub. The bishop hastened to assert, however, that this progress had not been at the expense of his spiritual duties, that he was preaching, baptising, marrying and burying. Lismore, he claimed, would soon be the most fully Christian place in all Dalriada – he did not say including Iona, but fairly clearly implied it. Colum smiled his acceptance of that.

They pressed on up Loch Linnhe and got as far as a small island, with almost the same name as Moluag's loch, Eilean Balnagowan, to pass the night. It had only two houses on it and so there was no question of danger from the inhabitants, as there might well be on the mainland – something they would have to reckon with hereafter.

Next day, soon after passing the mouth of what was obviously a major side-loch stretching away eastwards and flanked by high and shapely mountains, Loch Linnhe itself suddenly narrowed dramatically from over three miles to a bare three hundred yards, where there was a notable tide-race; and although it widened somewhat thereafter, it was to less than a mile. Some ten miles of this, and then abruptly, beneath a mighty humpbacked mountain to the east, quite the highest they had yet seen, snow streaking its high corries, they were at the loch-head, where three major rivers came in, from west, north and east.

Here was the end of their easy journeying, the long-ship

unable to take them further. Machar would return to Iona, for no one knew how long it would be before Colum's party would get back. There was a great unloading of coracles, paddles and gear, and more well-wishing.

At first, the central of the three rivers, opening northwards and called Lochy according to two fishermen they hailed, was deep and smooth-running, although swift, so that they could use their coracles – this enabling them to pass a fishermen's community near the river-mouth without having to explain who they were. This was very relevant, apart from avoiding danger, for Colum recognised that any major attempts at conversion at this stage would be unwise until they had seen King Brude; also unnecessary delay could allow word of their coming to get ahead of them perhaps, and prejudice their cause. So there was little advantage meantime in any unnecessary association with larger local communities, which might well be inimical anyway.

The eight of them paddled their way upstream, having to work quite hard against the current. The river was wide and without rapids, the mountains rising steeply on the west, less so and more wooded on the east. Not all would be as smooth as this, they recognised. Inexpert paddlers held the others up, but practice would improve that.

About four miles up, with the light fading, they had had enough, more especially Kenneth of Achabo, the oldest of them. On the west a deep, steep glen divided the mountain barrier, bringing in a rushing peat-brown torrent which no coracle could have negotiated. There was a small settlement at the mouth; but they did not need food yet and chose to go on a little further before pulling in to the wooded east bank to camp for the night.

That evening, sitting round a well-doing fire of dead pine branches, they heard wolves howling, for the first time, an unchancy sound – and one that drew nearer as the night got darker. A little concerned, for this was something of which they had had no experience but had heard alarming tales, there was some suggestion that they should perhaps cross to the other, steeper side of the river, or even go back to the village. But Colum was dismissive. They were here on God's purposes, were they not? He certainly would not allow any of His animal creation to impede it – whatever apostate man, made in His own image, might try. Nevertheless when, presently, Lugbe grasped his master's arm and pointed silently to the nearest woodland shadow where twin red pinpoints of light reflecting their fire gleamed at them, and then jabbed his finger further over again and then again, even Colum felt that they had better take some precautions. He suggested that they might build up their coracles and paddles into a semi-circle, close to the riverside, and then move their fire to within this, there to sleep, but one always to remain awake to keep the fire blazing. Some spare branches would help their barricade. All agreed that this might be wise.

Colum said that he would take the watch two hours before dawn, the most trying one. Seven of them slept. At some stage of the night the red eyes disappeared. Bishop Cormac, who had the watch just before Colum's, decided to let that man sleep on; but he awoke of his own accord. No wolves? Then he would do some praying.

Another three strenuous miles in the morning and they were able to launch out into another and narrower loch, still long and with the mountains pressing even closer. This made fairly easy paddling, and they felt that they were getting on very satisfactorily. This vast Glen More was a major help for travelling. They reckoned that they must be halfway to Inverness, and so far with no problems save inquisitive wolves.

But at the head of this narrow loch, their easy passage stopped abruptly. There was no large river flowing in from the north, only small burns coming in steeply on either side. One was just deep enough to take their coracles, but across this a barrier of timber was stretched, roped fast at both ends, with nothing accidental about it. There were houses nearby.

As the missionaries were discussing what to do, whether to go and enquire at the houses or just to lift their coracles over the barrier and proceed, a group of men came down to the water's edge, to wave and shout at them, led by a stout, fierce-looking character with a bull-neck and threatening manner. Colum paddled nearer to speak to him.

"Who are you?" this individual demanded. "Who enters my land unbidden?"

"Friends. From Ireland. Travelling to visit Brude mac Maelchon, your High King."

"Ireland? Then, no friends of mine! Scots!"

"No? But friends of your people. And of your king."

"You lie! All Scots are liars! You but want free passage."

"No. Never call me liar!" Colum's voice quivered. "We are not Scots, but from Ireland, I tell you. And we will pay toll, if we must. What is reasonable."

The other barked a laugh and looked at his men, who all grinned. "You will pay what I say – liar!"

No one had ever spoken to Colum mac Felim mac Fergus O'Conall of the Hy-Neill in that fashion in all his days. Fists clenched on his paddle, he all but choked. "Oaf! How dare you!" With an effort he restrained himself. "Let us past, I say – or it is *you* who shall pay, hereafter!"

The stout man gestured towards the coracle and two of his group moved down and into the water, wading out, clearly to grasp the boat.

Colum instinctively drove in his paddle and backed away.

Rejoining the others, he scarcely had to admit his failure. "Barbarous savages!" he exclaimed. "He denies us passage. A river-pirate."

"What shall we do, then?" Kenneth asked. "We cannot turn back now."

"We can lift our coracles over this barrier and paddle on, can we not?" That was Abbot Comgall.

Wordlessly Colum pointed. A little way up beyond the timber-boom, a couple of boats were drawn up at the stream's bank. Local men in those would quickly overtake coracles paddled against the current.

"Did he not say to pay?" Cormac asked. "I thought that I heard that."

"We do not pay that ruffian!" Colum's jaw was set, and he had a determined jaw.

The others did not argue.

"What, then?"

"We go back, yes – a little way. Down the loch. Then land, and carry our coracles back. To pass this village. They were made to be carried, were they not? Then return to the stream, higher up."

That was accepted. They turned back, to jeers and fist-shakings from the shore.

Half a mile down the loch, where a wooded headland hid them, they put inshore. They would have preferred the other, west side, for those men had been on this east side; but there were woodlands here only on this side, on the other bare hill-slopes where they would be seen.

So it was a matter of packing their gear into woven bags, slinging these on their backs, and then each man hoisting his coracle on top of that, to carry like a snail its shell, using the paddles to hold down the slings across their chests. They had practised this on Iona, but now, doing it in earnest, it was rather different, the load seeming heavier and more awkward. And once they started their walking, they knew the difference more direly still. For before they had walked on sands and tracks and level ground, not over wooded hillsides. To remain unseen from the lochside and riverside they had to proceed some distance up before heading northwards again, and there the going was rough indeed, thick undergrowth, fallen trees, outcropping rock and generally broken ground, with burns innumerable to cross, difficult enough going for unburdened men, but carrying coracles and all their belongings a major trial. Kenneth of Achabo in particular found it almost too much and was soon labouring heavily, stumbling, even falling. Colum grew anxious for him.

They came across the occasional path or track, made by deer no doubt; but most of these tended to lead upwards or downwards rather than contouring along, where the beasts went down to drink probably, so were only of marginal help – although they did, at times, deem it worthwhile to go down one and up another rather than labour straight along. It was all grievously time- and strength-consuming. Godly as they sought to be, they cursed those men and their barrier.

They reckoned that a mile up the riverside from its mouth ought to be sufficient for safety; but it took them a long time to get that far and they were weary indeed when at length they re-entered their coracles. But now they found this stream very different from the rivers they had used hitherto, shallower as well as narrower and swifter-running, with rapids occasionally. It was clear that this was no channel between two lochs but a true mountain torrent pouring down the glen for them to mount.

So the hard work must continue, beating against the current, dodging rocks and frequently making portages past rapids and small waterfalls. They did not get very far before dusk halted them, thankfully. At least they had seen no more communities on the way. Wary now of the local inhabitants and not wishing to draw attention to themselves, they did not risk lighting a fire. But with nightfall they could hear wolves beginning to howl again and deemed precautions necessary. Casting about they found not exactly an island in the stream but a spot where a massive tree had fallen into the water and where the current had built up a substantial bank of silt and small stones behind it. If they huddled close, this ought to be large enough to hold them and at the same time keep any wolves at a distance.

They made a less cheerful company that night. Despite all the energy expended, they had covered only a very short distance, they had met with opposition and they had discovered just how difficult travel in wooded mountain country could be.

It made an uncomfortable night for them all on that constricted raft, on to which any wolves would have to approach one by one along the gangway of the fallen tree. Not that they saw any wolves, nor even their gleaming eyes, however much they heard them. They did not actually take watch about this time, but in fact most of them were awake much of the time.

Colum wondered. Brude's armies had come down this Glen More, he had been assured. How had *they* come, then? Not in coracles, that was certain. There must be a route, better than this, for marching men. Either it was much higher, above the tree-line; or else it was on the other side, which was much less wooded than this. In the morning, he decided, they should cross over and investigate, for they could scarcely continue as they had done this day.

Stiff and chilled, they were glad to start early. The river itself was still impossible to paddle up, but at least they could find a pool to take their coracles across. At the other side, leaving the others with the boats, Colum and Lugbe set off directly uphill into the scrub and bushes of the mountainside.

They had to go quite some distance up the foothill slopes before, sure enough, they came on a quite broad track, well enough defined and clearly fairly frequently used, with horse and cattle droppings evident. This, then, must be their road hereafter, with due diversions to avoid the haunts of men as far as was possible – although all the dwellers in this Glen More might not be of the quality of those river-pirates.

One man always ahead some distance as scout, the party proceeded at this level, finding the going infinitely easier even though the weather had turned unpleasant, thin chilling rain, and the coracles were still all too awkward to carry, however carefully designed. There appeared to be no villages or even single houses in this difficult section of the great valley, where clearly they were rising to a summit or watershed, not to be called a pass, no cattle or sheep grazing. Deer they saw in plenty, great-antlered stags and the smaller roe-deer; also wild goats and many lesser creatures, such as squirrels, blue hares, foxes and an animal like a large dark-brown weasel. But, thankfully, no wolves and better still, no boars. Perhaps the former only revealed themselves at night.

Presently Diarmit, taking his turn ahead, halted to wait for the others. In front of them the track dropped steeply into something of a deep ravine – and when they got to the foot of this, they discovered that the stream there was flowing the other way, northwards. So somehow they had parted from their former river and now were over the watershed. This stream was no better for coracles than the other, however. But it was somehow heartening to have crossed the divide, the *Drumalbyn* or Spine of Alba, that the Dalriada people had spoken of.

Colum decided to go ahead with Diarmit, but not too far. River and road grew ever nearer. Then, in a mile or two they saw their first house since leaving the loch, a low-browed hut with byre and barn attached, a man watching their approach from a doorway. Nothing looked in any way dangerous. They went forward to speak.

The man, evidently a cow-herd, was friendly enough even though his dogs growled. They told him that they were travelling to King Brude's court, and asked where they were and how much further to Inverness. The man shrugged. He had never been to Inverness, but knew only that it was a long way. Trying again, Colum asked how far to the head of Loch Ness, at the foot of which was the capital. This the other could answer; half a day's walk – perhaps more, with those to carry, and he pointed at their coracles, clearly interested in their construction.

They agreed that the boats were a burden, although less heavy than they looked, the paddles almost more trouble. But they had been most useful in getting them thus far.

The man nodded, but added that they would not be much protection against the Water Horse.

They eyed him questioningly. What was that? Water Horse . . . ?

"The Water Horse – you have not heard of the monster in the great loch, masters? The terrible one! The monstrous horse that kills?"

The remainder of the party had come up now. They joined in the exclamations, questions, disbelief.

The cow-herd looked at them all pityingly. He gestured at their coracles. "The Horse will chew those up. So, if you go on the loch, keep close to the shore." Obviously the man was in earnest.

Colum said, "This, this creature, so terrible? You have seen it?"

"No-o-o. *I* have not. But others have. Those who lived to tell."

"What does it look like?"

"How big?"

"Where, on this Loch Ness?" They questioned.

But the man could tell them little more. Only that it was a monster, with the head of a horse but a body otherwise, and large. Like a dragon, men said. Since none of his hearers had ever seen a dragon, they were little the wiser.

Colum assured that they would look out for the Water Horse. But he was more concerned about less picturesque dangers. Men. Were the people of Loch Ness-side apt to be hostile to strangers – as back there at the river-barrier?

The other was interested in their experiences. That was the chieftain Leot, of Oich, a hard and cruel man, much feared. Oich was his loch and river; but his territory did not extend up as far as this. No, there were few like Leot, the gods be praised! Had they had to pay him dearly? As well that they had no women with them, for women Leot always took, there and then, in front of their menfolk, before he would allow them passage.

Colum grimly declared that he would remember Leot of Oich.

One more fact they learned from the cow-herd. Here, his house, was the very centre of Alba, midway between the oceans, the great divide. Five miles more and they would be at Loch Ness.

They left him with their blessing.

They had plenty to talk about thereafter – and more breath with which to do it, as steadily the road dipped downwards. Needless to say, this of the Water Horse produced most discussion. No doubt it was in truth just some druidical mummery designed to terrify and impress the ignorant peasantry. None really took it seriously. However, they soon had to consider that there might be something in it.

Presently the mountains opened out and the blue waters of a wide loch became evident ahead, and in sun and cloud, they came down to level land and greener country. At the loch-head was boggy ground where a larger river came in from the east. There were cattle grazing in the reedy marshland – but no houses. Then they perceived that what they had assumed to be a scatter of islets not far offshore were evidently, by their peculiar and regular shapes, not exactly that. They were artificial, built up of tree-trunks and stones and turf, with small houses upon them, each surrounded by a palisade of wood. The visitors had heard of these artificial islands which the Picts made, called crannogs, but had never seen any. When they observed a young man seeking to spear salmon whilst wading in the river-mouth – he already had two fine fish, both of which they bought from him – and asked about the crannogs and why they went to the trouble of building these when they could erect their houses on dry land, they were told that it was because of the Water Horse. Surprised, they enquired further. If there was in fact such a creature, would not a house in the loch itself be the worst place for it? Which the creature could easily reach? And were told that the palisades, built directly up from the water, prevented it from landing. Whereas it could easily land on any shore.

So the Water Horse was real enough, seemingly, to have demanded all this labour.

The young man, like the other, was interested in their coracles. Yes, he agreed, never having such small ones, it was the quickest way to travel. If not the safest. When, laughing, Colum asked if he was referring to this Water Horse, the other nodded seriously. They would be wise to paddle close to land, and at night sleep well up the hillside if not in houses. The missionaries thought that wolves would be more dangerous, but the other shook his head.

Glad of the salmon, and relieved that the people did not seem unfriendly, they pushed their coracles into the water and paddled out into great Loch Ness. There was said to be twenty-five miles of it. There was no current against them here and they made good time. The loch was over a mile wide, the mountains thronging closer on the left than on the right. They did not keep so very close to either shore, and saw nothing more monstrous than ducks and other waterfowl.

Encouraged by the friendliness of the cowherd and fisherman, they pulled in to pass the night at a place in the lee of a little headland on the east or right shore, where they saw three small cot-houses. A fair-sized burn came in nearby and they were preparing to set up camp beside it when Lugbe discovered a spring bubbling up like a well, with a stone beside it bearing one of the strange Pictish carved symbols. So good looked the water that he scooped up a handful, and found it ice-cold and delicious. He beckoned the others over, and they settled down beside it, all sampling the water, so refreshing after all their paddling. They were building a fire to cook their salmon, and Colum was about to go to the nearest cot-house for milk, when he was forestalled. A woman approached them from the house, looking respectful but concerned. Not to encamp there, strangers, she told them. And especially not to drink the water from that spring – never that.

Surprised, they asked why not?

"Because it is evil," she said. "Accursed. It will strike you with leprosy or blindness. Do you not see the sign?" And she pointed to the symbol-stone.

"Is that what that means?" Colum asked. "Leprosy? Surely not. Nor blindness. Leprosy is evil, yes. But it could never be carried by water. This spring is good, sweet, clearly coming up through rock – excellent."

"Accursed!" the woman repeated. "Evil. Of the Horned One, who gives leprosy." And she ducked a hasty little bow to the well and stone. "Many have suffered and died. And gone blind."

"Not because of this water, I assure you! See!" Colum stooped to scoop up another handful of the water to his lips. "It is as good water as any I have ever tasted. There is mineral in it, I think."

"Death!" the woman amended.

"Who told you that? The Druids?"

She did not answer.

"I think that it was the Druids. For their own profit!"

"It is of old. Always evil."

"Yes. But Druids are of old, also! Tell me – do the Druids

251

offer to try to *cure* the drinkers of this water? Of their leprosy or blindness? At a price!"

The other shrugged. "They do what they can, yes. They seek the gods' aid. Sometimes they succeed."

"But at their price?"

She spread her hands. "A calf. Or a lamb. Or some days' labour. Small price to pay not to be a leper."

Colum shook his head. "It is a deceit. A cruel fraud. The Druids play on men's fears. There is no ill in God's water, His good gift to men."

"Many have suffered and died, master. Whom the Druids could not save."

"Or did not pay! They would have suffered or died otherwise. Not from this water. From other sicknesses. And their fears. See – I bless this spring, in the name of the Lord Jesus Christ." Colum made the sign of the cross; and Cormac, smiling, dipped the leathern cup he used for baptising into the water, and drinking from it first, poured another cupful over his head.

A man had come up, to join the woman. He spoke. "You are of these Christians? We have heard of them."

"Only good, I hope, friend? Not that your Druids will speak well of us. For we come to end their rule of fear and cruelty. *We* bring God's love, and the blessing of His Son Jesus Christ. To *you*, and to all Albannach."

They eyed him unspeaking.

"Would you, friends, not prefer to worship a God of love and kindness, not cruelty? Of hope, not fear? Of everlasting life hereafter, not death and torment? Of giving, not taking? Would you not?"

The man inclined his head, but doubtfully.

"It is joy. And peace. And fulfilment. All to be yours."

"How, master?"

"If you but believe. Believe in Christ Jesus."

"How can I believe in what I do not know?"

Colum stooped to take Cormac's cup and scoop up more of the water. He drank of it, and then filled another for the man. "Drink – and believe," he said.

The other drew back. "No!" he exclaimed. And the woman shook her head.

"See – there is no harm in it, only good." Colum stepped into the little pool below the spring itself and splattered the water about him, washing his feet. "Believe, man – believe!"

"I cannot, master . . ."

"Very well. We go to Inverness, to see your High King, Brude mac Maelchon. To give *him* Christ's message of hope and love. When we come back, and you see us, and that the water has done us no hurt, will you then believe?"

They looked at each other, and the man nodded. "Then, yes."

"Good. Then I will hold you to that. We will come to see you on our return this way. And tell you of Christ."

They left it at that. Colum constructed a rude cross out of two pieces of pine-wood and set this up at the well above the symbol-stone.

Comgall wondered whether it was worth all this trouble just to convince a pair of humble peasants. But Colum asserted that it was. They were as important as others in God's eyes. And they would tell others, nothing more sure. They would be agog to learn whether the visitors had become lepers or gone blind. Such as this could serve the cause well.

The cottagers were sufficiently interested and friendly to bring them food and milk thereafter. Asked about the Water Horse, they declared that it was a great menace – but fortunately they were protected against its attacks. When their hearers wondered how that was, they informed that a Druid had given them a charm which protected them from the monster, a carved stone ball.

"Ha! One of those!" Colum exclaimed. "*Gave*, you say? Or sold?"

They admitted that they had had to pay well for it.

The missionaries were learning about these Druids.

Next morning, promising to call in on the way back, they resumed their journey down-loch, to warnings about the monster. They were now uncertain as to whether to take the Water Horse seriously, or to deem it just another profit-making invention of the Druids. They certainly saw nothing unusual as they paddled down the long loch.

In mid-afternoon they noted, on the left or west side, a large bay, the only one they had come across, fully a mile wide, with at its head a broch, a ramparted fort or dun and a sizeable township behind. They were thinking to pass this by, for safety's sake, when suddenly Colum changed his mind.

"Let us go in to this place," he declared. "Something tells

me that we should go there. Perhaps there is something for us to do. Some task, some opportunity . . ."

His fellow-travellers expressed reservations, but already he had swung his coracle round to head into the bay. The little flotilla followed, however doubtfully.

A number of boats were drawn up on a steep beach below the fort and broch, where the coracles landed. As they approached, they had been aware of a strange sound, a chanting which rose and fell, rose and fell, not tuneful like one of their own psalms but moaning, dirge-like, yet with a menacing note to it. The last time that Colum had heard a similar sound had been before the Battle of Cooldrevny, when the Druids had paraded in front of the Hy-Neill host. And, sure enough, hardly were the missionaries stepped out of their craft when a horn began to blow up there, behind the fort, in time with the chanting, rising and falling.

His companions were for retiring out into mid-loch forthwith, but Colum was determined. They could do so if they wished, he said, but he was going on to see what transpired. There was something here which concerned him, he was convinced.

Cormac declared that he would go on also; and none of the others actually turned back.

The fort, which was quite large, towered on a rocky bank above the waterside, not any hilltop dun but a strong position nevertheless. The newcomers climbed the bank by a series of steps cut in the rock, on the north side, and so gained access to a sort of wide terrace on the landward side of the fort. This proved to be full of folk, men, women and children, just standing, gazing towards the gateway of the fort itself. Between them and the ramparts a group of robed figures were parading up and down, one blowing a horn, some bearing poles with skulls and other symbols, some just chanting, Druids obviously.

None paid the visitors any attention. Colum picked out a man to question. What went on here, he asked?

The other looked at him strangely. "Do you not know? It is the Lord Emchat. He will not die," he said.

"Will not die? How mean you, friend?"

"He will not go. His spirit is sore troubled and will not let him go."

"Then why say that he is dying, if he is not?"

"He is dying, yes. Has been for days. All but gone, many times. But always he cries out in fear and will not go."

"Why all these to watch? And these Druids?"

"The Lord Emchat is greatly beloved, stranger. He is old and has ruled us for long, ruled us well. We would see him go in peace. He is torn with pain and fear. The Druids are doing all they can . . ."

"He is a good man, this Emchat? To be so well loved."

"None better. Kind. A good master. He deserves a good end. But the devils of the loch and the hills and the springs are fighting over him as to who shall have him, the Druids say . . ."

Colum glanced at Cormac and the others. "Here is work for us, I think," he said. "Why God brought us here. Come." And he pushed forward through the crowd.

They passed the Druid procession but were ignored. They entered the gateway in the outer rampart and were not challenged. At the inner gate guards stared at them, but Colum's authoritative bearing and purposeful striding presumably impressed them and they asked no questions. The hall-house door stood open ahead. To it the eight marched.

Within, the hall was crowded also, with servants and others, the great table set as for feasting, with skulls, each in a ring of candles, as decoration – presumably a death-banquet. All were gazing towards the north end of the large apartment where was a shut door.

Without hesitation Colum moved through the press, to the door, opened it and passed through, the others in his wake.

The room beyond was hot and stuffy, with torches blazing, and contained a large bed. Round this about a dozen people stood or sat, men and women. On the bed a shrunken figure lay huddled, moaning. One of the standing persons was a robed Druid, holding an entire skeleton, the bones realistically joined up by cord, and being rattled to the timing of the chanting outside. Otherwise there was silence in the chamber.

At the door opening, a youngish man, red-headed and well built, turned to look. They all did, save for the one on the bed, but the young man alone spoke.

"Who are you?" he asked, but dully, wearily, rather than angrily.

"We are sent by the Lord Jesus Christ, son of the Most High God, to aid the Lord Emchat," Colum said, with entire confidence.

255

The young man did not answer that, nor did any there comment, but all stared.

The newcomers moved over to the bed. The figure thereon was twitching as well as moaning but did not seem to be fully conscious, the eyes open but only the whites showing, a white-bearded, wild-haired old man, all skin and bone.

Taking the small bronze wedge-shaped saint's-bell from a pocket of his robe, the one he had made to replace that left in the cave at Ellary, Colum shook it above the recumbent figure. "Heed me, friend Emchat, heed me," he intoned. "I am Colum mac Felim, come from a far land to bring you the peace of Almighty God which passes all understanding. Heed, Emchat."

Whether it was the musical tinkling of the bell or the commanding, vibrant voice which spoke, something stirred the sick man and he straightened out a little and then gradually brought his eyes into focus, looking up. His lips moved but said nothing.

"You are Emchat, of this place? And sorely need help. Is it not so?"

The nod of the white head was only just discernible.

"So, Emchat. I am the Abbot Colum, of Christ's Church. From Ireland, beyond the seas. Sent by Christ God to give you what you need. You understand?"

The other's rheumy eyes searched the speaker's face. Again the lips moved, without sound.

"You have heard of Christ God? And the Christians?"

Again the faint nod.

"He is a God of love, not hatred. Of kindness, not evil. Of hope and not fear. He comes to you now. What is it that you need, Emchat? What is your wish?"

There was the faintest of whispers.

Colum bent lower. "I did not hear. No doubt God did – but I did not. Say again, Emchat."

"To . . . die . . . in . . . peace." The four words, wide-spaced, were just to be heard.

There were gasps and exclamations from around the bed.

"So you shall, friend – so you shall. That I promise you. But – you must believe. Do you believe? *Can* you believe?"

The other stared up uncomprehendingly but beseechingly.

"Believe, Emchat, that the Lord Christ Jesus, Son of the Almighty God, can give you peace now. And life hereafter, of joy and love. You have been a good man, they say, such as Christ loves. So He has sent us to you, in your need. The Druids and the devils cannot aid you, but He can. Or we would not be here. Can you believe that?"

The nod was a little stronger.

"Good. Christ Himself died, and not in peace, for men. In love, offered Himself as sacrifice. For you and for me and for all. And went to prepare a place for those who show love. Believe that, and you are saved. Can you?"

The eyes closed and there was no answer.

Colum, in his urgency, actually reached to shake the frail shoulder. "Emchat – hear me. God will give you the strength and faith you need. Then let you go in peace. Heed me. Are you prepared to believe? Willing?"

The eyes opened, and after a moment there was another nod.

"Praise be! Then say it. Say I believe in Christ Jesus. Who can save me, now and hereafter."

That was asking too much. The lips trembled and the head nodded. That was all.

"Try man, Emchat! *Try!* Then, go in peace."

Slowly words came, thick, hesitant. "I . . . believe . . ." No more.

"It is enough," Cormac exclaimed, at Colum's back.

"Yes. Enough." He turned. "Water. Give me water."

The youngish man who had spoken to them hastened to bring a beaker of water. Colum, taking it, made the sign of the cross above it.

"In the name of Father, Son and Holy Spirit, I bless this water. It is holy." Dipping his fingers in, he sprinkled some of the water on that straggle of white hair. "In the name of God the Holy Trinity, I baptise you, Emchat, into Christ's Church. You are His, now. He waits for you. Go in peace."

The old man did not speak. But slowly a smile spread over his wasted features.

All around people murmured and moved. The young man came forward, to grasp an old hand.

"Father . . . !" he exclaimed chokingly.

The smile persisted although no words came.

The son turned to Colum. "Stranger, Christian – I thank you!" he got out. "He has not smiled, not for long. I thank you!"

257

"Do not thank me, friend. Thank his Lord, and yours, Jesus Christ."

"I am Virolec mac Emchat of this Urquhart. He has been in sore affliction, torment. And death denied him . . ."

"He has been *waiting*, Virolec. For his Saviour's grace. Now he has it. The gift to all who believe. He can now go in peace."

"I think that he has gone already!" Cormac said.

They turned back to the bed. The smile was still there, but changed a little, for the bony jaw had dropped somewhat, to part the lips more widely. And the eyes had lost such gleam as they had had.

The young man bent over his father, close. "He, he does not breathe!" he declared. "It is done! He is gone. At last! In peace. Here is a wonder, magic . . ."

"No magic, friend. Only God's love. Your father has gone to a better place than this."

Others surging forward to the bed now jostled the Druid and caused his skeleton to rattle again. Colum turned at the sound, stared at the man, and then raised a commanding hand, to point to the door. "You! Go!" he ordered sternly.

Without a word the Druid left them.

Presently, after much talk and comment, they all moved out into the hall, to spread the good news. Virolec called for food and drink to be brought for the visitors and said that there would be feasting later, at which they would be the honoured guests. Acknowledging, Colum suggested that, in that case, those candle-ringed skulls should be removed. Also that the Druids outside should be requested to cease their chanting and horn-blowing.

Virolec went to do this, and to inform the crowd of the joyous outcome of the strangers' visit.

That evening, after the banquet, changed from a death-feast to one of thanksgiving, the missionaries took the opportunity to expound to the grateful new Lord of Urquhart the basic principles of the Christian faith, and had a receptive audience.

Well pleased with their day, they retired to comfortable beds in an attached guest-house within the ramparts. This Urquhart was evidently an important lordship.

In the morning, Colum offered Christian burial for Emchat; and while the family cairn was being prepared for this, Bishop Cormac baptised Virolec, his wife and child and most of his household, to much praise and psalm-singing. Then the burial-service upon a nearby knoll – although it was not exactly burial, for the body was not interred in the earth but placed in a stone coffin and taken inside a large artificial mound of stones containing stone-flagged and lined passages, these housing other coffins, each with its carved symbol stone.

When the little ceremony at the cairn was over, Colum pointed to one of these memorial stones and suggested that if they were going to make one for Emchat it should bear Christ's cross upon it, the first such in all Alba almost certainly. Virolec agreed gladly.

They left Urquhart, in their coracles, to a great send-off, but not without warnings as to the Water Horse. These Colum tended to dismiss as fantasy. They would be back.

Colum mac Felim was not always right. Some seven miles on they came, without incident, to the foot of the great loch, where it suddenly narrowed in to the River Ness. And here they were held up, not by any artificial barrier but by a great to-do of shouting and gesticulations from a crowd of people, a divided crowd for they were on both sides of the water, separated by perhaps one hundred and fifty yards. Clearly the visitors were being urged to land; but there appeared to be nothing threatening about the gestures. The coracles were nearest the west bank, so they put in there.

Well before they touched the shore they could hear that the shouts directed at them were warnings, and that the burden of them was the Water Horse, the Water Horse. They gazed around but could see nothing unusual.

Landing, they moved enquiringly up to the crowd – which was keeping notably well back from the waterside. Some of the folk were looking towards the river and loch but others were turned inwards, some stooping and even kneeling. Intrigued, Colum led on.

People were talking excitedly and pointing – but the new arrivals could discern nothing to look at. Colum asked what it was all about.

Many voices answered him, but one prevailed, that of a burly grey-haired man. "The Water Horse could have had you!" he declared, almost accusingly. "In those little boats. It could cut them in two with one bite. And you with them."

"I think not, friend," Colum returned. "We are Christians, and protected by Christ God. We fear no such inventions of the Druids."

The man hooted. "Christians! Stranger – the Horse would find you as tasty a bite as any other!"

Others loudly confirmed that.

Bishop Cormac spoke. "Good people, we have been warned about your Water Horse all the way down this long loch, and have seen no sign of it. We can scarcely believe in it."

"More fools you are, then . . ."

"Unbelief will not serve you . . ."

"Ask Donald there, if *he* believes!"

"Aye – ask Donald!" The last speaker pointed towards the inner huddle of stooping and kneeling men.

Colum looked and moved over. Pushing through the press, he saw that they were bending over a recumbent figure. Closer still, he perceived that the body was contorted and blood-stained; indeed one leg had been cut off at mid-thigh. The man was not moving.

Colum knelt, to peer. "Dead?" he asked.

Some there nodded, some shook heads. There seemed to be some doubt.

Colum reached out a hand. The body was warm. He leant over close, but could detect no breathing. Someone had tied up the stump of the leg tightly, to staunch the bleeding, but not entirely effectively.

"How long ago?" he asked.

Not long ago, he was told. This was Donald the ferryman. His house was just across the water. He had been rowing over, to collect a traveller, when the Horse surfaced, overturned the ferry-boat and attacked Donald, biting off his leg.

All there muttered protective incantations and made hasty signs, glancing about them fearfully.

Colum said that he knew something of wounds and their treatment, although he feared that it was too late in this case. He put his ear to the bloodied chest and shook his head. But he turned the body over, to kneel astride it, to supply in and out pressure to the lungs, at the same time calling for someone to tighten the binding on the raw stump.

It was the Abbot Kenneth who did this, although he too declared that he thought life extinct. Lugbe, standing above them, announced that that woman who was screaming, screaming, across the water, they told him was the victim's wife. Could they be doing anything for her?

"We could fetch her over, at least," Colum suggested. "Poor woman, I fear . . ."

"I will go and get her," Lugbe said.

"Yes. She should be here . . ."

"The Water Horse!" somebody exclaimed. "You cannot go. It will get you."

"I think not, friend . . ."

"No! No!" There was a chorus of dissent and warning. The monster was not far away. It could strike again.

Colum declared that Lugbe would be safe.

All there, save the visitors, decried this; and Colum, ever mindful of opportunities for the furthering of their message, declared that the Christian God of love would ensure Lugbe's and the woman's safety. When there was scoffing at that, he rose, leaving the body to Kenneth, saying that he would go over himself, in his own coracle, to prove the matter.

Now it was Lugbe's turn to protest. He had volunteered to go. It was *his* suggestion that the woman should be helped. It was his privilege to show these people the truth.

Colum acquiesced, but said that he would go with him to the water's edge and pronounce a blessing, that all might hear, see and believe.

So together they moved back down to the coracles, most of the crowd watching in alarm and agitation. The stretch of water before them was innocent, disturbed by nothing more than a swirling current that indicated depth. On the far side folk were still gathered around the wailing woman.

At the riverside, Colum raised his hand and his voice. "Hear, ye all!" he cried. "Hear me, Colum mac Felim, servant of the Living God, the Father of the Lord Christ. And of us all. In the name of Jesus Christ, I declare these waters safe, to believers. If there be evil in them, such evil to yield to God's power. Yield, I say! Amen." And he made the sign of the cross, and waved Lugbe to his coracle.

There were gasps and exclamations and head-shakings as the young man launched out cheerfully, paddle busy.

The current was strong and Lugbe had to work hard to keep from drifting downstream, northwards. But nothing save that current delayed his passage.

There was considerable outcry and comment on both sides of the water as he landed.

Despite that, Lugbe thereafter appeared to be having some

261

difficulty in convincing the woman to come back with him; or it may have been that her companions were seeking to restrain her. But eventually the pair of them moved down to the coracle. None of the others accompanied them.

The coracle was really a one-man craft, and getting the two of them in was not easy, with the woman reluctant anyway. The craft then sat very low in the water – which brought forth more head-shakings from the onlookers.

Lugbe pushed off, and now the coracle was more sluggish in countering the current, and noticeably began to drift north-wards however hard he paddled. Even with only one hundred and fifty yards to cross, it was obvious that he would come to land some way downstream. Colum was calculating how far, when yells from all around brought his head round. Folk were pointing as well as shouting, some indeed pressing back, horror and alarm prevailing.

Looking where they pointed, at the river-mouth, Colum saw what he thought at first was a log, or a couple of logs, bobbing in the current. Then he realised that these were making a distinct V-shaped ripple much more definite than could be caused by any current. And there were three black humps now, not two. They were moving fast, and gleamed a little in the sunlight. Even as he stared, from just in front of the first hump and V of the ripple there was a commotion of the water and out of it rose still another hump, which turned into an arching long neck supporting a head shaped like that of a horse, narrow, with flaring nostrils and what could be either ears or small horns set well back.

Colum blinked away his disbelief. The creature existed. It was coming near, at extraordinary speed. It was very large, obviously, for the last hump was many feet behind the head. It might be part of a tail, of course. The impression given was not so much of bulk as of length and serpentine motion. And speed. Clearly it was heading right into the river, and so for the coracle.

Amidst all the excitement, transmitted to himself now, Colum took a grip of himself. Lugbe and the woman were in evident danger. Drawing a great breath, he raised hand again, and shouted at the pitch of his powerful lungs.

"Go! Go! Back, creature – back! In the name of Almighty God, Creator of *you* as of us all – go! Turn! Leave us. Back, I say, in the name of Jesus Christ God!"

For dire moments thereafter the monster came on, and in those moments even Colum's faith wavered. Then, in an almost graceful motion that head and arching neck curved down into the river again, and there were only three humps, still moving fast. Then two, then one and then only the swirling water.

Amidst the cries of all, Colum waited, heart in mouth – all except Lugbe, who was paddling furiously. Would the beast surface again? Or was this submerging preparatory to getting underneath the coracle and overturning it? Or . . . had it been diverted, indeed?

Fearfully all counted the seconds. Lugbe in his desperation was now not so much trying to counter the current as to use it to carry him frankly sideways, slantwise across. No extra ripple disturbed the swirling surface.

Hardly daring to breathe, some part of Colum's mind assessed and calculated. Surely by now, at the speed it had been going, the Water Horse would have reached the coracle? Would it rise beyond the boat, attack from the far side? Or would it drive them into the shallows? Lugbe was fully two-thirds across.

More vital seconds, and Colum at last drew a long, quivering breath. "Thank you, God!" he exclaimed. "Thank you, my God!" The coracle was almost ashore. And the River Ness flowed on smoothly. Whether the creature had indeed turned back, or merely submerged to the bottom, there was no knowing. But it remained out of sight.

The other missionaries were racing down the bank to where Lugbe was disembarking; but Colum remained standing. He was actually trembling, something that he had not done, save perhaps in anger, for long years. He swallowed. Almost he had failed his Master, almost disbelieved, his faith tested and found less than strong. Never again, after this – no, never again!

Soon they were all around him, praising, congratulating, applauding, his own colleagues and some of the crowd. Almost harshly he rejected the adulation.

"Praise *God* – and seek mercy on me, a sinner!" he exclaimed hotly, and mystified everyone. Then he recollected his duty towards the sad widow whom Lugbe was escorting up to the corpse. He went with them, schooling himself to the pastor's part. Although Cormac would be better at that . . .

The Water Horse made no further appearance meantime.

A somewhat chaotic period followed, with the poor victim and his widow tending rather to be overlooked in all the excitement, comment and acclaim. Colum and Lugbe, the heroes of the hour, felt that they could not just depart on their way to Inverness – and needless to say, the former did not fail to see the opportunity for further conversions. So they decided to stay the night at this place, which proved to be named Dochfour Beg, and use the respect, even awe, in which they were now held, to expound the Gospel message. Also they suggested Christian burial for Donald the ferryman, the widow tearfully agreeing; and Cormac performed this that same evening. There appeared to be no lord, chief nor hall-house here – nor, evidently, a Druid. At least none showed himself. They slept in various cabins and hay barns.

Eight miles more, they learned, to Brude's capital.

14

The Ness was a strange river indeed, especially to be so major a waterway in importance and in breadth, if not in length. After its start at the foot of Loch Ness, in less than a mile it widened again into another very narrow loch, this named Dochfour, which extended for another mile. Thereafter the river proper flowed in a well-wooded vale, the mountains now drawn well back, only a further six miles to salt-water. This brief but main part of its course was through what clearly was fairly populous country, with villages and small communities dotting both banks, standing-stones and stone-circles in evidence where there were knolls and eminences clear of trees. There were no real rapids nor waterfalls to negotiate although the river made a number of great bends.

The coracles had rounded four of these major loops before there was a notable change in the scene, the land opening out before them into comparatively level country, the woodland retreating. They could not actually see the sea, or at least the

Inverness Firth, ahead, but they could sense it at no great distance. Between it and them lay what was obviously a major town, occupying both sides of the river but mainly on the east bank; while to the west, with the ground rising gradually to foothills, beyond the last of the houses were a series of isolated hillocks and green heights, all seemingly crowned by forts or ramparted structures. Furthest away, nearest the levelling off which indicated the firth, and some distance west of the river was, not the highest but certainly the most prominent of the hills, in that it was crowded with buildings, above the towers of which, even at more than a mile off, many banners could be seen to be blowing in the breeze, almost certainly King Brude's fortress and palace.

As the travellers approached the town, which seemed to be almost as large as Strathclyde's Dunbarton, and over which hung the smoke of fires innumerable, they were prepared to be halted and questioned. But nothing of the sort developed, and soon there were thronging houses on either side, the river-banks dotted with landing-stages and boats moored thereto, some of these quite large and obviously for sea-going. Yet there was little of the mercantile, trading aspect of Dunbarton.

Presently they came to a bridge, the first they had seen in Alba, quite long necessarily, and substantially built of massive timbers. Almost certainly this would be the High King's access from his palace to the main part of his capital.

Deeming this to be as far as they should go, by water, they pulled in to the west bank and drew up their coracles, an interested small crowd, mainly women, children and dogs, quickly gathering to watch. From amongst these, Colum asked the way to King Brude's house. As expected, they were directed westwards to the beflagged hill, Craig Phadraig it was called apparently. No hostility was evinced, as yet, and they thought it safe to leave their coracles unattended.

They set off, through the houses and hutments, fish-curing sheds, tanneries, storehouses and workshops, over level ground at first which began to rise, where buildings were terraced, Craig Phadraig now beginning to dominate the scene ahead, rising more steeply. It was not as impressive a site as was Dunbarton's Rock nor Skye's Torvaig, nor yet Conall's Dunadd nor An Tor, but it was larger than any of these, the flattish summit covered by buildings within three sets of ramparts and palisades.

There was fully half a mile of open rising ground after the last of the town's houses before the foot of the craig was reached, undoubtedly left that way as a defensive precaution so that any enemy approach could be observed in good time. By the same token, the missionaries' approach would also be evident, if anyone was interested. When, before they had gone very far, the wailing of horns reached them from ahead, which sounded as though someone *was* interested, the visitors eyed each other. Only Druids, in their experience, used those wailing, sobbing horns. Was their approach responsible? If their welcome was to be druidical, it was unlikely to be helpful. But how could anyone know of their coming?

Comgall said that perhaps they ought not to have lingered at Urquhart and Dochfour Beg, leaving time for hostile messengers to report on them. Colum admitted that this might well be so, although their lingering had been profitable.

The horn-blowing continued for all their way up to the gates of the first line of ramparts. They could not be sure, of course, that it was connected with themselves; it could be part of some druidical ceremonial going on. But when they reached the massive gates and found them shut, they were inclined to relate it to themselves; the more so when they shouted for admittance and received no answer – although they could hear voices at the other side. Surely the approach of eight men would have been noticed? Surely also the High King of All Alba would not always keep the gates of his palace shut and barred, as though besieged?

Colum raised his voice. "I, Colum mac Felim, Prince of Donegal, with the Bishop Cormac O'Lethan and the Abbots Kenneth of Achabo and Comgall of Bangor, all of Ireland, come to visit Brude mac Maelchon, High King of Alba," he cried. "Seeking his presence, we request admission."

There was no answer.

At a loss, they looked at each other.

Colum tried again. "Is the High King here? In residence? We have travelled far to see him. We request audience."

Still he obtained no least reply.

"We are friends. Not enemies. Come in peace."

They waited a little longer, in case the guards who were obviously just on the other side of the doors, had sent for instructions or authority to open. Nothing happened.

Losing patience, Colum went and hammered on the

timbers with his fist. "Are you deaf, within there? *We* are not, and can hear you speaking. Do you keep a prince of the Hy-Neill, a bishop and two abbots of Christ's Church, waiting like beggars? Is this how King Brude behaves?"

When that brought forth no response, Lugbe tugged at the angry Colum's sleeve and pointed up to one side. The earth-and-stone rampart was surmounted by a high palisade of wood. Above this, the heads and shoulders of a number of men had appeared. These were gazing down at them silently. The horns still wailed.

"So – all are not deaf, nor dead, within these walls!" he exclaimed. Then, swallowing his princely wrath, he spoke more civilly. "We seek an audience with King Brude, with important words for him. We have come far. Open to us, friends."

At last he got acknowledgement. A grey-bearded, rather fine-looking man in a colourful robe spoke. "We do not want you here, Christians," he said curtly.

"Ha – so you know of us! And who are your *we*, who do not want us? You are not King Brude, I think?"

"I am Broichan, Arch Druid of All Alba. And we want no Christian trouble-makers here."

"Trouble-makers? Whom do we trouble, Druid? Not the good folk of Loch Ness-side, of Urquhart and Dochfour. They welcomed us. We troubled their Water Horse, perhaps! And the supposed evil spirits of one of your wells. But none other. Nor shall we trouble King Brude. Open to us."

"No! Go! Leave this place, Christians."

"We have not come all this way to leave now, Druid. Without seeing the High King. And since you name us Christians, we name Christ God to you! The power of the Lord Christ is with us. Open, I say, or you and yours will feel it! As the Water Horse felt it, and fled. As the Fell Hound of Skye felt it, and died. Do you wish us to call down Almighty God's wrath upon you?"

The Arch Druid did not answer that, but there sounded altercation from the other side of the gates, voices upraised. Some there were not as confident as this Broichan, it seemed.

Colum remembered what he had said and sworn to at Dochfour. Never again would he doubt. Well, then . . .

He strode forward to the gate-timbers again, and smote them with the palm of his hand four times, up and down and side to side. "I make the sign of Christ's cross on this door," he declared loudly. "It shall open. And woe be to any who would keep it closed! Open, I say, in the name of the Most High!"

There were exclamations from within, shouts, the noise of bars being drawn, and when Colum pushed, the great gates swung wide.

Men stood there, armed men, staring. There were various expressions on their faces, but fear was the most evident.

Colum moved in, smiling genially now, hand outstretched towards the waiting guards, some of whom were making signs to ward off evil. "Thank you, my friends," he said. "That was well done, and wise. Now – take us to King Brude." He did not so much as glance up, right, to where the Arch Druid still stood, with some of his like, on the platform behind the timber palisade.

When the guards looked doubtfully at each other and then up at Broichan, and stood shuffling feet, Colum shrugged.

"Then we go and find him for ourselves," he announced, and moved on past them, his friends following close.

One of the guards, probably the senior there, came on behind. And Broichan and his Druids stepped down from the platform to come after them.

So they climbed up to the second rampart and its gate. This one was open however, although men therein stood watching. As the newcomers drew near, they saw a man running from the gateway uphill towards the last ramparts near the hilltop. The word would be spread. They were not stopped at this gate.

There was still another, open and apparently unattended. Colum was now leading something of a little procession. The horn-blowing had ceased.

Passing through the third gate they saw ahead of them, still at some distance, not one hall-house but three, grouped in a hollow square, over all of which the Boar banners of the High King flew. People were much in evidence in that open square and around. There were many other less imposing buildings, behind and at the sides. This Craig Phardraig was not so much a palace as a walled royal community.

Colum paused just inside the last gateway. This marching up to Brude's hall-door more or less unannounced might not be the best introduction, especially with the resentful Arch

Druid behind. Yet what was the alternative? At least they held the initiative. To wait and let Broichan hurry on and seek to further prejudice their case with Brude would be folly. They could only go on.

The matter was settled for them. Out from the central hall-house emerged a compact group of men, which moved on down towards this gateway, not hurrying but in purposeful fashion. They were led by a tall individual, wearing, above the usual Albannach multi-coloured kilt and leggings, a handsome embroidered tunic of rich golden cloth on the front of which was represented the stylised image of a wild boar, tusked and massive-shouldered.

As the two parties drew nearer, it could be seen that this foremost man was about Colum's own age, of rugged and masterful features and wearing at his throat two heavy gold chains. The gold necklace, not the crown, was the sign and symbol of Celtic kingship; two could only be worn by the High King. More than that became apparent. The leader, who must be Brude himself, had his hand on a sword half-drawn from its sheath. And behind him his well-clad party all had their hands similarly employed. The message was obvious.

This party halted presently to allow the visitors to do the approaching. Out of the corner of his eye, Colum saw Broichan now pressing ahead, and himself moved more quickly, to prevent the Druid from reaching the King first. He held up his hand.

"Hail, Brude mac Maelchon, we greet you with warm respect," he called. "Your fame is known to all. I am Colum mac Felim, come far to see you, Highness."

"They were let in by weakly, fearful guards," Broichan shouted, at the back. "After threatening them evil."

Rather than entering into any undignified wrangling about that, Colum turned and waved a mocking hand towards the Arch Druid, laughing easily.

The High King stood, hand still on sword-hilt, clearly uncertain as to procedure. He did not speak.

"I think that you have heard of our coming, Highness," Colum went on, approaching nearer. "Although you may have *misheard* as to our purposes and intentions; as this Druid would have it. We come in friendship and peace, eight unarmed men, seeking your goodwill and well-being." He gestured. "Towards us, followers of Christ, the Lord of love and peace, swords are scarcely necessary!" That also with a smile.

With something like embarrassment, Brude dropped hand from sword-hilt, although not all his party did likewise. He cleared his throat.

"I am Brude mac Maelchon, yes. Why have you come here?"

"To bring you a message, High King. A message from the one true God. To tell you that you are beloved of Christ and chosen for His service."

"I do not know, nor accept, your Christian god, Irishman."

"But He knows and accepts *you*, Highness. Which is what matters."

There were growls from behind the monarch, at that.

Brude stroked his pointed beard. He was clearly less than comfortable, unsure as to how to deal with this situation.

"I have heard of *you*, prince," he said. "Heard much of you. From near and far. From Skye. From Dalriada. From Fortrenn. From Strathclyde. And from . . . close by."

"None of what you have heard to your hurt, Highness, I say? Or to any man's, save those who deal in evil, cursing and devilry perhaps!" And he glanced round at Broichan.

"You say not? What of that of the boar, on Skye?"

"The boar . . .?"

"You slew a wild boar, with your own hands, it is said. Unarmed. None has ever heard the like. And you gave it to Cathal mac Coitir. The boar is the emblem of my house and throne. And now Cathal seeks this throne, and sees your slaying of the boar, and gift to him, as a sign that he shall have it."

Colum blinked. "Save us – nothing of that was known, Highness. Nor intended. The boar attacked me. If I had not slain it, it would have slain me! We took the carcase to King Cathal to show him that it was no Fell Hound, as he feared, only a dead pig. You cannot think that it had anything to do with you and the high kingship?"

"Cathal so thinks, I am assured!"

"Who told you this tale, Highness? I think that it would be Enda, Cathal's Druid. Who would send word to this Broichan, out of his ill will. And *he* made it into a threat against your throne. Is it not so?"

Brude glanced over at the Arch Druid and shrugged. "How

270

do I know that you do not lie, Christian? But make excuse."

"By my later acts, surely. You say that you have heard of me from Strathclyde and Fortrenn. If so, you must know what I was doing there? I was seeking to forge an alliance against Athelfrith of Northumbria, the Angle. To Alba's benefit. Alliance between Strathclyde, Fortrenn, Dalriada and, I hope, yourself. Against the invader who threatens you all. Surely King Gartnait of Fortrenn has sent you word of this?"

The other nodded briefly.

"That is, in part, why we have come. To strengthen that alliance. As well as to bring you Christ's message. You cannot think, Highness, that we wish you, or Alba, ill? We are your friends."

"Heed him not, Lord Brude. This Irishman has the tongue of a snake!" Broichan declared loudly. "He threatens all. It is all empty invention."

"Did your Water Horse so deem it, Druid?"

That produced gasps of dread, with the usual warding-off signs. Clearly the monster was as much feared here as on Loch Ness-side. Recognising it, Colum took the opportunity to press the message home.

"That turning back of the Horse was not *my* doing. It was the Lord God's. I am merely His mouthpiece. And in coming here, we are no magic-workers, as your Druids pretend to be, but humble servants of Jesus Christ. He, the Son of God, works His good and loving will. We but feebly seek to carry out His wishes."

Brude turned to look at his followers. "These are large matters. Of much concern to us all. Not to be decided on while standing here. We shall go back." To Colum he said, "You and yours, Prince – come. You will require refreshment, after your journeying."

The first hurdle was surmounted at least. They followed on up to the central hall-house.

Brude, after giving orders that the visitors were to be fed, left them in the great hall. His party went with him, Broichan and his Druids also.

Low-voiced, the missionaries discussed the situation and their further tactics. It was agreed that a fair start had been made, but no one underestimated the task ahead. How to retain the initiative, with Brude no longer present? They could so easily be pushed aside, ignored and then dismissed, if not worse, without opportunity to get their message heard. Brude had mentioned decision, which implied discussion; but this could well be behind closed doors, with his council, with Broichan making the running.

Colum decided that they had to do something. Finishing their meal, they would go outside into the courtyard and sing psalms, loudly. And keep it up until Brude appeared from wherever he might be. A pity that they did not have their cymbals; but perhaps they might take out some of these silver platters and beakers, and beat the time with them instead.

Nobody could think of a better plan, so they trooped out, with the silverware; the servants looking on askance but none interfering.

In the centre of the courtyard they started off with the forty-sixth Psalm, one of Colum's favourites:

God is our refuge and strength, a very present help in trouble.
Therefore we will not fear though the earth be removed,
and though the mountains be carried into the midst of the sea;
Though the waters thereof roar and be troubled,
though the mountains shake with the swelling thereof . . .

His great voice ringing out, the others sought to match it, clashing the dishes and mugs in stirring fashion, less effective than cymbals but beating the time resoundingly. And quickly they drew an audience, folk appearing from all around. Undoubtedly these had never before heard the like. Presently they had their reward when Brude himself, with sundry of his nobles, came to the central doorway to watch. Broichan was not there.

Object achieved, Colum did not end the recital, but launched out with increased vigour:

The heathen raged, the kingdoms were moved:
He uttered His voice, the earth melted.
The Lord of hosts is with us;
The God of Jacob is our refuge . . .

They had got thus far when Broichan's absence was explained. A loud wailing of horns sounded, and round to the courtyard entrance a file of Druids marched, blowing their hardest, Broichan in front bearing aloft a standard surmounted by a boar's head flanked by two human skulls. The horns did not actually succeed in drowning out the psalm, but they did create sufficient discord to render the singing tuneless and the words meaningless. Colum, recognising it, threw up his arm and changed voice to great laughter. He pointed to the Druids and laughed the more, his companions taking it up.

There was the most evident astonishment on all hands. Safe to say that never before had any there seen Druids laughed at. Still chuckling, Colum led the way over to the High King.

"Your Druids are jealous, I think, Highness," he declared. "Do they not sing? These horns howling make a dreary sound. *We* make a joyful noise unto the Lord. Worship should be a joy, not a weariness."

"Was that . . . worship?" Brude asked.

"To be sure. The Psalms of King David, of the Hebrews. A servant of the Most High."

"Your god likes singing?"

"Indeed yes. Why else did He give men and women tuneful voices? To sing on the land. As the birds in the air. And the seals in the sea. And His angels in Heaven. I swear that God sings for joy Himself — when He is not weeping for the ignorance and blindness, the sins and cruelties, of mankind created in His image!"

"What do you mean? A god weeping and singing?"

"Why not? Jesus Christ His Son wept and sang. His Father, and ours, would have us to sing and be joyful."

"You must tell us of this strange god. But not now. My council would discuss with you this alliance against the Angles."

Colum tried not to reveal his elation.

They went through the hall and two intercommunicating rooms to a large chamber in one of the adjoining buildings. Here the walls were hung with a sort of tapestry depicting various of the Cruithne symbols and other dramatic designs. At a great table on which were flagons and beakers, some other of the nobles were waiting. Brude took his place at the head, and all sat.

"This of Athelfrith and the Angles," he began. "What concern is it of yours? Why do *you* seek this alliance? You, an Irishman?"

"King Connall of Dalriada sought my aid in this, Highness.

273

He fears the Angles also. I agreed to it because I am a Christian, and therefore love peace not war." Colum paused. "I was, to my sorrow, involved in a battle. In Ireland. Why, need not concern us here. But men died, many men. And I have vowed to do all that I can to prevent war and battle wherever I can. Moreover, Dalriada and Strathclyde are Christian, and Fortrenn and your Alba are not. But if you can all work together against this fierce and warlike Athelfrith, then Christ's cause could be advanced." That was surely frank enough.

"Conall and his Scots are my enemies."

"They need not be. They do not endanger you. For long Dalriada and Alba lived at peace. You invaded there, and slew Gabhran – why, you know best! But *they* do not desire war with you. They would have this alliance."

"And how would it serve Alba?"

"I think that you know. Athelfrith will be King of Northumbria before long. He seeks to be much more, to rule an empire, no less. He has said that he will reign from Deira to the Orkneys. That includes Alba, does it not?"

There was a stirring and muttering round the table.

"He will not find Alba as easy as he finds Fortrenn!" Brude said.

"Perhaps not, Highness. But he could cause you great trouble. He has a large fleet of ships and so can strike deep into the firths of Forth and Tay. But equally he could strike at *your* coasts. You have firths leading into your lands too, I am told? Have you fleets to meet him?"

There was a silence.

"Orkney is yours, at least in name, is it not? But could you protect those isles? Athelfrith could take them with ease, I think. As he has boasted. And does not Orkney control your northern territories of Caithness and the Sutherland? Or so I have heard. So Athelfrith could have a base on your northern doorstep."

Brude drummed finger-nails on the table-top. "You are a strange priest, I think!" he said.

"I was born into a warrior house, Highness. That of Donegal."

"Yes. Gartnait mac Domelch said that you were offered the high kingship of All Ireland. Is that truth?"

"That was many years ago. It is true. But I believed that I could serve Almighty God better in a humbler role."

"Why?"

Colum had to be careful here. To say that he preferred men and women to be converted by belief and teaching rather than by a king's command could perhaps hinder their cause here. Where Brude's help would be all-important. He compromised.

"I know my own weaknesses, Highness. I feared that I might perhaps *compel* my Irish folk to be Christian if I was High King. I judged that they should be persuaded, not compelled. Christ Himself so taught. So I chose to be a priest."

Brude eyed him wonderingly. "You must believe, be convinced, very strongly, Prince, in your Christian god, to choose so. And to come here, seeking to make others Christian also – to your own danger."

"I do," he was answered simply. "Jesus Christ is all in all to me, my very life."

For long moments the High King stared at him, unspeaking.

Then he changed tone. "This alliance – how would it advantage me?"

"It would much restrain Athelfrith, the knowledge of it. But more than that. Strathclyde has much shipping. And I think that it is ships that you need, Highness. If you and King Roderick were allies, the Strathclyde ships could give the Angles pause."

Brude glanced round his councillors. Heads nodded.

"What would be required of us, in Alba?"

"Some armed aid to King Gartnait. And no further attacks on Dalriada, so that King Conall's forces need not always be watching their borders, and can aid in possible assaults on Athelfrith."

After a pause, Brude too nodded. "We shall consider this well. And inform you. And hereafter you can inform *me* of your singing and weeping god! Meanwhile, I hope that you will find the guest-house comfortable. Make your wants known to my servants." Clearly the audience was at an end.

Broichan had sat there throughout, but had not spoken a word.

The missionaries rose, bowed and left the chamber. They were escorted to the guest-house at the rear by a robed individual who introduced himself as a chamberlain.

275

As well as pleased at progress, Colum was distinctly surprised at much that they were discovering here. He had tended to think of the Albannach as not only heathen but barbarians, a savage and warlike people of little refinement. They had been learning something of their culture on the way here, especially in their stone-carvings and artistry; now they found a level of cultivation and behaviour not so very different from that of their own Ireland. This King Brude was obviously a civilised monarch, intelligent and open to reason. It was all encouraging for their mission.

They were well provided for at the guest-house and glad enough to rest.

Presently their converse was interrupted by more horn-blowing, of a different quality this time and at some distance apparently. Listening, they realised that there was chanting too, monotonous and dirgelike but not sounding threatening. It was too early for any sunset worship ceremony. And it continued. The missionaries sallied out to investigate.

They found the druidical group standing outside one of the subsidiary hall-houses, producing their dreary noises, Broichan not present. Their chamberlain had followed them round, and when asked what this ceremony meant, told them that it was the Druids' efforts to coax out the devils who had taken up residence in the body of the Princess Nessa, King Brude's daughter. She was sore troubled, much distressing her father. The Druids did this each morning and evening, after sunrise and before sunset.

"Devils?" Colum saked. "What sort of devils? What do they do? How does she suffer?"

"They tear her. She howls and foams, like a dog, a mad dog. She pines away, a young woman . . ."

"And this wailing misery does not aid her, I swear!"

The chamberlain shrugged, non-commital.

Colum turned to Abbot Kenneth. "How think you? Shall we go to see her?" Kenneth of Achabo had a reputation as a healer.

The other nodded, and Colum asked the chamberlain if they might see the princess.

That man said that he would go and see if this was permitted. He came back to say that King Brude was with his daughter and that they could come up.

Climbing the stairs to an upper room, they were aware of

strange noises ahead. A dog was barking, but there was moaning and gabbling as well.

They were shown into a chamber, to an extraordinary scene. On a bed a naked young woman sat huddled, rocking to and fro, sobbing and gibbering; and also on the bed, kneeling on all fours, was Broichan, barking like a dog. Beside the bed stood Brude and a young man, little more than a youth.

Astonished, Colum and Kenneth led the others in. So busy was he at his barking, and staring into the girl's eyes, that Broichan did not appear to notice them at first. Brude raised a hand, and the youth frowned.

Only when the newcomers moved to the side of the bed did Broichan stop to turn his glare on them instead of on the sufferer. If he felt foolish, he did not show it.

"My daughter is sore afflicted," Brude said. "Poisoned by dog-devils. The Magus, here, seeks to draw them out."

"Your pardon, Highness – but there are no dog-devils," Colum said. "Any more than there was a Fell Hound in Skye. They are but the inventions and imaginings of Druids."

"How can you say that, Prince? She is possessed. Greatly troubled."

"It is a sickness, yes. It could even *be* an evil spirit. But not dogs! The good Creator does not make His animal kingdom evil. That is left to man!"

"Then what of the Water Horse?"

"It is not *evil*. Any more than wolves are evil. Or boars! They are but wild, dangerous yes, but not evil. They can attack men, but not possess them."

"Heed him not, Brude mac Maelchon!" Broichan exclaimed, recovering his breath after his exertions. "He lies! All these Christians lie. They know nothing of the mysteries. Ignorant profaners of the sun's mighty power."

"If we are ignorant profaners, Druid, why does not the sun strike us down? Always the sun has shone on me most kindly!"

"It will strike you. Wait you, scoffer – wait you!"

"To be sure. But while we wait, we will not be inactive! Tell me, Druid – the sun you worship is bright as the day. It *makes* the day bright. Why should it do deeds of darkness? Spawn devils and evil spirits, phantoms and devil-dogs and the like? These are the enemies of Almighty God's blessed sunlight."

"Has not the sun two faces, fool? Light and darkness,

summer and winter? Half of the time the sun frowns or turns its face from us."

During this exchange, Kenneth had reached forward to touch the princess's arm. She jerked round, her back to him, her gabble rising to almost a scream.

Broichan, off the bed now, rounded on the abbot. "Leave her! Do not touch her," he cried. "She is not for you!"

"She is for Christ Jesus!" Kenneth answered quietly. "Christ can heal her."

"No! No, I say! Go! A curse on you!" He raised clenched fist above his head. "I curse you, trouble-makers!" he shouted. "In the name of all the powers of darkness, I curse you, waking and sleeping, coming and going, alive and dead, while the sun and moon endure!"

So passionate was his malediction, so filled with hate, that even some of the visitors crossed themselves. As for the girl, she yelled and yelled, practically in hysterics, rolling her eyes. Kenneth looked at Colum and shook his head. Clearly there was little that they could do in such conditions of excitement and rancour.

Colum turned to Brude. "Now we cannot help. At this time, Highness," he said, and had to shout, above the noise. "We can, perhaps, do something for her. At another time when . . ." And he gestured towards Broichan. "May we come and see your daughter again?"

The monarch nodded, and they left.

They asked their chamberlain more as to the princess's strange trouble. He told them that it had started some months ago. She had had a pet dog which had run mad, foaming at the mouth. It would not drink. She had tried to save it but could not, much as she cherished it. The dog died – and then its troubled spirit entered into the Princess Nessa. And brought in other dog-devils with it . . .

"Dog-fever!" Colum interrupted. "Dog madness. Did it bite her?"

"No. She was not bitten. But she ailed from then. She howls. She scratches herself. The devils have her . . ."

"We shall see."

In their quarters, they discussed this matter. A fever in dogs could kill humans, could it not? Kenneth agreed but thought not necessarily so. If this young woman had been close to the dog, been licked by it perhaps but not bitten, she could have been infected but not sufficient to die. Suppose that she had a prior weakness, for fits or spasms, this could cause grave worsening, fears and superstition and the Druids doing the rest.

The missionaries did not attend the sunset worship that night, but decided that early in the morning before the sunrise ceremony, Colum and Kenneth would go to the princess and seek God's help for her.

So the pair rose at dawn and found their way through the sleeping palace to the sick-room, the dozing guard at the stair-foot, having seen them the previous day, accepting that they had the High King's permission. They found the girl asleep, but twitching and tossing on her bed. They considered her, said a quiet prayer over her, without waking her, and then decided that they should sing a gentle, soothing hymn to waken her that way, without fright. Softly they began, and this having no evident effect, sang a little louder. She stirred and opened her eyes.

Smiling at her, they continued to sing, softly again.

She stared, eyes wide now, lips trembling. Then she began to whimper like a dog.

Signing to Colum to continue his singing, Kenneth moved slowly over to the bed. Fearful, Nessa started up, crying out; but he reached to stroke her bare arm gently, unspeaking. He kept on stroking. Gradually she relaxed a little. Presently she lay back.

"Nessa," Kenneth said at length, with Colum merely humming now, "fear nothing. We are your friends. Sent by the God of all men and women, and all animals, to help you. Sent from afar. You are to be well again. It is God's good and kind will. You will be well. There are no dog-devils."

How much of what he said she took in there was no knowing. But the quiet singing, the soothing voice, the stroking and the smiles had some effect. The young woman looked less troubled; and when Kenneth put out his other hand to take hers, fingers clasped his own.

Colum came, then, to the other side of the bed, to talk to her also, low-voiced, conversationally, with no urgency, taking her other hand. Between them they sought to comfort and reassure, to calm her fears, to give her some hope of betterment. They did not say much about Christianity – she was by no means ready for that – but emphasised the love of

God the Father; love and peace and joy as the true inheritance of all men and women, the folly and error of belief in devils and curses, magic and sorcery, and what the Druids taught. They had come to change all that, especially for her. But mainly they sought to get the message through to her that she was safe now, her troubles to be banished, a new life for her beginning.

Undoubtedly they had some success, in time. The girl had not spoken once, but she lay listening, looking from one to the other, clearly absorbing much of what they were saying. That is, until suddenly the Druids horns began to blow, for the sunrise ceremony – and immediately all was changed; she sat up, tense again, eyes darting, hands withdrawn to clutch herself.

Desperately trying not to show their disappointment, frustration, anger, the two men continued with their soothing ministrations, telling her that the horns meant nothing, merely a greeting of men for the rising sun, welcoming the new day, a day in which *she* would find peace. They kept this up throughout the period of the morning worship, perhaps fifteen minutes of it, with only partial success. And then, after a brief interval of blessed silence, with the young woman beginning to relax again, the horns started up once more, in the courtyard directly beneath this room – and all was lost. Nessa flung herself round in the bed, howling, eyes rolling, breaking out in a sweat, possessed once more.

Try as they would they could not affect her now. In fury, after a few more minutes, Colum rose to rush out, leaving Kenneth, and ran down the stairs into the yard, to storm at the horn-blowers, shaking his fist at them and ordering them to cease this wretched caterwauling and yowling, to begone, begone. Broichan was not there this time.

The Druids ignored him. He had difficulty in restraining himself from physically assaulting them.

Presently Kenneth came down to join him, saying that it was of no avail. He could do nothing with the girl now. She was wholly possessed again.

Colum angry, Kenneth sad, they returned to the guest-house.

They sought an audience with Brude so soon as they decently might – and had to wait for some time, for it turned out that he assumed they were wishing to expound Christian doctrine to him, and he had other priorities for that day. However, when he heard that it was about his daughter, of whom clearly he was very fond, he was sufficiently attentive. Seeking to keep his ire under control, Colum told him what had happened that morning, assured him that they believed that they could greatly help the princess, and permanently, and pleaded with him to order the Druids to keep away from her whilst they attempted it, with no more horn-blowing and chanting under her window – and certainly no more of Broichan's barkings. Given respite from the Druids' no doubt well-meant attentions, they believed that with Christ's help they could cure the girl. She had responded to them notably – until the horns restarted.

The monarch was doubtful at first. Broichan the Magus – as they appeared to call the Arch Druid here – was a notable and powerful man of much influence on them all, who had been his, Brude's, tutor and was now tutoring his son Maelcu. He would not like any such ban on him and his Druids.

Colum recognised that. But he pointed out that despite all the druidical ministrations, the princess had been getting worse, not better – whereas even in the short time that they had been with her this morning, she had shown marked improvement, become quiet, less tense, even lucid. Given a little time to work God's will with her, they might save her. Surely, if he, her father, loved and esteemed her, he would at least give her and them this chance. They suggested that if he agreed, he should come with them to her room presently, and see for himself what they sought to do.

That seemed to reach Brude's heart, and he acceded. He would give Broichan instructions, and come for them in due course.

Satisfied, but slightly apprehensive, they returned to the guest-house. Good as this was, it could of course turn out to be the reverse. If they in fact failed with the girl, their credit with Brude would go down grievously. And so much, even the success of their whole mission here, depended on the impact on the High King. So, in essence, this of the sad young woman could to a large extent make or break their whole mission.

The little party did some very intense praying thereafter.

When the High King came for them at noonday, Cormac and Comgall besought Colum that they should be allowed to go with him. He was doubtful of the wisdom of this, in the circumstances, but Kenneth said that a bishop's special ministrations might be valuable.

Before they reached the princess's room they heard the howlings and gabblings, and Brude shook his head. The door open, they found only a frightened female servant with the unhappy girl, whom they dismissed. Nessa's eyes were rolling wildly, and it was to be doubted whether she realised that they had come in.

Colum signed for the father to keep silent. Then he and his friends grouped themselves at the foot of the bed and commenced their quiet singing, low, slow and rhythmic.

For some considerable time this seemed to have no effect. The troubled young woman continued to yelp and toss. But they kept it up, and very gradually they began to sense some lessening of the convulsions, some quietening, modest but undeniable. They sang on.

After a while, Kenneth ventured nearer, to take Nessa's hand; and again, after a minute or so, her fingers clasped his. Presently they realised that her eyes had stopped rolling and were in fact regarding them. Kenneth began to speak, softly, soothingly, no particular phrases, just single, simple words, that of peace recurring and recurring. Colum, smiling as before, went to take the other hand, while the other two continued to sing.

Soon she was resting almost tranquilly, and her visitors themselves relaxing and feeling hopeful – and unfortunately this applied to Brude also, who could not contain himself at the improvement in his daughter and started up, to come to her side. Immediately she tensed up, presumably not having realised that he was present.

High King as he was, Colum signed to him almost peremptorily to stand back – and was obeyed.

When she was pacified again, Kenneth signed for Cormac to come forward. Still quietly singing, the bishop approached, with a beaker of holy water. Smiling to her, he waited until she was used to his presence, then dipping his finger in the water, stooped to make the sign of the cross on her brow. Gazing up into his eyes, she returned his smile in some measure.

Colum caught his breath at that, indeed they all did.

"If there is any evil sprit in this child of God, Nessa, or any other ill presence – come out of her, I command you, in the

Name of Jesus Christ!" he said, almost genially, conversationally. "She is the Lord God's and His only."

Amens were heartfelt, but these did not stop the singing. In time the princess's eyes closed. Whether she slept or not they could not tell, but she seemed to be at peace. Colum beckoned her father over and, most gently detaching his fingers from her clasp, offered her hand to Brude. That man took it, almost in awe, and so sat, gazing.

With the girl's deepened breathing indicating presently that she was indeed asleep, the men eyed each other questioningly. They decided in whispers that, whilst there was no point in them all staying, Nessa should not be left entirely alone, one of them always there. Kenneth volunteered to stay first, and Brude intimated that he would remain longer with his daughter. The others tiptoed out.

Colum, taking his turn at the bedside in the late afternoon, found Nessa more asleep than awake. She would be exhausted, of course, after all that she had been through and this untroubled slumber was probably to her great advantage. During her conscious spells she spoke little but seemed calm and content to lie either dreamily gazing at nothing or else wonderingly at the man. For his part, Colum spoke intermittently, easily, almost as though he was entertaining some sleepy child with a story of Jesus the loving Saviour who died for people like her and himself, that they should be delivered from fear and evil and men's cruel imaginings.

Brude came in again, and was now humbly content to sit watching, listening. There was no question but that he was both impressed and grateful.

When Comgall came to take over and Brude left with Colum, the latter asked if it would be possible for the sunset ceremony to be held somewhere further away than usual, where the princess would not hear the horns, which clearly troubled her. The king agreed that he could arrange that. He added that, after the ceremony, if Prince Colum came to his privy chamber, he would be glad to hear more of this Christianity and the kindly god who seemed so helpful.

So that very evening Colum and Cormac went to expound the elements of the Christian faith to a man prepared not only to listen but predisposed to hear favourably. Not that Brude accepted all they had to say without question or doubt; he was a highly intelligent man and had been tutored from boyhood in the druidical culture. But because of Nessa he now had, as it were, a hostage to fortune as well as an indication of the efficacy of this new faith.

So long as the princess improved, therefore, the missionaries could be optimistic.

For three days, accordingly, they concentrated their attentions on the girl; and had the satisfaction of seeing daily, almost hourly, betterment. Brude kept the Druids away; and the more his daughter improved, the more receptive he was to her benefactors' teachings. Broichan, no doubt, would seek to counteract this, privately, but if so was not successful.

When on the third day Nessa emerged, clothed and in her right mind, however diffident, and even ventured out into the open square, something unseen for months, the reputation of the visitors soared, and the High King's gratification with it. Nessa, however, clearly preferred the missionaries' company, particularly Lugbe's, who, nearer to her own age, seemed to have an especial affinity with her. This caused some ill-feeling with her brother, the Prince Maelcu, whom she tended to shun – just as she shrank away from anyone dressed in Druid's robes.

Colum had still one touch to add to their ministrations. He wished that he had his dog Gaul, left on Hinba with his mother Bridget; but there were many dogs around the palace area and he selected one, old and placid, and putting a lead on it, brought it to Nessa.

At first she looked alarmed, but at Colum's reassuring words and pattings of the animal's head, she let it come close. He handed her a piece of an oatcake from his robe's pocket, and gestured, smiling, to the dog. After a momentary hesitation she held this out, to have it taken with equal hesitation. That raised a laugh from Colum, and smiling a little herself she reached out to pat the creature.

Colum decided that she was cured. To celebrate, he decided to ask Brude if they might conduct a public service of thanksgiving.

The monarch could hardly refuse, although he was somewhat doubtful at Colum's further request that the Druids, if they chose to attend, should not be permitted to interrupt or make any demonstration. This was eventually agreed.

That same day there was something of a distraction, with the arrival at Craig Phadraig of the sub-king of the Orkney

Islands. This Wirp, an elderly small man with a defensive manner – at least on this occasion – had apparently been summoned by the High King to account for his failure to put down the sea-pirates who were plaguing the isles and the northern coasts of the mainland, even raiding as far south as this Inverness Firth. Brude was displeased, and showed it. The missionaries could have wished the timing of this visit otherwise.

However, whatever the monarchs had to say to each other in private, they both attended the thanksgiving service that evening, held in the palace courtyard – Colum had thought of holding it at the stone-circle on a nearby mound where the sun-worship was sometimes staged, but decided that this might be seen as unduly provocative. A large crowd had gathered. There might well be lesser Druids amongst them, but if so they were not dressed as such; not so Broichan, who was prominent and clad in his finest robes. He sat not with the kings but with the young Prince Maelcu.

The missionaries put on their most colourful and lively display – for it was that rather than a true service – recognising that this was no occasion for preaching, expounding of doctrine or even much in the way of prayer. Psalm and hymn singing, clashing improvised cymbals, processions with ready-made crucifixes, sprinklings of holy water, shouted acclamations of praise and brief addresses, were the order of the evening, and Colum kept all going with verve and *élan*. Whatever else the onlookers got out of it, they must have come to the conclusion that, unlike the druidical one, this Christianity was a cheerful religion.

The highlight of it all, however, was when Lugbe led on the Princess Nessa, hand in hand, to the shouts of approval and greeting of the crowd. It was sheerest showmanship, of course; but at this stage that was what was required.

Colum ended the session by declaring loudly that all who wished to hear more of Christ's message and God's will for the Albannach people should come, the next evening at this time, to the front of the guest-house. He added that Bishop Cormac would presently bless all, in the name of Christ Jesus – that is, those who wished for this blessing even though they did not wholly understand it all. Those who did *not* could now depart.

It was interesting and encouraging to note that, after some stir, fully half the company did wait, including both kings.

Brude, after the benediction, came for his daughter and took her away, apparently nowise displeased with the use made of her.

The missionaries were invited next midday to a meal, almost a banquet, given by Brude for King Wirp and his party. And thereafter, at the high table, Colum and Cormac became involved in a conversation which was to have unlooked-for consequences. It was King Wirp's assertion that most of the pirates who were causing all the trouble were not in fact Orkneymen at all but some Skyemen and more Norsemen coming from Iceland far to the north, that drew from Cormac the information that he knew Iceland, having visited it once on his travels, many years before. This was news even to Colum, who knew that his friend was a great voyager, almost rivalling St Brendan the Navigator; but not that he had penetrated so far into the cold and fearsome northern ocean as Iceland. It much interested both kings, neither of whom had ever been there, and who asked for details as to its land and its people, more especially who governed there, who was its king? Cormac told them that he did not think that Iceland had a king. The folk there had come from Norway and Denmark to escape kings' rule. They were very independent, sea-robbers of course, but brave, handsome, even hospitable, fire-worshippers. He had thought to go back and try to convert them to the true faith, but had never had opportunity.

Brude questioned him further. If they had no king, who ruled? They must have some leader. If he and King Wirp could make a compact with that ruler, to halt the piracy, it would be to great advantage. Did Cormac think that might be possible?

The bishop did not know, but saw no reason why it should not be tried. Their local leaders were franklins and presumably there would be chief franklins.

There followed questions as to how far it would be to Iceland, how long it would take to get there – and significantly, whether the bishop still would wish to make Christians there?

Colum, listening, wondered.

Then it came. If Wirp provided a ship would the bishop sail with him to Orkney and then on to Iceland, as envoy of the two monarchs? To seek agreement over this of the piracy. They would offer suitable terms to whoever ruled there. And he could, thereafter, teach the Icelanders about his peace-loving God – which also might help to lessen the piracy.

Drawing a deep breath, Cormac looked at Colum.

That man was thinking swiftly. He would miss Cormac – but here was opportunity unlooked for. And not only to spread the Gospel. For if he went as representing these kings, that must have the effect of, in some measure, committing them to the Christian cause. They could hardly use Cormac and his urge to spread the faith, and then deny opportunity to his colleagues here in Alba to do the same. This could be important for their cause. He nodded at his friend.

The bishop said that he would consider the matter well, and might accede.

Later, the missionaries discussed the situation at length, and all agreed that this was a development as hopeful as it was unexpected, to carry Christ's message to a people almost unknown to most of them and at the same time to greatly strengthen their own influence here. Cormac reckoned that it would be fully five hundred miles from Orkney to Iceland, possibly more. In a long-ship it would take perhaps a week, allowing for variations in the weather. How long he would have to spend there would depend on circumstances – but clearly to do any real missionary work would take time. He might be able only to lay the foundations of mission at this stage, then bring back word to Wirp and Brude, and return to Iceland another year for the main attempt. But it was a wonderful, God-given opening . . .

None disputed that. It was decided that he should go and that he could hardly go alone. One of the student monks should accompany him, and one, Sennell, immediately volunteered. Whether the rest of them would be waiting here for their return was uncertain, depending on how they got on with their own efforts. Colum did not want to be away from Iona for too long. Meantime, they would endeavour to set up a Christian base here at Inverness, and then seek to reach out further afield in the surrounding country. Here too, of course, they could only lay foundations, and come back later, on no doubt many occasions.

Next morning, Colum and Cormac went to Brude to give him their decision. The bishop was prepared to act ambassador to Iceland, if he was allowed to do some mission work in Orkney also; and in return Colum sought permission to proclaim the Christian message at large not only in Inverness but in all Alba, to those who would listen. The High King surprised them by agreeing without hesitation, and indeed declaring that when they held their first initiation service here, of baptism or whatever they called it, he was prepared to be one of the participants.

There was rejoicing in the Craig Phadraig guest-house.

15

In the weeks that followed, after a highly successful and exciting mass-baptism down at the side of the River Ness, where not only the palace folk but the townspeople of Inverness itself could watch the High King and many of his council and servants being accepted into Christ's Church, the missionaries spread their activities more widely, anxious to get their message and identity known over as great an area as possible, for future efforts, some of the nobles who had been baptised with Brude being helpful in this, sponsoring visits to their own territories, in especial Virolec mac Emchat of Urquhart, who had come to Inverness and made a most useful ally. Brude's own adherence, of course, was their greatest advantage, although Colum was concerned that there should be no mere token conversions, as it were by royal command, insisting on due instruction and acceptance and examination.

They did not have it all their own way. There was opposition, led by Broichan and the Druids, effective in preventing many from taking the great step and becoming Christians. Brude did not interfere in this, accepting Colum's claim that converts be sincere and therefore all free to make their own choice. It was noteworthy that this applied to his own son, for Prince Maelcu, much under Broichan's influence, would not adhere, and in fact became something of a focus for the anti-Christian cause. Nessa, of course, was considered to have been baptised from the first.

Oddly enough, it was another young woman who offered Colum a weapon against Broichan. This was a slave-girl in the palace, a nubile creature in her mid-teens, who listened in at one or two of the teaching sessions and then came forward diffidently at one of the baptismal ceremonies. It was at this that Broichan made his appearance and loudly interrupted the proceedings, to command the girl to leave, to come away with him at once, on pain of direst punishment.

Colum was not the man to accept this. He told the girl to wait where she was, that she was now Almighty God's servant and entitled to baptism if she wanted it.

Broichan countered by declaring that she was *his* servant, his slave, and she must do as he told her. That was the law.

"Not God's law, Druid! In His eyes all men and women are free. You may say that you own her body, but *He* owns her soul and spirit. Which is what we are concerned with here."

Broichan fell into Colum's trap. "I do own her body, have done for many a night. For that I bought her, for a good price. She is mine. None can deny it."

"So, Magus Broichan, out of your own mouth you are condemned! You, a man of fullest years, sixty-five at the least I would say, with a wife and sons they tell me, take to your bed this child fifty years younger! And claim to be a leader of this people in things of the spirit. I say shame on you! For I swear that she did not choose to lie with such as you of her own wish."

The Magus pointed a quivering finger. "She is mine, I tell you. To do with as I will. I *bought* her."

"Even you cannot buy human souls, Druid! They belong to the God of love who created them. And now this one has brought her soul back to Him. You will not, cannot, prevent it. As for her body, if you say that you can buy that – then so can I! I will pay you more than *you* paid – and she shall be free. So – leave us!"

As the crowd murmured and exclaimed, Broichan seemed almost to take a fit, in his fury and spleen, shaking, raising hands high and gasping for breath. Then he turned and stumbled away. The service resumed.

The girl, Lora, Colum handed over to Virolec to take back to Urquhart with him, to start a new life. He sent Broichan ample price.

In fact, when Virolec did make his return journey to Urquhart, Colum and Lugbe went with him, on a preaching tour of all western Loch Ness-side, with Kenneth and Diarmit taking the east side of the long loch, Comgall and the other student remaining at Inverness. So, for the first time, the party was split into four, Cormac off to Orkney and Iceland. Colum was inevitably again concerned with manpower, or the lack of it. Fortunately, Virolec was an enthusiast, and prepared to act acolyte meantime – but that would only apply to Loch Ness-side, for he had his chiefly duties to attend to. Somehow this problem would have to be solved, if much of Alba was to be Christianised. And Kenneth and Comgall could not remain here indefinitely, with their abbeys of Achabo and Bangor calling them back. He decided that he, Colum, must find the time and opportunity himself to go back to Ireland, to recruit a sufficiency of priestly helpers.

So they went back to Dochfour Beg, where Kenneth and Diarmit crossed by the ferry to the east side, with a new ferryman – and the Water Horse failed to put in an appearance. Colum held a service here and announced that there would be further teaching at Urquhart and a baptismal ceremony thereafter, to which all were invited, Virolec adding his encouragement. Then on up the loch-shore.

They made further fairly brief halts at the communities of Achculin and Brachla, spreading the Word, however limited their opportunity at present. They found that they required little of introduction, for all knew about them and their activities now, about Emchat, the Water Horse, Brude's conversion and Nessa's cure. News apparently travelled fast in Alba.

It was while at Urquhart, with the work progressing very satisfactorily, that Colum received a surprise – and more than that, something of a test, both to his imagination and his Christian charity. It came by a messenger from King Brude. Broichan the Magus was seriously ill. He had suffered a seizure, if not by devils then perhaps by the will of the Christian God. Could the Prince Colum help him? It was not to be doubted that it was because of the Christians that it had happened, upsetting all Broichan's life and power. The matter of the slave-girl Lora had been the final blow – since then he had grown ever worse. Now he might die. He had been Brude's teacher and guide from boyhood, and there was a bond between them. If Christ's Father was a God of love, as preached, could His servant Colum not pardon and heal?

Here was a challenge indeed. Colum was faced with a drastic self-examination.

He questioned the messenger, one of the High King's councillors. Broichan had apparently lost the will to live, eating nothing, breathing with difficulty, groaning and declaring that he was being eaten alive by Christian demons; some were even saying that the dog-devils driven out of the Princess Nessa had returned to possess the Magus's body.

Colum struggled with himself. If Broichan died, a great impediment to the Christianising of Alba would be removed. He had been their enemy from the first, and the lesser Druids took their attitudes from him. On the other hand, the missionaries were here to preach Christian love and forgiveness, as well as the *power* of God and Christ. Brude was invoking forgiveness. He, Colum, could scarcely deny it.

The fact that he did not *want* to help Broichan, and he had to admit it, was in itself a challenge and indictment. How could he go on preaching God's love of sinners if he himself could not forgive? And, after all, the man had only been seeking to uphold his own religion and beliefs.

So, he must do what he could. But what was possible? It was faith that could heal – but to a complete and determined non-believer such as Broichan how could that faith be brought to bear? To go and pray and sing over him, seek to minister as they had done for Nessa, would not be likely to be effective. Besides, there was the mission here at Urquhart all arranged, culminating in a great baptismal service, involving the saving of many souls, souls who were *choosing* Christ. He could not cancel that, or put it off, for the sake of one, their principal opponent.

Out of this debate with himself, Colum came to a conclusion. He must do what he could, but without hindering the work here. Broichan, whatever else he was, must be a believer in spells and symbols and magic, as were all Druids. He would not want the hated Christians at his bedside, praying over him. But he might well be affected by some *object*, some charm or token which he conceived to be magical. Might not the fight for him, therefore, be conducted with his own weapons?

Colum took Brude's messenger with him down to the lochside, and there picked up from the beach a white pebble. To make something of a ceremony of the business, he went back to the pool of the River Coilte where the baptisms were to take place, already consecrated. Here, ritually, he blessed the pebble, making the sign of the cross over it after dipping it

291

in the water. He handed it to the messenger, telling him that this was a sign and symbol of Christ's power over evil, pure in itself and now washed in holy water. Broichan and other devil-worshippers held those black, carved balls in their hands in times of stress, he had noted; let him hold this, instead, and let God's power for good prevail. He could also dip it in water and drink that. This could save the Magus, for a better life. He sent the councillor away.

The mass-baptism two days later was a great success, over one hundred coming, from the Urquhart area, Dochfour and elsewhere along the north end of Loch Ness, Lugbe and Virolec assisting and leading the local attempts at psalm-singing. There had been a slight to-do just previously when one of the parties coming down-loch from Bunlait spread some alarm by reporting that the Water Horse had been seen the day before swimming in the loch near their village; but when they admitted that no one had been attacked, Colum was able to reassure by declaring that the Horse was one of God's creatures, as were they all, and entitled to live its own life in the loch. The event at Dochfour Beg had not been an attempt to banish the monster from the loch but only to stop it attacking a Christian, namely Lugbe here. This explanation had its own effect.

The ceremonial over, they set about establishing the first actual church building to be erected, choosing to site it within the Urquhart stone-circle, Colum helping to labour at the preliminary work. There was some murmuring at this by those who were not accepting the Gospel message; and the second morning of the work they awoke to find that their efforts of the previous day had been destroyed, the hurdles for the wattle and daub construction pulled down and smashed up, the standard posts uprooted.

Virolec was very angry, and issued stern orders to his people that this must not recur. He suspected the local Druids as responsible. But when, the next morning, the havoc was repeated, he proposed dire punitive measures. Colum, however, suggested that they might try less drastic means first, for they did not want to create druidical martyrs. There was a large souterrain near the stone-circle, used by the Druids as a store for their standards, horns and other sun-worship equipment. If he and Lugbe and perhaps two or three others were to spend the next night therein, instead of in Virolec's hall-house, they might manage to surprise the raiders to some purpose. A little counteraction might be as effective as chiefly chastisement.

These souterrains were a marked if generally unseen feature of the Albannach settlements, underground chambers and corridors, earth-houses, after the fashion of the interiors of the burial cairns, carefully constructed out of masonry and stone slabbing, non-apparent save to those who knew of their location, entered only by hidden trapdoors. They were of all sizes and shapes, some large enough to contain a family, as refuge, or small enough to be little more than larders or cold storage for food. Every house had its souterrain, every community supplied with many. This one at the stone-circle was extra spacious and T-shaped, designed to house bulky materials, tables and other wooden structures connected with sun-worship, long poles and the like. Built into the side of a slight mound north of the monoliths, access was by a more convenient entrance than the usual trapdoor.

After dark that night, Colum, Virolec, Lugbe and three of the newly-baptised local men, made their way quietly to this earth-house, taking with them candles, flint and steel and tinder. The door was not locked or barred, for this place was allegedly protected by spirits. Over their arms they carried pale-coloured woven blankets.

Once inside, and the door shut again, they could light their candles without the glow being seen outside. The interior scene was grisly – heaps of human skulls and other bones, blood-stained chopping blocks, axes for sacrificial execution, knives, bowls for blood, large phallic symbols, the tips painted scarlet, and some of the druidical horns. In the eerie flickering light and shadow of the candles all this was off-putting in the extreme, and the newly-converted made hasty warding-off signs, even Colum not unaffected, the evil so palpable. However, since they might be in here for some time, he raised his hand to make the cross-sign and went through a brief exorcism exercise, after which they all felt better, as they settled down near the door to wait. They occupied themselves by detaching the phalluses and skulls from poles and then lashing cross-pieces to these to improvise crucifixes.

They had not long to wait. Presently they heard lowered voices outside and the sounds of stealthy assault being made upon their building work.

Colum gave the signal.

All within began to howl and yelp and wail, fairly loudly so that it would be heard outside, but rising and falling and varying in tone and volume. Then, two of them took horns and blew on these, seeking to make them sob and hoot, ·through the wailing and barking. Heard from underground, muffled, it would sound sufficiently weird. Ear to the crack of the door, Virolec said that he thought the noises of destruction had ceased for the moment.

They progressed to the next stage. Throwing the whitish blankets over their heads and shoulders, with only cut slits to see through, Colum and Lugbe opened the door quietly, each with one of the crucifixes to raise high and wave, while the howling and horn-blowing continued behind them. Silently, with swooping, dancing steps, they advanced towards the stone-circle.

In the semi-darkness of an early-autumn night they must have looked uncanny enough to affright even less demon-conscious characters than Druids and their assistants. Virolec was to follow on under another blanket, but before he could emerge with his crucifix, figures were plainly to be seen and heard bolting from the circle, some yelling in fear. When the trio reached the first of the monoliths they found all deserted.

Going back, they stopped the howling, and using sacrificial axes to sharpen points to the feet of the poles, planted their crucifixes one on either side of the souterrain doorway and one on the slope of the mound directly above. Then, laughing a little, Colum declared that he hoped that the good Lord would forgive them using the symbol of His cross in such mummery and child's-play, but thought that it would be quite effective in His cause. He doubted if there would be any more night-time attacks on their church.

Next day's building work proceeded satisfactorily and extra volunteers arrived to help, without explaining why they came. Watchers were posted the following night, but had nothing to report.

Oddly enough, their play-acting might not have been necessary. For the same messenger then arrived back from Inverness, bringing interesting news from King Brude. Broichan was much better in health. The white pebble was proving a great success, both to hold in the hand and to drink the water it was dipped in. The Magus had recovered his will to live. It was not suggested that he was likely to become a convert to Christianity, but he had to acknowledge that the Christians had some extraordinary powers.

Virolec made a point of promptly spreading these tidings abroad amongst his people, with encouraging results. The enmity of the local Druids and their supporters faded noticeably. It could be assumed that this would apply elsewhere also. Colum perceived that his distinctly grudging gesture of forgiveness to Broichan was proving unexpectedly helpful to their cause – and was, not for the first time, humbled as well as gladdened.

Now they moved on from Urquhart up-loch, Virolec accompanying them, on horseback now and finding progress therefore very different from heretofore when they had been water-borne, seeing the country in so much more detail, able to visit so many more houses and communities. Consistently they found that their identity and fame had preceded them, especially in the matter of the Water Horse, although Emchat's peaceful end, Brude's conversion and Broichan's miraculous white pebble were all talked about. Whatever other arts these Albannach had mastered, that of rapid communication was not the least, despite having no written language.

The second day out they themselves saw the Water Horse, some distance out in the loch. Colum and Lugbe would not have recognised it for what it was had not some of the party excitedly pointed it out, for it could have been no more than a tree-trunk bobbing on the surface – until the speed at which it was moving was appreciated. Sometimes two humps were visible, sometimes three, but always there was a distinct wake behind it. Colum, intrigued, put it to Virolec that this was fully twenty miles from Dochfour where he had encountered the monster before; could it be the same creature? Admittedly, moving at that speed, it could cover great distances; but was it not possible, indeed probable, that there was more than one such in the loch? Would only one of its kind be apt to exist? None there could answer that, indeed none was really disposed to discuss the matter, so deep-bred in the locals was the fear of the Horse.

Near the head of the loch they paid their promised return visit to the cottagers at the so-called leprosy well, and were kindly if shyly received. Even here, word of the missionaries'

295

activities had reached, and so their lack of symptoms of either leprosy or blindness did not provoke great surprise. The three households were given a course of instruction, for Colum had agreed to meet Kenneth's little party here, and waiting, they had time. Baptism for all duly followed. Using this place as a base, they spread their message farther afield in the area, before Kenneth and Diarmit at length turned up.

Kenneth, a quiet and self-contained individual, was nevertheless elated at the progress he and Diarmit had made along the east side of the loch. They had found the soil fertile, he declared, waiting to be tilled, no real opposition encountered. At a place called Inverfarigaig, in especial, they had set up what he hoped would be a centre for Christian endeavour for the district. If Columcille would come back with him, they might achieve much there.

So the united party turned northwards again, to follow the east shore of the loch. Colum, however, was becoming ever more conscious of the pressures of time, and anxious to return to Inverness and then to get back to Iona. Admittedly this of bringing Christianity to Alba was the principal objective of his exile from Ireland and should not be in any way scamped or cut short. But he had a major responsibility at Iona, their base, the well-spring of their corporate endeavours. Also they had now established cells, churches and communities in so many locations in the west and Hebrides, and these must be sustained by visits, never allowed to wither in neglect. Had he taken on too much, attempted more than could be maintained, too greatly dispersed his efforts? *Could* one overdo it in God's service?

Their progress northwards, therefore, was perhaps more hurried than Kenneth, for one, would have wished, although they did halt at a number of places besides Inverfarigaig to, as it were, confirm conversions started by Kenneth and Diarmit, and strengthen foundations laid. This east side was less populous than the west, but there were not a few small groups of houses, as well as Foyers and Inverfarigaig, where major rivers joined the loch. It took them three days to reach Dochfour. There they parted from Virolec and his men, who headed for Urquhart. They would however see him on their return journey to Iona.

At Inverness they found all well, save that Comgall had departed on a mission of his own, north-eastwards along the sea-coast towards the Moray Firth. Just where he had headed no one knew, but there were quite large lordships and even towns in that direction, such as Culloden and Balloch, Tornagrain, Cromal of Ardersier, Nairn and Barevan. It was this last name which had Colum thinking. They had heard that one of St Ninian's disciples, St Evan, had penetrated almost as far north as Inverness long ago, reaching the Nairn area. This Barevan, the height of Evan, could well have been the church he founded. Comgall was a traditionalist, and to seek to revive such an ancient foundation was just what would appeal to him. The chances were that was where he had gone. They were told that it was no more than fifteen miles away.

They had to wait, therefore, however eager Colum was to start the long road back to Iona. And Hinba – for he could not hide from himself the pull of that smaller isle. He did not kick his heels in the meantime, for there was plenty to do at Inverness. Brude's welcome back was more than formal, even warm. Indeed he held a feast for the returned missionaries – and summoned Broichan to attend. Clearly he was concerned that these two, his new teacher and his old, should not remain enemies. It was a dramatic moment when they came face to face at the king's high table in the crowded hall, Colum schooling himself to be civil if no more, and nowise indicating any sort of triumph over the matter of the pebble. Broichan, appearing somewhat shrunken in body, was stiff, obviously under strain. They bowed warily, as Brude looked from one to the other.

It was the Princess Nessa who acted as catalyst. Coming forward, she all but threw herself at Kenneth first and then into Colum's arms, in joyful, unrestrained greeting. And still clutching him, she turned to look at the Magus, almost defiantly. But as that man dropped his glance and bit his lip, suddenly she held out a hand to touch his arm, in a gesture of reconciliation.

If that girl could do it, surely a priest who preached God's love could. Colum also thrust out a hand, to close over hers on Broichan's wrist.

That man raised his head and then shook it, almost wonderingly. Finally he nodded, briefly patted both their hands, and turned away. But almost certainly to hide his emotion rather than dismissively.

Brude beamed on them all, and waved them to seats at the

table, placing Colum and Kenneth on either side of him, Nessa next to Kenneth, Broichan beside Colum. It was to be peace at Craig Phadraig, however little abbot and Druid conversed during that meal. Young Prince Maelcu, however, made no conciliatory gestures.

They had three days of visiting congregations of the converted in and around Inverness, baptising more, before Comgall reappeared. He had, as anticipated, been at Barevan, in the Nairn area, where he had reconsecrated the abandoned shrine of St Evan the Briton, and gathered together a little company to cherish it. Somehow they must find someone to maintain a ministry there, even if only diaconal. He had also established a group at Nairn itself, thanks to its lord, who was one of the chiefs who had accepted baptism with Brude.

Very much aware of all the unfinished labours that they must leave behind them here, the three abbots recognised that they must be on their way. There must be a follow-up fairly quickly if all they had initiated was to prosper and grow. Colum declared that he would be back in the spring, although the other two could not say the same, since already they had been gone from their abbeys in Ireland for too long. But at least they could then send over more priests to aid in the work here; and who knew, they might come back one day.

So the next day they called upon King Brude, to take their leave. It proved to be a remarkably moving occasion. The High King was most evidently sorrowful to see them go, and urgent in his wishes for their speedy return. He assured them of his active support of all they had started in his realm, of Christian endeavour, restated his conviction that their faith was the true one, informed that he had already sent word to King Gartnait and King Roderick that he would strongly support them in alliance against the Angles, and thanked Colum especially for acting envoy and for agreeing that his friend Bishop Cormac should make the long and hazardous voyage to Iceland as ambassador. Finally, he produced from a pocket of his royal robe an object which he handed to Colum.

"Here is a small gift, my friend," he declared. "What we call a brecbennach, that is *breagh-beannachd*, a fair blessing or benediction, to remind you of myself and my goodwill. I have had it made for you, Colum mac Felim."

Touched, and marvelling also, Colum took the proffered gift. It was a most lovely and remarkable construction. A casket less than five inches long and the same in height, in the shape of a little house; exquisitely crafted of wood, covered in thin plates of bronze and silver, and adorned with Celtic decorations in enamel, golden and red, these inset with jewels, and with a hinged handle, delicately carved, for carrying on a strap.

Exclaiming in delight at its beauty, Colum was instructed to open it. The roof part of the casket proved to be hinged also, and raising this, there within the wooden interior lay the white pebble from Loch Ness.

"Your precious amulet and healer," Brude said. "Returned to its giver. The shrine is unworthy of it – but the best that I could have made."

Much moved, and admiring, Colum shook his head. "I thank you, Highness – I do greatly thank you. This casket is a wonder, a delight. I shall always treasure it. But the pebble – it is not for me. God but used me to bless it. *You* keep it. Who knows – it may still serve you in some way "

"You say so? You are generous. But then, you could always bless another, could you not? My thanks, friend. I shall keep it safe, perchance to use it, one day."

Their other farewells over, an emotional one with young Nessa and a quietly grave one with Broichan, Brude himself accompanied the travellers down to the riverside and their waiting coracles. He had offered them horses and escort all the way to Loch Etive, but they declared that they would go as they came. Crowds saw them off, with cheers and waves, six coracles now, not eight. The sound of a psalm sung behind them by many voices, tone uncertain, sent them on their way.

16

Apprehensions as to affairs at Iona proved to have been well-grounded. Colum arrived back to find his people there in some distress and fear; Ernan, who had been left in charge, much concerned. Throughout that summer the island had been plagued by robbers, sea-pirates. These apparently were not from Skye, a notorious base for such, but from the much closer island of Coll. Their raids had been large and small, ranging from attacks by many men from long-ships on houses and farms, to steal goods and cattle and even abduct women, to individual raids on the monks' seal-raising islet to kill and make off with stock. Ernan had done what he could, organising watches and sentinels and patrols, but it all presented an almost insoluble problem; the raiders could strike anywhere and at any time, day or night. They had not so far attacked the monastic area itself, but they had been none so far off, growing bolder. Ernan had established a permanent watch at the seal-colony, now sadly reduced, but there the raiding had taken place in darkness and guards had found it difficult to stay awake night after night when most nights nothing happened. All they had been able to ascertain was that the trouble seemed to be caused by a single individual, for twice a coracle had been seen in the early morning heading away from the islet for the Mull shore, only one man visible. The larger raids were much more worrying, of course, and seemed impossible to deal with. Machar kept his long-ship in readiness to sail at short notice, to give battle; but no warnings given meant that he had been unable to intercept. Twice the farm of Colum's friend with the so similar name, Columban, at the north-west corner of the island, had been attacked. Now he had practically no cattle or sheep left.

All this had much upset the monkish community, naturally, and morale had sunk somewhat. Indeed they were saying that if Columcille was away, all went awry – which had not made things easier for Ernan.

Colum recognised that he was expected to put all to rights, somehow.

There was other news of significance. Diarmid mac Cerball, High King of All Ireland, Colum's enemy, was dead – and by an extraordinary chance, his slayer was now not far away, on the island of Tiree. This had come about in strange fashion. After the slaying – which appeared to have been little short of outright murder, with the man Black Aed mac Sween stabbing Diarmid to death with a spear at some inn – he had fled for safety to his friend, St Findchan. Findchan had been one of those who had been approached to come over to Dalriada to help in the missionary endeavour, but had put off.

Now, with the hue and cry for Black Aed's arrest, he had decided that the time was opportune to leave Ireland, and he had arrived at Iona in July, bringing this Black Aed with him. Not knowing what Colum's wishes would be in the matter, and with Baithen asking for another priest for a new monastery he had set up on Tiree, Ernan had sent the pair there meantime.

Colum was perturbed by this entire matter. He could by no means mourn Diarmid mac Cerball, who had now paid for Prince Curnan's murder, as well as that of many another; but murder, if it was indeed that, was not to be excused. And he knew of this Black Aed mac Sween, a high-born character of less than high morals, indeed known to be a man-lover, as well as quarrelsome – which made Colum wonder about Findchan. Were these the sort of aides Cousin Baithen required?

With much to see to on Iona, Colum could not spare time to go to Tiree at present. He told Machar to go and to bring back Baithen to see him. Also to make enquiries on Tiree, which was quite near to Coll, as to these pirates. They might know something which could be helpful.

Colum did not fail to make enquiries as to Hinba. All appeared to be in good order there. Ernan had indeed made a point of visiting the isle frequently, perhaps every two weeks. The Princess Eithne and the Lady Bridget were both well and apparently content enough. Although they did not remain isle-bound all the time, for they had paid visits to Ellary and Lismore during Colum's absence.

That man restrained himself from hurrying off to see them.

Instead, after a couple of days setting sundry matters in order on Iona, he, Lugbe and Diarmit made a little trip in their coracles across the sound to the Mull shore opposite the north end of their island. Colum reasoned that if the lone raider of their seal-farm had been seen twice heading in that direction, then the probability was that he had a base or lair somewhere fairly close to the shore, for he would not wish to have to carry his coracle and dead seals very far from the water. It was a practically uninhabited stretch of coast thereabouts and perhaps they might find some clue.

They had difficulty actually, in finding a suitable landing place – and that in itself might be helpful, since the raider would be equally restricted, the coastline here being rocky, all little cliffs and reefs. They landed at one of the few sheltered coves, pebbles not sand, and noted that there was a distinct track leading inland from it. Leaving their coracles, they followed this.

Soon they were in a wilderness of small hillocks dotted with scrub birch and oak. Colum shook his head. It would take them hours to search all this. The path they had taken here branched in various directions. It did not look hopeful.

They did climb two or three of the knolls, but all they could see from the tops were other similar knolls. Then the keen-nosed Diarmit smelt a whiff of wood-smoke. It seemed to come from behind them, he thought, nearer to the sea. It might be a house, where at least they might make enquiries.

So they turned back, and followed Diarmit's nose. Soon they could all smell the smoke, as it got stronger. And presently, not far back from the coast but further north than their cove, they found the source of the smoke – although there was little of that, in fact, only a small fire, more ash now than wood.

At first, disappointed, they conceived it to be deserted – although why anyone should light a fire in that empty landscape and then leave it smouldering, they could not think. Then Lugbe noticed that nearby there was a heap of bracken fronds, dry grasses and reeds, pulled obviously and recently, for they were not faded, presumably by whoever had lit the fire. They moved forward to inspect.

Suddenly Lugbe grabbed Colum's arm and pointed. Round behind a broom-bush was another of these heaps. But this one was less regular or, it seemed, less well made, for it had partly collapsed at one side, and clear to be seen therein was part of a sapling frame, such as they used in their building work, and stretched on this was a skin. And these three knew enough about drying and curing skins to recognise at a glance, even with only a small section showing, that this was sealskin.

Putting finger to lips, Colum moved quietly to the other larger heap. Close to, he could hear a faint sound and did not take long to identify it as a gentle snoring. He beckoned the others forward.

Carefully he lifted aside some of the greenery. Underneath was an upturned coracle. And from under this came the snores.

Grinning, he gestured to the other two. All three stooped

to pick up the coracle and put it aside. Beneath, the bearded sleeper opened his eyes, to blink, exclaim and sit up.

"We disturb you, friend," Colum declared. "You sleep soundly, for midday! I think that you must labour by night!"

The other, a man of middle years, short and stocky, stared wordless.

"Are you a fisherman? I see that you have sealskins. But you cannot catch seals by night, in darkness! Unless they are penned in a pond. I am Colum, Abbot of Iona yonder. And we have been missing seals from our farmery there!"

Still the man did not speak.

"We breed these seals for their skins, which are valuable, and for their meat which is good. I think that you discovered that, friend. How many have you stolen?"

The other found his voice. "I, I am a poor man. The seals are creatures of the sea. Any man can take them." That was half pleading, half defiant.

"Wild, yes. But these were reared by us, fed, cherished, all but tame. You did not come and claim them by day, but took them secretly by night. So you stole them, did you not? And knew that you were stealing. That is a sin, whether Christian or pagan."

The thief hung his head.

"So — you will come back with us to Iona. Up with you. We will take the skins and you will carry your coracle."

"What . . . what will you do to me, master?"

"You will see . . ."

They found half a dozen skins hidden away, and laden with these and some of the smoked meat, they headed back for their own boats, their unhappy prisoner burdened under his.

To prevent any attempt at escape, they tied the captive's coracle to Colum's, and paddled across to Iona.

There they took the man to the monastery's refectory and sat him down beside them for a simple meal – to his wary suspicion. Then Colum conducted him out to the infield.

"Pick two sheep," he instructed.

The other stared.

"Just two. Of your choice, friend."

"What . . . why . . .?"

"Do you not want them?"

The man shook his head. "Are they for . . . a sacrifice?" he got out. "To, to . . ." He left the rest unsaid.

303

"You might call it a small sacrifice. On *our* part. In a good cause. Choose you."

Still the other hung back, alarmed.

"What is your name, friend? And where are you from?"

"Erc. From the isle of Coll."

"Ah, another from that island! Well, Erc – if you will not choose your sheep, we must do it for you, Diarmit – pick two. wethers."

Little more confident than their prisoner, the younger man did as ordered.

"The feet tied, you can take these in your coracle. To Coll. Or is that too far?"

The man Erc looked utterly bewildered. "Take . . .?" he wondered.

"Why, yes. You will have a family, on Coll? You say that you are a poor man. Here, then, is some help, that you steal no more."

This Erc was clearly not a man of words. He looked from Colum to the other two helplessly. "I, I have no family," he muttered. "She died."

"Then for whom were you stealing?"

No answer.

"Do you not want the sheep, friend? They are yours, to take to Coll."

"Why? You mean it, in truth, master? Why?"

"Because you are poor. And have turned to theft. We are Christians, and our God is a God of love. So we, who are sinners ourselves, need mercy. And so seek to show it towards others. Take your sheep and go steal no more."

The man Erc, as he began to believe what he heard, still could not take it in fully. He stammered that it was too much, that he was not a good man, that he was ashamed, even that *one* sheep would serve, that on Coll they all lived by stealing . . .

"Then why go back to Coll, friend Erc? You have no family, you say. Why not stay here, on Iona? Become a Christian and learn better ways. Join us."

That brought forth more stares.

"You could have a better life here, I think. Since you know so much about seals, you could help to manage our seal-farm! Make good the damage done there. How say you?"

Erc did not say anything very clearly there and then, but he clearly was moved and not rejecting the suggestion made. Colum handed him and the sheep over to Diarmit's keeping meantime.

Lugbe found it in him to wonder, and to ask, whether Colum had been wise in this instance; to be told that there were more kinds of wisdom than one, as Jesus had taught them. This robber might have hidden virtues, and deserve a chance to reform. Moreover, he came from Coll. He might be useful in the countering of the pirates.

In the event, Erc did stay on at Iona, even if he never became an enthusiast for Christianity. But he did give them information about the Coll pirates who were so much more ambitious in their robberies than he had been. The lord of the island, Conall mac Donald, of the royal house of Gabhran, kinsman of the late king, was himself the chief pirate, although he was now getting old for it and his son, Ian mac Conall did most of the leading; a cruel man who killed as well as robbed. When Colum asked why they had recently started to raid Iona when not before, and yet did not apparently attack Tiree, which was adjacent to Coll, he was informed that Tiree was owned by the Lord Ferchar mac Tulchan, a kinsman of Conall mac Donald's, and there was an understanding between them. As for this Iona, Erc had heard that it was pirates from Skye who had advised raiding here. They had been driven out of Skye by the king there, Cathal, who was now under the influence of Christians. So they had come south to Coll and other islands thereabouts, and were hot against Christians.

It seemed that something would have to be done about Coll.

Machar came back with Baithen from Tiree, and the cousins held a conference about the situation concerning Findchan and Black Aed. The problem proved to be worse than Colum had realised, for Findchan was now desiring Aed to be ordained a priest and asking that Colum himself should do it. When that man demanded the reason for this, for such a notorious character as Aed, Baithen shrugged. It could be that he would feel safer from blood-guiltiness as a priest, that he wanted to start a new life. Or even that he had repented and sought to make amends. Who could tell?

His cousin was more than doubtful about that. From all that he had heard, this Aed was entirely unsuitable for the priesthood. Findchan must know it. Colum did not see how he could possibly agree to ordain the man. Nor agree that anyone else should do it.

Baithen tended to concur, but had some doubts nevertheless. If the man was truly penitent and anxious to aid in God's work, could they deny him? Were they entitled, or authorised, to deny forgiveness?

Forgiveness, no, Colum said. But ordination was a different matter. If Aed had indeed murdered Diarmid mac Cerball, could he ever be a priest? And his reputation was bad enough before that. And what of this of carnality? He was known as a lover of men. Were he and Findchan living together? Surely that must be sin?

Baithen did not know. It could be so – who could tell if they were? As to sin, it was to be feared that not a few in monasteries did the like, being denied women.

But Aed was *not* denied women, Colum insisted. He chose so to live. He was rich and of some power. He could have had women amany, or married, at any time . . .

They reached no conclusion, save that Colum was certainly unwilling to ordain, and recommended that none other should either. Baithen should keep an eye on the pair meantime. If, as he said, Findchan made a good priest and pastor in the new monastery – he had been a sub-abbot in Ireland and no known word spoken against him – then it might be that he could keep Black Aed with him there. But he, Colum, would be uneasy, even so . . .

Colum took his unease in this matter with him to Hinba in due course. He had a notable reception there after his long absence, although with some criticism from his mother for not having come to see them sooner. Bridget may have felt the same way but did not say so. And the dog Gaul went crazy with excitement.

The women had made great improvements to their island retreat, turning it into a place of delight and comfort, even if that was scarcely the original intention. Neither of them was nunnishly inclined or thought to equate God's work and purposes with austerity unless that was specifically called for by circumstances. So they set to and prepared a feast for their visitor which, they assured, would be none so poor a substitute for one of King Brude's. And while this was being made, Colum went along to his *diseart*, to pray there, almost guiltily

on account of the brevity of it and the feasting he was going
back to – and was touched to find his cell all clean, cared for
and decorated with flowers still – which in late autumn must
have been hard to come by on that rocky isle.

Guilt or none, he did ample justice to the splendid repast
provided, while he told them of the mission to Alba.

Thereafter, although it was not an evening for a sunset, he
and Bridget did take the dog for one of their walks, actually
back to the *diseart*.

After all the talk at the table, they walked along, compan-
ionably silent in the main, well pleased with each other's
company. But at the little cell itself, after thanking her for her
sustained attention to it, the man confessed to his earlier
feelings of guilt. He had chosen Hinba as a hermitage, a quiet
place of contemplation and spiritual renewal, in the wide sea –
and she, and his mother of course, had made it something very
different, a refuge from cares and worries, yes, but a place of
joy and relish and refreshment.

"Do you wish that we – or, at the least, *I* – was not here,
Columcille?"

"No," he answered frankly.

She smiled. "I think that you are too conscious of guilt," she
said. "You are strong – but you have your weaknesses. As
have we all."

"Do I not know it, woman!"

"To know, yes – but not always to blame yourself. As I
think that too frequently you do. If you judged others as you
do yourself, you could be accused of being a hard man!"

That gave him pause. "You think that I do not judge others?
Strange that you should say that. For I am concerned that I
may be judging others *too* harshly." And he told her about
Findchan and Black Aed.

She was silent for a while when he finished. "You have your
responsibilities as leader," she acknowledged "What are you
condemning in these two? Probable murder? Or bodily
affections? Or both?"

He thought about it. "Both, probably," he admitted.
"I . . . mislike such men."

"I am sure that you do, being the *man* you are! But others
may be . . . differently made. Is their sin so great?"

"You do not condone it? This of men and men? Or women
and women?"

"Who am I to judge? I do not like it, I admit. Indeed it offends me. But then, I am not made that way, any more than are you! Therefore, are we in a position to judge?"

"It is a sin, surely? Holy Writ declares it so."

"Are there not sins and sins, Columcille? Even some that *we* may on occasion commit! Murder, to be sure. Although you do not know that it *was* murder, do you? But this other . . .?"

"You say that I should overlook it?"

"I do not take it upon myself to advise the Abbot of Iona!" Then she laughed a little. "That is not quite the truth, is it? More sin! Say that were it myself, I should try to keep an open mind in this matter. Try to discover whether it was indeed murder. If so, that matter is settled. If not, and the man appears to be sincere, and anxious to aid in your work, God's work, then . . ."

"But, do you not see! It is not only myself. It is others, ordinary folk. If they believe this Aed to be a, a loose-liver, much less a murderer, it could hinder their faith if he was made priest, offend them as it offends you. And myself."

"I see that, yes. It is a hard decision to make. All that I can say is – do not be over-hasty."

"I have told Baithen that I will not ordain, meantime. And recommend that he does not, either. Nor others. And to watch them . . ."

They left it at that, Colum's problem little eased.

He mentioned that other and very different problem, of the Coll pirates. She had heard about this from Ernan, and was sympathetic. When Colum indicated that he was thinking of paying a visit to that island, to protest and seek to change their attitudes, she urged strongly against it. Old Conall mac Donald – to whom she was in fact distantly related, as were so many of the inbred Dalriada nobility – might possibly heed him; but his son Ian assuredly would not. He was a savage and evil man, a notorious killer, who slew for slaying's sake. Colum's life would not be worth anything on Coll if Ian mac Conall was there. No amount of preaching would affect him. Colum must not go to Coll, unless with a large armed band.

Perhaps God would look after him, Colum suggested.

"Would that not be a tempting of God? Knowing the dangers?"

"What, then? We cannot sit back and let him savage our people. Columban at Calva, has been raided three times. Two of his womenfolk and most of his cattle and sheep have been taken. Presumably because he is a Christian and his farm remotely placed."

"I think that you should approach Ferchar mac Tulchan. He is head of that house, of which Conall is a chieftain. Tiree is his, as you will know, although he does not live there. He will have influence with Conall, and therefore some on Ian – for he could take Coll away from them."

"Is this Ferchar a Christian? I remember, he offered us a place on Tiree, that first day at the council-meeting at Dunadd."

"In name I should think that he is. Like so many others here. But, in fact . . ?"

"What am I doing taking the Gospel to all Alba – when perhaps I should be devoting my time to the lost sheep of this Dalriada!"

She did not comment on that.

He agreed that he should go and see Ferchar mac Tulchan, who apparently preferred to live on the small isle of Gigha, near to Dunadd and the seat of power, and so was near neighbour to Ellary.

Making their way back towards the house, Colum asked about Ellary and Angus, and about her visit to Lismore, and learned that all was well there. Nevertheless, the man found himself just a little put out by what she told him. Angus was now back at Ellary, playing the chief; but she, Bridget, was just considering possibly taking his place on Lismore, where it seemed that Moluag had rather more use for women's services in matters of religion than had Colum mac Felim. Uncertain how to cope with this, after one or two false starts, he put it to her that he was not against women playing their due part in the Church – far from it. And not only as nuns. It was the distraction and complications of women *working* with men, that troubled him – and which, humanity being made the way it was, no amount of argument and disclaiming would alter. He knew *himself* well enough to recognise the dangers. Once a Church community was fully established and settled, it might be different, would be different. But at this mission stage . . .

"We have been over this before, Columcille," she said. "Let us not spoil our first evening together, after so long a parting, by such talk. I know your views on this . . ." She took his arm.

He was glad enough to leave it there, but retained some feeling of grudge – oddly enough rather against Moluag.

They went on in silence for a while, until she said, "Why do we so seldom walk together without getting deep into this so serious talk? Must we, always?"

"It is strange, yes. But – do you blame me? You are a woman of much understanding and sensibility. As well as other . . . good things. You *make* me talk."

"Perhaps it is just that you are missing your Laisran, your soul-friend and confessor in Ireland?"

"I do miss him, yes. Do I use you as confessor, then? In some measure?"

"It might be so. It must be difficult for you, as leader of all here. You cannot unburden yourself to those under you. The leader, like a king, is always alone. A wóman can perhaps help? Or . . . do I hinder rather than help?"

"Never! Never that, Bridget. Would I keep coming to you, if that were so?" Abruptly he put it to her. "Do you indeed intend to go to Lismore? To Moluag? To work for him there?"

"Would you not wish me to go?"

"I must be honest – no!"

"Yet Moluag finds work for me there, that you do not. He thinks to start a nunnery on Lismore."

"You are no nun!" That was jerked out.

"No. But this would not be an enclosed house. The women would go out. As you do. Out *behind* you. To nurture the seed that you and your missionaries have sown. You need such, do you not?"

"How think you that the new converts would receive women teachers?"

"*Other* women would, I believe. And half mankind are women."

"Perhaps you are right, as to converts. But what of those who will not accept and believe? Hard, cruel men. Defenceless women venturing amongst these could be ill-used, savaged, outraged. That I could not have on my conscience."

"But men also risk attack, death. You yourself, Columcille. Think you that I have not lain awake of a night, dreading that? If men can face that danger, so can women."

He shook his head.

"If Moluag can consider setting up a nunnery, on Lismore, for out-working women, could not you, on Iona?"

"We shall see . . ."

Back at the house they held each other close for a little before going within.

The implementation of Bridget's good advice to approach Ferchar mac Tulchan, on Gigha, was superseded by events. Colum got back to Iona the next day to trouble. A man had just arrived at the monastery, from the north-west end of the island, to announce that a raid was in progress, presumably the Coll pirates again, a long-ship with about thirty men.

Ernan had begun to assemble a party of monks to go to try to drive off the raiders, or at least rescue possible victims; but Colum said no. After what Bridget had told him of Ian mac Conall, if it was indeed he again, then he would have his crew of Christian-hating killers, and any protest in force by monks would probably merely provoke a slaughter, a massacre, for they could not hope to outfight these trained ruffians if it came to armed combat. No, he would go himself, alone. One man's protest or appeal might be more effective, as well as less costly. There was dissent at that; but he was determined. He would go alone.

In the event he did not go entirely alone, for Lugbe and Diarmit tailed along behind, just out of hearing range so that no instructions to turn back could be received.

Colum made across the central spine of the island, below Dun I, north by west, for Calva, Columban's farm. It was the largest on that coast and it had a natural harbour at Port Chlacha Dubha, the haven of the black stones, one and a half miles from the monastery.

He saw the smoke staining the sky as soon as he crossed the ridge. That was Calva afire, undoubtedly. Anger surged up within him.

Presently he could distinguish the long-ship in the harbour. Files of men could be seen, like ants, carrying gear and booty from burning farmery to ship.

He hurried, almost ran, that last half mile.

He was observed coming, of course, and not a few laughing men waited for him, laden with spoil, and shouting rudery. Seeking to control both his breathing and his wrath, coming up, Colum demanded, all prince now, who was their master.

His so evident inborn authority had its effect on those near enough to hear and see, and the laughter tailed away. One of the men pointed back a little way towards the farm, where a tall, youngish man came leading a calf. Towards him Colum strode.

"Ian mac Conall?" he jerked.

The man nodded, and all around others turned to watch.

"You, thief and robber, are the son of Conall of Coll, are you not? Think shame on yourself! Take that stolen calf back to where you got it. And order your ruffians to return all that they have taken." That was sufficiently imperative.

Even that hard-bitten character could only stare at first.

"I know of you, Ian mac Conall, and your evil ways. You will pursue them no more, on this island."

"Who . . . who are you?" the younger man got out.

"I am Colum mac Felim, a prince of Donegal and Abbot of this Iona."

"Ha – the Irishman! I have heard of you, also! You should go back to Ireland!" The other was recovering himself.

"While there are such as you to plague this land, I esteem myself needed here! That you, of the kingly house, should rob and ravish and burn your fellows, who have done you no hurt, passes belief. Are you so without respect for yourself, or so stricken with poverty on Coll, that you must descend to this!"

"Watch your words, Irishman! None speak me so!"

"*I* do. And do more than speak. I demand that you return to that ravaged farm all that you have stolen. And seek to make good all the harm you have done."

"Or . . .?"

"Or I lay a curse upon you, Ian mac Conall. In the name of Almighty God!"

"I do not fear your Christian god."

"Then the greater fool you! The Water Horse of Loch Ness did! As does Broichan, the Magus. And the King Brude."

"Then *they* are the fools. Be off, Irishman. While you still have your life!"

"My life is in God's hands, not yours, murderer. I have warned you . . ."

"And I you! Begone, before I set my men on you."

"You will not do that, I think. Lest I curse them each and all." He made that loud, for all to hear. "They will not all be so scornful of the Most High's power."

312

Whether the other recognised that this might well be so amongst superstitious fighting-men was not to be known. But instead of ordering his people to attack, he angrily waved them onwards, with their burdens, down towards the haven. He himself pushed on, with the calf, past Colum, unspeaking. There were only a few more laden men behind him. Colum followed.

Down at the shore all was busyness, with the long-ship being loaded up with spoil, livestock now either slaughtered there and then or with the legs tied together to be tossed into the ship like sacks, the man Ian directing all. Colum went up to him again.

"What makes you do this?" he asked. "Do you so mislike your fellow-men?"

"I mislike *you*, Irishman. I told you to be gone."

"You are entitled to mislike me, since I take you to task. But not all men, surely? Yet you steal and slay, rob others of their lives and goods. And need not. Others do not live so. Are you so differently made that you cannot live as do other men? You, son of a chieftain."

"Because other men are fools and weak, need I be? If men are fools enough to toil and labour and then not strong enough to protect what they have, then they deserve to lose it."

"That is the creed of the Devil! Not of man, made in the image of God."

"Then I salute your devil. Now – away!"

"You salute the Devil! Then, woe to you! Let the Devil protect you! I have warned you. God's power is infinite. As you shall find out."

The man Ian spat at Colum's feet, laughed at him, made a mocking sign of the cross, then turned to launch his coracle and paddle out to his ship.

It was that mockery of the cross which aroused Colum to fury. Trembling with it, he could find no words. Then he waded out towards the vessel. Water up his knees, he halted and raised both hands above his head.

"I curse you, Ian mac Conall!" he cried. "You, who have hated your fellow-men, slain, chosen the Devil and mocked Christ's cross, spurning Almighty God – now that God will spurn you! I curse you, in His holy Name. Go – and perish!"

Jeering and shouts of abuse came to him from the long-ship

as the oars were dipped in and the dragon-prow swung round to head for the open sea.

Still quivering from the strength of his emotions, Colum turned and waded ashore. For some time he stood there, in a strange state. Never had he done the like of this before. Often he had lost his temper, hot as it could be. But never had he been so consumed with wrath as scarcely to be in control of himself. That cursing – what right had he to curse so in God's name? The God of love whom he preached. Whatever the provocation. It was the sin he was told to hate, not the sinner. Had he himself sinned grievously in this? It was that of salute to Satan and defilement of the cross that enraged him. Was *he* the accursed?

He was standing in this state when Lugbe and Diarmit, who had watched all from a distance, ventured down to him. He stared at them but scarcely saw them. He did not speak. Eying him, nor did they.

Presently, silently they moved up to the ravaged farmery.

Columban and his few people, who had fled at sight of the pirate ship, had now come back and were seeking to extinguish the fires. Colum and his pair helped them, commiserating.

So busy were they all at this labour that they hardly noticed the change in the weather. It had been, for early November, a fine day, with high thin cloud and fitful sunlight. But presently, as the smoke of the burning buildings and hay-stacks thinned and faded, it could be seen that black, ominous clouds were piling up to the north, with the wind rising. They were the more concerned to get the last of the fires out before the wind fanned them, until heavy raindrops splashing down, they realised that this would douse the fires, and turned instead to other remedial work. But soon this was halted also and they all ran for cover where it might be found, so violent became the wind and rain, a sudden storm such as the Hebridean Sea can produce on occasion, unheralded but far from unusual; save on this occasion the wind came from due north, in savage gusts. Cowering where they could, they waited, for these squalls seldom lasted long. But this one went on longer than was normal, and presently they could hear, in pauses between fierce gusts, the booming of great seas on the rock-bound shore. And before, the sea had been comparatively calm.

Colum, listening, knew a further sinking feeling within him. This unlooked-for storm – could it be . . .? Any ship out in that, unless it could quickly find shelter in the lee of land or an island, would be in grave danger. Was his cursing responsible? Had he condemned a whole company, thirty and more men, to drowning? What had he done? There was no island to shelter a vessel between Iona and Coll, twenty miles – but many savage reefs and skerries, the tips of sea-bed mountains.

The storm ceased almost as suddenly as it had begun, although the thunder of the waves continued. With the light fading, Colum and the young men took their leave of the unhappy Calva folk and made their way back over the sodden ground to the monastery.

It was three days before the news reached them. Ian mac Conall's long-ship had never returned to Coll and was presumed lost with all hands.

Colum brooded on it all.

17

The winters were periods for consolidation, with travel and therefore mission work limited by weather and brevity of daylight. But none the less busy for that, with so much to be done in Dalriada as well as on Iona itself, and Tiree. And that last island produced a further question mark and occasion for soul-searching on Colum's part.

For, since Colum would not do it, and neither would Baithen, despite the former's prohibition, Findchan himself ordained his friend Black Aed priest. Whether he had the ability to do so authentically was doubtful, for he was neither bishop nor ruling abbot; but he had been a sub-abbot in Ireland and presumably considered that sufficient authority. When, in the New Year, Baithen came to tell his cousin, Colum was angry indeed. It not only was in direct disobedience to his orders but it went against all the rules and standards he had established for his mission. In his ire, he declared that the hand which Findchan had laid on Aed's head in blessing, was unworthy to bless and would, he asserted, bless no more. He sent Baithen back with orders that Findchan was to be suspended in his charge of the sub-monastery on Tiree, and given only minor duties, as penance; and that the man Aed was in no circumstances to be allowed to function as priest in any area where Colum had authority.

It took a month or so before the word came from Tiree that Findchan could not now use his right hand. It had become stiff, the fingers curling over claw-like, becoming set that way.

This news, after the matter of Ian mac Conall and his crew, set Colum furiously to think and question himself. Had he some power, some strange ability to bring down cursing on others? Was it just God using him? Or was it something other, something not good but in fact evil? A kind of possession of himself? By a power not of God and love but of anger and hurt?

He worried about this. He discussed it with Ernan and Baithen – Kenneth and Comgall had now returned to Ireland. His colleagues ridiculed his doubts. Did not Christ's own apostles do the same? God used their maledictions to punish evil-doers. Far from possible wrong, was it not a sign that God was with Colum to great purpose and power?

He took the matter to Bridget and long hours of spiritual wrestling at his *diseart*. The woman had few more doubts than Ernan and Baithen. But she did perceive possible danger to Colum himself in the situation, now that he was troubled with it. If he felt that he had this power, it could hold him back from strong measures when these were in fact needed. He could become afraid of it, dread its consequences, and so become even more concerned with guilt – which could be bad, for himself and for his cause, God's cause. Her advice, since he sought it, was to recognise it as God's gift and responsibility, but to use it very sparingly.

Colum's preoccupations that winter were not wholly with disobediences and self-doubts. He agreed, at last, to Bridget's suggestion to set up a nunnery of sorts, or at least a woman's missionary establishment, connected with his abbey. But he did not go all the way with her, in this as in other more personal matters. Still concerned over likely distractions, he would not put the place on Iona itself but on a small island offshore to the east, indeed much nearer to the Mull shore than their own, although still only half a mile across the sound. Bridget, of course, was to be the prioress here, and would work closely with himself and his monks; but at least the women would spend their nights on their own island. Bridget shook her head in a sort of exasperation over that, but accepted it.

So now there was enrolment to be dealt with. Bridget began with two or three converts from Iona itself, but went over to Mull for more, and sent for two of her own women from Ellary, so that she had ten to start with. The monks, of course, came across to the smaller isle each day to help with the building – they were already calling it Eilean nam Ban, the island of women – but Bridget insisted that her novices did much of the work of construction themselves, concerned that the 'helpless women' myth should be dispelled, or not allowed to grow.

They made a busy early spring of it.

Then, as Colum was preparing to start on his first mission of the season, back to Skye to see how Scandlann, Fechno and Grillan were faring, a strange long-ship sailed into the main haven, bringing Bishop Cormac back from faraway Iceland. The fact that this was an Icelandic vessel, not an Orkney one, seemed to indicate a successful embassage.

Cormac was full of news. He told of adventures with sea-serpents and monsters, one of which had actually smashed some of his ship's oars; of ice-mountains afloat in a strange ocean where leviathans blew fountains of water in the air; of land mountains which spouted fire and smoke above broad rivers of frozen water which cracked like mighty whips. Eventually, these dramatics over, he informed that the visit had gone well, after no less than a fourteen day voyage from Orkney, that the Icelandic franklins had agreed to Brude's and Wirp's terms to stop the raids on Alba and Orkney. He had set up Christian missions in both lands. He, Cormac, intended to go back there in two or three years' time, God willing; but meantime could Colum send someone to help to maintain what had been established?

That was asking a lot, when the Iona community was already stretched to the utmost. Colum could only tell his old friend that he would try, do what he could. But would

Cormac not do better to send people direct from Ireland when he got back there? This of manpower was a major problem.

The return visit to Skye was encouraging also, as well as interesting, in that Colum found the work going notably well, largely thanks to the support of Queen Sinech it seemed. Scandlann in the west, at Snizort, Fechno at Portree and Grillan now at Raasay, all spoke highly of her help. She was not at Dun Torvaig when Colum arrived, being off with Fechno apparently to the Sleat peninsula area to visit a cell they had established at Ord; but King Cathal was at home and greeted Colum genially enough for that man, and almost respectfully. He had not become any more Christian than before, it seemed, but clearly had no objection to his wife's beliefs and activities, indeed may well have found them convenient in keeping her occupied and so allowing him a freer hand in the womanising which seemed so important to him. The Arch Druid Enda was still in evidence, but kept his distance from the visitors.

Cathal had heard about events at Inverness and was considerably impressed – Colum was still intrigued by this the Albannach's so effective communication system and the swift passage of information over long distances. In particular, Cathal wanted to hear more about the Water Horse, which, after the Fell Hound and boar incidents, seemed to appeal to him. He was not greatly interested in Brude's conversion any more than in Broichan's cure – save in that he asked if Prince Colum would charm a white pebble for him also. He *was* concerned over Brude's health, however, asking searching questions. Colum remembered Cathal's excitement over the boar-slaying and its symbolism for him, as the emblem of the high kingship, and Sinech's revelation that he had ambitions to succeed Brude. He did not offer the monarch any hopes of Brude's early demise.

Another example of these people's faculty for gaining news, however it was achieved, much interested Colum. Cathal not only knew that the High King of Ireland had been killed but knew how and where it had happened. Apparently Diarmid mac Cerball had been raiding into Antrim, very much Hy-Neill territory, and at Rathbeg in that sub-kingdom had been celebrating the day's activities in riotous style at an inn – Cathal even knew the name of the inn-keeper, one Banban – when a group of Antrim men surrounded the inn and set it afire. One of these was Aed mac Sween, and when Diarmid rushed out, Aed thrust the High King through with a spear. Diarmid had fallen back into a great vat of ale, and then the burning roof collapsed on him. So he died the triple death prophesied – by steel, by fire and by drowning, which would ensure his damnation. And now another Aed, mac Ainmere, was to become High King of Ireland in Diarmid's stead. Cathal did not appear to know, however, that Black Aed was presently on the isle of Tiree.

This information made Aed's offence somewhat less grievous, since it could hardly be termed murder if Diarmid had been raiding and his death part of a reprisal by the invaded. So that was worth the knowing.

Colum went from Portree, through the central valley to Snizort, where he found Scandlann presiding over quite a well-doing community grouped round a church and monastic-type buildings, a cashel. Delighted to see Columcille, Scandlann proudly explained that this was only the centre for many other Christian outposts in west Skye. He would take him round them. All the converts would be greatly cheered and en-heartened to have a visit from the renowned Abbot Colum.

Asked about Grillan, Scandlann said that he was now settled on the isle of Raasay, between Skye and the mainland, and having success there. Colum would remember that he himself had been sent there at first, but had made little impression on King Cathal's brother who was chief there, and had left. But later Queen Sinech, a good friend, had taken him back, and she had much influence with this Fidach mac Coitir – who indeed was fairly obviously in love with his brother's wife – and they had been allowed to preach and convert. When Colum had sent him Fechno and Grillan as helpers, he had put Grillan in charge at Raasay and Fechno in Bishop Moluag's place at Portree. Both were prospering, and largely thanks to the Lady Sinech.

So for a few days Colum was escorted round Scandlann's west Skye communities, preaching, baptising and making new converts, much approving of all he saw – if reproving himself for his satisfaction on being taken to a loch, allegedly the largest fresh-water expanse on Skye, which was now being named after himself, Loch Columcille. It seemed that there had been a local belief that this loch was haunted by an evil creature, not exactly a water horse but a monster of some

319

sort, said not only to eat children but with powers to destroy them even in their mothers' wombs, so that they were either born dead or else defective in body or mind, and therefore were thrown into the loch by the Druids to placate the monster. On hearing of the Loch Ness deliverance, Scandlann had decided to try his own hand, or voice, at this; and using Colum's name to, as it were, reinforce Christ's in his exorcism, he had bade the creature begone and to trouble God's children no more. Whether or no he had been as successful as Colum with the Water Horse, Scandlann did not know; but there had been no appearances or troubles since, and the people believed. So now he had named the loch after Columcille and all accepted it as that.

However, whether it was on account of this incident or of other reports about him, Colum's name had in fact created at least one problem for Scandlann. There was an old chieftain named Artbrannan of Duntulm, in the Uig area, famous as a one-time great warrior although now very aged. He had been receptive to the Christian message and willing for Scandlann to make converts of his people; but he, in his pride, refused to be baptised by any save the famous Prince Colum himself. When he, Scandlann, had pointed out that in that case he might never receive baptism into the Church since he was old and unfit and there was no certainty that the Abbot Colum would be able to come to Skye in the near future, Artbrannan had declared that Colum *would* come, he knew it. And he would wait for him.

Colum, while agreeing that this was vanity and a totally wrong attitude towards the sacrament of baptism, pointed out that it still represented a sort of faith. The old man should not be denied entry to Christ's flock even if he was prideful. There were worse sins. He was prepared to go and baptise him.

Scandlann was doubtful. Would it not look like weakness, a pandering to unchristian values? And, since the aged chief was said to be very ill, it would mean Columcille going all the way to Duntulm, near the very northern tip of Skye, fully twenty miles away.

Colum remembered Duntulm, perched on its dizzy cliff-top, from his sail round the great island on his previous visit. He admitted that to go all the way, just to cater to the self-esteem of one individual, might seem weak. On the other hand, if the old warrior was sincere in his desire for baptism, they should not deny it him when he was near to death's-door.

A compromise, perhaps? Send him word that Colum mac Felim would come halfway to meet him. If he was truly eager, however ill and frail, a warrior like that would make some effort. If they chose somewhere as a meeting place where Artbrannan could be brought by boat, it would be a fair test.

Scandlann was scarcely enthusiastic, but agreed. Uig Bay would be about halfway. He could send word to meet there in, say, two days time. Although it would, in fact, be little more trying for Artbrannan to be brought directly here to Snizort, in his boat.

Colum said no. There should be the gesture on both sides. Halfway. Send the messenger.

So two days later they sailed down Loch Snizort Beg and into the outer loch, to turn in due course into Uig Bay, some ten miles. At the bay-head, where a small river came in out of Glen Uig, they landed, to wait. Scandlann had a group here, so their time was not to be wasted.

In mid-afternoon Diarmit, on watch, came to announce that a large curragh was approaching from the north. They all trooped down to the shore. Colum found a large flat stone, with a fresh-running burn beside it, and this he tapped with his cross-crossleted pastoral staff.

"Here is all we need," he said. "Here Artbrannan will enter his new life."

The curragh, pulled by six oarsmen, drew in to where the little crowd was gathered. Two young men waved, and with the help of the rowers lifted out a stretcher of sorts, on which lay a white-headed huddled old man, wasted of frame, eyes closed.

"Artbrannan's grandsons," Scandlann mentioned. "Both have been baptised. With their mother. Their father is dead."

Colum, as he greeted them and signed for the bearers to place the stretcher on the flat rock, was much reminded of old Emchat at Urquhart.

"Artbrannan, my friend. I am Colum mac Felim, from Iona," he said. "I understand that you wish me to baptise you into Christ's holy Church. And that you believe that Jesus Christ is the Son of Almighty God, who died and rose again to save us all? Is this true?"

The other had opened watery eyes, to peer. He did not answer.

Colum repeated what he had asked.

"Are you he? The Prince-Abbot?" the old man got out thickly.

"I am. But that is not important. I am but a humble servant of the Most High. As are all who accept Christ's teachings. As will you be if I baptise you." He spoke almost sternly.

"Not . . . in this . . . life." That was a whisper.

"Perhaps not, Artbrannan. But there is another life to come – eternity. Will you be servant then? Or must you always be the master?"

Silence.

"It is a hard decision for such as yourself, my friend, I recognise. But others have had to make it. *I* sought to do so, many years ago."

Again the whisper. "They say . . . you were . . . to be . . . High King of Ireland? And . . . would not."

"That is true."

"Then . . . if you could . . . I, Artbrannan . . . can."

"You are still proud, man!"

"So are . . . you!"

Colum paused at that, and then smiled ruefully. "Perhaps you are right. But I *try* to conquer it. Do you?"

"I . . . shall. Hereafter."

"Aye. So you believe?"

There was another pause as the eyes closed again. Then an almost imperceptible nod and a still fainter whisper. "Be quick! I have not . . . long."

"So be it." Colum stooped, to scoop up water from the burn in his cupped hand, to sprinkle on the old man's head. "In the name of God the Father, God the Son and God the Holy Spirit, I baptise you, Artbrannan, into Jesus Christ's Church and the company of the faithful. Be *you* faithful, in this life and the next."

The old eyes opened, looked from Colum to his two grandsons, and a smile of sheer joy and something like triumph spread over those wasted features. Then the white head fell back and the smile faded as breathing faltered and ceased.

All there watching, stared, and some crossed themselves.

"Glory be to God!" Colum exclaimed. "Receive the soul of Thy servant Artbrannan. And have mercy on ours. Amen."

When emotions had calmed somewhat and decisions had to be made as to procedure, the two young men came to the conclusion that instead of sailing their grandfather's body back to Duntulm, it should remain here, where so important an event in his life had taken place. Let Artbrannan's body rest here, where his soul had left it, on this rock. They would build a great cairn over it, to mark the warrior's last battle won.

Colum smiled over that. "More pride!" he observed, but not unkindly. And he helped with his own hands to gather and heap up stones from the beach to make an eye-catching monument.

He was not aware, as he said goodbye to the young men and with Scandlann re-entered their own boat, that he was leaving behind yet another legend – that the Abbot Colum had prophesied the old man's death on that stone, when they heard him say "Here Artbrannan will enter his new life." He had meant by baptism, but others interpreted it differently.

Back at Portree he found Fechno returned, with Sinech, another quite emotional occasion. The queen threw herself into Colum's arms, to Fechno's mixed amusement and disapproval – but not Colum's. He kissed her and held her from him, to say that she was a sight to gladden the eyes, more beautiful than ever. For a little while she could not answer that.

They had of course much to discuss and relate, and talked far into the night. But when Sinech offered him the bed in Dun Torvaig that he had occupied on a previous occasion, Colum smiled and announced that he would probably sleep more soundly on a harder couch down at Fechno's cashel. She made a face at him but did not pursue the matter.

Next day all three went in Machar's long-ship to visit Grillan on Raasay, a most pleasant interlude. Indeed Colum's guilt complex began to reassert itself over his frank enjoyment of this entire Skye visit – which was hardly meant to be a pleasure-trip. But that, he told himself, was foolish. Success and progress in a good cause, friendship, beauty, even stimulation of the senses, were not to be deplored, surely?

He found that he could not like Fidach mac Coitir, Sinech's brother-in-law, but was not ungrateful for the facilities he had afforded Grillan, for whatever reason. He found himself being critical of the man's so evident approaches to Sinech, despite the coolness of her reactions – and had to remind himself that this was no concern of his. Sometimes he all but despaired for himself.

They spent three busy days on Raasay, helping and supporting Grillan, who, like Scandlann, wanted assistant priests sent to him – this now becoming a general and continuing litany with Colum's colleagues.

Back at Portree thereafter, with Scandlann rejoining them, Colum and Fechno commenced a series of visitations of those parts of Skye not yet reached by the missionaries, Sinech accompanying them. Obviously she enjoyed these ventures, and she was a major help in gaining the men a hearing wherever they went, and the best of lodgings, since all must seek not to offend the queen. It was strange, however, to be accompanied also by four female warriors of the royal guard, strapping young women with little of maidenly modesty, but cheerful, and useful as camp-servants, cooks and grooms – for they travelled on horseback. Colum was uncertain whether they came along as it were to maintain the queen's dignity and status, or were sent by Cathal to keep an eye on all.

Skye was a huge island, the largest of the Inner Hebrides, with many long peninsulas divided from each other by deep sea-lochs, whereon were numerous isolated communities, some quite populous, the reaching of which was often difficult and time-consuming. But in early summer the beauty of it all was a continual joy, often breath-taking; and in good company their progress was almost consistently so pleasant that once again Colum tended to become nagged by the feeling that this was all too enjoyable to be right and suitable on a religious exercise – even though he was a great believer in the essential joy of worship. However, they did have considerable success in their evangelising wherever they went, which helped to still the doubts.

Sinech made good company, and although she made no secret of the fact that she would have liked to have a closer physical relationship with Colum, seemed to accept the limitations he prescribed and did not embarrass. Inevitably he found himself comparing her with Bridget, and sought not to do so. They were very different characters, not for comparison. Morever, Bridget was a free woman, a widow, and Sinech had a husband, however unfaithful – although that again was scarcely relevant, he reminded himself. Should such as he have favourite women anyway? Probably not.

But . . . Bridget was Bridget, and no amount of self questioning would change that for him.

He sometimes wondered about his colleagues in this matter of women. Presumably some would be as troubled and concerned as he was – or was he unusual? Others less so, undoubtedly. It was not a subject on which he felt inclined to question them – for, as leader and senior, what could he advise, who did not himself know the answers?

Despite all of which, when eventually his Skye mission was over, for that year at least, it was from Sinech that he was most reluctant to take leave, most upsetting the parting.

18

Iona, like the rest of Dalriada, was in a stir. King Conall thereof had died, when visiting his son Duncan of Kintyre. It was not his demise which was causing the unrest – for Conall had never been popular nor sought to be – but the question of who was to be his successor. The automatic succession of the eldest son did not apply in Celtic kingship, so Duncan mac Conall of Kintyre did not necessarily heir the throne, although apparently he was claiming it. Ewan mac Gabhran, eldest son of the previous monarch, would be the more acceptable choice, for he was well liked, and his father had died a hero's death; but his younger brother Aidan, with whom he did not get on, was also claiming it, and he was a very forceful young man. So there were three competitors, and the nation was divided in allegiance.

All this would have been of no great concern to the community on Iona had it not been that Ewan appealed to Colum – or at least requested Colum to *consecrate* him king on Iona. He it was who had offered the missionaries, at that first council-meeting at Dunadd, a site for their monastery on his isle of Colonsay, when his brother Aidan had objected. Ewan had since embraced the faith enthusiastically, whilst Aidan had not, although both were nominally Christians of course.

Colum was not averse to doing as Ewan suggested; indeed he recognised that the consecrating of the monarch, something which apparently had never before been done, would be an excellent innovation as far as the Church was concerned, enhancing its position and giving it an added authority in this realm. And Ewan would probably make a good king, whilst his being a strong Christian could only help their cause.

Oddly, it was Bridget who introduced him to an element of doubt in the matter. She informed that there was quite a strong feeling amongst the nobility that Aidan would make the better, or at least the stronger, king. The trouble was that Conall had been, not a weak but a retiring monarch, and it was feared that Ewan might be something of the same. With the threat of Athelfrith and the Angles hanging over them, and the alliance with Strathclyde, Fortrenn and Alba to be effected, Dalriada required a strong and warlike leader – and Aidan could be that. He was aggressive, self-assertive and could be difficult, yes – but he was a fighter, whereas his brother had shown little sign of that. Bridget herself was not taking it upon herself to recommend Aidan – although in fact her son Angus was doing so.

Colum, with no reason to like Aidan, was far from convinced. A truly Christian monarch was, he thought, infinitely preferable in present circumstances to any mere warrior. Such could be employed, surely, as commanding general in the field, without being king? Not that the matter rested in any way with himself, he pointed out.

Then word reached them that Duncan mac Conall had been killed in some raid in Kintyre. So the two mac Gabhran brothers were the only competitors. And Colum had no real difficulty in deciding to agree to Ewan's suggestion, and his consecration. He began to plan a suitable and impressive ceremony.

He was on Hinba when he had a strange and unique experience. He had gone to see his mother – who was greatly missing Bridget and was talking about leaving the islet and going to stay in the new nunnery on Eilean nam Ban. Hinba was not the same for Colum either; but at least he now made more use of his *diseart*; and he was sleeping therein that first night, after praying to be guided in the matter of Findchan and Black Aed, when he had a most peculiar and unsettling dream.

A being, an angel presumably, came to him bearing a book made of glass such as he had never before seen. Handing him this, he was bidden to read it. The open page proved to contain a list of the kings of Dalriada, starting with Fergus mac Erc, Lorn and the rest. And after Gabhran and Conall came the last entry – Aidan mac Gabhran.

Surprised, Colum dreamed that he shook his head and declared that here was, he believed, a mistake. *Ewan* mac Gabhran, a good Christian, should be Conall's successor.

The angel asked whether he thought that he knew better than his Creator, and Colum said no, but he knew Ewan and his brother and had no doubt which would make the better monarch. Whereupon the angel, if such he was, struck him hard on the side of the face, and vanished.

This woke Colum, who found his face stinging as from a blow.

Much troubled, he could not sleep again, and went walking instead. He did not tell his mother of the dream.

The next night he took the dog Gaul with him to the *diseart*. He had exactly the same dream, even the blow being repeated. Waking, he heard Gaul growling deeply in his throat.

Now deeply concerned, he did tell his mother. The Princess Eithne declared that it was nothing of *her* cooking which was giving him such dreams; he had always had too vivid an imagination.

He went fishing that day, from his coracle, finding fishing an aid to thought. Almost he fell asleep in the boat after two bad nights.

The third night he was almost afraid to let sleep take over, tired as he was. But eventually it did. And this time there was a difference in his dreaming, in that the angel *began* by slapping him again, and then announced that he had been sent by God to his disobedient servant Colum with this book; and that, according to the words he read in it, he was to anoint Aidan son of Gabhran to this kingdom. And if he refused, he would strike him again and again until he obeyed. With the angelic hand raised, Colum hastily capitulated. He would consecrate Aidan, he promised, not Ewan.

He awoke this time to Gaul licking his face where that cheek was stinging, and the beast whimpering as he did it, in much agitation. They went walking once more, later to return and sleep peacefully.

Colum went back to Iona with no doubts as to his duty, however difficult and against his own judgement.

First he had to go and inform Ewan mac Gabhran, no enviable task. He sailed to Colonsay, where he had promised, those years ago, to restore the cells and shrine of St Oran, and had never done it. Here was opportunity. They found that Prince Ewan was from home, at Dunadd apparently, in the furtherance of his claim to the throne, but he was expected back in a day or two.

So with Machar and his crew Colum filled in the time of waiting by building up the ruins, and constructing a new little chapel, on the adjacent half-tide island of Oronsay. They were still not finished their work when three days later Ewan mac Gabhran returned from Dunadd. Colum, reluctance heavy upon him, went to see him at his hall-house at Scalasaig. Ewan was glad to see him, but in a somewhat depressed state. It seemed that things had not gone well for him at Dunadd, with too many of the chiefs and nobles indicating that they preferred his brother as king. Whether he could in fact muster enough votes to achieve a majority was very doubtful. The trouble was that most of those who would have supported the slain Duncan mac Conall seemed to be now backing Aidan.

Sad as he was to have to further depress the disappointed young man, Colum told him exactly what had happened at his *diseart* and his consequent decision regarding the kingship. And he was rather surprised at Ewan's acceptance of the news. He took it quietly and without apparent resentment; indeed, Colum wondered whether he did not in fact detect just a hint of relief. Perhaps the prince had himself been having doubts, and saw this as settling the matter, taking the responsibility out of his own hands. All along the duties and obligations of the throne might have been weighing on the mind of one who was not of an assertive nature. At any rate, an interview which Colum had been all but dreading passed off with minimal discomfort.

Indeed, presently Colum was considerably impressed, even touched, when, on asking where he must go to announce the situation to Aidan, Ewan said that he would take him to his brother at Craignish and inform Aidan personally that he, Ewan, was resigning his claim to the throne and offering his brother his support. When Colum declared that this was a noble and generous gesture, in the circumstances, the other asked if it was not his Christian duty? Did not he, Abbot Colum, teach the like?

Next day, then, they set off in the two long-ships for the mainland, Colum sailing in Ewan's vessel. Aidan, it seemed, lived normally at a lordship some way north of Dunadd, the Craignish peninsula; and he had been there when Ewan left Dunadd. So the voyage was almost due eastwards, some forty miles, into the cluster of islands north of long Jura. When they neared there, Ewan's shipmaster carefully made a detour round the thrusting isle of Scarba, to avoid the Strait of Corryvreckan.

On the way, Colum learned more of an event about which he had heard only vaguely – and which was partly responsible for Aidan's advance in popularity. A great battle had been fought in the Cumbrian part of Strathclyde, at a place called Arderydd, on the River Esk near to Carlisle the Cumbrian capital, the first in the struggle against the Angles and their pagan allies. This while Colum was away in Skye. It was a major victory for King Roderick. That man, unwarlike as he was, had been forced into action when one of his own sub-kings, Guendoleu, stubbornly anti-Christian, had thrown in his lot with Athelfrith the Angle and attacked Carlisle. So Roderick had activated the anti-Anglian alliance which Colum had helped to forge; and Conall being at death's door, Aidan had been sent south with a small Dalriadan force. He had apparently distinguished himself in the battle, won Roderick's praise, and returned with his reputation considerably enhanced. The young man's choice to lead the Dalriadan force was not entirely on account of his fighting spirit, for his mother, Gabhran's second wife, was a Strathclyde princess, Lleian, daughter of King Brychan who preceded Morcant and Roderick. Ewan was son of Gabhran's first wife.

Past the screen of islands, they entered Loch Craignish. This was new territory for Colum, despite being comparatively near at hand, and very lovely, not unlike Loch Caolisport, but dotted with islets between green hills, high mountains rearing to the east.

Their arrival in the loch did not go unnoticed nor unchallenged. No fewer than six long-ships suddenly emerged from behind one of the islets – and all of them were flying the royal Dalriadan flag, however prematurely. When Colum commented, Ewan nodded.

"That is Aidan!" he said.

"But this is a fleet! Has Aidan so many ships? And men?"

"He has, yes. He is rich, you see. Or his mother is. Princess Lleian inherited much wealth and lands. From her own mother, of the Albannach, she inherited the entire province of Manaan in Fortrenn, as well as much land in Strathclyde. So Aidan lacks not for gold and silver. *I* am but his poor elder half-brother!"

"These riches could prove useful for Dalriada," Colum said thoughtfully.

The visitors were escorted past that first islet to another, in mid-loch, long, very narrow and craggy, along the quite high spine of which rose an extraordinary building, or series of buildings, to form a sort of terrace of housing. This, like the island itself, was lengthy and attenuated, above which projected no fewer than four flagstaffs flying the royal colours. In all that fair and fertile territory it seemed an unlikely and uncomfortable site to rear a house; but certainly the position was highly defensive.

At a haven, part artificial, halfway down the sheltered eastern side of the mile and a half long island, they pulled in at a jetty and went ashore, the six escorts lying off – so presumably Aidan was not aboard any of them. Ewan and Colum started to climb the zigzag track. Presently Ewan pointed. At the top, in a gateway through ramparts protecting the elongated building, a slim figure stood waiting.

Aidan greeted them warily, scarcely welcoming. Colum had not seen him since that first day at Dunadd years ago. He had matured noticeably, although retaining his slender, almost boyish physique. But there was nothing boyish about his jutting chin and hot eyes.

"So brother," he jerked, "we do not often see you at Dun Righ. And less often your Irish friend! If you have come to plead with me over this of the kingdom, you might as well return to Colonsay forthwith!" That was sufficiently frank.

"Not so," Ewan answered. "Quite otherwise. And I think that you could welcome the prince-abbot more kindly. Especially as . . ." He left the rest unsaid.

"God be with you, Aidan mac Gabhran," Colum said. "You are going to need His help hereafter. When you are king."

Aidan stared.

"We come to support your cause," Ewan added. "Myself, with some doubts. Abbot Colum with none."

"Is this mockery?" Aidan demanded. "You seek the throne yourself, do you not?"

"I did. But no longer. On Abbot Colum's advice."

"What is this . . . ?"

"I think, Prince Aidan, since it will take time to explain, it might be better if we were . . . elsewhere."

Without a word the other turned and led them indoors.

In a private hall they were seated and set food and drink, Aidan still distinctly suspicious.

"You are, I think, a baptised Christian, Aidan mac Gabhran?" Colum began carefully. He was going to try to extract the maximum advantage out of this peculiar situation. "How firm is your belief in Almighty God and His Son Jesus Christ?"

The other frowned. "Sufficient," he said briefly.

"I wonder? You are going to need considerable faith, I believe."

Aidan looked from one to the other. "Have you come here to preach to me?" he demanded. "If so, I do not need your preachings. I shall do very well without them."

"Will you? If you do not believe in what I tell you now, I cannot anoint you king."

"What . . . ?" That was almost a shout.

"Heed him," Ewan directed.

"I have what I believe to be God's direct command to appoint and anoint you, Aidan, King of Dalriada. But . . . only if *you* believe."

"Believe what, man?"

"Believe that Christ, the Son of the Most High, is your Saviour. That you are His servant on earth, and will be blessed hereafter in heaven. That Christ's Church is His body in this world and can claim your fullest support. As king." Colum emphasised those last two words.

"You would have me king?"

"Not I, but God. If you believe and promise to be His servant."

"Is this some trick, some churchman's artifice . . . ?"

"No. *This* churchman was against it! But – if you do not truly believe in God and His power, then there is no worth for you in what I have to tell you."

After a moment or two Aidan nodded. "Say on."

So Colum told him of his decision to support Ewan's claim to the throne, as the more devout Christian, and then of his three nights' dreaming and the angel's command to appoint and anoint Aidan instead, of his own reluctance, but his belief eventually that it was God's will and purpose.

Listening, Aidan's expression changed a number of times, as well it might. When the older man had finished, he remained silent for a while, looked at his brother, and then spread his hands.

"What do you expect me to say to this?" he asked.

"Only that you too accept it as God's will. That you will come for anointing, at Iona. And that, when king, you will support Christ's Church in this realm, And acknowledge His Gospel in deed as well as in word."

The other's hot eyes took on a calculating look. "Why think you your God chooses me? In preference to Ewan, or other?"

"I do not know. And say not *my* God. He is equally yours, from now on – and always was, even if you did not perceive it. I can only guess that you are chosen because you are a warrior, a fighter, and that Dalriada is going to need a fighter as king. Not, I hope, that you will fight without due cause, or for vainglory, but only for the good of the kingdom and Christ's cause."

Ewan looked doubtful.

His brother stroked his chin. "Very well," he said. "I am willing." That was all.

There seemed to be little more to say, save that Aidan should come to Iona for the anointing shortly after the council-meeting which would elect him monarch – and which, now that there was no other candidate likely to appear, was all but a foregone conclusion. There was no pressing on Aidan's part for his visitors to stay, and after only a brief interval they departed, Colum with an odd sense of anti-climax.

What Ewan felt he kept to himself.

Three weeks later the historic day dawned, unexampled, unmatched in the Church's story, as in that of all the northern nations, and remote Iona of the Hebrides was the scene. Here was to be instituted something new, something highly significant for generations and centuries to come, the State coming to the Church for its full and final authority in the appointment and ordination of its monarch. Here was Christ's Church supreme in a fashion hitherto unknown, the arbiter and ultimate reference in the nation.

Apart altogether from the constitutional significance of the occasion, Iona of course had never seen the like, even in the times of the druidical college there. The entire hierarchy, nobility and great numbers of the population of Dalriada flocked to the island, shipping so crowding the shoreline that many vessels could not find room to lie off there and had to send their people ashore in coracles and then retire to the shelter of the Mull coast, to wait. Fortunately the weather was good, fervent prayers for fair skies had been emanating from the abbey – as it was now being called – for days; just as well, for there would have been no shelter for nine-tenths of the folk who came.

With the ceremony due to start at noon, suitable for a people with a sun fixation, it was also suitable for Aidan to be almost the last to arrive, that he should not have to hang about waiting. It was equally required that Colum himself should not have to appear waiting on the shore for Aidan. So Ernan and Moluag, over from Lismore, and Baithen from Tiree, with Princess Eithne and Bridget, welcomed the monarch-to-be and conducted him up to the abbey, escorted by choirs of singing monks and nuns.

Colum, needless to say, had expended much thought and care on the details of this great occasion, to ensure that it all looked and sounded as important as it actually was. He had had special and splendid robes, vestments and copes fashioned for himself and his principal colleagues, in place of their plain black-and-white habits. In the past, inaugural celebrations for a new king had included ceremonies conducted by the Chief Druid and his subordinates, even in allegedly Christian Dalriada; and these had related it all to Echoid the Horseman of Heaven, and sun-worship, with great flourish and display, even human sacrifice. This all had to be, if not rivalled, at least countered and outshone.

So a resplendent Colum greeted Aidan, who had chosen to come dressed as though for war, amidst the crowd at the abbey threshold, and conducted him to the church-door. Since as many as possible were to see what went on, all was to be done outside; so there had had to be much moving out of furnishings and fittings, the altar, the abbot's chair to serve as throne, benches, utensils, canopies, draperies and the like. But most important for this day, Colum's own portable altar-cum-font. This was an extraordinary creation, fashioned out of a solid block of hard, marble-like stone, allegedly a meteorite, sent by King Brude as a token of esteem. Meteorites, having reputedly come from the sun, were greatly revered in the druidical faith, and this one, intricately carved with Celtic inter-lacing and cup-and-ring markings representing the sun in splendour, was a magnificent specimen. Of seat height, one of the flat faces had a distinct hollow, almost like a shallow basin; and Colum, in his desire to use it and, as it were, Christianise it, saw possibilities. That hollow could serve as a font for holy water and the flat surface act as an altar. There were carrying volutes contrived at each end for bearers, so that although weighty it was still portable. For special occasions one of these would make a notable and even awesome piece of equipment; and it could be carried on the back of Colum's old white horse.

This was indeed a special occasion and the meteorite could play its part. And not only Brude's meteorite but his brecbennach also, the little jewelled reliquary of bronze, silver and enamel, presented by him as a parting gift at Inverness. This was not made for holding liquid, but Colum had had fashioned a silver container to fit inside, and this, now sitting on the altar, held the oil for anointing.

Colum led Aidan to one of the benches and sat him thereon. Then, with Bishop Moluag on one side, Ernan on the other and Baithen behind, he signed for the singing to cease and unrolled a handsome scroll, painted and lettered in his own hand and, holding up a hand for quiet, commenced to read, in his strong, carrying, resonant voice.

"In the name of God the Father, God the Son and God the Holy Spirit! Aidan mac Gabhran mac Domangart mac Fergus mac Erc of the House of O'Neill, you have been chosen by the Most High God and elected by the high council of Dalriada to be King of Scots. I, Colum mac Felim mac Fergus mac O'Conall mac Niall Nine-Hostager, have been commanded by the same God to appoint and anoint you as king. Do you, Aidan, accept that appointment?"

The younger man nodded curtly. "I do."

334

"Do you accept that, although you are to be King of Scots, you are also God's humble servant, and protector of Christ's Holy Church in this realm?"

There was a slight pause. "I do." That was somewhat less definite.

Colum looked up from his reading, his own voice suddenly less warm, almost stern. "The protection of Christ's Church is your bounden duty and privilege, as king. Without it there can be no anointing, no enthronement. Do you understand that, Aidan mac Gabhran, and so accept?" There was a positive rasp in that, Colum at his most princely.

Aidan stared straight ahead of him. "I do," he said, almost grimly.

Colum resumed his reading. "Do you solemnly promise, before all these, to uphold and seek to advance Christ's Gospel and teachings in this your realm, and seek to sustain His other servants in their like efforts to advance the true faith?"

"I do."

"Then, Aidan mac Gabhran, I do hereby proceed to fulfil God's command and anoint you as king. Rise."

He took the other's somewhat reluctant hand and raising him, led him to the meteorite altar-font. "Sit on this stone of your destiny!" he commanded.

Aidan shrugged and sat.

"Now, I ask Bishop Moluag of Lismore to consecrate the holy oil."

Moluag moved over to the more usual altar whereon sat the brecbennach. He opened the little roof-like lid, made the sign of the cross over it and, intoning a petition and blessing, handed the reliquary to Colum.

That man dipped his fingers in the oil and drew the cross three times on Aidan's forehead. Then he laid his both hands on the other's head. "Aidan mac Gabhran, in the name of Almighty God, the Father, the Son and the Holy Spirit, I anoint you appointed and undoubted King of Scots. All men to see, note and give thanks. This day is great blessing come to this kingdom of Dalriada, I am assured. The son and grandson and great-grandsons of Aidan shall reign. And one day shall rule a greater kingdom than this. Praise God, I say – praise and thanks to the Most High!" That last was in the nature of a shout.

As the acclaim and cheering rang out, Colum took Aidan's hand again and led him from the meteorite over to the abbot's chair, to sit thereupon as though on a throne. And there Ernan came to place around Aidan's neck a substitute for the Celtic royal chain of kingship, while Baithen signed to the choirs and instrumentalists to strike up with the twenty-first Psalm:

The King shall joy in Thy strength, O Lord,
And in Thy salvation how greatly shall he rejoice . . .

It was a brief and simple ceremony for so momentous an occasion, but that was deliberate also. And a mass celebration of the Eucharist followed, for all prepared to take part, the priests circulating amongst the crowds with the bread and the wine, to the accompaniment of sweet music.

Thereafter there was feasting for all, a major effort and provision on the missionaries' part, whilst the nobles and chiefs and magnates lined up to pay their individual allegiances to the new monarch, commencing with Ewan his brother; Aidan still wary, reserved, as though he was not convinced that it was all true, genuine. The last to arrive on the island, he was almost the first to depart. He came to take leave of Colum.

"What have I to say now?" he demanded. "Have I to *thank* you for this day?"

"Not me, Highness. Thank your God," Colum said simply. "For, left to myself I would never have done it at all. Not . . . for you!"

"You believe in it, then? It is not all cunning artifice?"

"Believe entirely. You are God's choice, not mine. We must believe that He knows best!"

"You doubt it, still? You think that Ewan would have made the better king?"

"I do, yes."

Aidan smiled, and he was not a great smiler. "Then, I will prove you wrong, Colum mac Felim. You will see."

Hot blue eyes met clear grey ones, and held for a moment. Then Colum inclined his head. "I shall pray that you, and God, are right!" And he too smiled.

"I thank you, then." And as though the effort to say that had been almost too much, the king turned abruptly on his heel and strode off down to his waiting ship.

Behind Colum, Bridget spoke. "There goes a man who will drive himself hard to prove you wrong, Columcille. *I* am no prophet, but I see him challenging even your vigour and resolution, forcing your hand. But, who knows? You may come to love each other, I think!"

19

Perhaps Bridget was a better prophet than she esteemed herself. For within only a few weeks of that notable day, there was an entirely unexpected confirmation of her judgement, and with it a test of Colum's drive and commitment.

Unheralded, King Aidan arrived in person at Iona, in forceful mood. He wanted Colum to accompany him to Ireland, almost forthwith.

Astonished, Colum could only look, almost stare, at him.

Aidan was not really very good at explaining himself, tending to state rather than to elaborate. But by question and answer, the latter apt to be brief if not staccato, Colum was able to piece together the situation involved, a little of which was already known on Iona.

Three years before, a new King of Ulster had come to that throne, one Baetan mac Cairell, as forceful a character as Aidan; and he had been making his presence very much felt in Ireland. Now, the sub-kingdom of Dalriata, from which had come Fergus mac Erc and the first Scots to carve out Dalriada in Alba, was situated in North Antrim, part of Ulster. It had always been accepted as belonging to the Scots realm, and paid tribute in men, services and money to Dunadd. But this King Baetan was claiming it as wholly his, and had in fact invaded it. One of the last acts of the late King Conall here had been to write to the High King of Ireland protesting, and demanding action against the interloper. The High King, successor at Tara to Diarmid mac Cerball and, as it happened, also named Baetan, was an indecisive type, really a stop-gap monarch, and had done nothing effective. But the other Baetan, of

Ulster, had. He had sent over a fleet and armed force to raid the Kintyre part of Dalriada, as warning to the Scots to keep quiet; and it was this invading force which had in fact, at a battle at Delgon, slain Duncan, Conall's son, and so conveniently removed the alternative contender for the Dalriadan throne. The council had sent another protest to Ireland, threatening retaliatory action by a Dalriadan fleet, and this had produced some result. Colum's cousin and friend Ainmere of Donegal, who had fought at Cooldrevny, had died, leaving a son, another Aed, as king. This Aed mac Ainmere, although young, was the power behind the present High King; indeed it was accepted that the latter was only, as it were, keeping the high throne warm for him until Aed was old enough to occupy that prestigious position, unsuitable for so youthful a prince. Now Aed mac Ainmere, in the High King's name, had called a meeting, a convention, to settle the matter of Dalriada, asking King Aidan and King Baetan of Ulster to attend and put their respective cases. So Aidan had decided to go, and wanted Colum to go with him, since his name and influence meant so much in the Irish north, and Aed was his kinsman.

Colum was doubtful. He did not really want to return to Ireland even for a visit, with all the complications which would inevitably ensue. He had so much to attend to at Iona and in all the numerous subsidiary establishments now set up; and he had been planning a missionary visit to the Outer Hebrides.

Yet – there was an undoubted draw to take him to Ireland, apart from this of Dalriata in which he would entirely support Aidan. There was another matter; that of the Order of the *Filidh*, an age-old order to which Colum himself belonged. This was an important and admittedly privileged class in Ireland consisting of professionals in various disciplines, including poets, songwriters and storytellers, scholars, physicians and diviners and the like. From its ranks almost all the Druids had come and many Church priests likewise, especially the hereditary variety. The *Filidh* had a great many privileges. They were exempt from both taxation and military service; they were entitled to free board and lodging whilst travelling; all doors should be open to them, the custodians of the nation's culture. But as can happen with such privileged groups, they had become arrogant, prideful, overbearing and extravagant, demanding more and more and contributing less and less. Forbidden personally to own lands, many had nevertheless become very wealthy, and were rivalling the nobility in their trains of retainers and servants, for all of whom they were apt to demand free entertainment from ordinary folk. So bad had the situation become that in many parts of Ireland the people had revolted against the entire Order and its privileges, and the kings had had to take action. King Aed mac Ainmere had in fact banned all such from his realm, ordering its members to repudiate the Order or face banishment. Colum, although recognising the need to curb excesses, was concerned at this wholesale banishment, and feared that when Aed became High King he would apply it to the whole of Ireland, to the detriment of much of the nation's cultural heritage. Kenneth of Achabo and Comgall of Bangor, also members, had sent to ask him to use what influence he had with his cousin to prevent this. Here was opportunity.

He was still undecided when Aidan mentioned that Aed mac Ainmere had called the convention at Druim Ceatt. That clinched the matter. For Druim Ceatt was close to his beloved Derry of the oaks, the favoured spot where he had set up his first monastery. How many times on this Iona, lovely as it was, he had longed for just a glimpse of Derry. Now he could have it, conscience clear.

Aidan said that they would sail in four days time.

They did sail, in the royal long-ship, from Port an Deora, the haven for Dunadd, seen off by many of the council and nobility. Heading down Loch Crinan and into the Sound of Jura, Colum was interested to see which route they would take thereafter, north-about round that end of long Jura and Scarba, or south-about by the longer course past Islay – or even through the dreaded Strait of Corryvreckan, shortest of all.

Perhaps Aidan sensed this interest and question, and was concerned for his reputation as a man of spirit. At any rate, he ordered his shipmaster to head almost straight across the sound for the mouth of Corryvreckan, however doubtfully that man eyed him.

It was not a stormy day but there was quite a strong westerly wind, much more blustery than on the previous occasion when Colum had challenged the turbulence, the noise of which they had been hearing ever since they left harbour. He was still intrigued by it all, wondering how truly dangerous was the whirlpool, how much it was all dread and superstition. Aidan did not comment on it, so neither did he.

Their shipmaster, at the steering-oar himself, once in the strait, kept as close to the Jura shore as possible, away from the Scarba side. But even here the seas were not exactly rough but much agitated, their vessel tossed about like a cork. And despite the rowers' efforts and all the shouted commands, their bows kept turning northwards, towards Scarba. Fascinated, Colum watched. What caused it? Was there some strong undertow? Could the whirlpool even at a distance exert such drawing power?

By the time that they were halfway through, for all the oarsmen's efforts, the long-ship was in mid-strait and still trending northwards, the curious jabbly waves splashing inboard. All not rowing took to baling out the water, Colum included, although Aidan himself scorned to do so. It dawned on Colum that this was in fact a battle, not so much between men and the forces of nature – or of evil? – but between Aidan and himself, a trial of confidence and resolution. He was wondering when such contest might become irresponsibility, with men's lives endangered, and how he should react, when the shipmaster showed him.

"Master," he panted, wrestling with the steering-oar, "others can bale! Should not you be *praying*?"

Colum inclined his head. "Perhaps you are right, friend." He mounted the stern platform and raising his hand, and his voice to its most powerful, besought their Creator to look upon them and bring them safely past this dire conflict of waters, in the name of Jesus Christ.

Undoubtedly the rowers were enheartened, and pulled the more strongly. Water still came inboard and the vessel heaved and lurched as before, but the bows seemed less drawn to the north. Strangely, they were now close enough to see the almost smooth circle amidst all the upheaval of waters, which represented the centre and vortex of the whirlpool. But this, they all began to realise, was drawing no nearer. Relief was general, and sundry grateful glances were directed at Colum.

Aidan's glance was otherwise. "We were in no danger," he averred.

"Probably not. But men's spirits are none the worse for sustaining. Their muscles may pull the better!"

"Are you honest, then? Or is it all but mummery, man?"

"Honest, I hope and pray. *I* have faith in our Creator, and seek, by whatever means, that others should have it also. *Your* faith, Highness – where is it placed? In yourself? If so, I fear that you have much sad learning ahead of you!"

The other said nothing.

Once out of the Strait of Corryvreckan, they could turn prow due south-westwards, between Colonsay and Jura, with a clear course of some seventy sea miles to cover to the mouth of Lough Foyle and Derry. Unfortunately the wind was also from that airt, as so often it was, which meant that the sail was of little use, so the oars were necessary all the way, slowing their pace. The seas were head on and quite steep, so that the craft pitched in seesaw fashion throughout, but at least it did not roll, which, with oars in a shallow sided long-ship, made the most difficult progress.

In these conditions it took them eight hours to cover the distance, and it was early evening before they were able to make out the entrance to Lough Foyle in the long loom of land which was the North Antrim coast. The sight of it brought on a thickness in Colum's throat. It was eleven years now since he had left his native land and he had missed it sorely. He had known that he would, of course, which was why he had insisted on not settling until Ireland was no longer visible. Now he was back – and must ensure that sentiment was held in check.

In the sheltered waters of the great lough, for all that, he had to blink away tears – and hope that Aidan was not watching him – as he scanned the southern shoreline for the first sight of the woods of Derry.

They came to the abbey with the dusk, and great was the astonishment, joy and excitement at the totally unexpected appearance of Columcille, who, in the years of absence, had become an almost legendary figure, little less than idolised – a situation which fell to be amended, but not that night. From Dacuilen the Co-Arb downwards to the newest student-monks and serving brothers, all sought to surpass each other in adulatory service to their renowned superior, whilst King Aidan remained all but ignored. Colum perceived that he would have to be quite stern hereafter.

341

The long-ship's crew at least had no complaints to make as to hospitality.

Dacuilen knew about the convention to be held at Druim Ceatt in three days' time, even though Columcille's attendance was a surprise. Druim Ceatt, the ridge like a whale's back, was the site of one of the palaces of the Kings of Ailech and lay some fifteen miles east of Derry, near to Limavady, a large, rambling place which would house the contesting parties and their trains.

Aidan's train, or more truly Colum's, turned out to be larger than anticipated, for the next day there arrived at Derry Abbey none other than the Abbots Kenneth and Comgall, from Achabo and Bangor, come voluntarily to support King Aidan and to speak for the *Filidh* – and greatly surprised and delighted to find Colum there also.

Joy prevailed, the more so as Kenneth recounted how, a few days before, as they were preparing to sit down for their meal at Achabo Abbey, he had had a sudden premonition that Columcille was in danger from waters, and had delayed their dinner whilst all went to their chapel to pray for his safety. Calculating back, Colum could time this for Aidan's ship's entry into the Strait of Corryvreckan – which much moved him, and also set him wondering whether perhaps they had been in greater peril than he had realised.

So it was a large party, mainly clerical, which arrived at the palace of Druim Ceatt with King Aidan, to create a major impression. Already the place was thronged with folk, so that accommodation became a problem indeed. Kings Aed and Baetan mac Cairell were already present; also of course King Donald of Ailech itself, now growing elderly. Colum was welcomed by all with much enthusiasm, flattering indeed, so much so that he grew concerned for Aidan, who received considerably less attention; disconcerting no doubt for a proud young monarch. Colum explained that he was here amongst his own kinsfolk and friends. King Baetan, a bullet-headed, stocky man of early middle years, was understandably less than forthcoming towards either of them.

The convention opened the following morning in the open space before the palace, so many attending, of nobility, clergy and the *Filidh* to preclude any indoor venue. Young Aed mac Ainmere, acting in the name of the High King, was preparing to start the proceedings when Colum as it were pre-empted him by asserting that so important a meeting must surely be initiated with prayer to Almighty God for His guidance and blessing, and thereafter led a short religious service, with brief address and resounding psalm-singing from the churchmen, which had the effect of setting the scene satisfactorily, and more or less inserting Colum into a position of authority not previously envisaged.

The debate commenced with King Baetan declaring vehemently that Dalriata and Dalriada both were sub-kingdoms of his Ulster, the one deriving from the other. The fact that the ruling house of Dalriata had, of its own choice, fled from Ireland six generations ago to Alba, in no way could detach the said Dalriata from Ulster; indeed it had the effect of reducing the sub-kingdom's status to merely that of a lordship, since there was now no King of Dalriata in Ireland. That this lordship should be sending Irish tribute, rents and dues to Dalriada in Alba was quite unsuitable and he had demanded that this cease. When this was rejected, he had sent his forces to occupy the lordship, as was his undoubted right as King of Ulster. He asserted that none could deny it.

Aed looked at Aidan.

That young man did deny it, categorically – but unfortunately in his usual abrupt and overshort style. Because the ruling house of Dalriata had established a new kingdom in Alba in no way could injure their rights thereafter in Ireland and where the people acknowledged their royal sway and sent their dues. Ulster had no more authority in that sub-kingdom than it had before. Baetan had not only invaded Dalriata but restrained its people from paying their dues, confiscating them for himself – which was theft. Not only so but he had sent an army to attack Kintyre, part of Dalriada, and there had ravaged and slain, killing the Prince Duncan, son of King Conall – which was rapine and murder. He, Aidan mac Gabhran, demanded justice and compensation.

Baetan reiterated. If Dalriata in Ireland was a sub-kingdom of Ulster, then Dalriada in Alba must be also. The calf could not be greater than the cow. Therefore he was entitled and entirely within his rights to act as he had done.

Hotly, Aidan repudiated that but without further elaboration.

King Aed looked enquiringly at Colum.

That man spoke up, in marked contrast to the other two, reasonably, even smiling. A calf *could* be greater than a cow, surely? It could be greater, larger, stronger, produce more milk – or it could even be a bull! That produced the desired laughter. To claim that Dalriada in Alba was a sub-kingdom of Ulster seemed to him to be quite without foundation. Had Ulster ever had anything to do with its establishment? Had Ulster fought for its independence from the Albannach? As well say that because he and his friends had gone from Derry to Alba and established themselves at Iona, that Iona was part of Donegal! Dalriada undoubtedly was an independent kingdom. It had had its problems maintaining its independence against the assaults of the High King of Alba; surely it should not have to defend itself from those of the King of Ulster?

That produced murmurs of approval from much of the assembly, but an angry outburst from Baetan. Who was this priest, who had caused so much bloodshed at Cooldrevny, to lecture them on matters which were no concern of his? Why was he here, with his hymn-singers? This was a matter for kings, not clerks.

Aed mentioned that Prince Colum mac Felim could have been High King of Ireland.

Colum waved that aside. He was only a priest, yes – but concerned for *God's* Kingdom. And Dalriada in Alba was a vital outpost of that Kingdom, in the conversion and bringing to Christ of the great nation of the Albannach. Would King Baetan, who was not hitherto noted for his support of Holy Church, pursue with all his power and vigour the subduing of Alba, if Dalriada was his?

That gave Baetan pause. Without giving him time to think up an answer, Colum went on.

"I have heard it said, by some who seemed to know, that King Baetan's main object in desiring to take over Dalriada is in order to win control of its many hundreds of long-ships. Dalriada is largely an island kingdom, and because of that, and for its defence against Albannach pirates, it has to have a great number of ships of war. If indeed King Baetan is eager to lay hands on these, I wonder why? For what should Ulster need a greater fleet of ships than King Baetan already has? Could it be that he has designs on the high kingship of Ireland, by force of arms?"

That created a hush almost of consternation. Such a

344

suggestion, before all, was almost unheard of. Few would have dared to make it.

Colum, with a glance at Aed, the next High King designate, continued into the hush. "Perhaps I am wrong, misinformed? If so, I apologise to King Baetan. But if so, will he tell us why he wants all these ships, as I learn from sources in Ulster that he does?"

"Lies!" Baetan shouted. "All lies! Heed not this priest. I have no need of more ships to sail my armies across to Alba – as Aidan mac Gabhran has learned! I do not seek to be High King."

Aed looked from one to the other.

"Good! That is excellent, Highness, is it not? I am put to rights. King Baetan does not seek the high kingship, nor desires the Dalriadan fleet. So now we have the truth of it. So that there but remains the matter of Dalriata in Ireland. That sub-kingdom is undoubtedly in Ulster, although belonging to the Dalriadan throne. King Aidan does not contest that, nor could. He has an offer to make, I think, by way of token acknowledgement, for Dalriata only."

Aidan, on cue, nodded. "Seven," he jerked. "In token only. Seven soldiers. Seven shields. Seven horses. Seven hounds. Each year. That is all."

As all stared, at that brief declaration, King Donald of Ailech guffawed, his first contribution. Baetan looked uncertain, trapped.

Aed seemed to be repressing a smile. "Do you, Baetan mac Cairell, accept this token, which seems honest and fair? As due warranty of your position? Or not?"

"I . . . I require time. To consider it."

"Very well. I also shall consider my decision." Aed looked round the gathering. "Is there any other matter to consider?"

"Yes, Highness – this of the *Filidh*." That was Abbot Kenneth.

Aed frowned. "I meant matters of kingship and rule."

"Is not this of such matter? Since it concerns so many in positions of authority in this kingdom, and others?"

"I did not come here to discuss the *Filidh*, Abbot Kenneth."

"Nevertheless, I think that many here, Highness, would so wish it." Kenneth, mild as he generally was, could be stubborn.

Comgall backed him up. "This is important not only for *your* kingdom, King Aed, but for all Ireland. This convention ought to discuss the matter, I say."

Suddenly the entire assembly had a changed atmosphere.

"What is there to discuss?" Aed demanded. "I have made my decisions as to the *Filidh*."

"With all respect, Highness, there is much. For are there not more sides than one to any question? And in this, only one side has been heard – yours. Surely others should be, in especial that of Christ's Church?" And Comgall looked over at Colum.

That man was in something of a quandary. This was not how he would have dealt with the matter. A private approach would have been better. He did not want to offend Aed now, while the greater issue of Dalriada lacked a final decision and pronouncement. On the other hand, this of the *Filidh* did much concern him. And he wished to support his friends.

"Of your patience, Highness, I believe that good for all might well come of some discussion on this issue," he said tactfully. "Many of the *Filidh* have indeed behaved badly and deserve censure, although others have not and do not. But there is more to it than that. The very future of all Ireland, in matters of the spirit, is bound up in this of the *Filidh*. And so the Church has to be concerned."

Aed shrugged. "Very well. But . . . let it be short," he said curtly.

Colum waited. But all seemed to look to him. So he went on. "The *Filidh* however far many of them have strayed from their high calling, represent the culture, learning and scholarship of the nation. Remove that, and the nation, any nation, is in danger of losing its soul. And God's Church is concerned for the soul. However strong a nation may be, in men and arms and riches, lacking its soul, it dies. Even leaving the Church from it meantime, without the poets, the storytellers, the songwriters, the sennachies, artists, thinkers and the rest, what remains? Only brute force, the triumph of the strongest, the dark night of the spirit. You may say that poets and storytellers and players of instruments will arise whether or not the Order of the *Filidh* survives. But will they? For even these, born with such gifts, require teaching and training to play their parts to the full. The *Filidh* do that. So, rid Ireland of

346

the *Filidh*, and its kingdoms will have to replace them with some other body or order. How shall they do that? *Can* they do it? Will all the kings agree on what shall be done, and do it? And *pay* for it all? Would it not be wiser and simpler to *reform* the Order of the *Filidh* instead of banishing it, to prune back the Order like a fruit-tree which has grown too strong?"

There was applause, for undoubtedly many of those present were in fact of the *Filidh*.

Aed looked unimpressed, Baetan shook his bullet-head and Donald scratched his greying beard.

A voice spoke out from the body of the assembly. "The people have had enough of your *Filidh*. Of their greed and their pride. They want no more of them."

"Yet the people *need* them, friend. Or need some of them. Greed and pride and arrogance are evil, and must be controlled. But to cut down the entire tree of the nation's learning, history and art instead of pruning it, is folly; the tree which had taken all the centuries to grow. Control, yes – not banishment."

"How are the *Filidh* to be controlled?" Aed demanded. "I sought to control them in Donegal, before I banished them, and could not. They recognised no authority but their own. So they had to learn otherwise."

"How shall we kings restrain all the poets and storytellers, the physicians and the dreamers, Colum mac Felim?" Donald of Ailech asked. "They are a law unto themselves. They heeded us not – until the banishment."

Colum looked at his fellow abbots, and took a chance. "There is one authority even most of these must recognise, or risk their immortal souls – that is, Christ's Church! Let Holy Church control the *Filidh*."

There was a silence at that.

"How?" Aed barked, after a moment or two.

"The Church has its sanctions and disciplines. Penances, excommunication. The refusal of Christian baptism, marriage, burial. Many priests of the Church are already *Filidh*, as am I. Leave it to Holy Church."

Aed and Donald put their heads together. Then the former nodded. "As you will, Prince Colum. Let the Church control the *Filidh*. We will hold you responsible."

"Do you withdraw the banishment, Highness?"

"Yes."

There was a considerable stir in the assembly, mainly acclaim but some doubts also.

Aed took the opportunity to declare the convention adjourned until the morrow, and rose.

Somewhat alarmed himself at what he had so impulsively proposed, Colum was relieved to find that Kenneth and Comgall at least were wholly congratulatory and in favour of his suggestion. Here was a splendid and worthwhile task for the Church, something which could be used to advance Christ's cause as well as serving Ireland and aiding many good men. What arrangements had Colum in mind?

That man had to admit that he had none, as yet. It had been but a general idea. But they would think of something effective.

So that evening, after a banquet, the three friends, with sundry other clerics, got down to planning. What seemed to be required was to incorporate the Order of the *Filidh* as an organ of the Church itself, so that it would have sufficient authority over its members. This to be ruled by a standing council, carefully selected. They would, of course, not confine this to Donegal and Ailech, although they must start there. If the Church was to be in charge, then it all must refer to the nation of Ireland, which meant that they must have the direct agreement of the High King. Colum should go to Tara and persuade Baetan mac Ninnidh.

Colum agreed to do this, but pointed out that that must be the limit of his commitment. From Iona and Dalriada he could not play any responsible part in this matter. He would be interested and concerned, yes – but the actual leadership must be here in Ireland itself.

That was accepted – although whether Kenneth or Comgall would commit themselves to the leadership remained to be seen.

The resumption of the convention next morning proved to be surprising for most of those attending. For one thing, Colum's arrival on the scene was greeted by music, appreciative members of the *Filidh* producing what amounted to a concert in his honour. What King Aed thought of this was not announced, but he did delay his emergence from the palace until it was over, whether from annoyance or a desire not to cut it all short was uncertain. And when he did appear, with

Kings Donald and Aidan – no sign of Baetan mac Cairell – it was to announce, quite briefly, his decisions on the questions at issue. On the subject of Dalriata and Dalriada the ruling was that the former remained a sub-kingdom of Ulster, and this must be acknowledged by the annual payment of the dues, seven men, seven shields, seven horses and seven hounds; and that the latter was an entirely independent kingdom, in no way subject to any in Ireland. On the other matter, of the *Filidh*, he confirmed that the sentence of banishment was lifted, and responsibility for the Order transferred to the churchmen, with the warning that any renewal of its members' overbearing pride and extortions towards the people would result in a reimposition of the ban and harsh measures against the offenders.

With that he closed the proceedings.

Colum, to his embarrassment, found himself quite the hero of the hour, all the success of the occasion being credited to him, despite his disclaimers. Matters came to a head when, presently, the blind Dallan Forgaill, Chief Bard of All Ireland, was led up to him, to announce that, in his gratitude, and that of all bards, poets, storytellers and songwriters, he was going to compose a special Eulogy to Colum mac Felim, to be sung by choirs in his praise, for saving the *Filidh*. Colum, much concerned that he did not become an object of adulation, where folk should be ascribing praise to Christ and His Church, whilst thanking the blind man, declared that any such composition should not be voiced until after his death. However, Dallan's disappointment was so evident, and his announcement that he had already written the Prologue, caused Colum to relent and agree that at least they could sing this Prologue meantime. So the instrumentalists struck up and the singers gave voice, falteringly at first until they mastered words and tune, and then rendered the chorus in stirring fashion. They seemed to be going to repeat this indefinitely, so that, smiling, Colum had to call a halt; and repeated the injunction – not again until he had gone to his Maker.

Escaping from the grateful *Filidh*, he declared that he must get away from all this praise and flattery. Aidan, it seemed, was going to stay on in these parts for another ten days or so. Colum was to go to Tara and the High King. He also desired to see his former colleague and soul-friend Laisran, now an old man. Likewise he had new priests and students to enlist for Iona. Bishop Conall of Coleraine, there present, said that his seminary might produce some volunteers, all there being great admirers of Colum's endeavours. So a ten days tour was planned, Comgall and Kenneth accompanying him for part of it. They set out without delay. It was going to take Colum all his time to do what he wanted to accomplish. They went on horseback, necessarily.

As they rode through the hills, Colum was surprised to find that, wherever they went and it became known who he was, he was hailed with acclaim and something like reverence, his activities in Alba seemingly known to all, and no doubt exaggerated. It had never occurred to him that this would be so and that his exile from Ireland, almost in disgrace, would in fact turn him into something of a folk hero. He found, too, that all sorts of miracles were being ascribed to him, which displeased. Christ's cause must prosper without these. He began to feel that the sooner he was back at Iona, the better. But at least all this renown should help in the recruitment of new missionaries.

In fact, in this he was quite successful, not only at Coleraine but at other monasteries and religious establishments which they visited en route, enrolling over a dozen ordained priests, deacons and novices. These were instructed to report at Derry within the next few days.

From Coleraine to Bangor, near the mouth of Belfast Lough, was nearly fifty miles, and would in fact have been more speedily reached by ship. But they covered the distance in a long day's hard riding, which taxed Kenneth not a little.

Colum engaged two more recruits at Bangor Abbey. He left his friends there and, alone now, rode at his fastest due southwards, heading for Kells and Tara, fully eighty-five miles away. He must cover that in two days. His destination was not exactly Tara itself, for after Cooldrevny and the fall of Diarmid mac Cerball, Tara, his seat, had been abandoned. Aed mac Ainmere, his successor designate as High King, ruled from his own Donegal domains, only visiting the Tara vicinity for occasional assemblies. Baetan mac Ninnidh, however, resided nearby, at Teltown.

Colum reached his abbey of Kells in mid-afternoon of the second day, making excellent time, riding one of King Aed's best horses. Good as it was to be there, after so long an absence, he did not linger. He hoped to come back and spend the night there, after he had seen King Baetan – but that interview had to be his first priority.

Strangely, his programme developed otherwise. Riding along that well-known road from Kells, nearing the Hill of Tara, he became aware of a single figure walking slowly in front of him, with a staff, bent and unsteady of foot. Unwilling to seem to hurry past this pilgrim who went so painfully, Colum reined up, to ask him if he could take him up behind himself on the horse? When the other looked up, peering, there seemed to be something familiar about the haggard and worn features.

The old man, despite age and rheumy eyes, had no doubts evidently about identification. Staring, he wagged his white head.

"Colum mac Felim!" he got out, in a croak. "Come . . . come to . . . take me . . . to the next world!"

"Colum, yes – but scarcely to do that, friend! I should know you, I think . . . ?"

"Aye, you should!" Although a quaver, that was definite enough. "I am Bec mac De. Are you . . . dead, then? I had not heard . . ."

Colum blinked, gazing down at the former Arch Druid of All Ireland. "Dead . . . ?" he wondered.

The other bent over in a fit of coughing which shook his wasted frame so that only his staff saved him from falling. Colum dismounted. Clearly this frail creature would be incapable of climbing on to any horse's back.

"Bec mac De!" he exclaimed. "Of a mercy! So long since . . . that day! You are sick, man?"

"Sick, yes. Sick unto . . . the death. I did not think that you . . . *you* would be sent for me." That was almost challenging, however tremulous. "You who . . . cost me so dear."

"You think me sent for you?"

"Aye. When did you die?"

Colum shook his head in turn. "I am not dead, friend. I am very much alive! I came from Alba for the Druim Ceatt convention. Now I go to speak with King Baetan mac Ninnidh at Teltown. Why should I be dead?"

Bec mac De looked unbelieving.

351

"Where are you bound?" Colum asked. "On this road. A sick man."

"I go . . . to Tara. Where I . . . had rule." There was even a note of pride in that, however feeble the enunciation. "For the last time. Are you not sent . . . for me?"

"Sent *to* you, perhaps. In your need. For you require help, I think."

"Help? From a . . . Christian! I am . . . the Arch Druid!"

Nevertheless, Colum leading his horse with his left hand, took the other's bony arm with his right and gave him support as they walked slowly onwards.

"You have come far?" he asked. "In this state."

"Not so far as . . . I go!"

"You mean . . . ?"

"I have the sight. Christian."

"Perhaps. And what do you see, Bec mac De?"

"I see that there is something . . . that I must do. At Tara's hill."

"Can you climb that hill?"

"I must."

"Perhaps that is why I was sent, then. With this horse. To help."

They went in silence for a while, the green hill rising before them.

Presently, with the old man staggering, all but falling again, Colum, holding him up, said, "Must you go on, man? *Can* you? You think that you die?"

"We all . . . die."

"Yes. But some sooner than others. You have the sight, you say. Can you not see how long you have?"

"Seven years, Christian!" That was jerked out strongly, almost viciously.

Surprised, Colum looked at him. "Seven years is a long time. This of Tara – why today? You could climb Tara another day, when you feel stronger. You could do much in seven years, much that is good."

The Druid did not answer. But after a while he spoke. "What I told you is not true, Christian. I have seven *weeks* to live, not seven years."

"Ah! That is different. But still there is time. Another day. You can do much that is good in seven weeks."

Another pause as they moved slowly on. Then, voice

352

breaking and little more than a whisper, the old man got it out. "Never in my life . . . have I lied about . . . the sight granted me. Until now. But I have lied to you, Colum mac Felim. I had but seven *hours* to live . . . when I left my house!"

"So! Now I see it, friend. Then, let us spend those hours left together."

Silent now, both of them, but no longer in any enmity, they moved onwards. Then, at the roadside Colum perceived a fallen tree, a great ancient oak – and oak-trees were always his friends. To this he led mount and companion. Ranging the horse alongside the heavy trunk, he was able to assist the Druid up on to it and so, with his strong arms, to hoist him into the saddle. Then leading the animal, he made better time to the foot of Tara's hill, and up, Bec mac De swaying drunkenly but managing to remain mounted.

So they came to the hilltop and the abandoned ramparts of the ancient fort, where Colum helped the old man down and settled him against the walling, facing west towards the sunset. He was breathing erratically, much of the time with his eyes closed. Clearly he was more than exhausted. For long they sat in silence save for the odd panting breath; Colum's arm around and supporting the other.

Eventually, eyes opened, Bec mac De spoke, in little more than a whisper. "I go . . . with the Sun . . . I have served," he got out, gazing westwards.

"You go, friend, to the Son of God and Son of Man," Colum amended, but kindly. "And He will welcome you more warmly than *your* sun. That will rise again tomorrow, at our backs here. But you, you will stay with the Redeemer of all men, until all rise, at the last day."

"Too late, Christian . . . to convert . . . me now!"

"Never too late. Christ will do that Himself when He receives you, yonder. And show you love and peace."

"You are . . . very sure."

"Oh, yes – I am sure. *Your* troubles are over, my friend."

Bec closed his eyes again. "We . . . shall see. Tell me . . . when the Sun goes."

They sat, wordless again, until the sun went down in scarlet and gold, the old man's weight wholly supported now by Colum's arm. At last, as the final gleam of it disappeared behind the western hills, the latter spoke.

353

"It is gone now, friend. Go you in peace."

But Bec mac De had already gone, slumped against the other's side, breathing ceased.

Carefully Colum laid the frail body against the walling, there where so many druidical ceremonies had been enacted, and covered the face, saying a prayer over it. Then mounting his horse he rode downhill, to tell men to come for all that remained of his old enemy and Ireland's last Arch Druid.

He was a day late, therefore, in reaching King Baetan mac Ninnidh at Teltown. But that, in fact, did not signify, for the High King proved to be an amiable nonentity, carefully chosen by the lesser kings to be no trouble to anyone; and he acceded to the Church taking over the Order of the *Filidh* without argument, and approved the Dalriata-Dalriada decision.

In a way, Colum was sad to see the high kingship reduced to this, a mere constitutional convenience; but it was probably for the best. How Aed mac Ainmere would act and react when *he* became High King would be another matter.

Duty done, Colum turned his horse's head northwards again, for Lough Erne, some seventy miles.

On the islet at Devenish two days later, he found Laisran, no younger than Bec mac De but so very different in physical and mental state, living the life of an anchorite, alone, lame but cheerful and content – and overjoyed to see his one-time pupil and soul-friend. That Colum could spend only one night with him was sad; but he had promised Aidan to be at Derry in ten days time, and only two days remained, with forty-five miles still to cover. However, they talked far into the night, and in the morning held a little service together. Both knew this to be a farewell service in fact, indeed they called it that, for the probability of them ever seeing each other again in this earthly life was highly remote, but they knew that they would come together in a better place than even Devenish in due course, and would look forward to that. Colum had made his last soul-baring to his former confessor, and felt the better for it, with his Molaise warmly understanding and helpful over the doubts and problems which still worried his friend, even in the matter of Bridget nic Colman, whom Laisran instructed him to cherish as one more gift from God.

So they parted on the lough-shore, and if there were tears in Colum's eyes as he mounted and rode off, they were tears of emotion not sorrow.

He was back at Derry Abbey in time to cause no delay in Aidan's embarkation for their homeward voyage – and Colum did recognise then, almost to his surprise, that it *was* homeward for him, also; that Iona now meant more to him even than his beloved Ireland.

PART THREE

20

Colum's return visit to Ireland had made him very much aware of the passage of time, of the years gone, which, caught up in the ceaseless and demanding round of activities which was his mission and life in Dalriada and Alba, he had little thought of. This was further brought home to him when he got back to Iona, to find his mother ill and failing fast. The Princess Eithne, now a very old woman, was being nursed by Bridget at the nunnery; but declaring in practical fashion that her end was near, she requested that she be taken back to Hinba, to die there.

Distressed but practical as his mother, thither Colum took her shortly after his return, Bridget accompanying them. It was a strange interlude, less sad than it might have been, for Eithne had a serenity about her which could not but infect the other two. She declared that she was happy to be on her way to the next stage in her pilgrimage. She had had a good and a long life, and her old body, being now irritatingly feeble and unfitted for her still eager spirit, she would be glad to exchange it for a better and spiritual one, when she left Hinba, which little isle she looked on as a stepping-stone to eternity. She had really only been waiting for Colum to get back, to say goodbye, or she would have been gone ere this. And she was not going to die in any nunnery. In the face of this cheerfully pragmatical attitude to her departure, the others could not go long-faced.

That night, having seen his mother settled, and not wishing to go far from the house, Colum took Bridget and the dog only up on to the higher ground behind, where they could watch the Hebridean sunset, and told her of all his doings in Ireland; not omitting to mention Laisran's advice to cherish her as a gift from God – which earned him an impulsive embrace. And he heard from her much of what had been going on at Iona in the interim: of progress at the nunnery, with more novices arriving, and a women's missionary effort over in Mull; of visits by Moluag, Scandlann and Fechno – also of Ewan mac Gabhran, Aidan's brother, who was talking of becoming a priest and joining Colum's band; of the success of many of Colum's schemes for improving production on the island, such as the seal-colony, where the former poacher Erc was doing well; the bee culture, which the nuns had taken over and were expanding the wax-candle manufactory; the fruit-tree grafting which had greatly increased the yield; and the new salmon-ladders in streams over in Mull, much benefiting the fishing. And she added that he need no longer concern himself over Findchan and Black Aed, on Tiree, for the latter had gone; reverted to his former evil ways and gone pirating in Ireland, despite his ordination, and now said to be boasting that one day he would be King of Ulster in place of Baetan. Findchan was said to be desolated. So that was one less problem for Columcille.

In the morning, they found Eithne in a sort of coma, but with a half-smile on her face. She did not recover full consciousness during the day, her breathing fluttering. On one of their many visits to the bedside in the evening they believed that she had gone, her breath seemingly ceased, but then she stirred slightly. They knelt and prayed at the bedside – and presently perceived that she had indeed gone on, on her desired and so important journey, a blessed departure.

That vigil brought those two the closer together.

Colum's rapport with King Aidan now proved to be more time-consuming than he had foreseen, for he found himself frequently summoned to Dunadd in the capacity of adviser to the monarch and council. This, although it enabled him to help decide policy – and in that was all to the good – and to influence the Dalriadan nobility towards more enthusiastic Christianity, did tend to limit his missionary journeyings somewhat. But he did manage to carry out his long-projected visit to Kintyre, that lengthy peninsula stretching southwards from the Sound of Jura almost to the Firth of Clyde. He made this the opportunity to instruct his new recruits brought from Ireland, nearly a score of them, taking them with him to show them, as it were in the field, how he advised them to proceed in their conversion efforts and the setting up of cells, cashels and churches. Kintyre, of course, part of Dalriada, was already

nominally Christian, but in fact very superficially so. It would
be a good introduction for the newcomers. Of these, five in
especial Colum had high hopes for – Drostan, Donnan,
Fintan, Madoc and Cailtan, all well-born, able and responsible
priests.

The northern neck of the Kintyre peninsula was known as
Knapdale, and Aidan himself was hereditary lord thereof, so
the mission, able to use his name and authority, got off to a
good start. Moreover, Angus mac Riagan, whose territory
adjoined, himself came with them and was very helpful. They
found few churches, and fewer still which were in fact
functioning in any meaningful way, incumbents tending to be
old and dispirited where they existed at all. Colum almost
preferred the outright paganism of the Albannach, for that
was in fact worshipping something, however mistakenly;
whereas here they had to start from almost nothing, or at least
from failure, a vacuum, with the people practically devoid of
any belief or the need for any. This was made the sadder for the
missionaries in that one of the deserted churches they came to
on the South Knapdale coast was called Ardpatrick, founded
by and named after their own St Patrick on a visit to his
homeland from Ireland a century earlier. They started a
rebuilding and rededication of this there and then, and left two
of their number to serve it.

They found the entire shoreline area quite populous, and
dotted with a great many duns or former Albannach forts,
some now replaced by the houses of Scots chieftains, and very
many stone-circles and burial-cairns. So clearly this territory
had been important once. Inland, quickly the land rose in
green hills, not very high but quite steep, and now apparently
entirely empty. They revived churches, or established new
cells at several places, called Ormsary, Port Mhoirich (this
they named Kilmoluag, after the bishop), Ardminish, Dun-
more, this new one Kil-an-Angus (after their own Angus),
and Kennocraig on the long, probing sea-loch of Tarbert,
thereafter finding a broken-down sanctuary dedicated to St
Bride. This too they reinstituted, leaving Drostan to be its
priest temporarily, with Colum declaring that, because it was
named after Bride, and may have been founded by her all those
years ago, he would offer it to Bridget back at Iona, for her to
set up a women's mission, if so she wished.

On they went, founding cashels or merely cells at Dunskeig

and Ballochroy and Tayinloan, opposite the isle of Gigha, meeting with no opposition but little enthusiasm, before turning back. They could have gone on, but Colum ruefully realised that he had already used up half of his new recruits – and he had brought them for further missions to Alba proper, not the revival of the Church in Kintyre. Besides, this peninsula would much more effectively be dealt with by ship, he now recognised. They were still only halfway down the almost seventy-miles-long coast, to the Mull of Kintyre. That is, when he could find opportunity to return and tackle it.

Returning, he was preoccupied with the scale of all that remained to be done. So vast a task confronted him still, with manpower, as well as time, ever the limiting factor. Reluctantly he came to the conclusion that he would have to alter his methods. Instead of himself going out on the missions, as his every inclination urged, he would have to concentrate on teaching and training, preparing local men to act as priests. He could not always be enticing new people over from Ireland. The Albannach, and for that matter the Scots also, must provide their own priesthood. In place of personal leadership he would have to become an instructor, a trainer. Iona would have to become a great seminary for the production of missionaries, rather than he and his close associates being the missionaries themselves. Was his undoubted preference for this last a weakness in his character and commitment to Christ's cause? It was with something of a sinking heart that he came to this conclusion. He would have to discipline himself in this matter, he at last perceived.

So it was back to Iona, and have the call sent out to all his far-flung outposts, monasteries, and cashels – find suitable and energetic young men to send here to train for the priesthood, and send them quickly. He would have to become Colum the Teacher rather than Colum the Preacher, for some time to come. He recognised that in his inmost consciousness he had always known that it eventually must come to this, but had not admitted it. Bridget, after all, had said as much. Had he held the great work up by his obstinacy?

21

In the months stretching to years which followed, Colum
forced himself to adhere to this educative role of instructing,
tutoring and seeking to imbue with something of his own
enthusiasm the many volunteers sent to him from near and far,
Albannach and Dalriadans both – and not, in the process, to
reveal to them how this spirit chafed at the seeming inactivity
of it all for a man of restless energy and urgency for action.
Bridget at least approved, for it all enabled her to see a great
deal more of him, indeed her nunnery came to play an ever
more important part in the Iona scheme of things, the women
taking over many of the monks' duties to enable them to
devote ever more of their time to teaching; although the said
women went back each night to their own offshore island –
save in an occasional storm, which rumour alleged to be
prayed for now and again.

But the concept and discipline had its effective results. Large
numbers of new priests, deacons and workers were created,
and despatched to man the mission stations which Colum's
older colleagues were always establishing, so that a steady
progress was maintained. And the process of instruction and
exposition in itself had its rewards, in the watching of young
men growing in understanding and commitment and devotion – or so Colum assured himself.

All was not success and plain-sailing, to be sure. There were
failures, backsliders, disappointments, both in men and in
situations. Not all the missions succeeded, not all the students
finished their courses, not all the new priests lived up to their
vocations, not even all the senior ones. As when the handsome
and talented Fechno arrived from Skye, in great distress and
threw himself down on the ground at Colum's feet, to confess
his sin and disgrace. He had got a young woman with child, at
Portree, kin to one of the chieftains, and not all the interven-
tion and pleadings of Queen Sinech could save him from
obloquy and shame. He had been driven out, and his mission

and all his work brought into disrepute. Almost he had sought to take his own life – but suicide was a mortal sin, and adding one such to another would serve nothing.

Colum raised him up, and said, "Rise, my son. A broken and a contrite heart God will not despise. You will serve His Son the better hereafter. We all pay for our sins and weakness, but we are blessed if we can do the paying by serving the more devotedly all our days. I will send you to Tiree, where Findchan One-Hand is working out *his* penance. Perchance you can help each other, and glorify God in that isle instead of Skye."

He sent Cailtan to Skye to take Fechno's place, with a message for Queen Sinech.

Another matter for concern was Ernan's health. He was not an old man yet, only a year or two senior to his nephew, but for some time he had been less than well and was not improving. Refusing to give in to it, he sought to labour the more, and was clearly not fit for that, as all were aware. Colum sought to deal with this situation by sending his uncle to Hinba, the house there now unoccupied, to turn it into a retreat and hospice for the Iona community should they be sick, in trouble or dispirited. He had long felt somewhat uncomfortable about his private *diseart* there, so little used; now others could make use of it. The islanders on neighbouring Garbh Eileach would keep an eye on Ernan.

Problems were not confined to the missionaries. Aidan, troubled by the raiding of Orkney pirates, had protested to King Brude, who seemed to have done nothing. So he had assembled a fleet and sailed north himself, to teach the pirates a lesson; and whether by ill chance or on information received, Baetan of Ulster chose to invade and take possession of that outlying portion of the Dalriadan kingdom, the Isle of Man, with much slaughter and savagery, this in retaliation for his defeat at Druim Ceatt. And there were fears that he would not content himself with the Isle of Man.

In the general anxiety, and Aidan's absence with the fleet, the council at Dunadd sent to Iona to seek Colum's help. He was friendly with King Roderick of Strathclyde. And Strathclyde was much nearer to Man than was the rest of Dalriada. Would the Prince Colum go, on their behalf, to King Roderick and ask him to make a gesture against the invaders? He was supposed to be their ally, after all – Colum had contrived that. They did not ask that he actually went to war; he had many ships, and if he sent some to sail around the Isle of Man, and one or two flew the flag of Dalriada, Baetan would undoubtedly see the significance, and at least be warned about the dangers of any further advances, for even he would not want to risk war with Strathclyde.

Colum felt that he could scarcely refuse to do this; moreover, it would give him the chance to meet St Mungo, or Kentigern as he was sometimes called, who had returned to Strathclyde, something he had long desired. And a break from his teaching routine would be welcome.

It was now eight years since his previous visit to Roderick, which had so helped to contain that other warlord Athelfrith the Angle, his teeth by no means pulled but now confining his invasions to his southern and western neighbours. When he computed that interval, Colum could hardly believe it. He would be growing old himself before very long.

Meantime it was good to be on his travels again, sailing southwards in Machar's long-ship and gazing over at the Kintyre coast, recognising features now, and wondering how his new assistants were getting on. Rounding the dreaded Mull thereof, on this occasion presented no real hazards, if some physical discomfort, and then they were into the comparatively sheltered waters of the Firth of Clyde.

At Dunbarton, Colum was again distressed to see the effect of the years on his contemporaries. Was he himself showing his age, like so many others? He always assumed not, but perhaps that was folly, or vanity? Roderick seemed to have aged direly, his former bulky figure now sagging, his colour purple rather than ruddy, and now toying with his food where he had previously eaten so heartily. But at least he and his wife, Queen Langueth, seemed to be on better terms. She had changed also, notably, but in her middle years was still good-looking and markedly more kind and forthcoming than formerly, indeed going out of her way to be friendly towards Colum.

As to the object of the visit, there proved to be no difficulty. Almost casually Roderick agreed to send his ships to sail round the Isle of Man, some sixty miles from the mouth of the Firth of Clyde and a mere twenty from the nearest point of Strathclyde's Galloway. He admitted that his captains would no doubt be glad of the excuse to do something, now that

Athelfrith no longer menaced and their services in little demand. And, yes, they could fly the two large Dalriadan banners Colum had brought. The ships could sail in a day or two.

Errand so easily accomplished, Colum asked about St Kentigern. Was he still here, in Strathclyde, and a meeting possible? He was told that he was, but that Roderick understood that he was about to set off on some missionary venture in Southern Alba, Fortrenn. But that it was understood that he would be at Cathures, his old preaching base where the Molendinar Burn joined the Clyde, some eighteen miles to the east, for a day or two yet.

So the next day Colum sailed on upstream, further than they had ridden on that previous visit, past where the Clyde, narrowed now from firth to river, took a major bend south-eastwards through green, fair country, populous and fertile, Roderick providing a guide and escort.

As well that he did, for the Molendinar was no major tributary, a quite modest stream the confluence of which they could very easily have missed. It was explained that Mungo, almost forty years ago, had been guided by God to journey here, from St Serf's monastery at Culross on the Forth's estuary, to cross the waist of the land and halt where this little burn reached salt-water. So here, with his mother, he had set up his cell and begun his task of converting the Britons of Strathclyde.

Disembarking, and sending one of their escort ahead to announce their arrival, Colum's party moved inland a little way towards a slight ridge whereon could be seen buildings more ambitious than were the cot-houses dotted around. As they neared this, bells began to ring out sweetly, in a harmonious chiming such as Colum had not before experienced; and then a company emerged from the monastery, to come down towards them. As these drew closer, it could be heard that they were singing. Listening, through the bells' happy clamour, Colum recognised that it was the hymn 'The way of the just is made straight'. Smiling, he turned to his own people and signed to them to strike up, in tune and time, the next verse, his great voice leading, 'The saints shall go from strength to strength, Alleluia!' Thus, singing in unison, the two groups met. Leading the other party was a sparely-built, grey-haired man bearing a pastoral staff, clad in the white and black of an abbot, upright of carriage and singing heartily. To him Colum broke forward into a run, to embrace impulsively, to the other's shout of laughter and wide-armed greeting. Inevitably the two croziers got in the way, with a clatter, and, laughing in his turn, Colum grasped the other's staff and thrust his own at Mungo/Kentigern in exchange. Holding each other at arm's length, they stared, while their supporters stopped singing, to cheer.

Words seemed almost unnecessary at this juncture, both equally famous and having heard so much of the other. But Colum burst out, "Man, man – do I call you Mungo? Or Kentigern? Of a mercy – which?"

The other had a notably twinkling eye. "I was christened Mungo. The Welsh it was who named me Kentigern, when St David made me bishop. The Welsh are a people of much dignity, and Mungo, meaning manikin, was insufficiently dignified for a bishop! So I am Mungo the man and Kentigern the bishop!"

"What you were christened is sufficient for me, then, Mungo. My friends call me Columcille."

"May I so name the man who chose to be a priest rather than High King of Ireland?"

"If you do not, I shall smite you! And I am a larger man than you, Mungo!"

So these two, taking to each other like long-lost brothers, then made for the monastery of Cathures, which Mungo called his *glasghu*, his dear green place.

If there was no feasting thereafter, for plain fare was the rule, at least the feeding was adequate and garnished by a feast of conversation, recounting and anecdote. There was so much to learn, so much to tell, with these two, whilst their associates listened enthralled. Colum learned how, like himself, Mungo was of royal blood, albeit, as he cheerfully admitted, born in bastardy. His grandfather, King Loth, of a sub-kingdom of the Southern Albannach, now being called Lothian after him, was pagan and a hard man. His Christian daughter, the Princess Thenew, he had destined to marry a British prince; but Thenew had other ideas and was in love with one of her own people, a sheep-master in the Lammermuir Hills. Unfortunately or otherwise, she had become pregnant; and when her father discovered this, his wrath knew no bounds. He ordered her lover to be slain and she herself to be thrown over the cliff-face of Dunpender, at Traprain, his hilltop capital. But when she survived this drastic punishment, he decided that she must be protected by some powerful demon. But the disgrace she had brought on him and his house required that she be banished. He had her taken down to Aberlady Bay, on the Firth of Forth nearby, and there pushed off, alone, in a coracle without paddle. The outgoing tide carried her seawards until, near the Isle of May, it turned and she then drifted up Forth. Eventually the coracle grounded on the north shore, at Culross in Fife, near the blessed St Serf's monastery. Seeking shelter there, Thenew was shown pity by the saint, cherished and in due course her child was born, himself. He was given the name of Mungo by Serf. At Culross he remained, grew up and in course of time took holy orders; until, in his early twenties, with Serf dying, he was given the vision to leave, to go westwards and preach the Gospel to the Strathclyde heathen, taking his mother with him. She had eventually died also, and was buried near Cathures; and he, becoming too successful at his converting for the pagan King Morcant, Roderick's predecessor, had had to flee, and gone to Wales, to join St David and St Asaph. The rest Colum would know.

Colum, for his part, told of his upbringing, early adherence to the Church, the temptation over the high kingship, his founding of monasteries, Cooldrevny and the move to Alba and the task he had set himself.

This led to Mungo's forthcoming visit to the Albannach in Fortrenn, and when that man offered to postpone it, Colum would not hear of it. They would go together, for at least part of the time. He would like to see King Gartnait again, for he had heard that King Brude was failing, and almost certainly Gartnait would succeed him as High King, and he wished to make sure that the Christianising of Alba would go on. He could not be away from Iona for too long however. His long-ship would go to Dunbarton meantime to await him.

This was agreed, and plans and routes worked out. They would leave in two days.

In the morning, Mungo took them to see the Princess Thenew's tomb nearby, a handsome edifice and no mere cairn of stones, provided apparently by Queen Langueth, and they held a little commemoration service there. When Colum remarked that he would hardly have expected such a gesture from that queen, Mungo, in confidence, told him of the reasons for it. Langueth's morals, in the past, had not been immaculate, with a succession of lovers whenever Roderick was safely away from home. With one, in time, she was particularly indiscreet. This was one of the captains of the royal guard, and to him, foolishly, she gave as keepsake a special and unusual ring presented to her by her husband. One night, journeying, the King had occasion to visit that captain's tent, and there found him asleep, one arm outside his blanket, and wearing that ring. Roderick said nothing then, but later he found opportunity to banish the man from the kingdom, taking the ring from him, to throw it into the Clyde. Then he went to the queen and said that he had heard stories going about the court that she had been unfaithful to him and had given that special ring he had presented to her to one of her paramours. He was prepared to disbelieve this if she returned the ring to him. If not, he must judge her guilty, put her away, and she would be no longer queen.

In her fear and agitation, Langueth had come to Mungo, saying that he could help her if he would, and promising that if he did she would never be unfaithful again. He, Mungo, had been at a loss what to do, but in a dream it had been revealed to him. So in the morning he had gone to Langueth and told her to send one of her servants to fish for salmon in the Clyde. If he caught one, her problem would be solved. She did as she was bidden, the angler caught a fine fish, and there, lodged in its throat, was the missing ring. Since then Langueth had been a changed woman, and grateful. The ways of God were indeed wonderful to contemplate.

Colum, intrigued, told of the three nights' scourgings he had undergone at Hinba, to force him to anoint Aidan mac Gabhran as king instead of his brother.

On the morrow, the two principals much enjoying each others' company, they set out for Fortrenn. They journeyed on horseback, by the same route Colum had followed before, down Clyde to Bolline, then up through the Lennox hills to the Flanders Moss at the flood plain of the Forth, and so through the Highland foothills of Monteith to Strathallan. This time, however, instead of making for the royal palaces of Forteviot and Abernethy they swung off north-westwards into Strathearn, for Crieff and then due northwards through ever higher mountains of Glen Almond and Strathbraan.

Mungo was making for the former important Albannach druidical centre of Orrea, which on a previous visit to Fortrenn he had vowed to turn into a Christian community.

Colum was much impressed by the situation of this Orrea, when they emerged from Strathbraan into the great valley of the Tay. Rocky heights rising out of magnificent woodland created a tremendous amphitheatre where the rivers met amidst steaming waterfalls, and all to the north appeared to be closed off by an enormous barrier of steep mountainside. There was, in fact, a narrow high pass through it, Mungo explained, the only access to the further Highland fastnesses of Atholl in Alba proper – which was why Orrea was here, commanding the entry to the pass and all communication between Fortrenn and Inverness.

It proved to be quite a town, down there by the Tay, with fine buildings and monuments, surrounded by druidical stone-circles, temples and groves. The former college was now a hunting palace for King Gartnait, and the entire druidical influence in decay. But, as in Dalriada, Christianity had so far made little impact in succession, and Mungo was determined that this should be amended and that Orrea should become in fact the main generating place of the faith in Southern Alba, and had Gartnait's permission so to do, if he could. He had even got a new name for it, to emphasise its conversion to a Christian centre – *Dun Celidé*, the House of the Friends of God.

Colum was glad to assist in this work, although time pressed, and he wanted to make the journey to Abernethy also, to see Gartnait. It was an unusual situation for him to be assisting rather than leading, but the two friends, bishop and abbot, spent some rewarding and happy weeks together, using this dramatically exciting place as centre to missionarise quite a wide area, meeting with little opposition and spreading the Word of God down the Tay valley and into the upland area to the east, reaching into Blair-in-Gowrie and the verges of the mighty Strathmore in Angus, where, at Meigle, they came to the renowned King Arthur of Caerleon's wife's tomb, the errant Guinevere. And, in fact, Colum did not have to go to Abernethy, for Gartnait, hearing of the two famous clerics' presence at Orrea, came there to visit them, friendly and helpful. Colum had no difficulty in gaining his assurance that, if indeed he eventually succeeded Brude in the high kingship of Alba, the Christian endeavour there could go forward with his full support.

But, satisfactory as was this entire interlude, it had to be only that. The day came when Colum could no longer delay his return to Iona. To celebrate and commemorate their coming together and brief but effective joint mission, at Mungo's suggestion, Colum chose and blessed a fine spring of water welling up in a former druidical grove near the riverside a mile north of the township; his friend declaring that it would be called St Colum's Well for all time to come – despite the protests of a man who never used the term saint as connected with himself, however normal a title it was for Celtic Church missionaries. Thereafter, Mungo saw him as far as the head of Strathbraan, on the long road back to Dunbarton and the ship, in quite an emotional leave-taking. They assured each other that they would meet again one day, if not here – since they were both approaching their sixties – then hereafter, kindred spirits.

So it was back to being the teacher, the mentor, the schoolmaster – God forgive him for the reluctance!

22

With word that Brude mac Maelchon's health was worsening, Colum found excuse, the next year, for stretching those restless wings of his. He must see the High King, if possible, not only because of the calls of friendship and conversion but to try to ensure that it would be Christian Gartnait who succeeded him on the throne, not one of the other lesser kings or mormaors of Alba who would be quite likely still to be a pagan.

His planned departure for Inverness, however, was delayed; for King Aidan, whose expedition against the Orkney pirates had been a success, now decided upon a much more ambitious military adventure, the expelling of Baetan of Ulster's occupying forces from the Isle of Man. This, of course, would be a major undertaking, and there were grave doubts amongst the Dalriadan councillors as to its wisdom. But the king was determined, and sought Colum's support in council, on the grounds of their co-operation against Baetan at Druim Ceatt, and his help in getting Roderick of Strathclyde's co-operation with the shipping demonstration. Colum was very doubtful about advocating war and bloodshed, but recognised that such as Baetan had to be contained. He compromised, which was not really like him, by saying that he would support another demonstration, by Aidan's fleet descending on Man, but that actual battle should be avoided if possible. If a sufficient threat was posed, Baetan or his commander on the island, might well be prepared to negotiate or withdraw. After all, the Strathclyde gesture must have given him warning – and he had not risked any further invasion of Dalriadic territory.

Aidan had had to be content with that, but had gone ahead with his plans. And Colum had promised to have prayers for his success offered in all the churches.

In the circumstances, therefore, he felt that he could not depart on an inevitably prolonged visit to Inverness whilst the outcome of Aidan's venture remained in doubt.

It was during this period of waiting that Colum received an unexpected pleasure and encouragement – the arrival at Iona of Kenneth of Achabo, come to contribute another spell of missionary aid. Considering that Kenneth was some years older than Colum, this was quite a noble action. Achabo Abbey must be getting used to managing without its abbot. Kenneth would go on the Inverness visit, gladly.

Then Aidan returned in triumph from the Isle of Man. He had won a major victory there, completely routing Baetan's forces, and had driven the survivors back to Ulster, reinstating his sister's son, Brendinus, as sub-king. Some of the Strathclyde ships had come to join them. Sadly, Griffin, an illegitimate young son of Aidan, had been slain, in his first battle; but otherwise all was triumph.

So now Colum was free to sail. He brought Baithen over, to take charge at Iona and do the teaching, leaving the penitent Fechno to look after Tiree. He went to Hinba to take leave of Ernan – who wished that he was able to come with them. Then, in almost holiday mood, they were on their way. As well as Kenneth, Lugbe and Diarmit, Colum took Drostan, his nephew, now a fully-fledged priest. Also Machar, who was complaining that he was tired of being little more than a ship-master; he was promised that, when he had brought them to the end of salt-water at the head of Loch Linnhe, he could leave the long-ship in the care of another and come along.

Bridget and her nuns waved them off.

This time, when they took leave of the long-ship at the foot of the tremendous Great Glen of Alba, they did not take to coracles as before. But assured of the support of the High King, and displaying the personal banner of the Black Boar on silver which he had presented to Colum, they hired horses and obtained an armed escort from the local chieftain, and proceeded by the series of tracks and roadways – which followed approximately the chain of lochs and linking rivers in the gut of the mighty valley previously used – a vastly more speedy and comfortable progress. It was difficult to persuade Drostan and even Machar, and other newcomers, how different had been their earlier journeying. Colum made a point, however, of visiting their previous halting-places and meeting again such of those who had aided them and survived the years.

They reached the head of Loch Ness in excellent time, where they abandoned the horses and sent them back with the escort; and instead hired fishermen and two fair-sized boats from the village on the crannog or artificial island there, to take them onwards. They learned that the Water Horse was still being seen occasionally, but had not actually killed anyone of recent years and so was much less feared – thanks to the Prince-Abbot Colum.

They did not fail to call in at the various locations where they had made their mark, on both north and south shores of the great loch, in a zigzag progress. They visited the one-time evil leprosy spring, now being called Colum's Well and resorted to apparently, oddly enough, by lepers in hope of healing, a circumstance which much touched that man. Also, of course, they called on Virolec mac Emchat at Urquhart, and found there a thriving church acting as a centre of the faith for all that extensive lochside area. Here they spent two nights, in support of Virolec and his endeavours.

At Dochfour, at the loch-foot, they received a great welcome and found a tall, carved monolith erected by the riverside, displaying a fearsome creature with horns and a forked tail, as the Water Horse, and a not very flattering representation of Colum beating it with his pastoral staff, while an infant, presumably Lugbe, fled in terror. The latter, no longer a young man, pretended to be highly offended by this, to the glee of all.

Then it was directly onwards for Inverness.

They had been prepared for a change in King Brude's appearance, but were distressed nevertheless to find him so frail, bent and even broken in speech. But he greeted them warmly and put all at his palace at their disposal. His daughter Nessa, now a grown and attractive woman, particularly rejoiced to see them. She had never suffered more of her strange sickness of body and mind, and was now in fact her father's principal companion and support. Broichan was dead.

This ageing and dying off of those with whom he had long associated was coming to cast something of a shadow for Colum.

Brude well knew that his days were numbered, and was touchingly glad to have Colum there to ask about death and the hereafter. Colum could only tell him of Christ's teachings on the matter and his own complete faith in the immortality of the human soul and the fullest and more rewarding life beyond, the triumph of love in that better kingdom; that since God was love and all love was of God, in that kingdom those who loved in this one would be reunited. This was not just comforting reassurance, he insisted, but reasoned truth, God ordained. For love, order, beauty and truth were aspects of God, certainly not of man; and love the first, ensured by the other three. So let Brude fear nothing, as he himself had no fear of death. The dying itself might possibly be unpleasant, for a little, but no more so than so many other human experiences already undergone and survived; death itself would be a joy, release from present pains and frustrations to a wider and ongoing appreciation of living.

Brude received all this with most evident relief, and it enabled Colum quite easily and without discomfort to go on to the subject that preoccupied him – the succession to the high kingship. Brude himself was concerned about this, admitted that Gartnait of Fortrenn was his own choice, but that of course the election lay with the *ri* or lesser kings or mormaors; it was not for the *Ard Righ* to name his successor. There were seven of these – Moray, Buchan, Mar, Angus, Atholl, Ross

374

and Skye and the Isles. Fortrenn, with Fife, was a separate entity, independent. But it could be advantageous for both that the two Albannach main kingdoms should be united, all recognised. And Gartnait had another advantage over other contenders, in that his mother, Domelch, had been a princess of the Alban royal house; and it was their preference, if possible, to elect through the female in the royal line. Nevertheless, Gartnait's appointment was by no means certain, for there were two other contenders – Cathal of Skye, whom Colum knew of, and Bede, Mormaor of Buchan. Cathal was unlikely to win much support; but Bede was a notable warrior, where Gartnait was not, and some of the ri reckoned that it was a necessary quality in a High King.

As in the issue of Aidan and Ewan, Colum declared that surely the qualities of wisdom, good judgement, a love of peace and of morality were more important in the supreme ruler than was leadership in war, which could be provided by commanding generals?

Brude did not dispute that, but asserted that Bede could be a serious rival to Gartnait nevertheless. And the former unfortunately, was a pagan still.

Colum thought that perhaps this Bede might be a suitable subject for conversion. Was there nothing that Garnait could do to improve his chances?

Brude suggested that if Gartnait was to adopt a more warlike attitude, if but for a little while, lead an expedition against the Angles, or even make a move to check the excesses of some of his own Fife chieftains who had got out of hand after the Anglian raids, instead of all his hunting and womanising, then the other mormaors might view his appointment more enthusiastically.

That night, Colum and Kenneth put their heads together. The latter, who had been looking for somewhere to act the missionary as it were outside Colum's chosen territory, now had a location and an excuse; he could go down to Fortrenn and seek to persuade Gartnait to lead an expedition to this Fife area, which was allegedly still mainly pagan, and so perhaps achieve two objectives. And Colum could go to see Bede of Buchan and his people.

Brude, in due course, wished them well – but desired Colum not to be gone overlong.

The province of Buchan lay some eighty miles east of

Inverness, but on the coastal route to the south; so Kenneth could accompany them so far on his much longer journey. They went at first through the country where Comgall had operated on the previous visit, but which the others had not seen; and so were able to call at churches and cells then set up, and to assess progress. In most cases they were pleased, but in one or two disappointed. Success could not always be expected; but in the main Comgall's work had produced a goodly harvest. After the Nairn and Barevan area, however, a score of miles from Inverness, they were into new territory. There was a great temptation to stop and preach and spread the Word here; but they restrained themselves. They had business elsewhere.

It seemed strange to be travelling due eastwards for so great a distance, rather than southwards. They were largely hugging the lengthy Moray Firth coast, little to be distinguished from that of the open Norse Sea – this to avoid the inland hills, scarcely mountains these but awkward to cross. This seaboard could hardly have been more different from that of the west coast and the Hebrides, endless stretches of shoreline, unbroken by sea-lochs or even much in the way of bays, extensive sands backed by dune country or else cliffs, some lofty, some riven and shattered, some cavernous, but all this without major indentations. It was the land of Moray, the largest of the Albannach mortuaths, and fertile within, its mormaor an old man with no ambitions to be High King.

By Brodie and Findhorn and Burghead, by Duffus and Spynie and another Urquhart, by Cullen and Banff and Gamrie, they rode, along the long coastal plain, often with the roar of great breakers setting the air a quiver, the more so as they approached the Moray-Buchan border, with the coastal cliffs now growing ever higher and wilder, until the mighty Troup Head towered before them, the thrusting guardian of Buchan, where the bleak, featureless hills came down to the boiling sea in stupendous granite precipices, scored by deep steep dens and ravines.

Here, in this defiant terrain, they met with their first human challenge, fierce armed guards holding the narrow pass-like entry to the road into this dramatic doorway to Buchan. Clearly Mormaor Bede was not on the best of terms with his neighbour of Moray – which Colum philosophically took to be a good sign, one less vote for Bede, probably.

Greeted with hostility and suspicion, they requested to be conducted to the Mormaor, and this at least gained them entry and escort, however grudging. Their assertion that they came from the High King seemed to carry little weight.

Not anticipating any very enjoyable journey through this land thereafter, for Buchan they had been told was a large province, they were relieved to discover that Mormaor Bede elected to spend most of his time close to this northern gateway, at the fort of Dundearg, a mere five miles to the east. No doubt he had other palaces, but this appeared to be his chosen home. So at least they would know something of success or failure before long.

Down through the chasm-like pass they descended steeply to an extraordinary fishing township built on a narrow shelf at the foot of beetling cliffs, just a little way above sea level. It was noticeable how all the tight-ranked houses huddled endlong with their gables or shoulders to the sea; and it did not take much imagination to realise that in a storm those gables and roofs, not of thatch but of heavy stone-slates, would be battered by not only spray but actual wavetops. There was, however, a breakwater, part natural, part artificial, behind which the fishing boats could shelter; but surely, frequently, as a haven this would be unusable. The visitors had never seen such a place as Pennan.

Climbing out beyond, and over some miles of high, bare, cattle-dotted plateau land, they could look out over many a mile of similar seemingly featureless and more or less level uplands, semi-moorland. Far from attractive compared with the scenery to which they had become used in Alba. This Buchan was a territory unto itself, it seemed. Then, after perhaps three miles, they descended again, this time into a very fair, green and wooded valley hidden amongst the bleak heights, fairly narrow and dropping swiftly to the rock-bound coast, but pleasing – especially to Colum, when he perceived that the trees were in fact oaks. Their escort, when questioned, briefly announced that this was the Dour Water, with the village of Aberdour at its foot – *dour* being just another variation of Derry, Darrow, Darroch and Dair, all meaning a place of oaks. He, at least, felt better, enheartened therefore.

Only a mile further and they came to the spectacularly-sited fortress-castle of Dundearg, no palace this but a sea-eagle's eyrie of a place, perched on a narrow and thrusting promontory high above the waves, all stone battlements and parapets and towers; not large but most evidently strong, all but impregnable. That the lord of a large kingdom should choose such as his main dwelling was surely significant. Would a man of such mentality be suitable to be the High King of a great nation?

They soon came to a decision on that question. Within a short time of being presented to the Mormaor Bede, Colum came to the conclusion that here was another Cathal of Skye – and not only because he had a guard of female warriors, but also he used one of those carved stone balls to keep turning in his hand, a sign perhaps of an unquiet spirit. He was in his early thirties, red haired and fierce eyed. But Colum could not feel that he was a strong character, however able in war he might be.

Bede's reaction to his visitors was wary rather than hostile, but scarcely welcoming. He admitted that he had heard of Prince Colum from Ireland, and the man Comgall, and knew that King Brude was their friend and had heeded their teachings; also the matter of the Water Horse. He did not say that for himself he was not interested, but implied as much.

Presently Colum took the bull by the horns and asked if he had the Mormaor's permission to preach the Gospel amongst his people. Bede could scarcely refuse when, whether he liked it or not, Christianity was now in theory accepted as the religion of Alba, the Alba he had hopes of ruling. Since some other mormaors were Christian, it might tell against him in the election to be accused of rebuffing the missionaries. So he grudgingly acceded. That led Colum to ask further if he might set up his cell and mission-place at the village of Aberdour, the confluence of the oak-trees, adding that oaks had always been his especial trees. Shrugging, Bede agreed, perhaps thankful that the newcomers did not want to establish themselves at this his Dundearg.

So next day, they saw Kenneth and Machar on their southwards way – Machar, eager to prove himself as effective a missionary as he was a sailor, had asked permission to go on down into the province of Mar, where there was said to be a large city between the rivers Don and Dee, where Buchan ended, ripe for conversion. This city of Northern Mar was said to be a noted seaport, where much of Brude's fleet was based, and Kenneth hoped to get a ship there to take him on down to the Tay estuary and Abernethy and so to avoid the dangers of the high mountain passes of South Mar and Atholl. The pair took with them almost half of the little company, so that Colum was left with only Drostan and three helpers, to head back to Aberdour. So far he had made no attempt to convert Bede. That must await the guidance of events.

Aberdour, on closer acquaintance, was even more attractive than they had realised, a secluded declivity in open woodland, threaded by the Dour Water which twisted and turned in cascades and pools to its mouth between the jaws of cliffs, wherein nestled a little fishing haven, much less exposed than Pennan. Out of sight of this community, on a rock-shelf just above a bend in the stream, they decided to build a tiny church and the usual beehive cells. There was plenty of timber, sapling-boughs, sand and clay, so that construction would be simple.

Colum, so experienced now in establishing these missions, was not long in recruiting local labour, and at the same time seeking to instil in these workers the rudiments of the faith. He had found that working together was of major assistance in getting the message across and gaining trust. The fisherfolk of Aberdour were no exception.

Using this as centre they spread out to neighbouring villages and townships, including the extraordinary Pennan, meeting with fair response. Drostan was eloquent, personable and good-looking, and particularly successful with the young women, as was his uncle with their seniors. The work went well, and they were presently able to set up something like a permanent congregation at Aberdour of the Oaks.

Oddly, it was this matter of oak-trees which eventually brought the entire venture to a head. They had been moving inland ever deeper, up the valleys of streams which drained the strange plateau land, where the communities were of cattle-rearers and oat-growers rather than fisherfolk, and at one such, called Strichen, about ten miles south of Aberdour, the headman, a convert with whom they stayed the night, on hearing of Colum's interest in oaks, told them of another oak-wood not far away, the most renowned in all Buchan, called not Dour but Deer. On the South Ugie Water, it was large and beautiful and had been in much favour with the Druids.

Nothing would do but that Colum and Drostan must go and see this Deer – and they were duly impressed and delighted. It was indeed a place of beauty and character, an oak-forest rather than just a wood, but open, with glades and meadows along the riverside, almost parkland. There were no fewer than four stone-circles dotted around, a number of symbol-stones, cairns and other vestiges of paganism but now no one there, the village being a mile or so to the west – sun-worship in decline but not yet replaced. Uncle and nephew were at one in deciding that this should be their next and if possible their main centre – for Aberdour, although so pleasant, was too isolated on the coast, insufficiently central to serve the inland areas of Buchan. A monastery here would nurture a great area.

So it was back to Aberdour and then a visit to Dundearg. But Bede was now unhelpful. It might be that he was hearing of too much success on the missionaries' part and becoming doubtful about letting them go too far. He refused to let them have the Forest of Deer, or any part of it.

Disappointed, and not only on account of Deer itself but because of poor prospects for the hoped for influence in the matter of the high kingship, Colum went back to Aberdour. He would have to do some praying.

He and Drostan were in fact preaching and baptising in the Memsie area, some seven miles to the south-east, about a week later, using a great druidical burial-cairn there as pulpit, when they were surprised to have Bede himself arrive, at the head of a troop of armed men on hard-ridden, foam-flecked horses. Fearing trouble, possible prohibition of further pro-selytising, they stood their ground on that mound of stones and sought to still the immediate fears of the company of worshippers.

Bede dismounted and came up to them, long-strided and looking at his fiercest. But his words, jerked out, belied his looks. "Will you save my son, Prince Colum?" he demanded.

Colum blinked. This was his first intimation that Bede had a son; he had seen no boy about Dundearg nor heard of any family, or even of a wife.

"Your son . . .?"

"Maldoun, my son. He is sore stricken. Suddenly. Sick unto death. My wife says that you healed Brude's daughter. Will you come and heal Maldoun?"

"*I* did not heal the princess, Highness. God Almighty did that, in answer to our prayers."

"Then come and pray for Maldoun. Come, quickly."

Colum hesitated. This peremptory summons offended. Yet it could be but the man's manner, and resentment sinful pride. And a child – it could be no more than a child, with Bede the age he was – in need.

"Where?" he asked.

"At Inverallochy. Where he is in fosterage. Ten miles. Quickly. He may die if you delay."

"We can pray here, as well as at Inverallochy, Highness. God in His heaven is not concerned with miles."

Bede frowned doubtfully.

Colum turned to the watching company and raised both hands high. "Friends all," he cried, "on your knees, Christ's people. Pray to God for the child Maldoun mac Bede. Sorely ill. At Inverallochy. In great need. Pray that, in God's mercy, he may recover. Pray for Maldoun." And he sank to his own knees.

As all there, save for the staring mounted men, did the same, Bede looked about him uncertainly. Then, as Colum began to pray in a loud voice, reluctantly, almost shamefacedly, he too sank to his knees on the uncomfortable heap of stones.

Colum's prayer was heartfelt as it was simple. Suddenly he saw this as a test for *his* faith, not so much Bede's or these others'. He had asked for help and guidance in the matter of Bede's conversion and the high kingship, and here, all so unexpected, could be the answer. Did he, Colum mac Felim, sufficiently trust his Saviour? If so, then this public petition, thrust upon him as it were, could surely reveal God's will in the entire matter. All, he now felt, *knew*, rested on him and his faith, the child's life, Bede's conversion, Brude's succession itself. Here was test, trial, proof.

So, with all that was in him he prayed for the boy Maldoun, with a power, urgency and vehemence which communicated itself to all there in strange fashion, even surprising Drostan, the very air seeming to quiver with the intensity of his fervour.

He did not go on for long, could not, in that fashion. When he stopped, there was a great silence in that place, men and women waiting, for just what they knew not. But Colum himself knew something for sure, a notable sense of peace and fulfilment, as he got to his feet.

He turned to Bede as that man also rose, looking no more certain than before. "Go, friend," he said. "Go to your son. He will be well. Go to this Inverallochy – and thank God."

The other stared. "Go . . .? And *you*? You will come?"

"No need. I told you – God is not concerned with distances. He is everywhere. Your Maldoun is safe in God's hands. Go to him. We will stay and praise God here."

"No! *You* should come. My wife said to bring you . . ."

"There is no need, I tell you. Have faith. I have done . . . what I had to do."

"If he dies, I, I . . .!" There was sheer threat in that, as the Mormaor turned away and strode down and back to his waiting horsemen, to mount, rein around, and ride off without another word.

Drostan began to speak to his uncle, low-voiced, but Colum silenced him with a wave of the hand, and cried out, "Let us praise God for His mercy this day! Praise Him in the psalm:

> The king shall joy in thy strength, O Lord,
> In thy salvation how greatly shall he rejoice . . .

And he led off, his great voice resounding, his four colleagues at least joining in, as all the company gazed and wondered.

Later, on their way back to Aberdour, Drostan returned to his questioning. Why? Why had Columcille done this? Why had he not gone to this Inverallochy? To please the Mormaor, on whom so much depended? To pray over the boy. Why had he not even gone with Bede afterwards to see the boy? If he truly believed him bettered. To see? To gain Bede's gratitude, if it was true, instead of sending him away angry?

Colum shook his head. "I did what came to me," he said. "If it is God's will, as the answer to our earlier prayers, then this way was best. I did only what came to me, then. And . . . I have no doubts. For God's will will be done."

Drostan shook his head, in turn, and left it at that.

They were in their beds asleep when the clatter of hooves at the cell-door wakened them. They rose, to find Bede and his men there, dark as it was.

"All is well!" the Mormaor all but shouted. "Maldoun is himself again. He speaks, eats, laughs! You worked your magic, man . . .!"

"No magic, Highness – only God's mercy. *I* did nothing, only asked. He heard our prayers, *your* prayer also. That is all."

"All! I tell you, the boy is well again. Thanks to you."

"Thanks to your prayer, I say, as much as mine. All our prayers. For He is your God, and Maldoun's, as well as ours. Do you not see it, friend Bede?"

"I see that I owe you much – my only son."

"God gave *His* only Son for all of us. Thank Him. Is He not *your* God, now?"

The other drew a long breath. "If it is your will."

"Never my will, but His. He saved your son. And would save you also. Will you not accept His Son?"

"Very well. What must I do?"

"Tomorrow, I will come to Dundearg and tell you, Highness."

"Yes. And you can have the Forest of Deer. All of it."

"I thank you. But again, not for me. For Christ's Church."

"As you will. Come then, tomorrow."

Colum and Drostan did not go back to their couches there and then, but into the little half-finished church to give thanks.

In the morning they rode to Dundearg, two of their objectives seemingly attained. But how to win the third, that of the high kingship? Was it right, godly, to seek to make this matter the price of Bede's acceptance by the Church? Could that be God's will – or but Colum's own entirely human devising?

In the event, that man could not bring himself to tell the Mormaor that *he* considered it best that Gartnait of Fortrenn should be High King. After all, if Bede was Christian, might he not serve as well? He, Colum, was in dire danger of seeing himself as a king-maker, after the Aidan matter – and that would be prideful sin. God, who had intervened here adequately, might prefer Bede? So nothing was said on that subject, and Bede's indoctrination into the faith of Christ crucified proceeded without sanctions or even hints. A day was fixed for his baptism, along with his wife and son.

Before that important event, Colum and Drostan went southwards again to Deer, approving it the more and joyfully planning where their monastery was to be, its dimensions and features – for this, they envisaged, should eventually be large, an abbey indeed, as centre for all Buchan. Drostan would remain here as its abbot when Colum returned to Inverness, and would seek, in due course, to link up with Machar in Mar. One day, all Alba would be Christian.

So Bede and his family, with some of his chiefs, were baptised, and Colum, with Iona calling him back, recognised that he must go. With only his faithful Lugbe and Diarmit, he took his leave of Bede, that stiff-necked but grateful convert, kissed his nephew farewell, with his blessing, and took the road westwards for Inverness.

He found Brude neither better nor worse, glad to see him, also to hear of Bede's conversion, but reluctant indeed that Colum should proceed on his way back to Iona. They were friends now, and he wanted his friend beside him when he was called away to face the next world. But, moved as he was, Colum had to disappoint. It might be long enough before that day, and he had been away from Iona for too long as it was, the essential generating-place of all his aims and efforts. God's work must come first.

They made an emotional parting, as it had been with Mungo, both very much aware that it was highly improbable that they would see each other again in this life. But the next, that was different . . .

23

Coming to terms with death was, Colum supposed, the common requirement of all, and he himself had no fear of death, save that it should not happen before he had fulfilled, in fair measure, the task he had set himself – which was foolish, of course, and perhaps typically prideful, for if it was God's purpose, as he hoped and prayed, God would ensure its fulfilment, if not by him, by others. But were all men and women so concerned about the death of others, or not so much their deaths as their departure from the scene, *his* scene? Somehow, this dying off of those he had known and worked with was affecting him ever more grievously, not only the mourning their loss but the sense of impoverishment, the *emptying* of his scene, the constant reminder of mortality.

It was Ernan's death, not Brude's, which next so troubled him, even though in some way he was prepared for it – indeed, before he had set off on his last journey he had taken a possible final farewell of his uncle at Hinba, acknowledging that they might not look on each other again this side of eternity. In fact, Colum was barely back to Iona, on this occasion, when one of the Garbh Eileach men came hurrying up to the cell on Tor Abb breathlessly, to announce that the Prince Ernan had come. He was direly ill, and they had urged him not to, but he said that he had been given to know that Prince Colum had returned, and he was determined that, ill as he was, they should meet once more. He had ordered them to bring him here in their boat. He could no longer walk, and was down at the harbour waiting.

Colum immediately set off for the shore, but had only gone halfway when he saw a tottering figure come staggering up towards him. Astonished, he started to run, but while still a score of yards apart, the other toppled forward, fell and lay still. Colum reached him to bend down. His uncle was dead.

It seemed an extraordinary way to die, and presumably so chosen. When Bridget remarked on it, later, Colum said that he thought that it was in fact a final avuncular gesture on Ernan's part, wryly humorous, to prove to them both that his nephew was not always right, that when he had said that they might not see each other again this side of eternity, he was to be disproved. They had indeed seen each other – but only just.

So Ernan was buried on that Hebridean isle and Colum had a stone cross carved, to set up where his uncle fell.

He talked to Bridget thereafter about this perhaps unhealthy preoccupation with the removal from the scene of his contemporaries, and the feeling that *he* was going to be left alone eventually, as some sort of punishment. She told him that she thought that he was taking this altogether too seriously, that probably most others felt the same way as they grew older, particularly if they themselves were hale and vigorous. Let him just be thankful that he was so blessed in this matter. He was now aged sixty-five, was he not? Yet he had the health and energy of a man thirty years younger. God's gift to him. Let him not spoil it with such imaginings.

He sought to take her good advice. But when, not so long

afterwards, Grillan arrived from Skye with the word that Scandlann had died suddenly, and a replacement priest was required for the Snizort church; also that his own colleague Cailtan, at Portree was obviously failing – he found it difficult.

It took over a year for Brude to die. Machar brought the news on a visit to Iona to seek new priestly recruits for the church he had managed to establish in that city of Mar, between the mouths of the Don and Dee rivers, called, it seemed, Aberdeen. Brude had lingered on in physical weakness, but mentally alert to the end, and had indeed been able to persuade his mormaors, or most of them, to appoint King Gartnait in his stead, Bede and Cathal each only obtaining two votes. So that was satisfactory, and the outlook for Christianity in Alba good.

Machar was enthusiastic about his work at this Aberdeen and in Mar generally, a notable province, more populous than Buchan and not nearly so mountainous as they had heard; the high mountains were there, but there was much fertile land before these were reached, more than in any other part of Alba they had visited. Why the high kingship did not make this its seat instead of Inverness he did not know.

Machar left again, with four newly-ordained Albannach assistants. He was to return by Inverness and to convey to Gartnait Colum's congratulations and fullest support. When next he came to Inverness, if so it was wished, he could consecrate the High King as he had done Aidan here. He promised to visit Machar's establishment when he could.

Colum mourned for Brude, who had meant so much in his life's work.

Then it was teaching, teaching – and trying to accept that this was God's purpose for him now.

Bridget was his great help and consolation; her understanding unfailing, her encouragement constant. With so many of his original colleagues now gone, Baithen on Tiree the only one nearby, she was his stay, prop and ally, a woman of much common sense as well as of more endearing qualities, such as a man needed. And as Prioress of the nunnery, she now had a status in the Church which gave weight to her counsel – as well as enabling him to see a lot more of her.

It was not all one way, and frequently she came to him for advice and guidance. And they did not always agree. As in the vexed case of the woman Modwena. This was the wife of a small chieftain on Mull, who desired to become a nun. Her husband was elderly and their children grown up. She was a good Christian and wished to devote the rest of her life to God's service. Her husband, who was scarcely religiously-minded, did not want to lose her, but apparently did not absolutely forbid it. Bridget was prepared to admit her, but Colum advised not. He declared that the marriage vows, taken in God's name and presence, were sacred and were for life. This Modwena could not, or should not, wed the Church while her husband was alive and wanted her. Bridget thought that, in the circumstances, with the woman eager and conjugal life seeming to all intents over, she should be able to choose and not be tied. She had been a good wife for long years; was she not entitled now to follow her own wishes rather than the man's? They clashed on this, the unmarried man electing to support the sanctity of the marriage vow, the former wife and mother putting the woman's wishes first. They agreed to differ - but it was to be noted that Bridget did not in fact admit the woman to her nunnery.

On the other hand, Colum yielded to Bridget's judgement in the matter of Findchan, the one-time miscreant on Tiree. It was becoming evident more and more that Baithen was to some extent wasted on that outpost of an island, being needed frequently on Iona itself, to aid in the teaching duties and to take Colum's place when he was called away. He should be the sub-abbot there. But who to replace him on Tiree, which was now an important centre for the outer isles, with two monasteries and four churches? Baithen suggested Findchan who was now, it seemed, a reformed character. Colum said no. Someone who had behaved as he had done was not to be trusted, and should not be put in charge of others, particularly of young men. But Bridget convinced him to give Findchan a chance. Surely he would have learned his lesson, and should be forgiven? Let Baithen's judgement be trusted.

So Baithen came to be Sub-Abbot of Iona and Findchan was Prior of Tiree.

These domestic problems were dwarfed by national ones. With Brude dead and Gartnait moved to Inverness but not yet fully settled as High King, and leaving something of a vacuum at Fortrenn, Athelfrith of Northumbria saw opportunity to revert to his old ways and started raiding again into Lothian and Fife. Gartnait was anxious for his Fortrenn, and with

Roderick of Strathclyde now aged and lethargic, sent to ask Aidan if he would lead a Dalriadan army to aid his own Fortrenn forces in driving out the invaders, this under the Christian alliance. Aidan, who still saw himself as a warrior-king, was nothing loth; the more so as the sub-province of Manaan on the Forth estuary, inherited by him from his mother, was contiguous with Fife and therefore endangered. Colum himself was concerned, in that his friend Kenneth of Achabo was still in that area, seeming to have all but settled in Fife, establishing a monastery at Balrymond in Muckross, at the very eastern tip of that peninsular province where it thrust out into the Norse Sea. Athelfrith was a determined and bloodthirsty pagan, so there was cause for concern. Colum besought Aidan, if he could, to do his best to protect Kenneth and his establishment. Meantime, he would pray. Aidan, in that semi-cynical way of his, suggested that a prayer or two for *himself* and his army might do no harm, while he was at it!

There was a curious sequel to that conversation some weeks later when, during a forenoon teaching session in the abbey, Colum suddenly stopped speaking, stared away and away, and then called out to strike the bell, strike the bell. All were to enter the church and pray, pray unceasingly, for Aidan and his men. They were going into battle against the barbarians, at the foot of a high green mountain, and they were in dire danger. Pray for Aidan – pray!

All the students, the monks, the working brothers and such nuns who were on Iona at the time, flocked to the church at the clamant summons of the bell, and there prayed, in mainly silent but fervent petition. After perhaps two hours, Colum rose from his knees and turning to the congregation, cried, "God be praised! He has heard our prayers. Aidan has the victory. But . . . it is not a happy one. There is great loss, great loss. But the king is safe and the day his."

All stared at him, wondering, but few if any doubting. This was not the first time that their Colum had revealed himself as the possessor of the gift of second-sight as they called it, the strange faculty of awareness of distant happenings.

Afterwards, Bridget asked him as to his experience, the whys and the wherefores of it.

"I do not know," he told her. "It is just something which comes to me sometimes. It is no virtue in me. It is no prophecy. I but see something with an inner eye, as clearly as I see you now. Today, I suddenly saw a green mountain, steep, pointed. Not so high as the Alba mountains can be, but of notable shape. I saw Aidan and his sons, swords drawn, on foot not on horseback, and a great evil like some black thunder-cloud threatening them, and them crying to God for help. This, while I was speaking to the students . . ."

"And you are convinced that it was so? No doubts that it could be but some kind of waking dream? Had you been dreading such a thing . . .?"

"Not dreading, no. Or . . ." He paused.

"You had *some* forewarning?"

"Not, not of recent days. But . . . some months ago, Aidan asked me which of his four remaining sons I thought should be king after him, and he named them to me. Something then told me that it should not be any of the older three but the little one, the yellow-haired Eochaid Buide. I said so. Aidan scoffed, but . . ."

"And you think . . . ?"

He sighed. "As we prayed in the church I saw the older three fallen, amongst the heap of slain. Aidan should not have taken them with him, they were too young for battle. But he is always the fighter, the warrior, and would have his sons like himself."

She laid a hand on his arm. "So you fear . . .? Oh, Columcille – I am sorry! I would not wish to have such a gift as this of yours!"

"Nor I! Wishing does not come into it, my dear. And I do not fear – I *know!*"

Colum's distressful knowledge was sufficiently accurate, as was proved three weeks later when Aidan returned to Dalriada, bringing the bodies of his three sons with him, for burial on Iona. Sundry other bodies also, although the great majority of the Scots casualties had been buried on the spot, three hundred and three of them. Since Aidan's total force had numbered only two thousand, it had been a costly victory indeed, fought in marshland at the foot of Dunmyat Hill in Manaan, near the northern shore of the Forth. The enemy losses had been far greater, however, and Athelfrith's Angles were not likely to trouble Alba or Fortrenn again for some time, Aidan thought. But the price paid was over great. He now had only an eight-year-old as heir to his throne.

Colum could only seek to reassure him that Eochaid Buide at least would survive and bear sons.

That man now had a new preoccupation to worry him, as well as the dying off of his contemporaries – that he himself might be turning into a prophet of doom.

But at least there was good news of Kenneth at Fife Ness. Aidan had not actually got that far, but Kenneth had come to him at the rock of Snowdoun, near where Allan Water joined Forth, where the Scots were, as it were, licking their wounds prior to the long journey home. He had come to thank Aidan for this delivery from the Anglian threat, to condole with him over his losses, and to ask him to convey a message for Colum – that he must come and visit his thriving new monastery at Balrymond, where there was much that would interest and enhearten him, much to see and to do. Mungo had already been, and blessed the work. It was inconceivable that Columcille's name should not be linked with the great work also. Somehow he must find the time and opportunity to come to Fife, and before too long.

24

Kenneth was not the only one to feel sufficiently strongly about Colum's work in Alba to come back. For, the spring after Aidan's dear-bought victory at Manaan, who should arrive at Iona but Comgall of Bangor, to Colum's joy. He was Moluag's cousin, and brought two more priests to help on Lismore, and two others for their friend Kenneth in Fife. Not only these, but he had actually brought a woman with them, a nun named Eva, Sub-Prioress at the Bangor nunnery, who he thought would be a useful assistant for Bridget, whom he much admired.

Their arrival pleased Colum in more ways than one, for it gave him the excuse he had been seeking to go and visit Kenneth. They would make a great and comprehensive round of it, deposit the new recruits at Lismore, go on to Inverness and anoint Gartnait there, visit Comgall's own foundation at Barevan, proceed on to Aberdour and Deer, then see Machar at his Aberdeen and so on southwards to Balrymond in Fife, with the new men for Kenneth.

Comgall was delighted, and not at all alarmed by this major proposal. And now that Baithen was there to superintend the teaching at Iona, Colum felt less guilty in leaving. Bridget would have liked to come with them, and said so, but could hardly leave the new sub-prioress in charge for so long, so soon. But at least she could go as far as Lismore and see Moluag.

Colum had a new shipmaster now, named Tadg, an adventurous young man. He came up with his own suggestion. He would take the travellers to the foot of the Great Glen, at Loch Linnhe-head, for their journey to Inverness, then turn and sail back, and on up the Hebridean Sea right to the northern tip of Alba, and on beyond to the isles of Orkney, to see how Bishop Cormac's churches there were faring. Then back, to sail down the long east coast of Alba right to Fife Ness in Fortrenn, and there be waiting to bring Colum and Comgall back, by the same route. The longship's crew had been getting lazy and out of practice, lacking any major voyaging; this would get them back into form.

Cormac would have approved, so Colum did also; although Baithen, ever cautious, foresaw possible dangers and disaster.

So they sailed for Lismore, where Colum experienced his now normal reaction at the sight of Moluag looking so old and almost shrunken. But his pleasure at seeing them was undisguised, and he was proud to show the visitors all the progress made on that fair island, which was now indeed justifying its name of the Great Garden. He had established cells over on the mainland of Appin, and these also they inspected. Moluag still evinced a spirit of something like rivalry with Colum, which much tickled the latter, who entered into the game with alacrity, to the amusement of all, Bridget shaking her head over the pair of them. Moluag declared that he was going to invite Bridget to move her nunnery to Lismore, more suitable in every way, as the island was her son's – and there would be no nonsense here about siting it on any separate islet. Colum said let him try!

They stayed a week with Moluag, and left Bridget and the two new Irish priests on the island, to continue up the Firth of Lorn and then Loch Linnhe, to its head amongst the great mountains. Here they exchanged boat travel for hired horses and took farewell of Tadg, wishing him and his crew safe voyaging on their long sail through the wild seas known to prevail between Alba and Orkney.

Their own long journey to Inverness was now familiar and caused Colum little anxiety, with friends and churches to visit on the way. Even the wolves and other wild beasts seemed less of a menace, and as for the Water Horse, they almost looked on this as an old acquaintance which they might hope to glimpse – and did not.

Gartnait mac Domelch was glad to see them, recognising that Colum's friendship and support were valuable in consolidating his position as High King. He acknowledged the help given in bringing about his election and also was grateful for Aidan's prompt response against the Angles. He was happy to have a ceremony of anointing to his new throne, as witness to the Church's identification with rule and authority in government. The simple service, similar to that performed for Aidan, was watched by hundreds, and particularly appreciated by all at the palace, in that the consecrated ointment was taken from the brecbennach presented to Colum by Brude. It was Colum's hope that, after these two anointings, it would become the established custom for kings to seek anointing from the Church on their accessions, thus much strengthening the Christian influence.

They did not remain long at Inverness. Moving on to Nairn and Barevan, Comgall was delighted with progress there. They established two new cells, at Cantray and Auldearn, at both of which there had been druidical centres, with standing-stones and circles.

Proceeding on eastwards to Buchan, they visited Aberdour, which Comgall much admired; but Drostan was not there, now basing himself at Deer. They paid a courtesy call at Dundearg, and found Bede little changed in looks or manner, scarcely the glad host but not uncivil. His son, Maldoun, now on the verge of manhood, was well, with no return of his illness. Nothing was said about the high kingship election.

At Deer they were greatly cheered with what Drostan had achieved, both in building and in spreading the Word. With so much excellent timber available, the construction of the new abbey had gone ahead with remarkable speed and to notable effect – better indeed than anything they had on Iona. Drostan's energy and enthusiasm seemed to be infectious, and his band of helpers, mainly young and with a noteworthy proportion of women amongst them, were a lively and challenging crew. Colum was proud of his nephew – although some of his party were distinctly doubtful about the females. They had extended their mission far and wide through the province of Buchan, and Drostan asserted that one day Deer would be almost as important to the east of Alba as was Iona to the west – which earned him a rebuke from Comgall but not from Colum.

Fifty miles further south they discovered someone else to contravert Drostan's claims, with Machar declaring that his monastery and church at the mouth of the River Dee was going to lead in the task of Christianising the east. After all, Mar was much more fertile and populous than was Buchan, and was bound to have the greater influence as the major centre of trade. In a year or two he would have more churches and cells than Drostan – if only Columcille would send him more priestly helpers. This was all that was holding him up.

Colum approved of this healthy competition, although not all did.

They were impressed by this Aberdeen, set between the mouths of two great rivers which provided unrivalled harbour facilities, so that this was the principal merchandising centre of Alba, nearly on a par with Strathclyde's Dunbarton. Colum perceived that they ought to have arranged with Tadg and the long-ship to meet them here, and carry them on to Fife.

Colum was touched when Machar told them that he had chosen the mouth of the Dee, rather than that of the Don, only a mile or two away, as site for his church, not only because the harbour was here but because some declared that the name Dee was, like Deer, derived from oak-trees – although admittedly others said differently. Both rivers had been sacred to the Druids, but the Dee was his choice, for Colum's sake.

The travellers, to avoid the long and difficult land journey, decided to take passage on a trading ship bound for Dunedin in Lothian, which would put them ashore at Fife Ness in barely two days' sailing, a great saving of time. Promising Machar two new assistants from the next crop of Iona students, they went aboard.

Down a mainly cliff-bound coast they sailed, sharing the vessel with an odoriferous cargo of salted fish and untanned hides, but far from complaining. Never were they out of sight of land, even when they crossed the wide mouth of the Firth of Tay, the blue line of the mountains far inland ensuring that. Ahead were no mountains however but a comparatively level green land, sand fringed – Fife, and new country for Colum.

Their shipmaster, a Lothian man, knew the coast well and had heard of the Christian Kenneth, although himself a pagan. There was a haven at Balrymond of Muckross, where the missionary had established his strange company.

At first sight it seemed an unlikely place to base a mission-centre and religious community, at the very tip of a peninsular province jutting out into the ocean. But Kenneth must have had a reason other than the good harbour.

Landing at a natural breakwater projecting from a sandy beach below low cliffs, they found church and monastery perched directly above, a site anything but sheltered, especially in an easterly gale – which obviously could be common here – however splendid the views. What had brought Kenneth here?

That man was not present when they arrived, being apparently involved in the building of a new church at Strathkinness, a few miles away near the Eden River; but he was expected to be back that night.

Kenneth, at least, when he returned, gave Colum no pangs as to ageing and decrepitude, for, although a few years older than the latter, and never particularly robust-seeming, he looked just as he had always done, fit and quietly vigorous. Happy at seeing his unexpected visitors, he beamed and beamed, almost wordless.

The words came later, when Kenneth explained why he had elected to site his monastery here at Balrymond. When he had first come to these parts, he had thought to choose a more central position; but he was told by the local people that there was already a Christian tradition in this Muckross area at Fife Ness – and a resounding one, although it was now little more than a legend, insufficiently understood. The story was that in St Ninian's time, nearly two centuries before, one of his disciples, an Irishman variously named St Riaguil, St Rule or even St Regulus, had come and established a church here. As with all Ninian's efforts, the rising tide of paganism had swept this one away. But the memory here had lingered on for a special reason. This was that this St Riaguil had travelled to far distant lands, and had somehow acquired a most precious relic, a bone of one of the very founders of the Christian religion, one Andrew. This bone he had brought back to Balrymond, and with it, according to the local tradition, had worked great magic. So that long after Riaguil was dead, the bone was accepted by the Druids as a notable and potent charm. Where it was now no one knew; but its renown and the name of Andrew, lived on. So he, Kenneth, felt that here was the place for him to carry on the good work begun by Riaguil and to rescue St Andrew's name and fame from druidical witchcraft and superstition.

Needless to say, the visitors were much intrigued by this account, and full of questions. That part of the body of Simon Peter's brother should have found its way to this remote corner of a heathen land was a miracle in itself. Was there no notion or tradition as to where this celebrated bone was now?

Kenneth had asked that question also but got no good answer. The only hint was that the last Druid to operate hereabouts, an old hermit, had lived in a cave in the cliffs somewhere in the vicinity; but since he had allegedly put a curse on the cave for anyone violating it, and there were many such on this coast, it had not been discovered. He and his helpers had gone looking, of course, and had even found bones in caves. But who was to say what was a saint's bone and what otherwise?

None could answer that.

Kenneth was delighted to gain the adherence of the two new priests come all the way from Ireland, Monan and Ethernan. Like all the others, he required all the help he could get. Fife was large and well-populated, and there was no other Christian influence but his own at work. Along the southern coastline in especial, that of the Forth estuary, there was great opportunity for mission, with many fishing havens – Crail, Anstruther, Pittenweem, Abercrombie, Elie and others. He had always found fisherfolk more receptive to the Gospel than others – after all, Christ himself had found the same. Something about the sea – another reason why he had placed his monastery here, thrusting towards the ocean.

The travellers had come to help, not just to visit, and Kenneth decided that the best course was to take them along the string of aforesaid coastal havens to the south, to teach, preach and baptise. This would also give him the opportunity to take them to a notable *diseart* he had found for himself and his assistants, a fine island in the mouth of the Forth, named The May, or Inchmay, a place of birds and seals, but strangely different from the Hebridean isles.

They soon perceived why Kenneth was so taken with the series of fishing townships dotted along the sandy shores of Forth, places of individual features but similar character, each only a mile or two apart, on a fair coastline of attractive bays, strands and little headlands, nothing dramatic but consistently pleasing.

The first and most easterly was Crail, a little climbing community above a sheltered harbour where outcropping rock gave protection from the long seas running in from the nearby ocean. Kenneth had formed a little congregation here, and now hurried on ahead shamelessly to announce the arrival of the renowned Prince Colum mac Felim, of whom he had told them often, come in person, with the Abbot of Bangor in Ireland, to see them. Double the normal score or so of adherents gathered therefore, and the impromptu little service and exhortation was well received. Some new candidates for baptism came forward thereafter.

A similar programme was followed at Anstruther, the next village, really two separate communities divided by the outflow of the Dreel Water. So they held two services here, for there was a sort of rivalry between the east and west groups. Then on to Pittenweem where, tired but well content, they passed the night in one of the caves which gave the place its name – this, after arranging with some of the fishermen to take them out next day to the Isle of May, some five miles offshore.

This excursion was in the nature of a holiday for all, in breezy bright weather, much enjoyed. The island proved to be much larger than the newcomers had anticipated. When Kenneth had described it as his intended *diseart*, they had assumed it to be something of a rock, like the towering Craig of Bass which they could see so prominent over on the Lothian side of Forth a dozen miles away. But this May was well over a mile in length, girdled by high cliffs, and even cradling a loch at its centre. There were comparisons with Iona in size – but it was so very different in other respects, mainly naked rock with scant vegetation, those daunting precipices over one hundred feet in height, and all uninhabited save by birds. Of these there were thousands, sea-fowl in the main of course – divers, kittiwakes, guillemots, puffins, gannets with their screeching and clamour, the smell of their droppings also. At the south-east end, where the cliffs sank away and a landing was possible, round-eyed seals watched them from rocks and skerries and eiders swam with their flotillas of tiny, bobbing ducklings.

Ashore, they went exploring like boys out of school, prepared to be delighted with all they saw, clambering on the cliffs, leaping the rocks, stalking the seals, even bathing in the loch. But Kenneth told them that, pleasant as this place was on a fine summer day, in a storm it could be direly otherwise. Indeed this May had a notorious reputation for wrecking ships. Set right in the mouth of the Forth, it was a mile-long hazard at night or in mist and fog. He had often thought that to establish a beacon-fire on the summit ridge of this isle would be a very worthwhile and Christian act, with relays of watchers to keep it fuelled. But where to obtain the wood? There was none on the island, apart from the occasional piece of driftwood; and to ferry out sufficient from the mainland woods would be a major undertaking. Ethernan here declared that if Abbot Kenneth agreed, *he* would seek to make himself responsible for arranging the necessary supply of timber – they had passed much woodland on their way to this coast – and the bringing of it out here, for a warning light to shipping. Surely the fisherfolk would be glad to assist the Church in this matter? Kenneth said perhaps, one day . . .

They returned to Pittenweem in time for an evening service. Then onward next day to Abercrombie, where Monan, not to be outdone by his junior, Ethernan, was allotted the privilege of blessing the well for a baptismal session, and got the wording therefor mixed up, to the amusement of all.

Elie on its magnificent sandy bays was their next stop, and here their proselytising received some interruption again, whilst the missionaries went searching diligently not for converts but for precious finds of another sort, jewels, rubies or garnets, which were said to be found in one of the bays. They did discover one or two tiny red gems, which they might inset in a crucifix – but hardly worth all the time spent. They made up for it by the fervour of their evening preachings.

Beyond Elie were great cliffs, high and riven with caves and gullies, this named Kincraig Point. And from the summit of this, looking west by south, they could see across the Forth a strange isolated hill, like a crouching lion. There were other hill-ranges in the background, normal enough, but this one was outstanding, extraordinary, eye-catching although over a score of miles away at least. Kenneth told them that this was the Craig of Edin, a semi-legendary ancient British king, whose fort, Dunedin, was on a nearby rock-top. Its town was now the principal trading centre of Lothian. That land was still largely pagan and ripe for conversion – but probably St Mungo would look on it as his own responsibility, since he came of its ruling house.

Colum, always interested in islands, pointed out two which he could see due westwards, one large, one small. Kenneth said that in this Forth area these isles were called inches. The large one was named Inchkeith; of the smaller he did not know the name. Did Columcille wish to visit them? That man said only if time permitted.

In the event, after preaching and teaching at more of these fishing villages down that pleasant coast, they decided that enough was enough and that it was time to return to Balrymond. And then, Colum was told that not far ahead was another community called Aberdour. Intrigued that there should be another place of that name, and wondering about more of the so helpful oak-tree, nothing would do but that he must go there, to see.

This Aberdour proved to be almost as attractive as the other, with fine woodland around it, at the mouth of another Dour Burn – and so far untouched by Christianity. So the missionaries spent a further and profitable two days. Ethernan was especially eager to return, seeing it as virgin territory and an opportunity to rival Drostan's success up in Buchan, Colum not discouraging.

What pleased Colum almost as much as this development was the fact that the smaller of the two islands he had seen and asked about from Kincraig Point, many miles to the east, was here just offshore. The locals called it Inchgolan, the Swallows' Isle, a name which interested that man so fond of birds. So the second evening they got a fisherman to take them out the mere mile or so, and were rewarded by discovering a most delightful and sequestered retreat, half a mile long, crescent shaped, green and fair, like a Hebridean isle but uninhabited. Swallows there were, but more sand-martins, and eiders crooning their soothing evensong. All immediately saw it as a sanctuary, in conjuction with Aberdour as a monastery, with Ethernan claiming that it should be his *diseart*, if he was permitted to base himself here. Kenneth reminded him that he had already offered to do something about the Isle of May and establish a light-beacon there; but the enthusiast declared that he could and would do both. Colum, ever anxious to encourage zeal to match his own, supported and Kenneth acquiesced. Joyfully Ethernan began to make plans there and then for Aberdour and the island – which, he asserted, should have its name changed from Inchgolan to Inchcolum. He was now loth even to return with them to Fife Ness meantime; but this was necessary. It was time that they were gone.

Back at Balrymond, nearly forty miles, they found Tadg and his long-ship safely arrived, after the long and adventurours voyage. He and his crew were full of the wonders they had seen and experienced, the great fish which spouted fountains of water, the tide-races and overfalls of the Orkney seas which rivalled even Corryvreckan, the myriad isles of Orkney and their strange people, where St Cormac's churches were having a struggle to survive, the desolate empty level moors of north-east Alba where winds raged unendingly and waterfalls were blown like smoke. After listening to all this, the missionaries' own adventures and activities seemed modest indeed, if not tame.

Sad to part from Kenneth as they were, Colum was for off now, contemplating the long journey home to Iona, hundreds of miles. He asked Kenneth how long he himself intended to remain in Fife, so far from his own abbey in Ireland, and was told that this was in God's hands. They seemed to get on at Achabo very well without him, and he felt that he could do more useful work here than managing an abbatical establishment in Ireland. He would be given guidance in the matter he had no doubt.

So wishing their friends well, Monan and Ethernan in particular, the travellers embarked and set off for the north.

After all the excitements recounted by Tadg and his men, that voyage round Alba proved almost an anti-climax, sometimes laughably so, with the long-ship's crew next to crestfallen. In consistently good weather and with helpful breezes they made excellent time, with little of oar-work required. They kept about a mile or so offshore day after day, so that they could spot suitable places to move in to spend the nights, get fresh water and purchase food. Strangely this eastern seaboard of Alba produced practically no islands, while the west produced thousands, cliffs and long sandy beaches alternating, some of the former lofty and dramatic indeed. Colum composed a poem and two hymns as they sailed – which was some indication of uneventful journeying. Their only halt for more than the hours of darkness was at Aberdour and Pennan in Buchan, where they passed two days but did not see Drostan. The only time that they were out of sight of land was when they were crossing the wide mouth of the Moray Firth. They resisted the temptation to put in at Inverness. But at least thereafter they did see Tadg's smoking waterfalls, scores of them, cascading over the high cliffs of Caithness.

Even the long passage between the northern coast of Alba and the Orkney isles belied its reputation for storms and high seas, where the Western Ocean met the Norse Sea, giving them a comparatively smooth sail, with a following easterly wind, and the surprise of seeing the very lovely and colourful coastal scenery where they had expected it to be harsh and bleak.

The change, when they rounded the mighty headland which was the north-west tip of Alba and sailed down into the Hebridean Sea, was extraordinary, a different world, all islands, translucent waters, sands white not yellow, seaweeds multi-hued and brilliant instead of dark green, sudden rain-storms and exciting skies. Why should there be this difference, they wondered?

In familiar waters now they passed Skye and Rhum and Eigg and the rest, until the unmistakable outline of Mull's mountains reared ahead, and under their protecting heights Iona nestled. They had done it, circled Alba, almost the equivalent of the entire circuit of Ireland.

It was good to be home.

25

Bridget, a good listener, was interested in all the saga of Colum's travels and experiences, seeming impressed especially by the story of St Andrew's bone and Kenneth's decision to continue in Fife meantime. However, she made the point that probably the most important aspect of the expedition had been the anointing of Gartnait. Now that the High King and the King of Dalriada had undergone this ceremony of consecration, she thought that it was likely that other monarchs might seek the same privilege, and this must surely benefit the Church and the advancement of the Gospel message.

For her own part, she had various matters to report on. She was worried about Moluag. He had made a great effort whilst Colum and his party were on Lismore; but after they had gone he had suffered something of a collapse. She had remained on that island longer than she had intended, mainly to all but nurse him, for he was in fact an ailing man although he drove himself to continue his labours. She feared that he would not live long. Colum, concerned, said that he must go and see him, then, but Bridget was doubtful. Moluag was not exactly jealous of him; he was fond of him in his own way. But he had a deep-set urge, she felt, to show that he was as good and as able as Columcille, despite not being so high-born. The latter's arrival on Lismore again, on account of his own failing health, to witness his flagging powers, might well occasion him more distress than satisfaction. Colum was prepared to see the force of this, but it would be sad if he was to be prevented from seeing his old colleague again merely because of some stupid matter of pride. He would consider the matter.

Another clash of temperaments troubled Bridget. No doubt Baithen would inform him in detail when he returned from Tiree, where he was at present because Findchan was ill. While Colum was away, Donnan, one of the Irish priests who had been sent to help out on Skye, had returned to Iona to announce that he had decided to set up a centre and church on the Isle of Eigg, and wanted helpers for this project. Baithen was displeased and said that this could not be done without Colum's agreement, and Donnan must await his return, and go back to Skye meantime. But Donnan was urgent. He had already preached on Eigg, had chosen a large cave as temporary base and baptised his first converts there. It would be folly to leave it and return to Skye, where he was but one of many. So there was disagreement, and Donnan had rejected Baithen's instructions and gone back to Eigg, not Skye, but without the desired helpers. Bridget was sad about this and felt that perhaps Baithen might have had more sympathy for the younger man's enthusiasm. He was acting with strict rectitude, of course, but . . .

"Baithen was ever the cautious one," Colum said. "*I* would have said differently. But it was his decision to make, and should have been obeyed. Donnan erred in this."

"No doubt, in one respect. But is another not more important? That vigour and enterprise should be supported? Donnan is thirty years younger than Baithen. Is not that where the trouble lies?"

"Discipline there must be, in the Church as in any other company of men. Or women! You must know that, my dear, with your nuns. I left Baithen in charge here. So Donnan should have done as he said. So – is he alone on Eigg?"

"I do not know if he is alone. But he gained no helpers from Iona."

"I must go and see that young man. I have never landed on Eigg, but passed it often. But two days ago, indeed. A large island. To whom does it belong?"

"I know not. It is outwith Dalriada. Perhaps it is Cathal's, of Skye. Since Donnan went there from Skye. Might not your Queen Sinech have a hand in this? But . . . forgive me for troubling you with what is no real concern of mine, Columcille. When I *have* something of my concern to seek your guidance upon. A strange matter. Concerning my nuns. But which I think may have some bearing on what we have so frequently discussed – the role of women in the Church."

He eyed her, smiling. "You never give up, do you!" They were, as so often, sitting on Dun I watching the sun at its setting over the isle-strewn sea, one of the most rewarding of experiences for both of them. "What now?"

"It is further to what we have already spoken of – St

Bridget. You remember the sub-prioress, Eva, whom Comgall brought me from Bangor? She is an able woman and useful. But . . . I find that she has been teaching my young nuns strange doctrines – or strange to me. Regarding their behaviour towards men."

"Ah!" Wary suddenly, he rubbed his chin.

"When I spoke to her about it she was surprised that I knew nothing of it. Especially as my own name is Bridget. For this, she said, was St Bridget's teaching. And I remembered what you said, long ago, of Bridget's attitude to men."

He nodded. "I spoke of her monks and nuns working side by side in her abbey of Kildare and other monasteries, yes. Her beliefs, after all, helped me to agree to the setting up of your nunnery here."

"Yes, and I was grateful for that, and to her. But – did you ever see her writings on the subject? Or writings attributed to her?"

"No-o-o."

"Eva has a copy of one of these writings. She believes it was St Bridget's work. She showed it to me when I questioned her. It is . . . remarkable."

"Well . . . ?"

"In it is declared that, since there are as many women in this world as men, God's world, more perhaps since the men keep killing each other, God has as many and as great tasks for women in His Church as for men. Many are set down – not all of which I think you would approve, Columcille! But one in particular concerns me. You did mention it that time, this of the Church using women deliberately to test the strength of men's wills, and the control of their bodies' passions. This Eva has been telling my nuns – that they have been given persons, bodies, features, appearances and abilities which much affect and attract men – and for this purpose, as well as others. Not merely for the procreation of children – all women's attractions are not necessary for that, surely! They are there to give pleasure and satisfaction, yes – but also this testing of men's ability to resist temptation, especially churchmen."

"The Church has taught that, yes. But only on an especial occasion, to be sure."

"Perhaps. But there is more than that. This writing goes on to describe how women can most effectively use their bodies

403

and, and talents as they are called, to try men's abilities to resist, to seduce men indeed. And they are very . . . detailed. They make strange reading for young women – as apt, I think, to tempt the women as help them tempt the men! As a woman who was long married, I admit that I never thought nor heard of some of them. Surely this will tend to create an appetite in the tempter as much as in the tempted?"

"St Bridget did not write this, I think."

"That I do not know. Eva thinks of it as her writing, but that may not be so. Or it may be earlier Church teaching which she merely passed on. Not of her own devising. But – it troubles me."

"As it should. For this cannot be *Christ's* teaching – that I am sure."

"No. How think you that it could have become accepted in the Church, if it is? If you do not think that it was merely St Bridget's own strange notions? For you *admire* St Bridget, do you not?"

"What I have known or heard of her, yes, greatly." He paused. "See you – this may be but a mistaken rendering, not truly hers. Caused out of ignorance in those who followed her. Since she was strong on this of men and women working together. But this of deliberate tempting seems to me to be the *opposite* of what she worked for, the creating of division, hostility, conflict, as well as lustful passions, not unity of purpose and Christian witness. I would think that she would never train her women thus."

"How then has it become linked with her name, if the writings are not her own?"

"I can think of a reason – ignorance, as I said. Long before Bridget, Abbess of Kildare, that name was renowned in Ireland, before ever St Patrick brought us Christianity. I told you before – Bridget or Bride, after whom she herself was called by her pagan master, was a Celtic heroine, half-legendary, supposedly wed to a sea-god, a sorceress, but beautiful and capable of great deeds. The *Filidh*, the poets and bards, still sing of her and her seductions and amours. What more likely than that, in time, the two Bridgets should become confused in the minds of many, especially the ignorant? I have told you of that great weakness of the Irish Church, the hereditary abbots – aye, and abbesses also. In the south, particularly. These could well have been responsible for such confusion. Unlettered, with little or no training in true doctrine, this could well be their work."

"That could explain it, yes. Then – what do I do? Forbid further teaching on this?"

"To be sure. You are the prioress. Send this Eva to me, if you will, and I will give her my views. Comgall who brought her, also, perhaps."

"Very well." She smiled now. "If Comgall had brought this Eva with him on his first visit, and *she* had set up the nunnery, not myself, you would have had reason, I think, to fear distraction of your monks!"

"In that case, my dear, the nunnery would have been removed to the farthest uninhabited isle of these Hebrides, not set up a mile away!"

"Unless . . . you were not entirely proof against such temptation yourself, my Columcille!"

He eyed her. "What do you think, woman . . . ?"

They left it at that.

One problem at least solved itself. Some weeks later Angus mac Riagan arrived at Iona with astonishing news. He had paid one of his quite frequent visits to his island of Lismore and was amazed to find Moluag gone. When last he had seen him he had been an obviously sick man, however determined to be active still. Now he had allegedly recovered and departed on an expedition. And not on any minor visit to Appin or even Lochaber, but afar, to farthest Alba.

Angus had questioned the sub-abbot, Cathair of Tiree, left in charge at Lismore. It seemed that Moluag had felt a return of strength, and believed it God's token to him that he should undertake a last major task – to do what Colum mac Felim and Kenneth and Comgall had done, travel to the far limits of Alba and there convert folk who had never even heard of Jesus Christ. The others had tried to dissuade him, but to no effect. He was determined. He had a couple of men on Lismore who had been with Colum on his second journey to Inverness, and these would guide his little party, hire them horses, halt at friendly houses and so on. They would not be able to travel so fast, but God would sustain him. He would learn from King Gartnait where the Gospel had not yet been preached, probably *north* of Inverness, and go there.

Scarcely able to believe this, Colum had to restrain himself from setting off there and then in pursuit, so concerned was he. But that would have been useless. Moluag had been gone weeks now, apparently; and since his companions had not brought him back, collapsed again or even dead, by now, he could be at Inverness or beyond. Colum ordered prayer to be said continually in the Iona church, by relays of monks and nuns, day and night, for his obstinate but valiant old fellow-soldier in Christ's cause. He and Bridget did their own praying.

The matter of the Sub-Prioress Eva was settled amicably enough after an interview with Colum and Comgall, Bridget present – although who could tell what impact might already have been made on the minds of the younger nuns? But at least there would be no more erotic instruction. Colum and Comgall had discussed this question at length before the latter sailed back to Ireland – he had offered to take Eva back with him, if she was proving a disruptive influence, but Bridget said that would not be fair, for otherwise she was a good assistant.

The problem of Donnan, on Eigg, was less readily dealt with. Baithen, on his return from Tiree – where he had now installed Fechno as prior, Findchan now being dead – was unrepentant as to his reaction to Donnan. Once they allowed young priests to abandon the appointments and assistantships to which they had been sent on due authority, and to set up their own independent charges wherever they chose, that way would lie confusion and anarchy. Donnan's enthusiasm was admirable, but he should not have started off on his own without higher sanction. He, Baithen, could not give him that in Colum's absence, and told Donnan to wait and return to Skye meantime. But the young man had been as obstinate as Moluag – allowably a bishop and therefore independent – was being; and had gone back to Eigg. Such conduct could not be overlooked.

Colum was faced with a dilemma. There was no question but that he must uphold his cousin's authority, as his deputy. But there was a new congregation, established on Eigg, to think of, however unorthodox in its setting up, and these must not be the sufferers in any disciplinary action. And youthful impetuosity was not the worst of sins – and although Baithen might never have suffered from it, he himself had, and possibly still did, even at his ripe age. So he had to compromise. He told Baithen that he would go to Eigg to see Donnan.

It was a sail of about forty miles, and late in the season they made a rough passage of it – which pleased Tadg at least, who seemed to thrive on challenges. Eigg was a distinctive and unusual island, over six miles in length, dominated at its very southern tip by its single, notable upthrusting peak, the Sgurr, a landmark for leagues around, this seeming to be supported by strange columnar cliffs allegedly carved by the sea-gods. But the rest of the island was comparatively level and lower-lying, with much fertile land which sustained a sizeable population. It was, curiously, split into two clear halves by a long, north-south valley, the nick or *eag* of which gave the place its name. It was renowned for its caves.

The landing place was obvious, at any rate, a deep double inlet of the rock-bound southern coastline, guarded by an islet on which rose a dun or fort. Nobody challenged them therefrom however, indeed they could discern no sign of life there, and they sailed on into the forked bay beyond, which provided a sheltered anchorage. Houses were dotted around the shores of this.

Their arrival created something of a stir, with folk flocking down to meet them; and when Tadg announced brashly that here was the great Abbot Colum mac Felim himself there was considerable excitement – evidently they had heard much of him and his work, no doubt Donnan adding to the story.

They had no difficulty in finding that young man, for the villagers were eager to conduct them to him where, about a mile away beside a burn entering the northern horn of the bay, he and a crew of helpers were building a little church, of stone and thatch, these materials being more readily available on Eigg than saplings and clay for wattle and daub.

Donnan's joy at seeing Colum was great, and a little embarrassing in view of the latter's duty to reprove him. His pride in what was being achieved here was unbounded – and legitimately so, for he had indeed done well in a remarkably short time. Clearly he had made himself important to the islanders, of whom he claimed already almost half as converts, however elementary their faith might be as yet. The church building was well ahead, and he had also established a woollen-spinning and weaving centre, for there were a great many sheep on Eigg. This last fact constituted his one problem apparently, for it divided the population. Most were fisherfolk and small farmers, and as others had found before him, fishers were the most readily converted of people. But the inland minority were shepherds and their families, and on these Donnan had made little impact. The sheep were not their own but belonged to the chieftainess who owned Eigg and who lived on the mainland of Ardnamurchan. Donnan had not seen her yet, for she seldom visited the island; but her shepherds were not helpful, although they did sell wool for his spinning and weaving enterprise.

"So Eigg does not belong to Skye?" Colum asked. "Queen Sinech did not send you here? It belongs to another?"

"I heard of it on Skye, yes – but not from the queen. Seafarers told me."

"And you came, on their recommendation? Not seeing the chieftainess? Have you her permission?"

"Permission? Need I some pagan woman's permission to preach Christ's Gospel?"

Colum considered him. "You take permission too much for granted, I think, my young friend. That is unwise. Due authority falls to be recognised – even pagan authority. Render unto Caesar . . .!"

"If I had awaited permission I might not be here now. Nor all this."

"True. But that could lie in God's hands, could it not?"

Donnan did not answer.

Colum led him out of earshot of the others. "I think that you are not a great respecter of authority." he said. "Too much of it is not good, and could hinder God's work. But some there must be if disorder and schism are to be avoided. There is due authority in Heaven, but also on earth. You accept that?"

"Yes. But not of heathen over Christians!"

"Do you accept *my* authority, Donnan? In this of mission? Yet I have accepted the authority of Cathal of Skye, Brude the High King and Bede of Buchan, pagans all, and sought their permission to preach to their people."

"None could deny *your* authority. And you, a prince, could bring those other princes to your will . . ."

"Yet you ignored the authority of the deputy I had appointed, Baithen. He told you to return to Skye."

"I could not do that. I had already started my work here. I

408

only went to Iona for helpers. It would have been wrong to go back to Skye – wrong."

"Who decides what is wrong in our work – you, or Baithen? Or myself?"

"Surely every man must decide for himself what is right and what is wrong?"

"Do you tell that to your converts here? That they know what is right and true, equally with you?"

The other looked away.

"Think on these things, Donnan. Enough of it, meantime. You are doing good work here. Do not spoil it by spiritual pride."

They moved back to the others.

Colum spent three days on Eigg, viewing all, preaching and baptising. He went and spoke with some of the shepherds. He found them difficult, as Donnan had said. They were not, in fact, islanders but men brought out from mainland Ardnamurchan by the chieftainness, who all but despised the local people. However, he did make some impression on two of them, a father and son, the latter married to an island girl; and as a gesture, blessed a spring up on the high sheep-run at the northern end of the island, and baptised the pair there and then, beside their woolly charges, Donnan declaring that this would become notable as St Colum's Well and that other shepherds would in time come to esteem it.

They passed the nights in an enormous cave which Donnan had appropriated at the southern extremity, over two hundred feet in length, lofty and dry. He would build a cashel of cells in due course, near the church, but meantime this served very well. Indeed he had held services herein. It had been a druidical shrine at one time, and so was avoided by the ordinary folk.

The third evening, beside a fire of driftwood in the cave, with Colum going to leave in the morning, Donnan came out with a request, rather extraordinary in the circumstances and from so comparatively young a man. Would Colum honour him by becoming his soul-friend?

The latter was distinctly taken aback. Soul-friend was a very special relationship, part confessor. It could hardly be a mutual association between them, in the circumstances – and Colum hoped that *he* was not guilty of spiritual pride in thinking this. Nor was he so fond of Donnan as this would imply. He did not want to offend, but . . .

"I fear that would not be . . . appropriate," he said. "We are too far apart in age, if nothing else. Could I come to you, Donnan, for confession and absolution?"

"I could come to you."

"True. But that could be your duty, anyway, with myself your abbot. Friend, yes – but soul-friend is otherwise."

"Is this because I heeded not Baithen's command?"

"Only in part. You will understand one day."

"When it is too late! It is now that I need what only you can give me. If I am to fulfil all that God requires of me here."

Colum looked away from that young man into the inner recesses of the great cave, and a red mist seemed to form before his eyes. He closed them, and hung his head for a moment or two.

"I fear, I fear that you are going to learn hardly, Donnan," he said slowly. "I fear . . . a great sorrow. But perhaps I am wrong. Perhaps God's mercy will prevent it. Pray for a more humble spirit, Donnan – pray!" And gripping the other's arm tightly, he rose, to stare down, then turning abruptly, he strode out into the night.

It was long before he returned, with Donnan and the others asleep. For some time Colum stood in the faint light of the fire's embers, looking down at the younger man sadly.

In the morning, no more was said on the subject. Down at the long-ship, Colum blessed that island with a fervour unusual even for him, before farewells were said and they set sail.

26

It was a year almost to the day when Angus arrived from Lismore again, with the tidings that Moluag was dead. It was the summer of AD 592, twenty-nine years after they had come to Iona.

Strangely, the effect on all was as of the end of an era. Just why this should be was hard to say. Others of the original band had died earlier, without creating this impression. But all felt it now. It was not just mourning; something less personal as well. It was as a line drawn after a chapter.

Moluag, Angus told them, had achieved his purpose. He had reached Inverness and gone further, northwards into the land of Ross, where none of the Christian missionaries had actually penetrated. To a peninsula, known as the Black Isle, although it was in fact no island. He had settled at a coastal community called Rosemarkie, and there had set up a preaching centre and church. And there, after six months labours, he had sickened and died, allegedly well content, at last, to go. His helpers would have liked to bring his body back to Lismore, for burial; but it was an impossibly long way to carry a corpse, and he had been interred in his own new church there, to the great sorrow of all. Two of his people had returned, with the news, to Lismore. And now Angus was asked to persuade Colum to find two new incumbents, a senior for Lismore and a junior for Rosemarkie.

Bridget was greatly affected by Moluag's passing, for she had been closer to him than ever Colum had been, understanding him better, perceiving the forces which drove him, his different priorities. She went back, with her son, to Lismore, to help settle Moluag's unfinished work on that island and to advise the new prior on how best to take over most fittingly. Again she gently urged Colum not to go himself; Moluag would prefer it that way, she suggested.

Colum's own reaction surprised even himself. He had known for long, of course, that it was only a matter of time before his old colleague departed; yet he was not ready for the news when it came. And it had a far greater effect on him than he could have anticipated. No doubt subconsciously he had been making some preparation for what must happen – although it could not be certain to take place before he himself moved on. But the impact now took him aback and troubled him grievously. For it was not mourning. To be absolutely honest with himself, it was more like resentment, a feeling that he, Colum mac Felim, had been outwitted, outmanoeuvred, outdone.

At first he did not really recognise this. But gradually the truth of it came to him. Moluag had, in fact, gone on ahead, taken the lead in this the most important and vital step in a believer's life – and vital was the word. Moluag was now in the lead, not himself. Moluag had achieved his ambition and purpose, won his major battle here at great cost, and now was gone on to greater fulfilment and infinitely wider opportunities in God's next field of endeavour. Whereas he, Colum, was still running the old race, but at a lesser pace than heretofore because of years, most of his chosen tasks achieved but no real challenges ahead – except where Moluag had gone – only progressive slowing down to look forward to. And he knew himself for a man for whom that was not enough. Moluag had stolen a march on him.

Part of the trouble was, of course, that the teaching life had never appealed to him; and yet now most of his time was so occupied, and necessarily, for the supply of new priests and helpers was the prime need for the advancement of God's work in Dalriada and Alba, no question as to that. So this was the most worthwhile task that he could do, especially as he was now seventy-two years old, and not infrequently felt the onset of age. But his life was not satisfying his spirit. So he found himself thinking ever more and more of Moluag, wondering – and envying.

Recognising that this was probably, almost certainly, an unsuitable and ungrateful attitude, he betook himself to Hinba, alone, and spent three days and nights in his *diseart* there wrestling with his discontent, and seeking God's help and guidance, But despite all his fasting, prayer and concentration, he returned to Iona little more at peace than when he went, in little mood to resume his teaching duties. It is to be feared that his students must have wondered at their hero.

When Bridget came back from Lismore and reported to him on the situation there, and on how she believed that Moluag's work would continue and prosper, inevitably the subject of his discontent arose – for Colum had no one else to whom he could pour it out, his good and worthy Cousin Baithen being scarcely receptive to this sort of thing.

Listening to him and perceiving that his concern with himself was very real, she made no attempt to play down his trouble, to pooh-pooh it as a mere temporary reaction to an unsettling event, something that he would soon get over.

"These are the feelings of a man of great energy and drive, Columcille, towards advancing years," she declared. "The weight of the years comes to bear upon us all. Myself, I am very much aware of it – and I am ten years your junior. Your spirit has not aged, only your body; and that urgent striving spirit is caged within. More than that – you are a born leader of men, and you see your leading now largely done, over, the ends attained in the main, the prime work done, the churches and congregations established. It is not active, courageous leadership that is required now but steady, patient building up on the foundations you have laid – which is not your desired part. Is it not so?"

"No doubt. But – what *is* my part now? What is left for me to do? This teaching, teaching . . .!"

"Poor Columcille! I know how it tries you. Yet it is the necessary continuation of your great work, indeed in some measure the fulfilment of it. And you teach surpassingly well. You give your students what no others can give, kindling in them an enthusiasm, yes and love, which lesser men fail to do. Others can give the knowledge, the doctrine, but you do so much more. I know – I have listened to you. And heard my nuns talking. Never despise your teaching, my dear."

"But I cannot feel, Bridget, that this is God's will for me – to sit on this island and teach young people. I should be up and doing. And if this body of mine is beginning to fail my spirit, then the sooner that I am gone to where that body is exchanged for a new one, a spiritual one, the better! As Moluag has done. Can you not see it?"

"Ah – so we come back to Moluag! I used to wonder if he was jealous of you, of your power and vigour. And your birth. Now I think it is you who are jealous of him, in some strange way?"

"Not jealous. But sometimes I do envy him. Only now, when he is gone on. Ahead of me."

"Surely you do not wish that you were dead, Columcille? You, the most alive man that I have ever known! And . . . is it not a sin to wish that you were dead?"

"Dead! What is death but a word to frighten bairns and fools! We do not die, woman, in truth. We go on. We take a great step forward. To a better life. Where we can use to better effect what we have learned to develop and accomplish and create in this. That is Christ's message. When this life ceases to be fruitful, to progress, why cling to it, when a fuller lies ahead? To *take* one's life is sin, yes – but to long for the next, never!"

"So . . . you would leave us . . .?" That was thickly said.

413

He touched her arm. "Only for a short time, my dear. Until you join me again. Where love is, love will ensure reunion. Be sure of that. Love is the key to Heaven and all eternity, you see."

They sat silent for a little.

She found her voice again. "I must try . . . to be content . . . with that." And then, "What happens to those . . . who do not love. Tell me that. Not . . . that it will ever apply to me!"

He shook his head. "I do not know for sure. I often wonder. Christ did not tell us that. Save in the parable of the rich man and Lazarus. That man, who had failed to love, *wished* to come back, but could not. To do better. But that was only Abraham speaking – a man. Perhaps *God*, who is Love, in His mercy will give those who have not loved, who have rejected love for others in this life, another chance to love? To come back and do better."

"Reincarnation? Is not that something which the Druids teach? The coming back in a different form. Does the Church teach that?"

"No-o-o. It is but a thought. But one which could answer many questions. I do not know. As I *know* that love survives death and goes on beyond triumphantly."

Again she could not speak.

"So", he went on, "what am I to do until my time comes? Only teach? Leave others to do the real work? That would destroy me, I think – *me*, if not my body. Moluag could not face that, I think. And so he went. He went, to die fighting!"

"And you think to do the same?"

"I have not decided . . . yet."

She took a deep breath. "Could *your* fight, your last perhaps, not best be fought here on this Iona, whose name you have made to ring throughout Christendom? Here, where you belong as no other does. Fight on here, where you have brought God to so many, and God will surely show you the way He would have you to go. Oh, Columcille – it is not for me to teach *you*. But – trust your God in this, as in all, to the end. Then so shall we all. And then, and then . . . our end will indeed perhaps be our beginning!"

He turned to her, heeding that broken husky voice, and stared. Then threw his arm about her and held her close. "Bless you, Bridget – bless you!" he exclaimed. "You are right. God have mercy on me, a weak and doubting sinner!"

He all but shook her, and suddenly laughed aloud. "*You* should be the teacher, not me, woman! I shall come and sit under you, in your nunnery, and learn. Re-learn what I have forgotten. Will you have me as a student, lass . . .?"

She could only shake her head, wordless now.

EPILOGUE

It was five years after that conversation before Colum recognised the call to move on, however often in the interim he had wished and prayed for it, as his bodily strength waned and his urgent spirit rebelled. Not that even so he had been in any way inactive, nor confined himself to Iona and its immediate vicinity. Indeed he had paid a visit to Skye and Queen Sinech – to find her an old woman but still attractive and in a lot better state than was her husband, Cathal being now a poor and mumbling shadow of his former self. But that voyage brought it home to Colum that such travel was no longer for him; he had found it trying in the extreme and realised only too clearly that he was become a burden on his companions. Henceforth his voyaging must be in the mind and spirit – until the great adventure should at last take him on his longed-for way.

Then, on the night of Good Friday, 597, he dreamed a dream of release, of summons, of the call to advance. And waking, had no more doubts. His time had come, and he was ready, more than ready. Only one question troubled him. This was Good Friday, the day of sorrows, although he had no sorrow for himself. But in two days it would be Easter, the time of rejoicing for Christ's Church. If he allowed himself to go now, then for all on Iona that Easter would be a time of sadness and pain, not joy, he knew well. He prayed for guidance on this and came to the conclusion that, if it was not against God's will, he must seek to delay his departure until Eastertide was over, that the festival might not be spoiled for others. So, whatever his pains and weaknesses, he must wait a little longer, until Pentecost perhaps. He had come to Dalriada at Pentecost thirty-four years ago, the Feast of the Holy Spirit. What better time to leave it?

So, frail and progressively feebler of body but active, clear and eager of mind, he passed those days, harbouring his remaining strength, seeking to enter into his people's celebrations with as much normality as he could muster, and writing, writing, especially at yet another transcription of the Psalms of David, his favourites, for one or other of the churches requiring them. This at least he could still do, even if he had to peer at his writing.

By the night of the Friday before Pentecost Sunday he realised that it was going to take him all his time and determination to last out another day. So when Diarmit, faithful Diarmit, still his acolyte and personal attendant although now a man of middle years, came up to the cell on Tor Abb to seek to minister to his needs next morning, he asked that the wagon which they used to carry the milk jars from the byres to the monastery should be brought, for he intended to pay a visit to various places on the island where work was in progress, and did not feel capable that day of walking, or even mounting a horse. Diarmit said then why not wait until another day when he was feeling stronger? But shaking his head, Colum besought him to humour an old man. He would go this day.

The cart, with its old white horse – not the same animal which Colum had trained to travel in the long-ship all those years ago, but an equally venerable successor – was brought, and Diarmit helped his master up. He had provided a pile of sheepskins for the passenger, so the travelling was less bumpy than it might have been.

They went, first, right across the island to the south-west-facing bay where first the visitors from Ireland had landed, and where now monks and students were working to save the machair, or grassland, from erosion by the tides, erecting stone-and-turf banks. After watching them for a while, and absorbing all the beauty of the white-sand shore, listening to the crooning of the eiders and rejoicing to see a heron stalking the shallows, he raised a hand to bless the place, the men and their work, before turning away, tears in his eyes – tears not of sorrow but of strong emotion nevertheless. He had always looked upon this stretch of coast and its background of skerries and islands as especially a foretaste of Heaven. Soon he would be in a position to compare.

Then they proceeded north-eastwards to fields where men were cutting the hay this fine June day, to bless this labour also. He had intended to go further, right to the northern headland, to visit the seal farm, but reluctantly recognised that this would be beyond him, his strength, such as it was, running out. So back they headed for the monastery; but Colum asked to be taken first to the granary, the great barn where the island's harvest was always stored. There again he blessed not only the building but the two great heaps of golden grain left from last year, observing that he foresaw in this plenty that the monastery of Iona would progress and endure, under God's smile, its provender, material as well as spiritual, not to run out.

Exhausted now, he was taken back to his cell.

Diarmit, wondering, asked why this curious tour, these benedictions? He was told only that it was a form of thanksgiving, a survey in gratitude. But now he must sleep, for he was very tired. Mystified, the other was leaving when Colum called him back. After he had eaten, would Diarmit row across to the nunnery and ask the Prioress Bridget if she would kindly visit him in the afternoon. But . . . not to tell her of their forenoon's activities meantime.

He was still sleeping when Bridget arrived at Tor Abb, and she eyed him long and thoughtfully before touching his shoulder. Strangely, he looked extraordinarily happy, as though his dreams were joyful indeed.

He awoke, but it was clearly some moments before he fully realised where he was. He apologised and struggled to sit up.

"I sleep too much, these days, Bridget. Forgive me. Sloth is a sin. But . . . there may not be much sleeping ahead of me."

"You mean . . .?"

"That where I am bound I will be very active, I think. More active than I have been for long. No more sloth!"

"Dear Columcille!"

He pointed across the cell to a small simple wooden chest, in which she knew he kept his few personal belongings. "Bring me, my dear, the package that is on top."

She went and lifted the lid. There lay a parcel tied up in faded parchment. Taking it out, she noted that underneath lay the exquisite brecbennach which King Brude had presented.

Taking the package from her, he sought to untie the cord fastening it, but his hands shook overmuch and she did it for him. Inside was a sheaf of manuscript sheets, worn, stained and tattered with age and use.

"Do you know what this is?" he asked her.

Bridget shook her head.

"It is the *Cathach*. The Battle Book. You have heard of it? My first copy of the Psalms . . . which caused so much trouble, long ago. Those papers we used as banners, at the Battle of Cooldrevny. Carried them aloft, as against the Druids' skulls and symbols. Perhaps I should not have kept them, but burned them? I do not know. But . . . they are yours, now. To keep. Or to burn. As you see fit."

Wide eyed she looked from the sheets to him. "Why?" she demanded. "Why? Why me?"

"Because you are a woman, my friend, and good. And represent peace not war. These were used in war. Men died under them – a burden I have been carrying ever since. Why I kept them – to remind me of what I did. The Battle Book became celebrated – better that it should not, perhaps. I want it to speak no more of battle. Men may so esteem it. So I give it to a woman. For women hate battle and war."

She hung her head, biting back words and sobs alike.

"What you do with it is your concern, my dear." He leaned back and closed his eyes, as though the effort had been almost too much for him.

"Columcille," she got out. "You do this, now, because, because . . .?"

"Because I wish to," he said. "My heart is that much lighter now. I should have done it before, or burned it."

"I did not mean that. I understand that. But why now, today? Is this . . .?" She could not go on.

"Say that this is a day for lightening the heart, Bridget. The Eve of Pentecost. It seems a good day for, for sweeping out, for tidying. Tomorrow is the Holy Spirit's day. We must be ready for that."

She looked at him, biting her lip. "I think . . . that you are being less than honest with me. Is that all that you have to tell me?"

"Not all, no. I could say much more, Bridget – of what you have meant to me, will always mean to me. But I think that you know that. Words are poor things, so often. And today my tongue is . . . less than nimble. I am a little weary. But one day I will tell you all that is in my heart. One day . . ."

"Is that a promise, Columcille?"

"A promise, yes. When I am less tired, lass. When we will be . . . without distractions." He achieved a smile.

"Distraction – that is a term which has come between us for too long, my dear. Not much longer now."

"I have tried . . . not to distract."

"I know it. Any fault has been mine. I will do better . . . hereafter."

When still she eyed him more than doubtfully, he spoke almost pleadingly. "Bridget – this of the Battle Book. I should not have brought you across the sound from your nunnery just for this. But it was on my mind, my conscience. Now I feel better. Will sleep again . . . more at peace. To give me a little strength, for tomorrow. Tomorrow, lass, tomorrow . . .!"

"Tomorrow." Slowly she nodded. "Tomorrow, then. You would have me to go now, Columcille?"

"Would not, but must, I fear – the flesh is being . . . very weak. But only until tomorrow, my dear – Pentecost!"

She stopped to kiss him, and a single tear fell on his brow. "I go, then, since you ask me to – cherishing your promise." Turning, she hurried from that cell.

He lay, eyes closed, but he did not, in fact, sleep. That was but a poor farewell to take of Bridget nic Colman; but he had to try to spare her the pain of it. Had he done so? She was an intelligent woman, and loved him. Perhaps she knew it all . . .?

After a while he reached down for the little bronze bell on the floor beside his couch, that which had summoned so many to service and Eucharist, and tinkled it. Diarmit, never far away, appeared.

"Fetch me Baithen, now," he requested. This at least should be easier.

Baithen, stockily stiff, the years but seeming to make him the more rigidly upright, came presently.

"How goes it with you, Columcille?" he asked, jerkily unsentimental as ever, a man who seemed suspicious of emotion.

"Well, Cousin, well. Never better – for I am on my way, at last. I think that you know it."

"I have seen you failing, yes. I am sorry."

"No sorrow for me. Iona is a good place – but I go to a better. *You* will take up my burden here, whilst I go light-of-foot!"

"If you say so, Cousin."

"I do. Bring me that box there, Baithen."

The other carried over the little chest whence had come the *Cathach*. Colum took out the brecbennach.

"This is now yours," he said, handing it over. "The symbol of authority entrusted to me. From this kings have been anointed, and will be hereafter. You will cherish it well, I know. As you will cherish all, in love and peace, from this little isle to far beyond. So much to cherish, Baithen – a great responsibility, as I know, but a precious one. You will find the strength, and the blessing, of it – and better than I have done, perhaps. And I shall be praying for you."

He paused, eyes closing again. Extraordinary that even talking should so tax him, he of the ringing and vigorous voice. Baithen, who was otherwise, nodded.

"I shall do my best," he said.

"I know it." Colum pointed across the cell. "There is my staff. Tomorrow, yours. And there, the altar-font. I see it taking on a strange importance in the future – I have seen this more than once. That stone will speak, I think, to generations to come, not always in love and peace, alas – a peculiar destiny. So cherish it also." It was at his portable shrine that he pointed, a seat-like block of dark stone, a meteorite it was said, which had been decorated with fine interlaced carving and hollowed out on top to cup water for baptism, as well as serving as an altar. Heavy as it was, it had travelled many miles on the broad back of that old horse, as of its predecessor.

"All I will care for, Cousin. Have no fear of that. You feel that your end is near?"

"Never the end, man – never that. I but hand over to you, that I may go forward freed of my burdens. As will you, one day."

Baithen nodded. He put the chest back in its place. "Do you require anything, Columcille?" he asked, practical ever.

"Nothing. I am well content. I shall attend vespers, if I am permitted. If not, Cousin, say to my children, this. Have true love between yourselves. And peace. God, the gladness of the good, will strengthen you. And give you not only your needs in this life but the prize, the prize of eternal good things also. Tell them . . . no new message. But, I think, my last here."

When Baithen had gone, Colum lay waiting. Then he realised that he was in fact counting, counting minutes, wishing time away, wondering whether his little stock of remaining strength could last sufficiently long. This would not do, surely no way to approach eternity, in feebly idle counting of the hours. Pentecost was still six hours away, when the Holy Spirit, he prayed, would come for him. Six hours . . .

He dragged himself up and reached for his paper, quill and ink, always nearby. The psalm – at least he could be transcribing his psalm.

He wrote slowly, painfully, trying to control his shaking hand – but thankful that he did not require to consult another copy, for he knew most of the psalms by heart. When he reached the line.

They that seek the Lord shall not lack any good thing,

He found that the pen was wandering, misforming the words. He lowered his head and dropped the quill. So be it – Baithen would have to finish what followed

He must have slipped into something between sleep and unconsciousness thereafter, until a sound, a continuous sound, brought him back to awareness – the ringing of the vespers bell, at the monastery for evensong. It was a summons, awaited, and he must answer it, if he could. With a great effort, he managed to get to his feet, reaching for his crozier.

To the cell door Diarmit came hastening, all concern, saying that this was not necessary, not wise, too much. Colum ignored that, but took the other's arm, to go slowly down the hill towards the church. The bell had stopped ringing, so they were going to be late for the service. But to hurry was out of the question.

Halfway, indeed, Colum feared that he would get no further, and had to sit down on an outcropping stone, breathing irregularly, Diarmit saying that they ought to go back. It was then that he found an access of strength however, from an unexpected quarter. It was the old white horse, released from its cart, and cropping the grass nearby. Seeing them, the animal moved over to them and, ignoring Diarmit, came and stood over Colum, lowering its head to rest it lightly against his chest, nuzzling gently. Diarmit would have driven it off but Colum restrained him and raised a hand to stroke the creature's head.

"See you that," he said, and showed where a single great tear had splashed on to his hand. "Never before have I seen a horse to weep." It was the second tear shed that afternoon – so probably Bridget had known also. "God, it seems, has given dumb animals gifts that He has withheld from men. This one, of whom always I have been fond, knows that I am on my way, and comes to say God-speed."

"God-speed, Master . . .?" Diarmit faltered.

"Why, yes. You did not know it, then? As this creature did. This day I do my leave-taking. For tomorrow I move on, old friend. But . . . see you, do not you weep also! For here is a joy, not sorrow, or, one little sorrow, for me. Lugbe. I sent him to Aidan, at Dunadd. You and he are close, and both have my love. Tell him so, Diarmit – tell him so, when he returns. Now – if our old friend here will let me rise, on to the church. For we are late – and our Baithen does not like late-coming . . ."

They moved on slowly, the chanting from the church drawing them, and enabling them to enter and take a place right at the rear without overmuch disturbance of the worship which Baithen was leading.

They did not wait until the end of evensong, for Colum knew well that the climbing of Tor Abb again, little hill as it was, would demand the very last of his strength. Besides, all his children would come to flock round him in well-wishing, and that he could by no means face.

So, in the half-light of evening now, they made their halting way out and upwards. Why had he, long ago, elected in prideful zest, to place his cell up there?

That cell, at length, Colum reached thankfully. But before he entered, leaning on Diarmit's arm and his staff both, he turned to survey that scene. It might look still better, hereafter, from another stance, but even so he loved it dearly. It is never really dark of a June night in the Hebrides, and the filmy curtains of the dusk did no hurt to the beauty. From north to south he gazed, seeking to absorb it all, picking out favoured landmarks here and there, lingering for longer at Eilean nam Ban, the women's isle where was the nunnery, before moving on to the monastic buildings, the *Reilig Oran*, the haven, the farmery and barns and all the familiar reminders of thirty-four years of endeavour. Then, releasing Diarmit's arm, he raised his quivering hand, and spoke.

424

"I see it all, and give thanks. This small place, mean in some men's eyes. Yet here much homage shall be paid. Not only by the kings of Scots and of Alba but by others. The rulers of strange and even heathen nations and their peoples. And by Holy Church itself. For long, for all the generations to come. I see it all. Thanks be to God. This . . . my last words here, I think."

Stumbling round, he groped his way into the cell and collapsed upon his couch.

It was the ringing of the nocturne bell at midnight, signifying the new day, Pentecost, which awakened Diarmit, where he had been sleeping just outside Colum's cell. Debating with himself whether or not it was his duty to go down for the brief service or to stay with his master, he rose and looked in at the cell door. It was dark in there and he peered, then exclaimed. No, there was no one there, the couch empty.

Astonished, alarmed, he hurried out, to gaze around. Nothing to be seen, only the still shadows of the night, save for the pale blur which was the white horse below. At a loss, and heeding that bell, he went running downhill. Could it be . . .? The church? Ahead he could see now the lanterns moving. That would be the procession of monks and students coming from the dormitories to celebrate the midnight service of thanksgiving for Pentecost and the coming of the Holy Spirit to mankind. He could hear the chanting as they walked.

Diarmit reached the church first and hurried within. It was dark, dark. Staring, seeking to pierce the gloom, he shouted, "Father! Are you there? Father Columcille – where are you?"

There was no answer.

Almost, he went out to await the procession, to tell them, ask them. But something took him on, right up to the altar. And there he all but fell over the body. With a groan he sank down, to gather up that beloved body in his arms, and so remained.

Then the lights appeared, with the chanting brethren, Baithen leading, and Diarmit called out. Hurriedly the lanterns were brought forward. They revealed Colum stretched out on the floor below the altar, his head on Diarmit's lap, a smile of purest joy on his face.

"He came. Alone. But, but breathed his last . . . in my arms!" Diarmit declared. "He is gone. I felt his spirit go out of him. I tell you, I felt it. I, the least amongst you all – and the most blessed!"

The midnight bell ceased its tolling. It was Pentecost.

AUTHOR'S NOTE

Colum mac Felim, or Columba as the succeeding Roman Catholic Church chose to call him, did not labour in vain. It can have been given to few men to achieve so much of permanent significance. The light he lit has never been extinguished since, not only in what is now called Scotland but in England also, where his disciples and successors went on to carry the torch.

His anointing of monarchs was, of course, of enormous importance, linking Church and State in a symbolical act which has persisted. Iona became a place of pilgrimage, and to it have flocked millions, not only the kings and princes and great ones – it is claimed that forty-eight kings of Dalriada and Alba lie here, four kings of Ireland, eight kings or princes of Norway, one of France and one of Northumbria; all this may well be something of an exaggeration, but certainly here were interred the Scottish monarchs from Fergus the Second to MacBeth, including Kenneth MacAlpine who united Picts or Albannach and Scots. The clerics and the religious have come in their thousands; but these as nothing to the ordinary folk coming from all over the world, many of whom today have no links with the Church, but few of whom can leave Iona without some feeling of wonder and respect and even peace. The Iona Community, founded and based here, has now spread world-wide, with its message of love, hope and unity.

It has not all been joy and peace, of course. The Vikings, who savaged the Scottish coasts so direly in the eighth, ninth and tenth centuries, attacked Iona several times, sacking all and slaying the monks. Such of the precious relics as survived were brought for safety to Dunkeld in Perthshire, which became the new centre of the Columban or Celtic Church, and later to Scone, which was established as the coronation place of the Scottish kings. Of these, of course, the Stone of Destiny was the most famous, and is thought by some experts to have been Columba's portable altar. The lovely brecbennach, sometimes called the Monymusk Reliquary, since it was long deposited at Monymusk in Aberdeenshire, and was carried by the Abbot of Arbroath before the victorious Bruce at Bannockburn, is now in the Museum of Antiquities, Edinburgh. The Book of Deer and some of Columba's writings, went back to Ireland. What became of the Battle Book, this author does not know.

It is perhaps significant to note that in AD 617 St Donnan and his helpers were massacred on Eigg at the hands of the chieftainess, owner of the island and those sheep. It is recorded that, as the missionaries were celebrating mass when the lady's warriors arrived, he requested that they should be allowed to finish the service before the slaughter took place. This was permitted, and then all were slain.

No doubt there will be those who will criticise this novel – and it *is* a novel, I emphasise – on the grounds that not only is it insufficiently well-written, as I am the first to acknowledge, but in that it misses out so many of the miracles said to have been worked by Columba. This is quite deliberate. Not all novel readers today are prepared to accept and believe in miracles; and far be it from me to limit admiration and esteem for Columba by question and disbelief. The man's life and achievements are sufficiently miraculous in themselves, for me: and his faults and weaknesses will only make him the more acceptable to many. Where I have invented, or transgressed otherwise, please forgive.

Nigel Tranter
Aberlady, 1987

NIGEL TRANTER

PRICE OF A PRINCESS

After young James the Third's accession to the Scottish throne, the ambitious Boyd family of Kilmarnock seized power in a bloodless coup.

Mary Stewart, James' eldest sister, was at first unwilling to marry Thomas Boyd, future Earl of Arran. Eventually, however, she learned to love him, and when he was sent to the Danish court to negotiate with King Christian, she discovered a unique talent for diplomacy. In exchange for Princess Margaret of Denmark marrying her brother, Princess Mary at length persuaded the Danes to hand over the islands of Orkney and Shetland to Scottish dominion. But when the Boyd regime was finally toppled, Mary's position became severely compromised.

In this riveting tale of romance, treachery and heartbreak, Nigel Tranter shows how, irrespective of their individual desires, the lives of royal young women were all too frequently used to forward national or political alliances.

HODDER AND STOUGHTON PAPERBACKS

NIGEL TRANTER

BLACK DOUGLAS

It was almost inevitable that in the 15th century the new Scots royal House of Stewart would have to come to a reckoning with the great and puissant House of Douglas.

Young Will Douglas, the eighth Earl, was born to vast power, influence – and trouble. And with a boy-king on an uneasy throne, and scoundrels ruling Scotland, the death of Will's father plunged him suddenly into a world where might prevailed and the end justified the means.

'A stirring story of stirring times'
Times Educational Supplement

'Nigel Tranter captures the spirit of the times and writes with an absorbing attention to detail'
Yorkshire Evening Post

HODDER AND STOUGHTON PAPERBACKS

NIGEL TRANTER

DAVID THE PRINCE

Set in the 12th century, this is the incredible story of one of Scotland's greatest kings.

Half-Celt and half-Saxon, King David determined to take hold of his backward, patriarchal, strife-ridden country and, against all the odds, pushed and dragged it into the forefront of Christendom's advancing nations. It is a story of independence, singlemindedness and hard-headed leadership. But also, through the turbulent years of his reign, it is a story of devotion: to the woman he admired and loved, Queen Matilda.

'He has a burning respect for the spirit of history and deploys his characters with mastery'

The Observer

HODDER AND STOUGHTON PAPERBACKS